T0267317

PRAISE FOR

RED CHAOS

"Be ready to be catapulted into the real world of international intrigue that keeps national security experts up at night. A world where leading international oil executives are assassinated. Oil tankers are sunk in the Straits of Hormuz. An attack on the Suez Canal closes shipping for a year. Who benefits from actions like these? You'll find out in *RED CHAOS* by Fuller and Grossman, and all-too real scenario with heart-pumping action from Washington to London, the Arabian Sea to the North Atlantic, Russia to China. Areas where I served, that remain in the headlines today. You'll be swept along with *RED CHAOS* as I did. It's the fastest read on the shelves in a long, long time!"

WILLIAM GRIMSLEY
MAJOR GENERAL US ARMY (RETIRED)
· SECRETARY OF SOUTH CAROLINA
DEPARTMENT OF VETERANS AFFAIRS

"Turn off the news channels right now, crack open Ed Fuller and Gary Grossman's incredible new thriller, *RED CHAOS* and be prepared to stay up all night reading—you will be catching your breath as you turn the pages. Fuller has the inside track on bringing his experience in the field to the page. I know. I spent time with him in Iraq and you better believe he's one of the best of the good guys. Together with Grossman they weave together a web of lies, murder, and treachery that reach to the highest levels of government in Washington. Back at the center of the action is international hotel executive Dan Reilly who must decide whether a nefarious Chinese fixer is trying to help America or bring it down—it all feels so real. It's a read written from the inside out. A winner—Second Place is not close."

FRANK HEMLICK
LIEUTENANT GENERAL US ARMY RETIRED

"Just when I thought Fuller and Grossman couldn't turn up the heat any more after their award-winning *RED DECEPTION*, along comes *RED CHAOS*, with a spot-on, globe-hopping plot. Ed Fuller comes to thriller writing from years as an international hotel executive. On top of that, he had a heavy dose of anti-terrorism experience. His collaboration with Gary Grossman delivers ticking clock scenarios that play out real because so much of it is real, or just on the edge of reality. *RED CHAOS* is a top flight thriller that will have you spell-bound from page one!"

DOUGLAS F. MULDOON, CHIEF OF POLICE (RETIRED)
CITY OF PALM BAY POLICE DEPARTMENT
2013 FBI NATIONAL ACADEMY ASSOCIATES PRESIDENT

"Having been impressed with the first two books of the *RED HOTEL* series, I eagerly awaited reading the next volume. With *RED CHAOS*, Ed Fuller and Gary Grossman exceeded my expectations. Their third work is a timely fictionalization of the volatile world we live in. It is both exciting and accurate; a 21st century thriller and a must read! *RED CHAOS* if particularly close to me as I was the commander of an F4 squadron on the USS *Midway*. I know what America's Navy can do with its air power in a crisis."

TOM KOEHLER

COMMANDER, F-4 PILOT, RET. USN

"There have been more terrorist attacks on hotels around the world than any other target. Ed Fuller was there, lived it and dealt with it. *RED CHAOS* is much more than a delight to read. It's a textbook in dealing with crisis management from someone who literally wrote the book. I worked for Marriott for 35 years. From 1989 to 2012 I was the Vice-President of Safety & Security on Ed's team. With a close relationship from several government entities, we established security protocols for our international hotels (including over 200 "threat condition RED" hotels). When I retired from Marriott we had 2,000 International hotels in 200 countries."

ALAN ORLOB

FOUNDER & CEO

ORLOB GROUP

"*RED CHAOS* is a timely, pulse-pounding thriller that exposes the complex and dangerous web of espionage, international business, and geopolitics. Five-star hotels are at the epicenter of the secret deals that shape our lives, and, as a hotel security executive, former US Army intelligence officer Dan Reilly is uniquely positioned to see what goes down in the bars, lobbies, and lavish private suites everywhere from London to Beijing. When a Russian oil magnate is assassinated at one of his London properties, Reilly launches an investigation that could expose treachery and violence at the highest levels of multiple governments—and puts him in the crosshairs of men willing to kill to cover it up. This is a tour de force by authors Fuller and Grossman that will leave readers clamoring for more."

DANTE PARADISO

AUTHOR OF *THE EMBASSY: A STORY OF WAR AND DIPLOMACY*

"*RED CHAOS*, Gary Grossman and Ed Fuller's newest thriller, vividly draws us into two worlds: one where Washington's power-hungry walk the halls, scheme in back offices, and lurk in the shadows of the White House and Congress, and another fraught with the intrigue and occasional inanities of international business. They engage us in the machinations of a talented assassin, an empire building, oil-crazed autocrat in the Kremlin, and a fixer in China. We see the morally ambivalent and morally bankrupt—from Moscow to Macau to Washington. Readers will cheer their richly drawn hero and heroine, international hotel executive and sometime spy Dan Reilly and Secretary of State Elizabeth Matthews as they continue the fight for right in this entertaining series firmly rooted in the real world."

LINDA PEEK SCHACHT
FORMER WHITE HOUSE PRESS AIDE
FORMER COMMUNICATIONS DIRECTOR,
US SENATE MAJORITY LEADER
FORMER GLOBAL VICE PRESIDENT,
THE COCA-COLA COMPANY

"In *RED HOTEL*-and *RED DECEPTION*, my Marriott colleague and global nomad, Ed Fuller, brings his love of politics and his experience in the Vietnam War and deep inside knowledge of the hotel and travel industry including crisis management to build another political thriller with Gary Grossman, an acclaimed novelist and TV producer and journalist. Pour some of the current global uncertainty into this cocktail, and you have the combustion of *RED CHAOS*."

KATHLEEN MATTHEWS
AMBASSADOR FOR WORLD TRAVEL & TOURISM COUNCIL
FORMER ABC NEWS ANCHOR
FORMER MARRIOTT INTERNATIONAL SENIOR EXECUTIVE

"I've been engaged in national and homeland security for over 45 years, I seldom read fiction. When I do, it is historical fiction. It most often provides opportunities to learn interesting facts in an enjoyable way. While *RED CHAOS* is not an historical novel, given today's news, it affords the reader an extremely compelling, most realistic and fast paced story. In crafting this riveting read, Ed Fuller and Gary Grossman have written a thriller that reflects their impressive knowledge of today's strategic global dynamics. But they must be seen as prescient given the events happening at this moment: The real-world implications of climate change on global trade and national security, and the fragility of the world's avenues for commerce. *RED CHAOS* is a timely must read for those seeking a book that is both stimulating and eye-opening."

WILLIAM CARWILE
COLONEL, US ARMY (RET)
FORMER ASSOCIATE ADMINISTRATOR, FEMA

"Put the Do Not Disturb placard on your door and settle into the latest thriller in the *RED HOTEL* series, *RED CHAOS*. And trust me, chaos is ready to break out in Fuller and Grossman's most timely novel yet! This team of masterful authors race us through one heart-pounding scene to another with prescient vision of the world as it is and things to come. Trust me, *RED CHAOS* delivers as a page-turning thriller that also waves a red flag at real geo-political issues we better pay attention to now!"

ROGER DOW
FORMER PRESIDENT & CEO U.S. TRAVEL ASSOCIATION

"*RED CHAOS* jumps out of the gate with real fury and delivers a scenario where patriots and scoundrels clash on a worldwide playing field. From my perspective,

Fuller and Grossman's latest thriller tests how far the long arm of the law can really reach and whether justice served is justice denied. *RED CHAOS* is a fast-paced international thriller that comes right back home. It's going to have you flying through the pages to find out who, what, where and when."

MARK MORGAN

CAREER MILITARY AND LAW ENFORCEMENT OFFICER

U.S. MARINES, FBI, LAPD,

FORMER ACTING COMMISSIONER OF CUSTOMS

AND BORDER PROTECTION

"Gary Grossman and Ed Fuller have done it again in *RED DECEPTION*. Plot, characters, and details are gripping and captivating. A page-turner by authors who might as well sit on the National Security Council. A fantastic read!"

PAUL DEBOLE

FORMER AIDE TO SENATOR JOHN MCCAIN
AND SENATOR LAMAR ALEXANDER
ASSOCIATE PROFESSOR, HISTORY, LASELL UNIVERSITY
AUTHOR, *CONSPIRACY 101: AN AUTHORITATIVE EXAMINATION OF THE
GREATEST CONSPIRACIES IN AMERICAN POLITICS*

"Laced with drama culled from recent events, *RED HOTEL* places the reader directly into the role of intelligence analyst and operative as well as business and political strategist. Read *RED HOTEL* and it's doubtful you'll ever travel again without conjuring up possible intrigue from observations that used to seem like normal occurrences."

JOHN TIERNEY

FORMER MEMBER OF THE U.S. HOUSE OF REPRESENTATIVES
MEMBER, HOUSE INTELLIGENCE COMMITTEE AND CHAIR,
NATIONAL SECURITY SUBCOMMITTEE
EXECUTIVE DIRECTOR, CENTER FOR ARMS CONTROL
AND NON-PROLIFERATION

"Grossman and Fuller deliver gritty insider detail in their thriller *RED HOTEL*, bringing fact and fiction together in an explosive mix. *RED HOTEL* is a must read for international travelers and anyone seeking to understand the new Russia."

K.J. HOWE

BEST-SELLING AUTHOR
THRILLERFEST EXECUTIVE DIRECTOR

"*RED DECEPTION* provides an in-depth and realistic ground level view of the type of asymmetric Nation-state sponsored threats faced by the Agencies tasked with protecting the United States both domestically and abroad. Thoroughly researched with thrilling pacing, it follows a worst-case scenario with the resulting fallout and a complex investigation that unfolds all over the globe."

EDWARD BRADSTREET

SPECIAL AGENT- DEPARTMENT OF HOMELAND SECURITY

HOMELAND SECURITY INVESTIGATIONS (HSI)

"Forget 'ripped from the headlines,' because *RED DECEPTION* threatens to write its own! Everything a great thriller is supposed to be! High stakes, incredible action scenes, a deadly plot, and a dynamic hero in Dan Reilly. Gary Grossman and Ed Fuller have crafted a relentlessly riveting tale that hones in on our greatest fears and takes us right to the brink in breathless fashion."

JON LAND

USA TODAY BEST-SELLING AUTHOR

"*RED HOTEL*, a terrific, fast-paced, stylish, eye-opening spy thriller, with a knowing, insider's look at the intersects of terrorism, the CIA, and world politics. *RED HOTEL* will forever change the way you look at hotels, and use the phrase 'Road Warrior.'"

BRUCE FEIRSTEIN

JAMES BOND SCREENWRITER, VANITY FAIR CONTRIBUTING EDITOR

BEST-SELLING AUTHOR

"*RED DECEPTION* is a Thriller with a capital "T"! Not for the faint of heart. "The doomsday scenarios depicted in this fast-paced, can't-put-down nail-biter are real-world accurate and truly scary. Dan Reilly is a terrific new hero for today's troubled times!"

"As the former Director of Intelligence (J2) for the U.S. Pacific Command in Hawaii and Joint Chiefs of Staff in the Pentagon, I know these dangerous scenarios are plausible, which makes *RED DECEPTION* all the more thrilling. Infrastructure attacks, Russian aggression, bumbling national leaders, North Korea malign activity, Venezuelan dangers—Fuller and Grossman's exciting story mirrors reality!"

"*RED DECEPTION* is an adrenalin-laden thriller and as true to life as it gets. As a former intelligence operative (linguist/analyst—Soviet/Warsaw Pact) with assignments to Field Station Augsburg, Germany and the Defense Intelligence Agency at the Pentagon, I know that all of the explosive events, all of the alliances, and all of the deceit detailed in this book are realistic. This book just can't be put down. Outstanding!"

"Russia is a country masquerading as a gas station."

"Whoever controls oil controls much more than oil."

JOHN MCCAIN

UNITED STATES SENATOR

FORMER CAPTAIN, UNITED STATES NAVY

RED CHAOS

ED FULLER

GARY GROSSMAN

BEAUFORT
BOOKS

Hardcover ISBN: 9780825309878
Ebook ISBN: 9780825308666

For inquiries about volume orders, please contact:
Beaufort Books, 27 West 20th Street, Suite 1103, New York, NY 10011
sales@beaufortbooks.com

Published in the United States by Beaufort Books
www.beaufortbooks.com

Distributed by Midpoint Trade Books
a division of Independent Publisher Group
www.ipgbook.com

Book designed by Mark Karis

Printed in the United States of America

I dedicate this book to my lovely wife Michela, who has exemplified being the best wife in good times as well as difficult times. I also dedicate RED CHAOS *to our family Scott, Elizabeth, Alex and our grandchildren Cameron and Nolan. Also, to "Candy" our special and unique puppy.*

ED

For Helene, my wonderful wife, whose writing career is flourishing, and whose creative voice is reaching far and wide, and making a difference. I'm so proud of you.

GARY

PRINCIPAL CHARACTERS

WASHINGTON, D.C.
DAN REILLY
President, International
Kensington Royal Hotel
Corporation

ALEXANDER CROWE
former U.S. President

RYAN BATTAGLIO
U.S. President

MOAKLEY DAVIDSON
United States Senator

ROGER WHITFIELD
National Security Advisor

ELIZABETH
MATTHEWS
Secretary of State

PIERCE KIMBALL
National Security Advisor

BOB HEATH
CIA Case Officer

REESE McCAFFERTY
FBI Director

GERALD WATTS
CIA Director

TASHA SAMUELS
Congressional Aide

SHERWOOD BAKER
Reporter, The Hill

MIKAYLA
COLONNELLO
U.S. Senator

U.S. ARMY GENERAL
ZARIF ABDO
Member of the Joint Chiefs

SEAN ALLPHIN
Speaker of the House

ADMIRAL RHETT
GRIMM
Chairman, Joint Chiefs
of Staff

BRADLEY SNAVELY
Secretary of the Interior

DOMINIQUE DHAFARI
A hotel guest

SHEILA JOHNSON
DOUG COX
BUDDY MULDOON
FBI Agents

BEIJING, CHINA
HUANG ZHANG
Colonel, Chinese People's
Armed Police Force

SKIP LENCZYCKI
Former CIA operative

EY WING LI (AKA
SAMMY)
A fixer

YIBING CHENG
Private security consultant

MATTHIEU LEFEVRE
Tourist

YICHÉN YÁO
President of China

SUEZ CITY
DAE-JUNG WOO
GYEONG SONG
Operatives

RUSSIA
NICOLAI GORSHKOV
President, Russian
Federation

GENERAL VALERY
ROTENBERG
FSB Chief

DR. ARKADY SECHIN
Russian Oil Advisor to the
Russian President

LONDON, ENGLAND
WALTER GRÜN
Hotel Assistant Manager

IGOR KRITZLER
Russian oil executive

ALAN CANNON
VP, Global Safety and
Security

CHICAGO, IL

EDWARD JEFFERSON SHAW
President/CEO
Kensington Royal Hotel Corporation

BRENDA SHELTON
Dan Reilly's Executive Assistant

CARL ERWIN
Former CIA Director
Kensington Royal Crisis Committee

BD COONS
U.S. Army General, ret.
Kensington Royal Crisis Committee

DONALD KLUGO
Private security consultant
Kensington Royal Crisis Committee

LOU TIANO
Kensington Royal COO

CHRIS COLLINS
Senior Vice President, Legal
Kensington Royal Hotel Corporation

PAT BRODOWSKI
Kensington Royal CFO

CHIP SNYDER
Kensington Royal Domestic President

NAIROBI, KENYA

JAYO MENG
Chinese oil company executive

BAETE DE SMET
Belgian Tourist

GATIMU KAMAU
Police Detective

NORTH ATLANTIC

ANDREW POLICANO
Commander, USS *Hartford*

MARCEL JAMES
Sonar Operator

BORIS SIDOROV
Commander, *Admiral Kashira*

ALI SHIRVANI
Cmdr. *Karim Khan*

ADMIRAL BRANSON STUCKMEYER
Commander, U.S. 2nd Fleet

PART ONE

LINE OF ATTACK

1

"Reilly, get down!"

The volley of automatic gunfire in the hotel lobby made the order almost impossible to hear. But Dan Reilly didn't need any warning from the hotel security assessing his options—if he had any at all.

He breathed heavily. His pulse raced as he rewound the previous minute in his mind, piecing together the events as they had unfolded. He'd seen an older couple checking out. Vacationers with too much luggage. A young woman glancing at her watch expectantly, then opening her purse. Probably for a lipstick touch-up before heading out on a date. A man at the bar working on a Bloody Mary. A seven- or eight-year-old girl wearing a bright yellow dress sitting on a couch, well into her *Goosebumps* book. Two hulking characters flanking her tightly. A boy carrying a skateboard, undoubtedly ready to get away from his parents. A concierge at her desk arranging theater tickets or giving directions. Some twenty other people also in sight, spread throughout the lobby.

Then five men entered. Five huge men with shaved heads, all wearing long, loose-fitting leather jackets. One marched purposely toward the front desk. The remaining four split up and headed directly to the far corners of the lobby.

Reilly watched and concluded, *They're taking up strategic posts.* He tapped the officer beside him on the shoulder and whispered,

"Look—there!" He nodded to the near corner. "And there." The opposite corner. "Something's going down."

The officer didn't immediately pick up on his concern. The concern was that Reilly saw people who were armed, and he wasn't.

Reilly took in the entrance in one sweep. A dangerous choke point; poorly designed with two narrow manual doors that would become instantly clogged in a mad rush. Reilly feared that kind of chaos if things truly turned bad. He'd seen it before. Young and old, people died. Just then, a sixth man entered wearing a long leather coat that was definitely not in season. He stopped five steps into the lobby and scanned the space just as Reilly had. He exchanged a nod with the man who had taken up position at the front desk. A signal. A signal that told Reilly the figure who just arrived was the head of the snake.

Reilly glanced back to the front as the man removed what appeared to be an AK-47 from under his coat. Then, without warning, he raised the weapon and fired five rounds into the ceiling.

That was ten seconds ago. Everyone ducked, some faster than others. One of the two men sitting with the little girl on the couch threw his body over her. Reilly dropped behind a couch as the security officer crawled to the nearest man standing. But not just a man—an assailant with his version of the same weapon as the leader.

For now, there was nothing Reilly could do. That was not his way.

Dan Reilly, forty-three, President of the international division of the Kensington Royal Hotel Corporation, was touring the Capitol Hoganville Hotel outside of Washington, D.C.—a friendly visit, though experience told him never to be complacent.

At that moment panic struck. A woman close to the entrance rose and ran toward the door. The leader grabbed her with his left hand and pulled her in. A shield. With his right, he swept his weapon across the room. "You behave, you live," he shouted. "So in the interest of your own health, sit down. Better yet, lie down."

Reilly heard a German or Slovakian accent. It was cruel and dangerous. All too familiar in tone.

No one responded.

He fired again.

"Have I not made myself clear?"

Those nearest offered a meek yes.

"Everyone!" He repeated, "Do … you … understand?" punching every word.

He heard compliance except from the young woman at the front desk. From her standing position she slowly inched toward a door behind her as others lay down. The move caught the eye of the corner man near Reilly.

"No!" the gunman shouted. The woman panicked. She turned and bolted. The terrorist closest to her turned and shot her in the back.

Men and women screamed. The security officer with Reilly removed his gun as he knelt. Reilly was surprised he even carried. But aiming quickly, he took out his near-corner man. Then he stood, spun right, and shot the terrorist near the front desk. It would be his last kill. Crossfire over the huddled captives took him down from the other three corners.

His Glock fell three feet from Reilly. He dove for it fast, pulled the pistol in, and rolled to the right against a man lying face down. Reilly caught his breath. He saw the woman who had checked her watch and her purse lying low a few feet away. She gritted her teeth. Reilly put his finger to his lips indicating she should stay still. She blinked confirmation. Reilly controlled his breathing. He knew the room. Where his targets were standing. Where civilians were most vulnerable.

No more than thirty seconds had elapsed since the first gunshots. It felt like an eternity to Reilly. Combat was like that—elongated, exaggerated.

"You see what happens when you don't listen," the leader said, stepping further into the lobby and purposely walking toward people to his right.

The terrorist continued to bark instructions, but Reilly shut him out. He had to concentrate and draw on his experience in battle. His mind raced back in time to more than a decade ago, to his service with the U.S. Army in Afghanistan. To an ambush that should have never happened. He lived to talk about it, except that he couldn't. Command quickly clamped down. The mission was stamped classified because of two participants. Very few people knew the truth. He had also been in dangerous situations since. In the past eighteen months, Reilly's work had taken him into danger zones in Asia, South America, the Middle East, and Europe. To hotel bombings, street shootouts, interrogations by rogue military officers. He faced an assassin in Brussels and chased down a killer in Stockholm. He'd squared off with a Mexican cartel leader and stood up to a Russian spy. Not the typical work of a business executive. But Dan Reilly was nowhere near typical.

He remained low, watching the leader's legs as he crossed the room. Reilly figured his best opportunity, perhaps his only one, would come after a few more steps when the gunman passed his position; facing away. He could get him, but he likely wouldn't survive the next round when the three corner men found him in their sights. He might get one. Beyond that? Still, he felt he had to try.

As he began to rise to take his first, and perhaps only shot at the head of the snake, he heard the wail of sirens. Police were on the way. Possibly hostage negotiators or the SWAT team. Now he felt it would be better to wait. *Stay down,* he told himself.

That would have been fine if the next thing didn't happen. The civilian closest to Reilly saw that he had the security guard's weapon. Suddenly taking him as one of the bad guys, he screamed, "No, don't shoot me!" Acting on impulse, he jumped up and headed for the entrance. Others saw the opportunity to follow. The old man with all the suitcases shouted for his wife to follow. Bloody Mary man rose and rushed forward with the growing crowd. Head of the snake fired and dropped him and the old man's wife. The choke point choked.

Outside, the sirens stopped. Reilly heard doors open, the orders shouted. But getting in would be impossible, and the assailants had multiple ways to leave once their mission, which had become clear to him, was accomplished.

Now with the cover of others standing, Reilly got to his knees, then to full height. He stepped over the woman he had motioned to be quiet, maneuvered around the crowd and found a target. His aim was good. The leader took two hits to the chest. Reilly then found the two corner men at 45-degree angles. He got one. He missed the second.

More screams. More panic.

The last remaining terrorist grabbed the boy with the skateboard and used him as protection. He began shooting indiscriminately. Reilly tracked him. He willed himself to wait for the best shot; a safe kill. *Safe kill.* The phrase had always struck him as such a contradiction in terms. He shook it off. He suddenly had opportunity; a side angle. But as quickly as the opportunity arose, it ended when people pushed against one another and blocked his shot. *Wait ... wait.* The remaining attacker hustled to the office door the front clerk had hoped to make. He pushed the boy down and raced ahead. Reilly steadied his right wrist with his left and breathed in.

A shot echoed in the lobby. It wasn't from Reilly's gun. The young woman he had motioned to remain quiet, the woman with the large purse, large enough to contain a Smith & Wesson M&P T4E, expertly put two shots dead center into Dan Reilly's chest.

LONDON, ENGLAND

The first bullet had been enough. Professional. The second was purely personal. Igor Kritzler fell back onto his bed in his Kensington Royal Mayfair suite in London.

Barely four minutes earlier, Kritzler's two wrestler-sized Russian security officers had cleared a man into his suite who had identified himself as a hotel assistant manager. He had a winning smile, appropriate for a hotel executive delivering an unexpected treat. He was gloved and smartly dressed in a dark suit, wearing a name tag they couldn't pronounce. He looked to be in his late fifties with mid-length wavy gray hair and a close-cropped beard. He rolled a cart with items that seemed absolutely appropriate for someone of Kritzler's stature as a Russian oil magnate—a bottle of Dom Perignon with, as he revealed, an extravagant food plater.

"Compliments of the house," Walter Grün warmly explained with a slight German accent. "May I?"

It was certainly in keeping with what they had seen before. Expressions of hotel staff largesse, including complimentary food and drink, limousines at the ready, and depending upon the country, women waiting for him in the backseat or in his bed upon his arrival.

One guard, the bigger of the two by forty pounds, knocked. A few words were exchanged in Russian without opening the double doors.

"*Da,*" came curtly from inside.

The smaller guard swiped the electronic room key allowing Assistant Manager Grün to enter.

"Thank you."

Nods, but no smiles.

Grün pushed his cart forward. He turned, smiled to the guards, and said, "I'll just be a moment."

The big guard shrugged and gave him a *whatever* look.

Grün closed the door and saw Kritzler spread across the couch in the huge living room portion of the suite. He was fat and irritable. He wore a silk bathrobe and mink slippers. Grün assumed he had nothing on underneath.

"Mr. Kritzler, On behalf of the Kensington Mayfair, welcome back. We've prepared something we hope you'll like."

"Fine, fine," Kritzler said like a man who expected people to lavish gifts on him. "But not here. In the bedroom. I'm expecting someone. Put it on the corner table and leave."

"Of course." The assistant manager replied. He crossed the suite to the bedroom. "A nice nightcap."

"Open the bottle, then go."

"Certainly, sir. But there are great delights. You should come see them."

Grün parked the cart just inside the bedroom, removed the metal cover and described the assortment of cheeses, the truffle pâté, the crispy artisan crackers, strawberries, and fine chocolates from Roast + Conch, one of London's newest shops. "The cocoa beans are from St. Lucia. They're positively delicious."

This brought Kritzler to the bedroom. He reached into the open box, rudely grabbed a handful, and filled his mouth.

"They're really to die for."

"Yay, yay, now finish and go."

Kritzler sat on the bed ignoring the man who was clearly below his station; little more than a mid-level functionary doing his job and talking far too much. No tip for him.

Kritzler found the TV remote, turned the set on, and flipped through the channels until he settled on RT, the English-language Russian propaganda channel. In the background, a report on oil futures.

Grün cleared his throat. Kritzler shushed him and turned the sound up.

"I'll pour your champagne!" Walter Grün said, his back now to the Russian lout.

Kritzler ignored him. Grün slowly came around. The television audio drowned out the muffled pop. Not a pop from the champagne. The man posing as an assistant hotel manager held a Makarov 9mm pistol with a suppressor he'd hidden in the cart drawer. The first shot was between Kritzler's eyes. The second was between his legs just because he had been so rude.

Chocolates oozed out of his mouth as blood leaked from between his legs.

He'd been right; Kritzler had nothing on underneath.

Grün backed out of the suite door, pulling his cart. He gave a pleasant thank you to the guards, wishing them a good night. He was certain it would be anything but a good night when they checked on their boss later. They'd be recalled to Russia and once there likely *questioned to death*.

In the hotel kitchen the killer removed a backpack he had also stored in the cart and casually walked to the service door leading to the loading dock. There, he transformed into a completely different identity by removing his fake beard and gray wig, swapping out his jacket for a London Monarch's football sweatshirt, putting on a pair of tortoise-shell glasses, and popping in an ear pod. All in the shadows; all within thirty seconds. He instantly looked some thirty years younger, now more like a student on his way to a pub crawl in Piccadilly than an assassin leaving a successful job.

STAFFORD, VIRGINIA

"The paintball hurt, didn't it?" FBI agent Sheila Johnson said, standing over Dan Reilly in the hotel lobby.

"Yes, it hurt," Dan Reilly replied. "Like being clobbered by an iron fist. Twice."

"You made a fatal error, Mr. Reilly."

This appraisal came from FBI Agent Doug Cox, who had been watching the exercise on CCTV cameras from a command trailer.

"Just one?" Reilly shyly smiled.

"Oh, there are others. We'll go over them."

Cox turned to an associate, hostage expert Buddy Muldoon. The pair had set up the practical exercise, which was only half done. The debriefing ahead was equally important to Reilly's grading. "Let's just say you did better than some, not as good as others. But not as good means you took two in the chest."

Reilly acknowledged Cox's critique. That's what he had come for: lessons from members of the FBI's Hostage Rescue Team (HRT).

"All right" Muldoon said with his hand out. "Time to get up and stretch those bones." The agent, a friend from college, helped Reilly. "Johnson will get you looked at. Make sure you're okay, then we'll review the recordings."

"Sounds good," Reilly replied. He rubbed his chest. He'd have welts to show for his mistakes.

They walked out of the hotel, past the woman who had killed him and the rest of the terrorists. They all nodded hello. Reilly returned the gesture.

Agent Johnson walked Reilly down the main street of the crime capital of the United States. Diagonally across from them was the most-robbed bank in the nation. It averaged at least five break-ins a week. The luncheonette a few doors down saw regular gang shootouts. The jewelry store was subject to night-time assaults by drug dealers, the movie theater to domestic terrorist attacks. This was Hogan's Alley.

It was a street in a town, but not a town, with a hotel that was no more a real hotel than the bank, the drug store, the movie theater, the barber shop, the laundromat, the pool hall, the deli, the warehouse, or the row of homes and apartments. Hogan's Alley was where more bad guys stalked more local and state police, FBI agents, and members of the military than anywhere in the world. It was where trainees and recruits learned what to do, and as Dan Reilly found out, what *not* to.

The challenges covered a vast array of practical scenarios, from employing defensive tactics to surveillance. In one form or another, Hogan's Alley had been around since 1945, named after a cartoon of the 1890s that featured an alley in a tough neighborhood. Early on it was equipped with mechanically controlled pop-up cutouts and hidden obstacles. Within a few years, the challenges became more demanding, with moving figures that would appear at the windows, at doorways, and around corners. Trainees had to instantly distinguish friend from foe.

As the facility evolved and the need for even more realistic training increased, cardboard and wooden targets were replaced with actors; actors armed with hard impact paintball guns or laser-firing weapons, the latter of which Reilly would have preferred today.

Hogan's Alley of today was designed with the help of top Hollywood set designers. The layout provided opportunity for real-time, live, authentic scenarios. Agents could be dropped into tactical situations that they must explore, evaluate, and survive. They're immersive and stressful, demanding, and ever-changing, just as actual danger zones are. The goal was to teach survival, incorporating basic operational tactics, investigative practices, and firearm skills. Equally important, trainees developed defensive skills in scenarios intended to demonstrate how wrong decisions could lead to quickly deteriorating situations. Trainees learned to tactically clear areas for safe entry, eliminate threats, and neutralize the enemy. The last three points were euphemisms for killing the bad guys.

The facility was created to challenge even the best, with gunmen—and as Reilly discovered—women, very seriously playing their parts to resist arrest, be unpredictable, and shoot to kill.

All of this at Allmed Drugs, Bank of Hogan, Hogan's Alley Post Office, and for Dan Reilly, the Capitol Hoganville Hotel. A trip through Hogan's Alley could make a difference, saving lives domestically and internationally. That's why Reilly came. To learn more. To be better prepared for his work.

He rubbed his chest.

"It stings," Johnson noted.

Reilly grimaced. "Yeah."

"Good," Johnson said. "Pain teaches."

Absolutely. His ribs ached.

"You'll be smarting for a while, but you'll be fine."

Smarting for something stupid. Another of those contradictions in terms. "Thanks."

Johnson, one of the bureau's leading instructors, had watched Reilly during the mock assault on closed circuit cameras with agents Muldoon and Cox. They had prepared an elaborate scenario to test his judgment, creating a realistic hotel lobby inside a warehouse. It had all the appropriate trappings familiar to Reilly: check-in, bar, couches and chairs, artwork, even flowers and vases. While highly trained FBI agents acted as the terrorists, the guests milling about were mostly, but not all, civilian hires. "One in particular wasn't," Johnson noted.

"The woman who got me," Reilly admitted. "She was an inside plant."

"Which you should have recognized," Johnson said, "through how she acted. What she did. She was different from the others. Her expressions, her movements. Her reactions were slower than others. You'll see when we look at the video."

Dan Reilly had experience. He wanted more. He would get it here, under the watchful eye of Johnson and her bosses. They trained students of all military and law enforcement stripes to evaluate threats, to think like the enemy, to minimize casualties, to secure zones, and to survive. Survive was what Reilly hadn't managed in the day's exercise.

"Question, Mr. Reilly. Was there anything that could have tipped you?" Johnson asked.

He closed his eyes. *Oversized purse. Not enough to make him suspicious. The fact that she was alone? A lot of people in a hotel lobby are alone.* Then he hit on something.

"As a matter of fact, yes. She ducked a fraction of a second before the gunshot. Like she expected it."

"Good," Johnson said. "And what should that have told you?"

"She knew what was about to go down. I should have anticipated exactly what."

Reilly had served in Afghanistan. He'd faced fire and returned it. He was not afraid. But he knew he had to be better at what he did for the sake of his company, company guests, and his own well-being.

"Then back to your fatal errors. Errors—multiple," Agent Johnson said as they walked toward the command trailer.

Reilly now had his paint-splattered suit jacket over his arm. He listened.

"You made a bad situation worse. Help was on the way. You heard the sirens. You didn't wait for backup. You tried to play hero. You were armed. The enemy didn't know that. You should have stayed low. Waited. Your opportunity would have come when the SWAT team stormed. You could have created a diversion within, pulled eyes off the incoming. Helped—and that's the key word, Mr. Reilly—you could have helped, helped to save the day. Instead, you were taken out."

Reilly wasn't so sure. "May I?" he asked.

"Certainly," Johnson said.

"First of all, I had no comm. I didn't know when or how SWAT would come in."

"Go on," Johnson said without agreement or disagreement.

"In combat I learned if an opportunity arose, you don't hesitate. If you can make a difference to save fellow combatants, do it. If you can reduce the odds, reduce them. You have one job. Take the enemy out."

"All well and good, Mr. Reilly, but you are on a very different battlefield populated by terrorists willing to be martyrs, mobsters with a code to follow, and crazies who lack any true conscience. No enemies in uniforms."

Reilly understood ... and didn't. Following the bombing of his Tokyo hotel, he walked among the dead. He saw children's toys that wouldn't be played with again, jewelry never to be passed down, watches that had ticked for the last time. Had he been there to prevent it, he would have done everything in his power to stop the terrorists.

"What's more, your action today could have precipitated a suicide bomber detonating a device. Killing everyone."

Reilly stopped walking and faced his instructor. "There was no bomber. No one intent on suicide."

Johnson was intrigued. "Oh?"

"The age of the team. The manner in which they entered. Their authority. Military training. Chain of command. They weren't terrorists. They had another purpose. And they planned on leaving alive."

The FBI agent smiled. "And their purpose?"

"Kidnapping. In and out, minimum civilian casualties. The wild card was the security officer. He escalated the situation, not me. For the sake of the exercise, it was choreographed, likely to see what I would do. But I had already identified their purpose. A subject of interest."

Johnson looked down and shook her head. Not a *no*. "And who was that?"

"The young girl in the yellow dress sitting on the high-backed red couch. She was reading a *Goosebumps* book. Two guys, linebacker size, sat on either side of her. They were obvious and definitely not the uncle type. I pegged her as the daughter of a diplomat with a light protective detail. As soon as the bad guys came in, the man to her right whispered something to her. Probably a rehearsed code to get small within her space. Then he pushed her head down and laid over her. The kidnappers—"

He paused. Johnson neither confirmed nor denied his assumption.

Reilly continued, "The kidnappers scanned the lobby in a way that told me they were looking for their package—the girl—not counter threats. The corner man at my 3 o'clock saw her and gave a silent signal to the lead who began his walk forward. That's when things went to shit."

Agent Johnson was impressed. Reilly was more than he appeared. "Very observant, Mr. Reilly. How did you miss the woman who took you out of the game?"

"I'm asking myself that, too. You're right; she anticipated the maneuver. I saw it, but I just didn't put it together in time."

"In time," Johnson said. "Something you should have measured more carefully."

"Except," he continued.

Johnson tilted her head, not expecting a rejoinder. "Yes?"

"It was a false scenario from start to finish. Kidnappers would have taken her on the street, not in a hotel lobby. Too much muscle. Too much risk. Yes, I went down, but they wouldn't have escaped and here's where you really went wrong with your scenario. Our security doesn't carry guns except in places like Russia."

"What about the service entrance out the back?"

"SWAT would have been there. Same with the side entrances. It was a blown mission. One that professionals never would have allowed themselves to step into. And I was set up to fail." He stopped there.

Johnson smiled. "I suppose we'll both have to take into consideration what we've learned today. You might even be able to help us."

"I'd like that. I want to study the video. Then can we set up another scenario for tomorrow?"

Johnson nodded. "That won't be a problem, but you should have your chest looked at." She waved to a bureau paramedic to come over. Reilly never got examined. A phone call from Chicago changed his plans.

"Hello."

"Hello, Mr. Reilly. Please hold for Mr. Shaw."

The call was from Chicago—Nancy Barney, the assistant to E. J. Shaw, President and CEO of the Kensington Hotel chain, one of the world's largest hotel corporations. Shaw was Dan Reilly's boss.

"Dan, we have a problem," Shaw said.

We. Reilly immediately knew the *we* was about to become *he; his* problem.

"Where? What?"

"A murder in our Mayfair property. In a London suite."

"Oh God!" Reilly's mind raced. The hotel was hosting a regional oil conference. He started to ask for detail, but Shaw interrupted.

"A visiting oil minister. A Russian no less. Nasty guy. A brute according to our staff. But still—"

"Got it. Scotland Yard there?"

"All over it. And the Kremlin is already complaining. "

Reilly sucked in a deep breath. "Suspects?" he asked. This was well within his bailiwick. He traveled the world evaluating markets, over-seeing purchases and sales, solving personnel problems, and meeting with foreign dignitaries. He was also responsible for establishing the new five-tiered Red Hotel threat assessment plan, RED being the highest degree of protection.

Reilly brushed back his black hair and knew that his day had suddenly gotten more complicated.

"According to the Russian's detail outside the suite, a man posing as an assistant manager gained entrance with a rolling cart containing a food plate and a bottle of champagne. All normal looking. Friendly. Supposedly compliments of the house."

"Poison?"

"No. Gun. Two shots strategically placed. One in the head did the job, the other in a rather indelicate place."

Reilly shivered. "An assassination and a personal statement."

"Like I said, the victim was a brute. Pissed off everyone."

"Motive?"

"None so far. Scotland Yard is working it. I imagine Interpol before the day is out."

"Alan on it yet?"

Reilly was referring to Alan Cannon, head of the company's security and his friend.

"Yes. He's at O'Hare for a flight out."

"Good. I'll meet him in London. Brenda can book me, too."

"Tonight?" Shaw asked.

"No, tomorrow night. Alan's better at the advance work and talking to investigators. In the meantime, we'll pull together the Crisis Committee members and set a meeting for tomorrow afternoon in Chicago. Say two o'clock. That should give almost everyone ample travel time."

Reilly was in full work mode now. He went through a list of pre-established protocols starting with putting the London hotel on *Red* status. That was the highest threat level assessment. With it came removing any American flags, deploying bomb sniffing dogs, requiring IDs from all guests and visitors to access rooms, baggage and body scanners, using metal detectors as well as placing concrete bollards in front of the entrance and all ground floor windows. There were other defenses that civilians wouldn't see. On one hand, the heightened security was designed to be a visible deterrent to discourage attackers. On the other, it put management, staff, and even guests in a defensive posture. All Dan Reilly's design for property and guest safety.

"Good," the CEO said. "I'll have accounting prepare the cost analysis and—"

"Hold for a second, boss." FBI Agent Johnson was returning. Reilly held up one finger and mouthed that he needed a moment. Returning to Shaw, he said, "I'll call you back. I have to wrap something up here."

"Where's here?"

"D.C. Doing some brush-up work." He decided less was best. Reilly said goodbye.

"We're on for tomorrow," Johnson declared.

"We're off," Reilly said. "Sorry. Work. But I'd still love to see the video before I go and come back later for more training."

"Not to pry, Mr. Reilly, but you're a hotel exec. Does your job really demand this kind of training?"

"Increasingly," he said, aware that the current situation in London underscored the point.

Agent Johnson nodded. Reilly had been cleared at the director level to take the FBI course. That made him a VIP. The presence of Muldoon and Cox further emphasized his status.

"Well then, before you leave let's take a good look at why you died today."

3

200 NAUTICAL MILES OFF THE COAST OF MAINE

PRESENT DAY

The commander knew he was being tracked by an American sub. It was intentional. *Play it like he didn't know. Make some stealthy moves. Disappear, and let the American find him again. All in a good day's work,* he laughed inwardly.

It was a match played daily around the globe and in virtually every ocean by Russia and the United States, the U.S. and China, the U.S. and Iran, and increasingly, American and North Korean subs. Lessons were taught on land and practiced at sea. Surviving a future war depended on training now.

Sometimes luring came within yards before withdrawal. Usually, however, there were miles between the alternating cats and mice.

However, on this mission, brinkmanship would take three nations' submarines to the edge and only one man knew the ulterior motive. He was Boris Sidorov, veteran commander of the new nuclear-powered Russian vessel *Admiral Kashira*.

"Range?" he asked sonar.

One-nine-two-three meters, commander."

For now that was a perfect distance. Just under two kilometers. Room to operate. Room to hide when the time came.

Based on the acoustic signature of the pursuing submarine, his sonar operator reported their tail was the USS *Hartford*. According to the sub's onboard intelligence file, Andrew Policano was in command. *A more-than-worthy foe to engage.*

Heading to the rendezvous point from another direction was the *Karim Khan*. Though the Iranian sub's captain Ali Shirvani and his shipmates wouldn't know it, they were destined to become a *sheep in wolf's clothing*, collateral damage, a victim of circumstances beyond their control.

"Steady as she goes," Sidorov commanded. "We act like we don't know they're there."

ABOARD THE USS *HARTFORD*

"No change," Petty Officer Marcel James reported to Commander Policano. "Continuing on course."

No change because he's heard us or no change because he's fucking with us? Policano wondered. He'd been advised topside by 2nd Fleet command that Boris Sidorov had been seen in the Kremlin just before deploying. "Find him. Stay on him, Commander."

Not an unusual order. *All in a day's work*, he thought, until—

"Course change, sir."

James called it out. Subtle, but significant. Sidorov was taking a turn toward the ridges of the New England Seamount, an extinct ocean volcanic mountain range off the Massachusetts Atlantic coast. It extends more than 670 miles south from the Georges Bank with peaks that rise to over two miles from the seabed. The mountains can provide cover for a submariner trying to hide. Hiding here would put one of the world's most stealthy subs within 150 miles of Cape Cod.

For Andrew Policano, his orders suddenly carried more weight. *Admiral Kashira* was too close to the mainland, with too many places to hide.

4

THE KREMLIN, MOSCOW

SIX MONTHS EARLIER

No one in the room would ever describe Nicolai Gorshkov as merely power hungry. Power ravenous perhaps. Power addicted. Power obsessed. Then again, no one in the room would ever say any of those things aloud. Even showing an expression that hinted at that could lead to an immediate dismissal. And dismissal meant more than mere early retirement. For that reason, everyone under Gorshkov's direct eye had become especially adept at wearing their poker faces and hiding their inner thoughts. That's how they stayed alive.

"Sit," the President of the Russian Federation said with no expression and no eye contact for the five senior officials who filed in. It was an indication that there would be no levity and that they were due for a lecture, or worse, a reprimand.

The group, all men in their fifties, flanked Gorshkov, who sat at the head of his large Kremlin conference table. Each of them had his own assigned seat. There were four empty places at the table—recently made empty by Gorshkov.

"First my displeasure, which should be abundantly obvious."

He swept his right hand across the table, pointing one-by-one to the empty chairs.

"Recent efforts fell short of expectations. While some initial operations succeeded, they were outnumbered by utter failures."

Gorshkov avoided saying anything specific, but the members of the inner council knew. Russia had employed North Korean operatives to attack America's infrastructure, targeting the 14th Street Bridge across the Potomac, the Lincoln Tunnel under the Hudson, the Stan Musial Veterans Memorial Bridge spanning the Mississippi, and other bridges in Pittsburgh. But plans to destroy the Oakland Bay Bridge, and an even greater objective, Hoover Dam, had failed miserably. Some of the terrorists remained in the United States. Most were killed. Nothing pointed to Russia.

There was one other achievement that also remained unspoken—the assassination attempt against U.S. President Alexander Crowe. Although Crowe lived, the ingenious plot led to the accession of Ryan Battaglio. Battaglio was a lesser man, an egotistical narcissist whom Gorshkov had quickly manipulated with great ease.

"In time, we'll activate other efforts aimed at American vulnerabilities," Gorshkov continued. "However, we are at a historic crossroads. Some of you are already aware of this ongoing operation. Now you all will know. I like to consider it a gift from the environment."

There were nods, but no notetaking. Gorshkov didn't allow written records of his meetings.

"Since the dissolution of the Soviet Union, we have been viewed as a poor excuse for a democratic republic and a haven for thieves, thugs, and mobsters. We have been undermined by feckless administrators." He paused for the impact he wanted to place on his next critique. "And for decades we have suffered under America's endless sanctions and stood by as the expansion of NATO threatened our security. We have fought back on both conventional battlefields and in cyberspace. We have begun to restore our sense of pride, our position in the world. Because of our efforts, Russian exceptionalism is returning. It is time for us to guarantee our future."

The five had heard this kind of speech before. So had the full nine and others before them. Still, President Gorshkov was building to a dynamic point, raising his voice and gesticulating widely with a sense of enthusiasm that was undeniably infectious.

"Gentlemen," Gorshkov continued. "We do this by digging down hard. By relying on our own … resources."

Arkady Sechin, Gregor Moloton, Igor Bazalvonov, Markov Kudorff and General Valery Rotenberg were well aware of Gorshkov's goal—to further Russia's creeping expansion in Europe; to take back what had been theirs. What was lacking was money. This plan and the resources he suggested would lead to fulfillment of the goal.

Gorshkov stood, commanding attention. "Together we will create the new, economically independent Russia by letting nature take its course, and, when necessary, speeding up the process with a little push here, a little shove there, and sinking a few ships along the way."

Rotenberg smiled. He was overseeing this aspect.

Gorshkov picked up a TV remote on the table, fired up the monitor, and pressed play. "Now for a preview that we'll be showing on TV soon." A video began, starting with a view of Earth from space.

Nicolai Gorshkov had ascended to the presidency of the Russian Federation through strategic and calculated moves. From Cold War spy to advisor to his predecessors, to billion-dollar oligarch, to a classically maniacal leader who would kill to have the job.

He was the ruler of all things Russia. Under the separation of powers established by the Constitution of the Russian Federation, the government was divided into legislative, executive, and judicial branches, presumably independent of one another. That was how the document read. That was not how Gorshkov, now in his sixties, ran things.

He was the guarantor of human and civil rights and freedoms. Except he no longer guaranteed them. He was charged with ensuring the coordinated function and interaction of all state government bodies, which he didn't ensure. He was elected for six years, but continuously found ways to make the citizenry forget how to count. According to law, he could be impeached by the Federation Council on the basis of high treason brought by the legislature, the State Duma. But Nicolai Gorshkov was above the law. His five top advisors knew it. Someplace, their four former colleagues, and thousands of dissenters, knew it as well.

The video, a combination of news clips, military footage, and CGI animation, ended with a swelling dramatic score and a shot of the Russian Federation flag flying over the Kremlin. The nine-minute presentation, narrated warmly but authoritatively by a woman, offered history focused through a Gorshkov lens and the fast-approaching future as he ordained it. It covered today's international alliances and changes that blew with global warming winds especially favorable to Russia's tomorrows. Of course, the video lacked detail on the precise timeline or the manner of execution. But these men knew the dates and the means to the end. They had them on their calendars. They had been draftsmen of Gorshkov's grand design to reshape the world's economy. The key component was oil. The black gold that would line Russia's coffers. Oil would flow through thousand-mile pipelines and be shipped through the Arctic's open waters. Oil that would suddenly stop flowing via traditional routes. Oil that was destined for the world's number-one customer with 1.4 billion users. The world's most populous nation, the thirstiest—China.

The video ended and Gorshkov received the standing ovation he sought.

"It will galvanize spirits," Sechin proclaimed.

"And shake the markets," his banker Bazalvonov added.

Rotenberg said what Gorshkov really wanted to hear. "You will change the world."

5

WASHINGTON, D.C.

J. EDGAR HOOVER BUILDING

PRESENT DAY

There was no confidence in the air at the FBI. No answers to lingering questions on the identity of the perpetrators who had planned and executed the attacks that targeted America's infrastructure, disrupting transportation in major cities. There were guesses as to who was responsible for the attempt to poison President Alexander Crowe. But no proof that tied the attempt directly to North Korea.

FBI Chief Reese McCafferty had hundreds of investigators working around the clock in Las Vegas, Pittsburgh, San Francisco, Washington, D.C., New York, and St. Louis—wherever the terrorists had struck.

They had footprints, but no fingerprints. Receipts from bomb-making purchases, discarded battery wrappers used for powering remote detonators recovered by an astute Virginia motel housekeeper. Stolen credit cards used to pay for lodging and to rent cars, trucks, and watercraft. The FBI had taken down perpetrators on the Oakland Bay Bridge. But they were ghosts well before they were killed.

All objective and subjective signs pointed to North Korea as a culprit. *The culprit,* McCafferty wondered, *or a puppet?* But who? *Iran, China, or Russia, because a puppet has to have a master.*

McCafferty called Gerald Watts, his counterpart at the CIA. "Anything new on your end?"

"Nothing," Watts said with resignation; without proof there was nothing to take to the White House. And even if they had evidence, Watts, like McCafferty, wasn't convinced the new president would act on it.

"Gerald, this was an immense operation. I wouldn't be surprised if all loose ends were eliminated."

This call ended as others had in the weeks before. The agency and the FBI continued their investigations, and life moved on with people outside the affected cities already forgetting.

THE DIRKSEN SENATE OFFICE BUILDING

The attacks were in the front of the minds of members of Congress, particularly Senator Mikayla Colonnello, chair of the Committee on Homeland Security and Governmental Affairs.

"Elizabeth, we need to talk."

"Of course, Mikayla."

They were on first-name basis on the phone but fell back on titles whenever they were in public.

Elizabeth Matthews continued, "I was expecting I'd be hearing from you."

Colonnello and Matthews shared respect for one another over their terms in Washington. Colonnello, a California native like Matthews, was born and bred in Orange County. She'd earned her master's degree in international business at the University of California, Irvine, risen from CFO to CEO ranks at a startup Santa Monica Silicon Beach tech firm, oversaw its sale to Amazon, and used her earnings to bankroll a run for the U.S. Senate. Now midway through her second term, she'd distinguished herself as fiercely independent, yet a loyal friend. It was Senator Colonnello's committee work, first as a junior member, and for the last four years, as chair, that solidified their relationship.

Though eleven years in age separated them, Matthews never treated

Colonnello as a junior. They often shopped together and regularly met for dinner. Usually it was casual. Today's call definitely wasn't.

"Too many questions I can't answer," Elizabeth Matthews said.

"Interesting phrasing, Elizabeth."

"You know what I mean."

Senator Colonnello did.

"Call Watts and McCafferty."

"They're on the list, but so are you. Nothing I can do. America was attacked. Do you have any idea how much of the infrastructure bill money has to go toward rebuilding the bridges and the Lincoln Tunnel?"

"Of course I do," Matthews shot back. "But I can't. Get me off the list."

Matthews heard Colonnello take a deep breath.

"The State Department report that laid out the targets—"

"Leaked by a staff member on an intelligence committee? Used by a foreign power. We still don't know who."

"Then come and testify to that."

"And look like a fool? No thank you. Watts and McCafferty," she said again.

"How about we talk about this over dinner? I'll see if I can come up with any solutions."

"Give me a few days. And promise me that solution will keep me out of it."

"I'll work on it."

Right after hanging up, Matthews made two quick calls. The first to FBI Chief Reese McCafferty, the second to CIA Director Gerald Watts. The conversation was the same. Glum.

6

EGYPT

Dae-Jung Woo worked at a Baba Ali Café on Al Arbaeen in the city of Suez for two months without missing a day. Soon he wouldn't show up. When ordered, he would activate his team of three who had similarly filled their time with menial day jobs. Together, they would assemble their stored supplies at a warehouse on Al Shoda Street, retrieve scuba gear, and prepare for their assignment—blowing the outer and inner steel-plated hull of a tanker ship in the Suez Canal. They knew precisely where to plant the bombs for maximum destructive impact: under empty gasoline compartments where a combination of fumes and air would create an explosive mixture.

Roughly an hour north, Gyeong Song was also waiting for the signal to gather his crew and the equipment kept in another port warehouse. They'd strike in the dead of night along canal-hugging 23 July Street. Armed with shoulder-fired Light Anti-tank Weapons (LAW), costing a mere $350 each, they'd fire at specifically marked shore-facing containers loaded with explosives. Song and his team were the insurance policy, or more appropriately, the assurance that their target would go up in a fireball and down in the Suez Canal.

Once their mission was completed, the teams under Woo and Song would fold back into their jobs for a short time before returning home to be celebrated as national heroes to family and country.

Or so they were promised. The two leaders had been instructed to eliminate the problem of too many people knowing too much. Eventually there would be one, and then none.

MOSCOW

TWO MONTHS EARLIER

There's a saying that particularly resonates in the world of espionage. Three people can keep a secret if two of them are dead.

The adage wasn't lost on Gorshkov's inner circle. It wouldn't be recognized in time by those carrying out his plan.

The agents, the operatives, and the sleepers had all come to Russia under false pretenses. Better non-Russians than Russians for purposes of deniability. They'd been told they were serving the interests of their own countries—the Democratic People's Republic of Korea and the Islamic Republic of Iran. But they really were in Nicolai Gorshkov's employ while living, working, and waiting in Central America, Egypt, in the Atlantic, and the Persian Gulf.

They were professionals both on the ground and under the sea: munitions experts and veteran commanders. The North Koreans were promised unimagined luxuries for their families. For the Iranians, rewards they wouldn't have to wait for the afterlife to enjoy. They were told they were on missions to strike fear in the cold hearts of the West's infidels. Stealth ops and holy errands. Stories they could share with the children and grandchildren to come.

Within a very short time, the world would hear how loud a noise sleeper spies could make.

"Gentlemen," Gorshkov said, "I am ready. Are you?"

One-by-one he heard a resounding yes from his men around the conference table.

"And after we have struck?"

"The world's economy will tip in favor of the Russian Federation. Imagine what we will accomplish with a blank check and a little help from our friends.

PANAMA

A hotel cook, an Uber driver, and a warehouse worker, all Koreans with stolen American IDs, awaited orders from their unit commander regarding which ship to board. When the signal came, they had two hours to meet, change into port inspector uniforms, and take control of a harbor pilot boat, kill the crew, and board the designated tanker. They had made trial runs for months, here and abroad, and were excited to finally fulfill their mission and return home.

7

WASHINGTON was the globe's acknowledged home for these kinds of meetings. A furtive walk-and-talk along Rock Creek Park, down the National Mall, through Meridian Hill. This morning, Elizabeth Matthews met Dan Reilly at Chesapeake & Ohio Canal National Park.

The trail began in Georgetown and stretched all the way to Cumberland, Maryland. Today their walk would take them just a mile. Twenty minutes. Their conversation would begin with light chatter—How are you? Getting any rest?—then ease into the real agenda except when bikers and joggers approached. They would never raise their voices beyond a conversational volume. Those were the rules. Not just for Matthews and Reilly, but for the dozens of similar conversations occurring today within the 258 miles of Washington Beltway between handlers and spies, reporters and their confidential sources, lobbyists and members of Congress, and even hookers and Capitol Hill clients.

Elizabeth Matthews didn't travel alone. She couldn't. She was the United States Secretary of State under President Alexander Crowe and the man who replaced him following an assassination attempt that ended his term well before it was over. Now she worked for Ryan Battaglio, a president she considered just short of incompetent. And yet, remaining in his Cabinet was more important than leaving. At least for now.

Matthews was in her mid-50s with a bright political future ahead. She was warm on camera and tough behind closed doors. She dressed for the job; conservatively, though her politics tended more centrist. But to really understand Matthews, all insiders needed to do was to look at whatever brooch she wore on a given day. The pin itself always held meaning, as did the way she wore it—right side up, upside down, or to the left or right side. Everything said something to people smart enough to notice. It wasn't an original idea. Madelyn Albright, President Bill Clinton's Secretary of State, had started so-called "pin diplomacy" with flair and distinction. Matthews turned it into high art, keeping everyone guessing what she was thinking whether they were close friends, political rivals, or the press. She always left it to speculation unless she was trying to communicate a specific message to a specific person.

Today Matthews wore an enamel bear pin designed by a Native American artist. From the time they first met at 7:50 a.m., Reilly wondered what it meant.

"Madame Secretary, nice to see you," Reilly said.

"And you, Daniel. Thank you for joining me for a little morning constitutional."

She was aware he was eyeing her pin.

"Just something I picked up on a trip to Denver."

"It's never just something," Reilly said. "Let's see. Bears hibernate. Bears eat salmon and people who get in the way. They have a keen sense of smell. We equate Russia with the bear. Am I in the ballpark?"

"One national park," she said. "We should also keep our eyes out for dragons and lions."

"Cagey."

"Uncaged," she said. "Let's take this at a faster pace."

"The conversation?" Reilly asked.

"The walk. I'm not getting enough exercise." Elizabeth Matthews immediately sped up and Reilly double-timed to keep in step.

Matthews and Reilly were friends, nothing more than that. But friends who deeply cared about one another. Matthews quickly established that this walk was going to be all business. She signaled to her handlers, agents of the Diplomatic Security Service, the State Department's police force, to widen out. They did so and watched for joggers and bicyclists, for friendlies and threats.

"I take it you didn't just want me for company on your morning jaunt. What's on your mind?" Reilly asked.

"Not that I don't enjoy your company, but yes. I'm hearing things. Things that you should know about."

Dan Reilly had worked for Elizabeth Matthews when she was an Undersecretary of State. She'd taken him under her wing, hoping he'd continue working in the State Department. However, a job in the private sector took him out of government service, but never far from Matthews. As he traveled the world for Kensington Royal Hotels, he served as an additional unofficial source for her. On a more formal basis, he also provided information to a friend at the CIA. That made his life complicated. In one sense he was an informant. In another, he was informed. Intelligence flowed both ways. He got and he gave. Today, he felt he'd get.

"Daniel, you know what they say about a butterfly flapping its wings."

"Yes. We'll see the effect here from halfway around the world."

"And if the flapping begins here?"

"What are you saying, Elizabeth?"

"There's an ill wind blowing, and if you can't feel it, then it's time to turn in your secret decoder ring."

"I don't have a secret decoder ring," he said.

She laughed. "We'll work on that. Everyone in the Diplomatic Security Service has one."

"I'm not ..."

She laughed again. "Sure you're not."

They continued to walk. He was right. She gave him a good deal to think about.

THE WHITE HOUSE

President Ryan Battaglio sat at the Resolute Desk. He was above all things, resolute to a fault. Battaglio had not been elected president. He had succeeded Alexander Crowe after his predecessor was poisoned in the Oval Office by a still-missing assassin. Crowe lived but turned over the government to the lesser Battaglio, whose nomination as Vice President had been a political compromise to solidify the party. The ticket won and now Battaglio was president, ill-prepared for the office but arrogant enough to run amok within it.

He was already limiting intelligence department access to his phone calls, looking into replacing Crowe's cabinet members with interim appointees who wouldn't require Senate confirmation, and developing new political alliances that would serve his vision of America. His new best friend was Russian President Nicolai Gorshkov.

So for the fourth time in two weeks, Battaglio placed the call himself. No one else was invited to listen. Not even a translator. Nonetheless, even Battaglio figured the call would be monitored by the National Security Agency, which he headed. Considering there would be a record and undoubtedly a recording, he would take care with what he said.

The phone rang five times. Battaglio waited, measuring his breaths. This was still all so new to him. He had to show strength.

On the sixth ring a woman answered. "Hello."

"Hello," Battaglio replied. "Who is this?"

"Just one moment, Mr. President."

It was a friendly voice. In English. "I'll have President Gorshkov for you shortly."

One minute later, Ryan Battaglio, President of the United States, was speaking with Nicolai Yurievich Gorshkov, President of the Russian Federation.

"So glad you called, Ryan." Gorshkov said in perfect English.

"Mr. President."

"Please, I insist we must keep this on a first name basis when we confer in this manner."

"Of course. Thank you, Nicolai" Battaglio said.

"It's so good to hear your voice again," the Russian president said. "We can do great things together."

"I share your opinion, Nicolai. It's nice to chat—just the two of us without all our aides. Much freer."

Battaglio couldn't see how wrong he was. Gorshkov had four chief advisors—Sechin, Moloton, Bazalvonov, and Kudorff—along with the Director of the Federal Security Service (FSB), General Valery Rotenberg, listening silently. They sat opposite the Russian leader, eager to see how the conversation would play out.

"So, what can I do for you, Ryan?"

"First of all, I'm sorry I'm calling so late. I didn't check the hour."

"Only eight hours ahead of you. Not even dinner time."

Battaglio realized he should have known that.

"Besides, Ryan, it's never too late for us to speak."

"Thank you, Mr. President."

"Please. Again, I must insist. It's Nicolai."

"Thank you, Nicolai."

Battaglio took a strained deep breath that he hoped Gorshkov wouldn't catch. He didn't want to convey any anxiety. After all, he believed he had forged a good relationship with Gorshkov only weeks earlier in Stockholm. But he had to maintain an air of authority, never sounding weak.

"I'd like to talk to you about the election in Ukraine," Battaglio began.

Gorshkov immediately replied, "Yes. Encouraging."

It wasn't the response Battaglio sought. It threw him. He couldn't afford to get thrown. He had to show resolve; be *resolute*. Battaglio cleared his throat and measured his response.

"Nicolai, at the Stockholm summit we agreed to have a fair and open election."

"Of course, we did. It forged our friendship."

Battaglio agreed to Gorshkov's proposal to hold elections in Ukraine. This was against the advice of NATO negotiators, the U.S. Secretary of State Elizabeth Matthews and National Security Advisor Pierce Kimball who argued unsuccessfully that Gorshkov was empire building with the goal of reclaiming the former Soviet satellite nations. And true to form, Gorshkov put another plan in motion, accomplishing what his predecessor had begun—the complete political realignment of Ukraine into the Russian Federation.

"May I be perfectly honest with you, Ryan?"

"Certainly."

Gorshkov put a smile in his voice. "You see things more clearly than your predecessor. The big picture. The way we can make the world a safer place. A new world of nations built on respect for national needs. Geographic needs. Historical needs."

He paused to let Battaglio think about the point, but not too long.

"We can be a great benefit to one another. It won't be easy. We will have to quell debate amongst our brethren, but just imagine the business success we can create. But I'm getting ahead of things, and after all, this was your call."

Battaglio cleared his throat. A habit. He had no idea that a Russian psychological profile on him noted that he did that when nervous, uncertain, or confused before speaking. *Irresolute.*

"Nicolai," he began, "you are quite right, it won't be easy. And hence the reason to talk with you."

"Oh?" It was a polite *oh*. Not one designed to shake Battaglio.

"We need to come up with something that will be of benefit to me." He immediately corrected himself for any NSA ears. "For the United States. I can't have Congress nipping at my heels over this."

Nipping at my heels? Nicolai Gorshkov wasn't certain what the idiom meant. But he did understand the position he had put Battaglio in. Step by step, the former KGB and FSB spy was marching toward restoring Russian control over Eastern Europe. Battaglio needed something in return. That was to be expected. But the American would never get the better of him. That was certain. The reason was decades old.

"I suppose I have presented you with certain domestic political challenges, Ryan. Please let me know what I can do to help you." Gorshkov paused, stifling his snicker. "Do you have anything specific in mind?"

"Yes, Nicolai. I don't like my Secretary of State."

OUTSKIRTS OF WASHINGTON

"It's worse than imagined," Elizabeth Matthews continued on their brisk walk. "Gorshkov played Battaglio masterfully in Stockholm earlier this year." She was referring to a meeting Battaglio took as Acting President after the unsuccessful attempt to assassinate President Alexander Crowe. "He was unprepared for the meeting. Unprepared to negotiate. And, I'm not alone in saying this, he's unprepared to be president. It's going to be a long two years until the next election. The man can do a great deal of harm in the meantime."

"He's teachable. Teach him."

"Not possible. He needs to go, but we can't risk tipping our hand. If we do, we'll be replaced. And while it's inevitable that will happen anyway as Battaglio reshapes the administration, we want to postpone that day."

"We?"

"A very small group of us."

"Which you want to expand?"

Matthews smiled but didn't answer the question directly. "Daniel, Battaglio sold out Ukraine. Gorshkov has advisors in Kyiv who will control the polls. The elections will go badly. Ukraine will fall just like Crimea. Nicolai Gorshkov will be one nation closer to redrawing the political map of Europe."

Nicolai Gorshkov's motives and history were well known to Reilly. In the late 1980s, Gorshkov had earned a brutal reputation in East Germany as a young KGB lieutenant colonel luring, recruiting, blackmailing, and manipulating foreign journalists, professors, scientists, politicians, and executives. Once compromised, they'd do Gorshkov's bidding, stealing whatever intelligence there was to steal, reporting whatever there was to report—from state and military secrets to corporate plans and think-tank studies. When the Berlin Wall fell and it became apparent a divided Germany would become whole without Russian governance, Gorshkov was ordered to burn all of his records and drop his assets. In the last hours of his time in his last post, Potsdam, he burned boxes upon boxes containing intimate reports, titillating audio tapes, and salacious 16mm film. Everything he had used to control his network.

The collapse of the Soviet Union became the watershed in Gorshkov's political life. His guiding principle came down to the fact that the old men in the Politburo sold him out in Germany. They'd sold out the legacies of Lenin and Stalin. They'd sold out Mother Russia.

Gorshkov returned to Russia hating the regime. But this was not his time for revenge. It was the time to plan for the future and to plot his own ascension. Married, with two children, he was assigned to St. Petersburg to take a post in Leningrad State University's international affairs department. At least that became his latest cover story. Aside from relatively meaningless academic duties, his principal job was to recruit moles and spy on students; work he knew all too well.

This led him to an even better opportunity. Gorshkov became deputy mayor of St. Petersburg and earned more political currency in the reconstructed Russia.

He cashed some in after the dissolution of the Soviet Union, heading a committee to bring overseas businesses to St. Petersburg. As a port and a home to the state-owned shipbuilding and defense contractors, there was money to spend and money to make. Nicolai Gorshkov worked both sides of the deals for years, parlaying his ever-expanding position into higher political circles.

Decades later, guided by unfailing faith in his own right to rule, Nicolai Gorshkov became the natural heir to the Russian Federation presidency. At his side, he had a network of people loyal to him. Those who dared conspire against him had short-lived terms in the Kremlin.

Now Gorshkov was closer to fulfilling his dream of reestablishing Russia as a true world power. To ultimately succeed, he needed two things: the former Soviet satellite countries returned to Kremlin control and cash. The border countries were already beginning to fall one by one through the combination of the rise in nationalism, the promise of protection from Moscow, voter fraud and intimidation, and strategic military moves. Money would come with the sale of oil and natural gas, through increased sales to Europe via his personally brokered deals with Russian oligarchs. These relationships gave Gorshkov ultimate authority over the near markets. But his real goal was the Far East. Gorshkov wanted to lock out all other nations and become the single supplier to the world's most oil-starved country—the People's Republic of China.

The press, which Gorshkov controlled, carried every story as he wanted it reported. Every lie. Every bit of propaganda. He had no organized opposition, and he viewed the world as his for the taking.

As Elizabeth Matthews talked, Dan Reilly reflected on the one time he had met Nicolai Gorshkov. It had been little more than a year ago at a reception in Moscow. Gorshkov exuded charisma and telegraphed pure evil. Since then, their paths had crossed through agents Gorshkov sent to do his messier bidding—an assassin and a spy. In each case, Reilly managed to walk away; his direct involvement unknown to the Russian president. He feared that his invisibility wouldn't last forever.

And then there was Ryan Battaglio. Reilly knew him, not just through reputation, but through experience. He had history with the man—a disastrous history, all too quickly blown past and buried in government red tape. It went back to his service in Afghanistan.

"Dan, it's bad," Elizabeth Matthews said, bringing Reilly back to the present. "Doing nothing is not an option."

Reilly touched her arm lightly. "You're playing with fire."

"I am. But I want to know I can rely on you."

"To do what?"

A member of her security detail twenty feet in front pointed to her waiting Town Car and her SUV escorts. She acknowledged the signal. "Another minute."

"To do what?" Reilly repeated.

"To put disparate pieces together."

"About?"

"Battaglio. Anything you hear in your travels. Anything that relates to Gorshkov. Anything that appears more important than what most people might consider."

"You've got more eyes and ears around the world than anyone," Reilly offered. "And access to Langley."

"Yes, I do. But I want yours. I trust you. I need you."

Reilly now considered sharing his experience in Afghanistan when then-Congressman Battaglio toured the war zone. But she had to leave. It would hold for another time. So he did all that he really could do for now—he nodded.

"The last car can take you back. Stay in touch, Daniel. Pay attention." She touched the bear pin over her heart on her tailored black jacket.

Reilly thought he finally got the meaning. It came to him in a roundabout way. Back to an Army unit he was assigned to—the 250th Intelligence Battalion. The colorful insignia of the unit included seven stars forming the Big Dipper constellation: Ursa Major, the Big Bear. The motto below in gold: "KNOWLEDGE POWER FREEDOM." Bears, he had learned, have a sense of smell well beyond a dog's and eclipsed human ability by a factor of 2,100.

"You're following a scent, Elizabeth," he said.

She lowered her hand. "Am I?"

"And you want me to help."

She tilted her head to the right and gave a half smile.

"Okay, a trade."

"Oh?"

"I have an itch."

"Allergies?"

"Only to things I don't understand."

"And in this case?" Matthews asked.

Reilly said without hesitating, "Three questions. Who would put a hit out on a Russian oligarch? Why in one of our hotels?" He paused.

"That's two," she replied.

"The third. What can you tell me?"

"Nothing."

"Meaning you can't, or you won't?"

"I don't have anything yet. The report hit my desk last night. You may know more."

"I don't."

"Then," she touched the pin again, "we both have things to sniff out."

MOSCOW

THE KREMLIN

Nicolai Gorshkov had a grip on Russia even tighter than his predecessor's, more money than anyone else in the country, and more operatives than any Soviet premier had during the Cold War. He was charming and ruthless. Married and unfaithful. A father and a son of a bitch. As a spy, he surveilled and he killed. He hadn't stopped either as president of the Russian Federation.

"Gentlemen," Gorshkov asked. "Comments?"

The Russian president was known to invite comments as a means to gauge loyalty, though everyone in his inner circle knew to take special care not to tell truth to power. Accordingly, Rotenberg measured his words carefully. He was only recently appointed to the high-level post. Just three weeks earlier, his predecessor had the misfortune of not stepping out of the way of an oncoming bullet. His death saved the Russian Federation the cost of a short trial and years of prison meals. He wasn't guilty of state crimes, but recent events in Stockholm resulted in the death of one of the FSB's superstars and another deep mole in the United Kingdom. An unforgivable mistake. A waste of years of training. A fatal mistake. Gorshkov blamed the FSB director, and his fate was sealed.

Now Rotenberg was in at the top, with, he hoped, a longer life ahead. He was fifty-six, ten years younger than Gorshkov, but no less ruthless. He had risen in the ranks with the president, most recently serving as FSB deputy director following a decorated career as general of Special Operations Forces. Even more important, he was the president's brother-in-law.

"Valery, don't hold back. What did you see in Battaglio's manner?"

"Most of all inexperience, sir. Hesitation as well. He's looking to you for solutions."

Gorshkov turned to his advisors. Dr. Arkady Sechin was his oil expert: a professor at Moscow University and a man who earned a great deal more from consulting for Gorshkov than he did from teaching. He was the architect of Gorshkov's working plan. Markov Kurdorff and Gregor Moloton competed to run Gorshkov's businesses: those on the books and those off. All of Gorshkov's gains were somehow funneled through his banker, Igor Bazalvonov, into hidden bank accounts around the globe. General Valery Rotenberg, director of the Federal Security Service, was charged with watching them all carefully.

"You have given him a tactical approach with calculated, timely wins he can boast. He will look like the victor in a very difficult negotiation. In reality, you will own him, Mr. President. For that reason, he will do as you say so long as he thinks he's manipulating you."

Gorshkov nodded. The men had heard the conversation as he had. Battaglio was in his pocket. He excused everyone but General Rotenberg. Once the civilians were out of the office, Gorshkov smiled. "Can I trust them?"

There was no right answer. Yes or no; either could be wrong. The newest FSB chief chose another approach.

"Compartmentalize information, Mr. President. No one knows everything you're thinking. If you ever suspect disloyalty, you plant a seed and see if it takes root."

"Spoken like a true spy, General."

"I shall take that as a compliment."

"You should. Now to your man?"

"Busy. London was a success. We're on schedule for the others."

"You're certain he can't be traced to us."

Rotenberg shot a confused look.

"If he gets caught?" Gorshkov asked more specifically.

"He's not the type who gets caught. But I also put on another hire to take care of your additional request."

"With the same sense of confidence?"

"Actually, there will be a different outcome."

"Oh?" Gorshkov raised an eyebrow; a signal that he required more information.

"We will be laying down breadcrumbs. Clues to be followed. A dead end. I am not worried."

"A word of warning, General."

Rotenberg listened.

"You walk in the shadows of predecessors who did not worry enough."

"My apologies, Mr. President. I misspoke. I should have said, there will be no mistakes."

Gorshkov smiled. "Very good. No mistakes it is. Tell me when this new hire has completed the assignment."

"I won't have to. You'll hear it on the news."

8

ARLINGTON, VIRGINIA

Reilly cleared security at Reagan National Airport for his mid-morning flight to Chicago. He pulled a single rolling suitcase and, with briefcase in hand, headed directly to his gate with the day's *Washington Post* tucked under his arm. He read the *Post, New York Times, Chicago Sun-Times,* and *Wall Street Journal* every day online, but he still liked real paper for the plane.

The nonstop United 11:45 a.m. flight would get him in just after 1 p.m. He'd be a little late for his meeting at two o'clock, but the team should be well past small talk by the time he arrived.

He had thirty minutes before boarding—time to check in with his assistant, Brenda, and time to read the front page.

"What do you have for me, Brenda?" Reilly asked.

"Most of your Crisis Committee can make it in person."

"Who can't?"

"Mr. Klugo. No surprise. He'll call in from Morocco. General Coons is recovering from an eye operation, but says he'll be on the phone and can come in person if we need him by next week."

"Okay. Did Alan make it to London?"

"He landed this morning."

"Have him Zoom in online," Reilly said.

45

"Already have."

"And Shaw?"

"No noise from his office. But Nancy promised to warn me if he gets concerned."

"Tell her I'll stop in to see him before hitting the meeting. I'll need fifteen."

"Done."

Reilly hung up and browsed through the paper. He stopped at page five. The headline below the fold, left column, caught his eye.

London Police Investigating Hotel Shooting

The report summarized the shooting. No names, but the story identified the Kensington Royal Mayfair. Reilly knew that Chris Collins, the company lawyer, and PR Vice President Patricia Brodowski would be knee-deep in their own crisis management.

"Not especially good news."

The voice came from over Reilly's shoulder. He smiled and quietly responded without turning around. "Yup. Anything you can add between the lines?"

"Just my opinion. A well-staged professional hit. Clean in and out. Something someone paid good money for."

"Motive?" Reilly asked.

"Russian oligarch. Possible power play, or maybe he outlived his usefulness."

"Want my two cents?" Reilly asked.

"Always."

"Kensington is hosting oil conferences around the world. What if this is just the first, with others to follow?"

"Any reason to believe that?"

"No reason to ignore it."

"Then we won't. I'll be in touch if I come up with anything. And if you do—"

The man left the rest unsaid, but Reilly completed it in his head. A thought echoed what Elizabeth Matthews had said: *Stay in touch.*

When nothing else was said, Reilly looked over his shoulder. Bob Heath was gone, returning to his office at Langley—back to the CIA.

* * *

At the same time, a passenger was disembarking a flight from Singapore via Brussels. The story would be simple for the young Asian traveler at U.S. Customs. "Student. I'm on holiday. Touring the area, visiting the museums, then an interview with graduate schools."

It was narrative told dozens, if not hundreds of times a day at Dulles. Rarely questioned. Rarely checked. Simple follow-up would be to detain the traveler, call the schools, and confirm the appointments. But that took time, and Customs Agent Will Lindo didn't want to hold up the line for someone whose visit seemed perfectly normal.

Still, he thought, *maybe one question just to see…*

"And where will you be staying?"

"Exploring at first, but then in the city. It's …" It took a moment to call up the name on the cell phone itinerary. "The Kensington Capital."

Good enough, Lindo concluded, stamping the traveler's passport. "Hope all goes well. Welcome to the U.S."

"Thank you."

With that United States Customs and Border Protection cleared a foreign operative with quite a different agenda than the lie told to Agent Lindo.

CHICAGO, ILLINOIS
KENSINGTON ROYAL HOTELS CORPORATE HEADQUARTERS

Brenda Sheldon handed Reilly a cup of freshly brewed coffee. She knew just what Dan Reilly liked; moreover, she knew what he needed. That included a packed suitcase with two suits, five shirts, jeans, turtleneck, and Vans that he wore when he flew. He exchanged suitcases with her. Reilly also knew what she liked when he traveled. Chocolates. Today's came in a colorful box, a delicious thirty-piece assortment from Artisan Confections in Arlington.

"Coffee for chocolates," Reilly said, "I think you get the better of the deal."

Sheldon laughed lightly. "I hope you don't ever see that as a problem, Mr. Reilly."

"I know my place."

"You're smart, for a man," she joked.

"Compliment accepted," Reilly responded.

"With room to grow."

"Point noted."

Such was the banter Reilly enjoyed with Brenda Sheldon. She'd worked with him since he joined Kensington Royal from his job at the State Department. She was devoted to him as a boss, he to her as his assistant and confidant. She respected his need for discretion, because her husband was a police officer and a sometime contact for Reilly. Accordingly, she worried about the two men in her life.

"You're a fast learner. Like I tell Mr. Shaw, you have real possibilities."

Reilly laughed. "Anything I need to learn now?"

"As a matter of fact, according to a birdie, Mr. Collins has been with Mr. Shaw since eleven-thirty."

"Not a surprise," Reilly responded.

"And expecting an onslaught, he's lining up lawyers."

"From?"

"Gazplux, the dead Russian's company. They're blaming us."

Reilly sighed deeply. Collins should have waited for the Crisis Committee to come together. "Jesus! Collins is getting way ahead of his skis again. He knows he'll get recommendations from the group—which he's on. Okay, thanks. Should I thank your birdie before I head in to see the boss?"

"No need. You've already sent her flowers. Anonymously, of course." Sheldon knew how to work the system. "Third bouquet this month."

Reilly laughed again. "This anonymous person is really thoughtful."

"He has someone really sharp looking out for him," Brenda replied.

"And with that, I'm heading upstairs. Clear the way."

"Mow 'em down, Mr. Reilly."

Dan Reilly took his first and only sip of his coffee, puffed out his chest, and steeled himself for the meeting in EJ Shaw's office on the twenty-first floor.

"Your suitcase is ready when ..."

Reilly was out the door running to the stairwell as she finished saying, "you come back."

Brenda opened her box of chocolates and decided on a square decorated with red geometric designs. *Yes,* she thought, *Mr. Reilly learns well.*

* * *

Reilly bounded up the stairs two at a time, barely altering his breathing, thinking at least he was in decent shape. He exited on the twenty-first floor, turned down the hall and counted off the forty steps to EJ Shaw's outer office.

"Good afternoon, Mr. Reilly," Nancy Barney said. "Mr. Shaw is expecting you."

Reilly started toward the closed door. "Oh," she continued, "Mr. Collins is with him."

"I know."

She knew he knew. The fresh flowers on her credenza were the evidence.

"Hi, boss," Reilly said with a broad smile. He saw Collins sitting opposite Shaw. "Hello Chris."

Collins, five years younger than Reilly, was pure Brooks Brothers, while Shaw, twenty-five years older, was dressed in his preferred white shirt with a red tie and black sweater-vest. Shaw looked relaxed, Collins tense. His forehead was lined with worry, his teeth showing signs of grinding day and night. As much as the senior lawyer often sounded like a contrarian, Collins actually gave more than he obstructed. Nonetheless, Reilly always started conversations with him cautiously.

"Dan, welcome." EJ Shaw rose from behind his large oak desk, immaculate as ever. Nothing out of place. A yellow pad for notes in the left corner. A Montblanc author series fountain pen lying across it. To the right, an antique green-glass banker's lamp. To the left of the desk on a sidebar was his 27-inch iMac. Behind him, a bookshelf with a collection of historical novels, travel books, and even a row of his childhood Tom Swift, Jr. books. Framed on the wall were photos of his family from around the world, a picture of him at Notre Dame, where he served as a trustee, and photographs with each of the last five presidents in the Oval Office. Reilly doubted Ryan Battaglio would ever be part of the collection.

"Good flight?"

"Quick. Next one will be longer." He now addressed Chris Collins. "Hello, Chris, care to share what you're planning?"

Collins cleared his throat like a kid caught talking behind the teacher's back. "EJ and I were just reviewing legal strategy."

Reilly said nothing.

"Weapons down, Dan. Just a briefing," Shaw said. "I wanted to understand what kind of legal action we're likely to face. So let's all sit and talk."

Shaw took his leather-backed chair. Reilly, the empty seat next to Collins.

"I wish you could have waited," Reilly replied.

Reilly and Collins were colleagues, but often at odds with one another. The differences were apparent to Shaw: Collins always conservatively out to protect the company, Reilly determined to do the same while also committed to protecting clients. Together, they made the operation more secure, but it didn't mean that they didn't constantly butt heads.

"Dan, Chris put some thoughts together at my request." He repeated the last point: "At my request."

"Sorry. I have a lot on my mind."

"We all do, Dan," Shaw said softly.

"Okay, what do you have?" Reilly asked.

Collins replied, "Gazplux lawyers called this morning. Multiple lawsuits on the way."

"When?"

"They're working on paper now. Probably within the week."

"Based on?"

"Lack of adequate security."

"Jesus, Chris. Gazplux had two guys posted. They're the ones who let the shooter in."

"…who identified himself as a hotel assistant manager. He looked the part, right down to the nametag."

"And they let him in the suite!"

"And that will be part of our defense, which we may win in court, but cancellations are another matter."

"And?" Reilly asked.

"They're adding up."

"Okay. Understood. But we're upping the threat assessment to Red at the Mayfair."

"Doesn't that make us look guiltier?" the lawyer asked. "Not prepared?"

"It's SOP to go Red after an incident like this," Reilly quickly declared. "We've got the record to prove it. So Red at Mayfair, and we should consider what other properties to elevate—foreign and domestic."

"Jesus, Dan, overkill!"

"Just the opposite," Reilly countered.

"All right, gentlemen. Time to get out of your corners and make nice," Shaw said refereeing.

Reilly and Collins nodded. Shaw dialed the phone. A man answered.

"Steven, I need you."

Steven was Steven Hauber, VP of Risk Management. Collins gave an audible sigh of relief. Shaw summoned the wunderkind, plucked from Harvard B School with national debating championships under his belt. He was the executive to argue the company's case to the insurance company.

Hauber arrived just four minutes later, wearing a business suit and Air Jordans. He said he liked to get around fast. Shaw brought him up to speed.

"Steven, you have to make it clear that the police are viewing the London shooting as a criminal act, not terrorism."

"Was it?" the risk management specialist appropriately asked.

"Not according to initial reports," Reilly said. "So far London authorities are treating it as a targeted murder."

Reilly knew how important the distinction was. Insurance against terrorism required a separate, and significantly more expensive policy, far and above liability coverage. Moreover, for a company-owned and managed property, as the Kensington Mayfair is, the greater liability burden would fall on the hotel if the attack was regarded an act of terrorism.

Reilly continued, "Kritzler had his own security, Steven. The killer talked his way past them."

"Good for us," Hauber noted. "Not good for them."

Reilly had the same feeling. The two guards would likely not be heard from again.

Hauber had another pointed question. "Would Kritzler have been killed if he'd been staying anywhere else?"

"Yes, it was a hit," Collins declared. "One and done."

"And what are you hearing, Dan?" Hauber pressed.

Reilly hoped Collins was right but shared what was already in the works. "Steven," he emphasized, "we are taking precautions at our other locations, particularly where we're hosting oil conferences. Kritzler was there for one."

Hauber raised an eyebrow. "You've scaled up to Red Threat status, Dan?"

"Red in London, Red for venues hosting the conferences. Other international properties, Yellow."

"I'll let the carriers know."

The meeting wrapped up with Hauber about to put his debate skills to good use on Zoom. Shaw excused everyone but Reilly. As Collins was leaving, Reilly stopped him. "Sorry, Chris. This thing has me on edge. I'm actually worried that this might not be an isolated incident." He offered his hand.

"Better not be," Collins replied.

"Don't know."

They shook hands and the lawyer left. After the door closed, Shaw noted, "You're hard on him, Dan. He's doing his job. You're doing yours. Ease up."

"I will. It's a lawyer thing, not a Chris thing. We'll have dinner as soon as I get clear."

"When you get back from London, make it so." Shaw employed a term from his Navy service as captain of the guided missile cruiser USS *Lake Champlain* in the mid-80s.

Reilly responded accordingly. "Yes, sir."

Edward Jefferson Shaw, EJ since Boy Scouts, was soft-spoken, easygoing, and accessible. But anyone in business who took that as weakness ultimately regretted it. He was as shrewd as any other Fortune 500 CEO, but he retained the business ethic on which he founded Kensington Royal. *Everything mattered. Everyone mattered. Nothing is too insignificant to ignore.* It fit his company decades ago when he started out with ten employees and one food truck in Chicago. It defined the corporation on the New York Stock Exchange today.

"Now, the same question to you that I had for Chris. What do you think we're facing?"

"Hopefully a manageable PR problem and the legal issues that Chris can make disappear."

"Do you sense there's more that could come down the pike?"

Reilly took a moment to gather his thoughts. He wanted to correctly frame his response.

"Boss," he began slowly, "the Russian was in London for a European cartel session in advance of the full meeting in Riyadh next year."

"Yes, that's what I understand."

"Well, there are three other regional meetings this month. In Kenya, China, and Washington."

"Aren't they ..."

Reilly interrupted. "Yes. We have the contract. Maybe London was one and done. Maybe not. I want to elevate each of the other properties to RED status. I'll be taking that to the Crisis Committee."

"Okay. Good decision," Shaw observed. "Any intelligence to support your concern?"

The mere fact that Shaw used the word *intelligence* indicated a general awareness of Reilly's outside contacts.

"I haven't heard anything, but I have shared my concern."

Reilly stopped. He didn't want to say too much. Shaw would ask if he wanted more. He did with a raise of his eyebrows.

"We don't know why the Russian was taken out. It could have been an internal power play. It wouldn't be beyond Gorshkov. If that's the only reason, then he's just shuffling the deck, and there's little to worry about. But if this is part of bigger plan—"

"Bigger?"

"Let's just say we need to be prepared. There could be more down the line. That's the reason I don't want Chris to act too quickly. Talk, yes. Then stall until we know more. Doing that job will help us."

"Okay," Shaw said. "Make the point. I'll reinforce it. Now I want to talk to you about your job."

Reilly waited for a follow-up.

"How would you describe it, Dan?"

"It's a hard job that always gets harder. We're an American company with an open door around the world, and that invites trouble."

Kensington Royal wasn't alone in that department, but it was more prepared. Attacks on hotels had occurred somewhere in the world almost every month over the past twenty years, putting tens of thousands of guests at risk. In the course of the attacks, hundreds had been killed. And while the London shooting was different, Reilly looked at every attack through a wide lens.

"Could the shooting have been prevented?" Shaw asked. "And why in the room? Wouldn't it have been easier on the street?"

"First question: it could have been prevented if Kritzler's guards had actually done their job properly—not let anyone pass without first checking downstairs. But then again, that might have earned them each a bullet. As far as the room, no cameras were inside. And to answer your second question, London's huge network of CCTV street cameras would have likely captured the hit. So it was pulled off exactly as I would have planned it—in our room."

Shaw raised an eyebrow.

"That's what makes us smarter," Reilly added.

"And *us* is precisely what I want to get to. Just who is *us*, Dan?"

This was the question Dan feared he'd finally have to answer.

"Us?" Reilly fixed his eyes on Shaw. "There's *us* and there's the U-S."

"Go on."

"You sure you want to know?"

"It's time I should know. I'll tell you when to stop."

Reilly swallowed hard. He looked around Shaw's suite. Tall windows overlooking the Loop. Modern clean furniture. Original fine art. Everything comfortable. Like the man himself. It might be his, once Shaw retired. Reilly was conceivably one of the people in line. But he had never been very good about waiting around for things. Reilly lived in the moment. In the Army and in State Department service he lived on information. Information made him smarter. Information is what made his work for Kensington better.

He had inside contacts and with that came an open exchange of intelligence. Reilly's relationship with Elizabeth Matthews was one channel. The other was Heath at the CIA. Neither considered him a spy. More a conduit. And through the association, he reported things he saw and learned things he needed to know. But increasingly, even Reilly couldn't deny it. He was spying for the United States government. And now EJ Shaw wanted Reilly to admit that he served multiple masters.

Reilly began with a simple topic sentence. "Sir, above all else, you must recognize that I'm dedicated to my work."

"I've never doubted that."

"Then I hope you also know that everything I do is designed to make our business strong. Strong and safe."

Shaw nodded. Reilly drew in a deep breath.

"The country has enemies all over the world. They freely walk the streets with hoodies and backpacks, intent on making political statements with bombs and guns. They're religious radicals and military leaders, extremist groups and rogue nations, lone fanatics and presidents and premiers. If they have a credit card, they're welcome to a room. Come on in. Use the pool, eat in the dining room, and then blow up our building. Pretend you work for the hotel and shoot one of our guests. I know you're familiar with each of those scenarios."

"I am."

"Sir, we do a better job because I am informed. I have personal sources. And while we are not alone in intelligence mining, thankfully we are ahead of most."

Reilly hoped that this would be a stopping point. It wasn't.

"Who are they Dan? And what do they get in return?"

Reilly leaned back in his chair. Explaining this required care if he were to keep his sources confidential and his relationships general.

"As I noted, all major international operations have affiliations with intelligence organizations around the world. Mostly we get advisories. State Department warnings. A heads-up from Interpol and metropolitan police departments. These come in as discreet conversations. Sometimes they lead to nothing. Other times, we're grateful for the advance word. In turn, when we uncover or observe something suspicious—an unusual number of battery wrappers tossed in room trash, note pads with calendar dates, or unusual receipts—we pass that along."

He thought a sharper example would help. "If our surveillance cameras pick up someone taking an inordinate number of photographs in a lobby, it might be reconnaissance for an attack. Alan is routinely informed by our security. He reports to local authorities and tells me. We decide whether to launch it higher up for analysis."

"Higher up?"

"Higher up," Reilly repeated not wanting to provide specific names. "People who will do what local police in a country might not—check against photos of known enemies. If a high-risk ID pops up, we're more prepared. We move to an elevated alert status. That's what happened in Athens, Amman, and Mumbai. As a result, the bad guys go looking for another, more favorable target."

Reilly let the thought linger. He hoped he had said enough. Since Shaw gave him no indication to stop, Reilly continued.

"It's a necessary part of business. I just happen to have the background and certain friends who can give us a greater leg up."

"Such as?"

Now it was definitely getting uncomfortable.

"State Department relationships from my time there."

"Just State Department?"

"Like Alan, I've worked with the FBI," Reilly said. "In fact, I was at a training session at their Quantico campus before I came here." He hoped volunteering that would hopefully deflect further conversation.

"What kind of training?"

"Real life. Terrorists taking a hotel lobby. Guns out, ready to kill."

"Why you, Dan. I could see Alan doing this—"

"He has. With the FBI and the ATF. I felt I needed to as well," Reilly sighed, "to be better at spotting trouble."

"How'd you do?" Shaw asked.

"I died."

Shaw stifled a laugh. "I guess that pretty clearly answers *why*."

"Oh yes," Reilly said again, hoping that would put a period at the end of the conversation.

It still didn't.

"We need to come to an understanding, Dan."

Reilly pursed his lips but remained silent. Time to listen.

"I'm not blind. And I'm not unaware of the contact you haven't mentioned. Your friend at the CIA."

Reilly tilted his head. An acknowledgment.

"You see, I have relationships, too."

Reilly nodded.

"But I am concerned about the line you walk between what's legal and what's ethical. Or to put it more bluntly, the line you cross between what's illegal and unethical. And for the work you provide these unique relationships—"

Here it comes, Reilly thought.

"Are you salaried?"

"No, sir, I'm not."

"Do you need to disclose anything to our chief counsel?"

"I've been reporting to Chris regularly."

That drew a nod from Shaw.

"Finally, do you tell these relationships things that would violate any Kensington Royal corporate confidences?"

Reilly really hoped that was his final question; that Shaw didn't want to know more. Not specific details about his contact with the State Department and the Central Intelligence Agency, not his personal and political relationship with Secretary of State Elizabeth Matthews or CIA operative Bob Heath.

"Absolutely not. Never."

"Then I think I'm satisfied for now."

Reilly heard how his boss pronounced *for now.*

"So, here's what's on my mind," Shaw said directly. "I want *you*. You're too good to lose. But I can only do so much, protect you so much. I want to make sure I don't have to make excuses to the board. I have to have answers. The right answers, Dan, that your connections help us run our business more safely."

"They do."

Shaw studied Reilly in a way that invited a still greater response, more clarity. Reilly recognized the cue.

"It's a two-way street. We share. Sometimes they have a lot and I have a little. Sometimes, like I said, it's the other way around."

"I'm grateful for all that, Dan. For what you and Alan do. Safety depends on intelligence. I get that. It's when it crosses over into politics."

Reilly showed a blank face.

"We both know what I'm talking about. Your relationship with the Secretary of State. Your affair with the Russian agent who worked for Barclays."

EJ Shaw had focused on the two women he had trusted. One alive. One dead. Elizabeth Matthews who was absolutely a confidant, a source, and an ally. And Marnie Babbitt, an FSB agent planted deep inside the London bank. She had entrapped him with the goal of ultimately turning him. In the end, she died, conflicted over duty and love. Reilly thought Shaw didn't know. Glancing again at the photographs of his boss with past U.S. presidents, he realized he was wrong to believe Shaw wouldn't have the means to find out.

"I'm sorry about the woman. It will make you smarter."

"Yes, sir."

"As to your friend at the State Department, beware. Ask yourself the same thing. What are her motives for bringing you into her circle?"

Reilly frowned.

"Yes, she has motives, too. I don't want to see you go down with her."

"Sir." It was the fourth time in the conversation he referred to Shaw as *sir*. It helped punctuate his response. "The State Department has a standing hotel committee. Alan and I are plugged in. Have been for years. We give and we get. But we don't get enough through open channels. My relationships put us in a better position than other hotel companies. Hell, better than most international businesses. You have to trust me."

"Dan, I do. But since I began, this business has changed beyond all comprehension, especially since we went global. Terror for no good reason. Bombings, mass shootings, and yet we still keep the lights on. As you've told me, we're as much in the hotel business as the anti-terrorism business. Our reputation depends on us being smarter and safer than the next guy. You're dedicated to that. Unquestionably. But if I've heard certain things, it's not inconceivable that others will too."

Shaw was tipping his hand. His contacts—whoever and wherever they were—were warning him. He was warning Reilly.

"What do you want me to do?" Reilly asked.

"Two things. Two very important things. First, be careful—for your own sake and ours. Second, I'm starting a clock."

"A clock?"

"All right, a calendar. One year to see how this goes."

"EJ—"

"One year, Dan, to see how things work with one foot in and one foot out of," Shaw searched for the right terms, "... the swamp, the mud, whatever you choose to call it. The Beltway."

Reilly remembered how nervous he was first meeting Shaw eight years earlier. Not EJ, not Edward Jefferson. It was "Mister Shaw."

Shaw recruited him out of the State Department. A high-priced search committee identified Reilly based on the needs outlined by the company: international experience, critical thinker, team player, business degrees, language skills, and military training preferred, willing to travel.

Reilly checked all boxes and had passable proficiency in Arabic, Russian, and Mandarin. Kensington Royal made the offer, and Daniel J. Reilly joined the firm as an associate vice president and was given a company credit card with a $25,000 limit. Over the years that turned into an unlimited amount.

"Mr. Shaw, it is an honor to work with you," Reilly said on their first meeting in the Chicago tower.

"Prove it!" Shaw shot back.

Reilly was used to such banter from his Army service and what he had to do for then-boss, Under Secretary of State Department Elizabeth Matthews.

"I will, sir."

"Good. When I see it and feel it, you'll get a big bonus."

Reilly raised an eyebrow when he heard the inducement.

"Oh?"

"Yes, you get to call me EJ."

Now all these years later, EJ proposed another arrangement. "Got that? One year, Dan."

"It won't be a problem," Reilly replied without any notion if it were true.

"Good. Do what you need to do in order to keep us safe, but with the promise that you will not put this company in legal or moral jeopardy. Ever."

"You have my word."

"And you will let the people who are trained to carry guns carry them."

This was a harder question. He wondered if Shaw actually knew everything that had happened in Brussels when he chased down an assassin and in Stockholm after Marnie Babbitt was killed in the hotel explosion.

"I will." He decided to add one absolute truth. "Besides, I can honestly tell you I'm sorely out of practice." Reilly flashed back on the woman who shot him at Langley. It wasn't real, but it could have been.

9

LONDON

Timothy Eckhart put the book he was reading on his lap. The young woman next to him started talking to him. She was attractive, obviously educated, and alone. She sat next to him on the train out of London's St. Pancras Station. He seemed like a safe companion. Someone who definitely wouldn't hassle her.

After talking about the weather—rainy, their destination—Paris, Eckhart added to the obvious. He was a priest. He'd recently graduated from St. Augustine's Seminary in Toronto, and while awaiting his assignment from the Roman Catholic archdiocese, he had a few weeks to tour Europe. After seeing London, he was excited about taking the Eurostar through the Chunnel to Paris.

"And what do you do?" Father Eckhart warmly asked.

"I'm an art history doctoral student at King's College. Working on my thesis. Off to the Louvre," Miranda Schiller said with a delightful lilt to her voice.

"What area of study?"

"Neoclassicism. The arts that draw influence and inspiration from the historic works of ancient Greece and Rome."

"How interesting. So much to study."

"I could say the same for you."

"Well, yes," Father Eckhart replied.

He smiled at the young beauty next to him. He wondered whether she had other considerable talents. Probably. He considered her eminently fuckable. He wished he could, but it wouldn't end well for her, and it would be a tactical mistake. The priest's only job was to pass through French customs easily, not draw any undue attention, and catch a flight to Nairobi for an important appointment. The meeting would end with a religious experience. Father Eckhart would send his next target to heaven. Except by that time, he wouldn't be a priest anymore.

By last count, he had developed more than twenty distinct identities. Old and young, straight and gay, men and even women. He was a master of disguise and a very successful assassin, one of the world's best.

There was always work for a man with his talents, especially one who owed no allegiance to any one country. He had his favorites, but he considered himself an equal-opportunity assassin, originally trained with British pounds, but comfortable spending rubles, drachmas, dollars, yuan renminbi, yen, euros, and on the right occasion, even North Korean won.

He spoke five languages fluently and another four for the sake of business. No one knew where he lived or how to talk to him directly. He made calls to specific contacts he'd made over the years. If there was a job, they had fifteen seconds to tell him. He would figure out how. Then another call to arrange payment.

He was approaching his thirty-eighth birthday and planned to retire by forty-five. He killed with no remorse, turned down children, and would take out political figures for a premium. Guns were his weapon of choice. Poisons were acceptable. He wasn't a huge fan of knives or box cutters. Too messy. Arson and bombs were okay under the right circumstances. He was that discerning.

His most feared enemy was facial recognition. He was particularly careful at airports. He could spot CCTV cameras along streets and inside buildings. He knew how to turn away from their view without appearing suspicious.

The assassin had weapons stashed in warehouses around the world. He meticulously planned his executions and his escapes. In addition to being exceptionally proficient at what he did, he put his faith in people who knew how to manage finances. He had accounts in five safe countries, invested in Bitcoin and stocks. Well positioned and diversified. Of course, none of his money managers ever had direct contact with one another.

Seven more years and he would leave it all behind. All the disguises, all of the murders. Maybe he'd even settle down and start a family. It wasn't beyond the realm of possibility, he thought, as he returned to the thriller on his lap—the latest Jack Reacher novel. He smiled. *The author got so many things right. How did he know so much?*

10

THERE'S MORE TO A PERSON than what's in a resume or a corporate bio. And then there are people whose resumes aren't published, but their reputations precede them.

For example, a freelance assassin, a CIA operative, or a business executive with a background that doesn't show up in D&B Hoovers' database.

Dan Reilly is also one of those people. The National Security Agency had followed his Army career ever since he entered intelligence school. That wasn't listed on his CV. It wasn't until he was recruited by the State Department that Reilly learned that *followed* didn't begin to describe the agency's interest in him. They had groomed and primed him from beyond arms' length for years. Also missing from his resume—they made sure he had a job offer with the State Department when he retired from the Army with the rank of captain. Just another unknown step in their long-range plan for him. But Reilly decided on his own to get out of government work after years on the inside and the completion of a report on America's vulnerability as a State Department special program analyst. That fact was now circulating in closed circles.

Reilly left for the private sector, where he could use his experience and make more money. The Kensington Royal Hotel Corporation was interested.

Outside of government, he was still able to keep his contacts. One of those contacts, his former State Department boss, became more important to him. Elizabeth Matthews was two years his senior, but every bit his equal in bed. The attraction they'd had for one another at work remained unfulfilled. However, once he was out of government, the walls tumbled and they took to each other. Yet as fast as the romance began, the flame burned out. Matthews was rising in State Department circles, and Reilly was constantly on the road. Her security made it more difficult to remain discreet, and he wasn't happy keeping everything secret.

Though their short affair ended, their friendship didn't. They vowed it never would. Two years later Reilly married. Matthews was present for the wedding and also on the phone with him three years later, helping him through the divorce. Such was the relationship between Matthews and Reilly right through to her current position as United States Secretary of State.

Reilly also thought about whether he'd finally have to give up one job for another. Would conflicting loyalties finally get in the way of his ability to function as the international lead for Kensington? He worried about that. EJ Shaw worried about that. That's why his Kensington Royal boss gave him a year to figure it out. The bottom line—he was damned good with all the masters he served, but he was going to have to make a decision.

11

CHICAGO

"Thank you, everyone." Reilly addressed all the participants at the conference room table on the twentieth floor of the Kensington Royal Chicago offices. "I had hoped that we would not be meeting so soon, but circumstances have dictated otherwise."

Joining Reilly in person, to his right, was fifty-six-year-old company Chief Operating Officer Lou Tiano. He put down a prepared summary and displayed a look that showed he was taking the murder seriously enough to warrant discussion by the Crisis Committee. Next to him was Patricia Brodowski, the company's shrewd sixty-something CFO who helped shape KR's global footprint.

To Reilly's left, Chris Collins. Next to Chris was the company's Director of Media Relations, Lois Duvall: just thirty-three, but with the savvy of someone twice her age. Duvall had come from CBS Television with contacts and confidence. She was effective in the corporate office and as an on-camera spokesperson. At six feet, one inch tall, she commanded attention. Her shoulder-length brown hair, open face, and piercing eyes delivered the message and helped make the news.

Beside Duval sat Carl Erwin, former CIA Director, former Navy SEAL, and now a well-paid private consultant. He was arguably one of the most knowledgeable anti-terrorism experts in the country and a go-to talking head on CNN who never held back.

Continuing around, there was former Assistant FBI Director Tom Reardon. In his fifties, and more than a decade younger than Erwin and Coons, Reardon was a walking encyclopedia on terrorist tactics.

On Zoom, retired U.S. Army General BD Coons and Donald Klugo. Coons sat comfortably in his Texas ranch, recovering from his surgery. It wouldn't keep him down long. Prior to serving on the Joint Chiefs, he had commanded Special Forces in Afghanistan and Iraq.

Klugo was perhaps the most interesting member of the team as president and CEO of GSI, Global Security Initiatives. His company operated not so quietly out of Jordan. Klugo was careful who he took on as clients, careful because of the muscle and weaponry in his arsenal. Men and guns for hire. GSI was a mercenary outfit with boots able to hit the ground quicky in danger zones around the world. Their speed at deploying came from the two Airbus Beluga Super Transporters, evidence that GSI had very good-paying clients. One of them was Kensington Royal.

So far absent was Kensington Security Chief Alan Cannon. He promised he'd call in.

"Ladies, gentlemen, the subject is 'Why Us?'" Reilly asked. "Why was a Russian oil oligarch taken out in our hotel? Retribution? A change in management? A message? Strictly internal or something bigger? Theories?"

"I've talked to a contact at Scotland Yard," the retired FBI agent offered. "They're leaning toward Russia. Some sort of Gazplux house-keeping. Expertly planned and executed. Digging further. Calls out to Interpol."

"Thanks, Tom. Anyone else?"

Everyone heard someone clearing his throat on the conference line. "You know how I think."

It was Klugo, phoning in from Amman. The international security operative was well known for his blunt assessments.

"I wake up suspicious and I go to sleep worried. This doesn't go down like this without an underlying reason. Feels to me bigger than a company shuffle."

"Against us? To embarrass Kensington?" COO Tiano wondered aloud.

"Possibly, but not a good enough reason."

At that point, an alert sounded on the conference line. "Cannon here."

"Alan, thanks for calling in. We've got most of the usual suspects with us." Reilly ran through the participants and caught him up. "Anything new in London?"

"Just pulled into the hotel, but I've been talking to our team on the way from the airport. Nothing newsworthy. But in ten minutes they're going to walk me through the crime scene, which I'll do for you when you get here. Screening house footage later today to see if anything jumps out to me that the police might have missed. Of course, I'm pissed that Gazplux rushed Kritzler's security and his aides out the door as soon as they were finished giving their statements."

"Out of the hotel and out of the country?" Klugo interrupted.

"Don't know. I suspect their first stop was the embassy and from there to the airport. Any chance you can find out?"

"On my list," Klugo said.

"Thanks, Alan." Reilly then added, "Unless there's a change here, I'll be with you tomorrow, late morning."

"Good. I should have a better feel for everything by then."

"Okay, back to theories."

Klugo picked up where he left off. "As for staging a killing in the hotel, it made escape easier than pulling it off on the street in full view of London's extensive CCTV network. At least that would have been my mission decision."

This seconded Reilly's opinion.

Klugo cleared his throat again. "Alan, I'd be curious what his exfil route was and whether he went out as he went in."

"Meaning?"

"Disguises. It would help me draw up a list of suspects. This was a professional hit. Not everyone could pull it off so easily."

"Good questions. I'll check."

Reilly brought the conversation back into the room. "Where are we with the media, Lois?"

"Manageable with facts. Until we have more, we're just repeating what the police have already put out," Duvall said. "We've got our standard language about security and the well-being of our guests, along with our support for the ongoing investigations. Our position is we're open for business. So far, the only inquiries have come in from London papers and TV. No U.S. reporters, though the story has hit the wires."

"Saw it coming in."

"On the positive side, it's been pretty drowned out by the Ukraine vote and whatever noise the cable nets are shouting about."

"Need a statement from me?"

"Probably not yet Dan," Duvall replied. "Referring everything back to London police."

"Okay, back to theories. General Coons?"

"A personal observation." His deep voice exuded authority on Zoom as it did in command under fire. "I met Kritzler at a dinner in Moscow. At that point I was out of uniform, and he probably didn't really know who I was. He had more than a few drinks and was talkative. A little about business. Mostly about sex. This lined up with the Pentagon briefing paper I had on him. He always had a woman on his arm. He might have become an embarrassment to his own company, which would support the internal decision to quiet him."

Cannon spoke up again from London. "As a matter of fact, Kritzler's next visitor that night was a hooker. She's the one who discovered he was dead."

"Could she have killed him?" Tiano asked.

"No," Cannon stated. "Doctors determined Kritzler was dead before she arrived."

"Then the timing only gave the killer a limited window," Reilly noted.

"Wouldn't that mean the assassin had his schedule?"

It was a point no one had considered.

"That could play into Gazplux knowing more and wanting to move someone else in."

"They needed to kill him to do that?" This question came from the company lawyer.

"Fewer problems, Mr. Collins," former CIA Director Carl Erwin proposed. "No pension. No complaints. No risk of secrets sold to a competitor. A clean out for the company."

"Another thought," Klugo added over the phone. "Kritzler may have been planning a power play against another company, or even more dangerous, against Gorshkov. All reasons why it would be good to eliminate the problem outside Russian borders."

"Or it could be any number of other countries," Coons suggested.

"Or corporations," Tiano added, amending his notion.

"Too many threads all in a ball." Reilly's observation. "What's the best way to unravel them?"

"We play out all the possibilities into zero-sum scenarios," Erwin continued. "We identify the principal participants and anyone in the shadows. How are they involved? Are they essential or expendable? Ultimately it all comes down to one question: *Cui bono.* Latin for "who benefits?" It suggests that the greatest probability of someone being responsible for a certain event is the one who stands to gain the most from it."

Erwin believed, and Reilly concurred, that bouncing ideas among a diverse group of experienced critical thinkers was far better than just plowing ahead with one line of thinking. It also helped to have someone who could open everyone assembled to the possibilities and ultimately the probabilities.

Erwin explained. "In my early days at the CIA, we hired an analyst from NYU to consider more than a thousand predictions. He was twice as effective as our own people. His forecasts helped us shape Middle East policy, predict the actions of Islamic radicals, accurately name successors who would replace fallen leaders and terrorists, and who we should influence along the way. His insight helped us see through the fog."

Reilly added, "My experience has taught me that culture trumps strategy. We have to understand the core beliefs of foreign opponents, in war or peace, politics or business. What have they been taught … what do they want … what do they need? From our point of view, their actions may seem totally irrational. To them, they're reasonable and will be totally within their moral code. Let's face it, we don't have the same value systems as the people we're up against today. For that matter, we didn't with Hitler or Hirohito either. The same must be said for how we evaluate the Russians, the Chinese, the North Koreans, let alone terrorist organizations and lone wolf assassins.

"Our goal is to spot the person or country's gains that exactly equal the net losses of another's. For example, how might a political attack from one party lead to huge fundraising from another? How is religious zeal used to eliminate, eradicate people viewed as less pious or as nonbelievers? Mr. Erwin is right, ladies and gentlemen. *Cui bono*—who benefits?"

For the next three hours they weighed winners against losers in theoretical matchups and came up with dozens of possibilities. But the nation that topped most of their lists was China.

Reilly argued for another. "Russia," he said. To him, all roads led to Moscow, and all roads within Moscow led to the Kremlin. From there they went up to the cavernous Presidential Executive Office and to Nicolai Gorshkov, who was already speeding down a one-way road. "He wants to turn back the clock to when Russia was a major power and had control of all Eastern Europe."

Erwin went to a white board and wrote down China and Russia with a blue grease marker. "For the sake of argument, I'll add a third, USA."

He had the team's attention.

"China first. They've got money, people, and tech. It equals twenty-first-century power. Their business holdings around the globe are huge. And they're even expanding beyond Earth, satellites, the moon, Mars landings, who knows what else. But China lacks one natural resource in a major way—oil."

He circled USA. "We've got money, people, tech, and oil. Our power comes with a deep postwar pocketbook, but China holds much of our debt. We can argue that China is eating into our power with its own money, people, and tech. But we still deal in oil diplomacy.

"Now for Russia. Gorshkov doesn't have the cash, but they have people, tech, and oil. *Cui bono?* Who benefits in this Venn diagram? I'm with Mr. Reilly."

"I love what Senator McCain said about Russia," General Coons offered. "Russia is a gas station posing as a country."

"Right," Erwin said.

Pat Brodowski had drawn three circles on a pad of lined Kensington paper; a Venn diagram with overlapping and interconnecting circles. Within each, the name of a country. Her sketch had two circles that shared the most space: Russia and China. The U.S. only cut in a little on each. She cleared her throat. "China needs Russia's oil. Russia needs China's money," she declared while unconsciously tapping her paper.

Erwin recreated Brodowski's version on the white board. He switched from blue to a red marker and wrote OIL in large block letters. "Helluva win," he said. "Worth killing for?"

The question hovered in the air. The answer was obvious.

"Damned straight," Klugo added from Jordan. "Gorshkov is a mean son of a bitch who learned from the best. I don't mean best as a compliment. He learned from Soviet tactics. He learned from Lenin and Stalin. The lessons for us—never underestimate the lies he will spread, the deals he will make, and the military forays he'll attempt."

"Now let's see what else we can come up with," Erwin said. After another hour, energy was draining from the Crisis Committee. No new practical theories emerged. Erwin called for a break, recognizing another important lesson. Think tanks and the think tankers within often tanked.

Reilly stood. "I apologize. I have to leave. But up to this point, we really haven't answered my question. Why us? Please focus on that. You've all got my number. If you can't find me, Brenda will. Also, we're a corporation, not the U.S. government. But that doesn't mean we aren't inextricably linked to global issues. Come down from the jet stream and make sure you land on what our exposure is before something else happens."

Reilly didn't say it, but he left for O'Hare worrying that another attack was already in the works.

12

THAT NIGHT

The 8,500 ton, 300-foot long *Alexi Rykov* slipped out of Admiralty Shipyard at 0200 hours. The ship was named for Alexei Ivanovich Rykov, a Russian Bolshevik revolutionary who succeeded Vladimir Lenin after his death. He became the first premier of the newly established Soviet Union. But the ship had greater importance than the name on its hull. It was a technical marvel, a nuclear-powered, weaponized icebreaker enroute to the ever-warming Arctic to join its sister ships slicing lanes for Russian's ever-expanding interests.

The ship combined the functions of an icebreaker, a tugboat, patrol boat, scientific vessel, and warship. Armed with cruise missiles, a portable antiaircraft missile system, a helicopter launch pad, and electronic warfare akin to a destroyer, *Alexi Rykov* upped the Russian Federation's Arctic fleet, joining some forty other ships in the region and securing President Gorshkov's preeminence in the Ice Cold War. It could smash through six-foot-deep ice and get Russia all that much closer to controlling the NSR, the Northern Sea Route, the link between Asia and Northern Europe. It also made it easier for Russia's submarine fleet to carry out its operations.

* * *

Six time zones east, along the frozen landscape of the New Siberian Islands, activity picked up at Andropov Clover military base on Kotelny Island. The three-tiered complex houses up to 350 servicemen with enough supplies to operate and survive on their own for a year.

The base, closer to the Arctic Circle than to Moscow, was the latest of Russian President Gorshkov's 480 Russian bases above the 75th parallel. Andropov Clover, like the *Alexi Rykov*, gave Gorshkov immense influence and muscle across the massive coastline. From Kotelny Island, military personnel could quickly deploy with offensive and defensive armaments capable of operating in temperatures below -50C.

With Russia laying claim to nearly 50 percent of the total Arctic coast, the mission was to protect Russian Arctic interests as global warming created more access through the melting ice.

The clock was ticking in favor of Russia and against the West. The ground forces, the weapon systems, and ships would soon guarantee that nothing could pass without Russian permission. Nothing including oil.

To the press and the world, Gorshkov said he was expanding the Russian economic zone to cut shipping time from Europe to Asia by 40 percent compared to going through the Suez Canal. But there was more to it. The Kremlin would require any ship seeking to navigate the route to submit a forty-five-day notice, carry a Russian pilot, and pay transit fees.

Communism was dead in Russia. But like his predecessor, Gorshkov mastered capitalism, and soon his accounts receivable would be looking very good.

13

THE KREMLIN

Nicolai Gorshkov had CNN International on one TV and Russia-1, his state-owned entertainment and propaganda channel, on the other. CNN reported on renewed protests and riots in Ukraine. Russia-1 continued to falsely report on Ukraine's welcome liberation from Western tyranny. He knew one to be true, and it wasn't his own country's coverage.

Today, Gorshkov's own audience consisted of three senior military officials. Around the conference table sat General Ilya Alexandrov, commander of Russia's 150th Motorized Rifle Division, posted in Ukraine's major cities and border crossings. Beside him was General Ivan Zalinski, one of Gorshkov's most ruthless military leaders who headed the Southern Military District, which controlled the middle of Ukraine to the Black Sea. His forces now included more than 600 tactical aircraft, 440 helicopters, and the two tank regiments known as the "steel monsters" that leveled homes during the invasion.

Also at Gorshkov's disposal were Il-76 heavy-lift transport aircraft from the 7th Guards Airborne Division under General Arkady Bolonguv. They had flown out of Dzhankoi Air Base in northern Crimea, along with BMD-2 infantry fighting vehicles that had driven across the Kerch Strait Bridge. Bolonguv also commanded Su-30 and Su-24 attack aircraft, supported by S-300 and S-400 air defense batteries transported from Crimea into Ukraine.

Despite all the Russian troops and firepower, insurgents fought back, mostly with stealth strikes, some crippling, though never covered in Russian media.

Gorshkov was convinced Battaglio, inadequate and faint-hearted, would do nothing. The bitch Matthews, Battaglio's left-over Secretary of State, was another thing entirely. She was smart, with ambitions all her own: a player to remove from the table.

Gorshkov thought about ways to do that. His new FSB chief, General Valery Rotenberg, now entered.

"Valery, sit. I have an assignment for you."

"Yes, sir. Of course."

"You'll find it interesting, and it may take some of our established resources. I have utmost faith that you will succeed." He explained that he suspected that Matthews might run for U.S. president against Battaglio. For that matter she could very well win. "I want contingency plans to prevent that."

Rotenberg heard, *You know what will happen if you fail.*

"Yes, Mr. President."

"All options on the table."

Rotenberg also understood what *all options* meant: funding opposition candidates, the manipulation of social media platforms, digital psy-ops, campaign cyberattacks, and even a bullet from a sniper rifle. *All options.* "Your timeline?"

"Now. Plan accordingly. Do it right."

Once again he heard Gorshkov's not-so-veiled threat. *You know what will happen if you fail.*

"Okay, moving on," the president said affably, "Now, let's talk about the NSR."

14

WASHINGTON, D.C.

"The NSR? Never heard of it," Ryan Battaglio declared.

"Now's as good a time as ever," Elizabeth Matthews said. She had requested the briefing, which was important and timely. Joining the session in the Oval Office were familiar faces: CIA Director Gerald Watts, National Security Advisor Pierce Kimball, Defense Secretary Vincent Collingsworth, Chairman of the Joint Chiefs Admiral Rhett Grimm, and Chief of Staff Lou Simon. They all had a piece of the story to share. Matthews had instructed them to take their time, use photographs and charts, and remember KISS –keep it simple, stupid.

Admiral Grimm placed a map on an easel the president's secretary had ordered for the meeting. "NSR is the abbreviation for the Northern Sea Route; it extends along Russia's northern coastline roughly 3,500 nautical miles from the Kara Sea, along Siberia to the Bering Strait. The route lies within Russia's economic zone and within Arctic waters. Russia views the route as an internal waterway. We see it differently. And yet, the NSR is fast becoming the major transportation link between Europe and Asia as melting ice makes the Arctic more navigable. In the process, it literally gives Russia the high ground over Arab oil."

Battaglio nodded. "Competition is good."

"For Russia. They control the passage and require a forty-five-day approval of who and what goes through. But sir, it's what Russia is transporting through the NSR and what they're doing to secure the route that is particularly important."

"Go on," Battaglio said.

"Russia's interest in the Arctic goes back to the sixteenth century and its conquest of Siberia. It's all wrapped up in Russia's endless quest to acquire more resources and secure and control trading routes to build its economy. It's lost on most historians, but the modern oil industry was born in the Russian Empire. In 1846 they drilled the first oil well on the Absheron Peninsula in the Baku Region. In the nineteenth century, the Rothschild family and the Nobel brothers struck black gold and ruthlessly vied with each other for supremacy.

"Through the early twentieth century, the Russian Empire proved to be one of the world's top oil producers, controlling 30 percent of the market. The 1917 Russian Revolution led to the nationalization of the oil companies. With the Rothschilds and Nobels suddenly on the outs, the Communists made deals with Standard Oil of New York and Vacuum, the company that ultimately became Mobil. So rich were the Russian reserves that Winston Churchill noted, "If oil is queen, Baku is her throne."

"Of course, Nazi Germany wanted Russia's oil, and Hitler was willing to fight through the winter to get it. He didn't succeed. Following World War II, new oil regions were discovered, including vast territories in Western Siberia and along the Arctic Circle. The postwar increase in Soviet oil exports led to a dip in world oil prices and was a key reason for the establishment in 1960 of OPEC, the Organization of the Petroleum Exporting Countries.

"And now to more recent times," Grimm said. "Elizabeth?"

The Secretary of State stood next to the easel with a map. It showed the Pacific from the Arctic Circle and Alaska down through the Pacific coast, including Canada, the U.S., and the nations around the Pacific Rim.

"During the Cold War we were especially concerned about Russia's proximity to Alaska. At the nearest point it's only fifty-five miles—closer than Cuba is to South Florida. Close enough for missiles to launch, subs to harbor, troops to advance. Fortunately, none of that happened. As relations improved with the fall of the Soviet Union, tensions eased. But along came new dictatorial regimes and ultimately Nicolai Gorshkov. His rule erased any hope of cooperative engagement with the West. Gorshkov's well-known goals: protect Russian borders from further expansion by NATO while stretching its own influence, strengthen the Russian Federation military, and return Russia to superpower status.

"Perhaps more than anything else, the Northern Sea Route provides Nicolai Gorshkov with the means to fund all his world-building plans, both defensive and offensive. The NSR gives him a quicker, cheaper oil shipping route to China. It halves the time it takes containers to reach Asia through the Suez Canal.

"I can't put it any more directly, Mr. President. This faster delivery route solves Gorshkov's money problems. It wipes out any sanctions we've imposed against Russia, the oligarchs, and Gorshkov personally."

"Like I said, good for trade," Battaglio replied dismissively. "They've created a less expensive way to get their oil to Asia."

Matthews pushed ahead. "Mr. President, along with its newest Trans-Siberian pipelines, Russia stands to improve its economy thanks to a combination of global warming and their commitment to transiting the route. Currently oil and gas account for upwards of 60 percent of Russia's export business and 30 percent of its federal budget. Their commitment to the Arctic waterways has made strategic sense. I can't stress it enough. Increased oil profits give Gorshkov the cash he needs to reestablish control over his border-country neighbors well beyond Ukraine."

"That's quite a mouthful, Elizabeth and a rehash of Cold War scare tactics."

"Actually," National Security Advisor Kimball said bolting up. "It's more a possibility than ever considering—"

"Considering what!" Battaglio demanded.

"Considering our recent posture."

The words hung in the air and enveloped Battaglio.

Battaglio's nose flared and the veins in his neck flared out. Kimball had said the unspeakable truth in four words, thought by everyone in the room. Eyes shifted.

"Perhaps a better way to put it, Mr. President—"

Battaglio surprisingly smiled. "No need, Pierce. I think we all get it. Sit down, and let Elizabeth make her own bed."

The National Security Advisor obliged. Matthews kept her composure.

"Mr. President, recently President Crowe worked with NATO command and the U.N. to explore new treaties, a right-of-passage agreement, and free trade routes with the Kremlin."

"And—"

"Gorshkov has not been receptive. Russia has launched new icebreakers for the region—more than forty."

"How many do we have?"

Admiral Grimm, Chair of the Joint Chiefs, quickly responded: "Two."

The president sighed. "Forty to two. And you expect me to solve that difference with a wave of my hand?"

"Not a wave, sir. But an understanding of the impact and the need to address it. Moreover, Russia has built new and better bases and brought in additional troops and hardware to protect their trade route, which is becoming more accessible each year."

Matthews looked at Defense Secretary Collingsworth. It was time to change presenters again. "If I may?" Collingsworth stood, unbuttoned his suit jacket, and put a stack of large photographs on the easel.

"As Secretary Matthews noted, trade and military bases, Mr. President." He began flipping through the photos. "Gorshkov seeks both market position and military superiority over the region. In the last eighteen months, we've seen an unprecedented build-up: construction of new troop facilities and below-ground storage spaces. We've observed Russia's Northern Fleet testing anti-ship cruise missiles not far from our bases. Here are satellite photographs of a new Russian nuclear submarine base with advanced Poseidon missiles and torpedoes. They've expanded their network of radar installations and upgraded their Arctic Trefoil base. It's a permanent facility on Franz Josef Land, a desolate ice-covered archipelago that now houses hundreds of personnel. All of those troops are not in the oil business. So, to the meaning of this, Mr. President, they are prepared for commerce and for war."

Collingsworth removed his visuals. CIA Director Gerald Watts stood with another set. The first was a satellite image of a submarine base. "Russia has three principal military interests in the Arctic. Number one, establishing a more powerful ballistic missile submarine second-strike capability on the Kola Peninsula, home to seven of their eleven ballistic subs. They have achieved that. Second, protecting the Russian Federation's ability to operate in the European Arctic and the North Atlantic should NATO decide to raise the stakes. They're very close to owning the route. Third, protect Russia's ever-expanding commercial interests in the Arctic. They will have that if we do nothing.

"The undeniable fact is the Arctic is essential to Russia's Northern Fleet, its income, and its plans for empire building."

Matthews studied Battaglio's reactions. He showed nothing. No surprise, no concern.

Watts continued. "We call it bastion defense, Mr. President. That is to say, securing strategic territory to ensure freedom of operation. But to be clear, Russia's military operational capabilities in the region have definite offensive potential, which Gorshkov is testing now through intimidation. Provocative maneuvers, snap military drills, even poking at the Danish and Norwegian borders with submarine and air patrols. Hell, they've even used aggressive tactics to harass our air operations off the coast of Alaska. All to say, we have the power; don't fuck with us.

"To put it another way, Mr. President, admittedly there is no longer an Iron Curtain. But Russia's dangerous Arctic military posture has created an Ice Curtain—cold and calculated with the ultimate purpose to freeze us out of the Arctic."

Admiral Rhett Grimm took over again. "I'd like to cover the prospects for Russia's success and the threats to us."

"That would help," Battaglio stated.

"Russia is on its way to expand its oil and gas exports to Asian markets."

"You already said that."

"Yes, but increased sales to China will offset ongoing current U.S. sanctions and any around the corner. With cash reserves, Gorshkov will have the resources to threaten its neighbors. Note that I said, *will*, not *might*, Mr. President."

"You can't be suggesting that we start a war over icebreakers and oil tankers?" the president fumed. "Hell, tickling a few Baltic nations' borders and creeping up on our fighters is nothing new. You can't tell me we haven't done the same. Have you seen anything that suggests Gorshkov's motives aren't anything but economic and peaceful?"

"Sir, I'll answer that." Secretary of Defense Vincent Collingsworth replied. "One, Wrangel Island." He nodded to Grimm who placed a satellite photograph on the easel. "It's located 300 miles from the Alaskan coast and houses a network of advanced radar early-warning systems." He dropped the image on the floor and revealed another. "Two, Kotelny Island off the northern Siberian coast. A regional command and control operation and home for missile launch vehicles." A third satellite photo. "Three, Alexandra Land in the northeast Barents Sea. This is Russia's northernmost military post. Its position asserts Russia's complete control over the NSR with proximity to Greenland, Iceland, and Norway. The base has the ability to disrupt vital NATO sea lines of communication between North America and Europe, striking the U.S. military. And this fourth photo shows Kola Peninsula. It's Gorshkov's golden goose with extensive firepower. Kola's proximity to Russia's Gazhiyevo submarine base, huge weapons bunkers at Okolnaya Bay, and Severomorsk-1 Air Base make it the epicenter for Russia's strategic Arctic initiatives."

Battaglio had enough lecturing. "Excuse me. You obviously came very prepared and coordinated. There is one thing I fail to understand."

Everyone looked at the president. It was his meeting now.

"Have you all lost your minds? I am not going to war with Russia because Gorshkov is protecting his borders and wanting to sell oil to the Chinese? F'christsake, we sell to China, too."

Matthews raised a finger. "Mr. President, no one is suggesting we go to war. Not in the conventional sense."

"Get to the point, Elizabeth. Better make it good."

She decided to appeal to his ego.

"You're effective face-to-face. That's your strength. Meet with our allies. Start formulating a strategy to contain Russia. Develop an alternative for Venezuela. Make it harder for Gorshkov to achieve everything he wants."

Battaglio stood and striking a presidential pose, gazed through the windows of the Oval Office to the Rose Garden. Matthews waited for an answer. It came thirty seconds later.

"Thank you, Elizabeth, I'll give this some thought."

The Secretary of State instantly knew the subject was dead.

15

DAN REILLY AWOKE with the English flight attendant's announcement.

"Good morning. We'll be landing in at Heathrow in about one-hour. We'll raise the lights slowly. Nothing too quick," she cheerily said. "In a few minutes we'll be coming through with a light snack."

For Reilly and the other first-class passengers, breakfast would be heartier. And for him, needed. He had fallen into a deep sleep before dinner was served on the overnight flight. Deep but disturbing. He dreamt that he was back at Hogan's Alley. The FBI's training center was just as it had been the day before: people casually milling about in the lobby, then terrorists storming in. Guns fired. The warnings. The security officer going down. Reilly recovering the gun. The woman he had misjudged rising with her weapon in her right hand. He now saw her face, which looked so familiar. She was a beautiful brunette. In his dream she called out his name. "Dan, it's me, Marnie." He smiled, lowered his gun, and walked toward her. Her eyes widened. She smiled back lovingly. She had a cocktail in her free hand and offered a toast. "To us, Dan. To our forevers." He raised his hand and what had been his weapon was now his own cocktail glass. "Yes, to us, Marnie." Then he saw that her drink was a gun. She fired. From the outside looking into the dream, he saw his own surprise. Surprise punctuated with a question: "Why?"

Reality was buried in his dream. The FBI player in Hogan's Alley became Marnie Babbitt, the Russian sleeper spy who had stalked and entrapped him and died as a result in Stockholm just weeks earlier. He had fallen in love with her and believed that in the last moments of her life, she truly loved him. A silent nod gave him a chance to take down a Russian agent who had come to kill him.

Reilly awoke. It took him a few minutes to get a sense of where he was—not at the faux hotel lobby but in the seat of his Chicago-to-London nonstop United flight. As he stared straight ahead he thought of Marnie and their short time together. *Marnie Babbitt.* He never learned her real name, and the lie that he told himself—that he had left her behind in the rubble of the Kensington Royal Nordiska Hotel—was just that. A lie.

* * *

Customs took longer than he'd hoped. It pushed Reilly behind schedule. He wanted to get in, meet with Alan Cannon, and check out the murder scene.

"Good flight, Dan?" Cannon asked when he finally arrived at the hotel.

"Fell asleep quickly." He didn't tell Cannon about the dream that woke him up. "How are things going?"

"To most, like nothing has happened. Which I suppose is good. As kills go, this was as clean as it gets."

"Okay, but show me the dirty stuff."

Reilly left his single rolling suitcase with the bell captain. It would be in his room on the seventh floor by the time he arrived. The desk was always offering higher floors. Reilly's rule was to stick with lower ones: floors that could be reached by most cities' hook-and-ladder fire trucks.

They put their conversation on hold as they approached the elevator. Reilly smiled to a family that loaded in with them. After they departed on the fifteenth floor, Reilly asked, "Any leaks from the staff?"

"I've talked to department heads and made it abundantly clear that if they're approached by press, send them to Brightman's office." Spencer

Brightman was the hotel's general manager. In turn, he kicked requests back to Chicago and Lois Duvall. "Of course, that doesn't stop some tabloids from getting unattributed statements from staff. But so far, it's been okay."

"So far," Reilly replied. He knew all too well about the world of leaks. A confidential study he'd authored while working for the State Department had recently fallen into the hands of terrorists. The report resulted in attacks on America's bridges in Washington, St. Louis, and Pittsburgh, and one of New York's tunnels under the Hudson River. Attacks on two more targets were foiled: the Oakland Bay Bridge and Hoover Dam.

The FBI ultimately discovered the source of the leak, and today that mid-level Congressional Intelligence Committee aide is finding her life much harder in isolation.

"Security looked good when I came in. We're up to Red status?"

"Orange now. We'll be at full Red tomorrow night."

"Good. I want the same for the other hotels that are hosting oil conferences. Nairobi, Beijing, even DC if domestic agrees."

The door opened to the twenty-fourth floor of the Mayfair Kensington Royal. A London cop stood at the door to Kritzler's suite. He'd met Cannon but didn't know Reilly. Reilly produced his Kensington ID.

"Okay," the uniformed officer said after examining the credentials. "Same thing as before. Don't touch anything."

Cannon swiped his house key card and, ducking under orange police tape, Reilly entered a large living room. Cannon held him up from going further.

Cannon nodded toward the door they'd come through. "It all seemed normal to Kritzler's guards. Someone who identified himself and looked the part of a hotel executive gained entry without difficulty. According to Kritzler's security, he wore a nametag. One of them remembered was Walter Grün. We have no Mr. Grün working for us. Once inside, he announced himself to Kritzler. His security waited to leave until Kritzler sent them back to guard the door. Kritzler appeared satisfied with the royal treatment."

Cannon led Reilly further inside. "From here they went into the bedroom. Kritzler apparently decided to have the spread set up close to the bed for later."

"Later?" Reilly asked.

"Yes. Thirty minutes later. That's when his next guest, the escort, arrived for some transactional fun. No doubt he had ideas about what to do with the strawberries and chocolates on the cart."

"I'm sure."

"The assassin acted quickly and left as if nothing had happened."

Cannon recreated where the assassin had stood, the angle of the shots, the position where Kritzler ended up on the bed.

"No fingerprints? No shells?"

"Nothing," Cannon said. "A white-gloved hotel executive just doing his job and heading down the service elevator with a smile."

Reilly wondered whether Kritzler's security could have been involved and whether there was a promotion waiting for them. Then again, there were few employment benefits for Russian security who knew too much. "Any questions before we move on?"

"Video from the hall cameras?"

"I'll show you when we're through. Our friend was aware of them, but not in a way that might have flagged security watching live. He kept his head down and away from full view."

"Wait," Reilly interrupted. "We had live eyes on the floor?"

"Yes and no. They had screens in front of them. But were they watching? I'm still working through that. They should have checked against housekeeping. Obviously they didn't."

"Excuses?"

"They said they just missed it."

"Are we checking if they've received any sizeable drafts to their bank accounts?"

"We aren't. Scotland Yard is. But I think it wasn't intentional. It's another hole we have to plug when we have VIPs. More training, additional staff."

Reilly had long ago realized the learning curve would never flatten out. Every experience taught them more about the demands for better security.

"Okay, now let's take his route out."

Cannon and Reilly left the suite and walked down the hall to the service elevator. When it arrived, it opened to three walls with laminated posters showing photographs of a diverse group of hotel employees standing beside big block letters advising, IF YOU SEE SOMETHING, SAY SOMETHING.

Cannon continued his narrative on the way down. "The killer, still looking the part, went to the basement where he began his disappearing act. He casually pushed the cart through the kitchen, again head down, drawing no attention. A new face among a staff used to new faces."

"Anyone talk to him?"

"No. The route is all on camera. After the kitchen, into this storeroom."

They stopped at the storeroom door. Police tape barred them. "Inside, he transformed into a totally different person. He came out looking some twenty years younger. We have images of the before and after. Both have been entered into criminal databases. Nothing's come up according to investigators I've heard from. And for my money, these are identities no one is likely to ever see again. He changed. Outer clothes went into the suitcase he had underneath the cart. Leaving, he pulled it along, looking like a tourist, not an assassin."

"Again, no one raised any concern?"

"Concern? No. One housekeeper saw him. He looked lost, like he got off at the wrong floor. The elevator was opening when she got close. Then he was gone. She's probably alive because she didn't engage him," Cannon maintained.

They boarded the same elevator up. It opened to the lobby. "From here he left, looking like a typical check-out."

"Without checking out," Reilly smirked. "Do we have any security cameras of him scouting ahead of his mission? Testing the route?"

"If we have, we haven't seen it yet. We're reviewing the hard drive as far back as a month. Nothing so far. And quite frankly, I'm doubtful. This guy is good. More than good, a real pro. He kept his head down at every turn, which makes me believe he made multiple surveys, each with different disguises, and had any number of ways to escape."

"How did he know Kritzler's room?" Reilly asked. Before Cannon answered he added, "Never mind." Reilly knew that was one of the easiest bits of information to get. It could have come from a desk clerk who talked too much, the concierge, who gave a delivery to a bell captain casually observed by a passerby, or even a housekeeper who kept a computer open too long for prying eyes.

"What about London CCTV cameras? They had to pick him up leaving the Mayfair."

"They did. All the way to Piccadilly. Then, like clockwork, he got lost in a theater crowd. All perfectly."

"And the suitcase?"

"Probably also tricked out with a fake exterior. Contact paper or something like that. Easy to change its appearance. Dan, this guy's a chameleon. Someone paid top dollar for this hit."

"Russian mob?"

"Possibly, or perhaps another oligarch. Maybe a Saudi prince, a Venezuelan oil baron. Or take your pick of anyone with oil interests in China, Iran, or even the U.S. My Interpol contacts will be watching the markets closely. Then, of course, it could just be a very dramatic firing. Kritzler may have pissed off people in Gazplux. The fact is, we may never know. Either way, we have our own sack of rocks to carry."

Reilly agreed. And the sack was constantly getting heavier.

16

Baete De Smet walked up to the front desk wearing an engaging smile. He said hello to the check-in clerk, a young woman, who greeted him in kind. Her name tag read Nakesa.

"Welcome to the Kensington Nairobi Premiere." Naming the hotel Premiere was a calculated decision that reflected long-standing cultural and historical considerations that went back to 1824. The then-nation of Mombasa became a British protectorate, and in 1825, British East Africa. The road to independence took nearly seventy years and cost many Kenyan and British lives. In 1963 a new nation was born, and anything related to the word *royal* recalled the British rule and remained an anathema even years later when the hotel was built.

"Thank you, Nakesa," De Smet said with what sounded like a French accent.

He put his rolling overnight bag by his side but kept a tote strapped over his shoulder. Check in proceeded as he turned over his identification—a Belgian passport and a credit card from Nationale Bank Van België. De Smet was booked in the hotel for five days.

"And what is the purpose of your visit?" the clerk asked trying to get a feel for the new guest. She mostly observed that De Smet appeared positively vanilla. White hair, glasses with clear frames, white shirt, white suit, topped off with a white Panama hat. She couldn't look over her desk, but she was certain his socks and shoes were also white. Beyond his clothes, there was nothing memorable about the seventy-something man. Nothing distinctive other than how bland he was.

"I'm on holiday. Well, actually I am permanently on holiday. Retired professor, traveling to places I've only read about. Making new friends, maybe over a few games of chess." He patted the shoulder bag.

"Well I wish you a most pleasant stay and successful games, Mr. De Smet." Nakesa made an adjustment on her computer, adding, "And you're in luck. I've been able to upgrade your room to a junior suite."

De Smet thanked the beautiful Kenyan woman, declined a second room key, and took his ID and card back.

The clerk added, "Oh, one more thing. Don't be surprised if you see additional security. We're hosting a regional oil ministry conference. They'll be here for another three days."

It was no surprise to De Smet. In fact, that's why he'd come to Nairobi.

* * *

De Smet set up his chess board on a lobby bar table with a match already in progress and yet no competitor. He simply studied the pieces, sipped an aperitif, and appeared to strategize. Every so often he made a move only to take it back and shake his head. People walked by without comment. The man in white was apparently deep in thought, patiently trying to figure out a tactic to a lost game.

As De Smet was into the end of an hour, a middle-aged Asian man in a three-piece suit strode through the lobby with a contingent of four countrymen whose constantly shifting glances took in everyone and everything in their surroundings. They saw De Smet and moved beyond him without concern. Then they similarly evaluated a pair of businessmen at the bar, a family organizing their day, and a group of executives congregating around the concierge desk. No issues. No threats. The lead whispered to the man they guarded and continued to the elevator bank. While waiting, the Asian looked back through the lobby. He saw an older man alone at a table twenty feet away packing up chess pieces into a leather case. He watched and even took a step forward, but when the elevator arrived, his men quickly ushered him in.

De Smet caught the Asian's interest and smiled inwardly. He'd played this first gambit masterfully. Recognition would lead to engagement. If not today, tomorrow. If not tomorrow, then the day after. He was patient. The time would come. He knew the temptation would be too great to ignore. Most importantly, he had thoroughly researched the Asian and knowingly worked out all the moves in advance.

* * *

The next morning, the Asian had his head of security ask about the chess player in the lobby with the Panama hat. Nakesa good-naturedly explained that he was a Belgian on vacation who spent part of the day taking foot tours, visiting the National Museum and galleries, and relaxing in the lobby with his chess board. "He said he was hoping to find challengers. I haven't seen anyone with him yet."

The Asian guard bowed in thanks and reported what he learned to his boss, Jayo Meng, president of China's second-largest oil and petroleum company, Sino Propulsion.

De Smet was back in the lobby with his chess pieces positioned just as they had been the previous afternoon. The Belgian tried multiple moves with his queen and knights. Nothing satisfied him. He returned the pieces to their previous positions. His frustration was visible. For long minutes, no one who walked past the man and his chessboard understood. Then one did.

"Excuse me, but I couldn't help notice that you're struggling with Shirov's bishop sacrifice."

De Smet peered up, looking over his glasses' frame. He tilted his head to the right but said nothing.

"I'm sorry," the Chinese man said. "I shouldn't have interrupted you. Accept my sincere apologies."

"Oh heavens," De Smet replied with a smile. "I welcome your interest. You must be a chess player of great distinction to recognize the board."

"How could I not? It's one of the most celebrated endgame sacrifices. Grand Master Alexei Shirov's famous move, considered one of the best ever."

"Which still astounds me. I find myself staring at Shirov's stratagem for hours. I understand that Black's bishop merely stands as an obstruction to the king, but Shirov's decision to simply give it up? Astounding, all the more incredible because, as much as I study all other options, it remains the only way to win."

Jayo Meng, without invitation, settled into the seat opposite De Smet. "My friend, I see we share an appreciation for Shirov's extraordinary play." He examined the board to calculate alternative moves. "White must try to capture the bishop, but he can't move the king past f2. This allows Black's king to reach e4." He picked up the Black king and moved it accordingly and continued. "Unstoppable. Brilliant beyond all consideration. A bishop and pawn ending."

"Would you honor me with a game?" De Smet proposed. Without hesitation, he began resetting the board.

Meng waved for one member of his three-man security detail to come forward. A solid officer, properly dressed in dark blue and without an ounce of body fat, approached. Meng motioned for him to bend down. He whispered in his ear. The guard frowned. Meng then brushed him off. The guard went to the other two men who formed an equilateral triangle with each posted some twenty feet away.

"My apologies. Sometimes the employees consider themselves the boss."

"They must have your best interests in mind."

With that he reached across the table and offered his hand in friendship. "I'm Baete De Smet. Only a moderate player and a fairly good, but retired college professor."

"My name is Meng. I'm here for a conference." He didn't explain further. "Don't tell anyone, but it is boring beyond all description. You give me a needed diversion. I hope to be your worthy opponent."

De Smet smiled. "And you mine."

They began. Midway through the match, De Smet ordered two top-shelf whiskeys. Macallan no.6. Meng toasted to long life and happiness. De Smet clinked, smiled, and enthusiastically repeated, "To long life and happiness."

De Smet gave up the first game intentionally. He asked for a second. Meng enthusiastically agreed. And with it came a second scotch and a win for De Smet.

"We could leave it at one each," De Smet said, knowing full well that Meng's sense of competition would not allow him to walk away from the table.

"Yes, one more please. But we must make plans to engage again before I leave."

"Of course," De Smet lied. There would be no more games after today.

Meng won the final game over a third drink. The man named De Smet felt it only right to give him something to go out on. That afternoon, Jayo Meng returned to his room satisfied but tired. He told his men he would rest for two hours. They should wake him in time for his dinner with fellow oil executives. When they returned, he appeared to be sound asleep. He wasn't. Meng was dead. His security immediately had the hotel summon paramedics. A team rushed in within fifteen minutes, but they were unable to revive Meng. Under other circumstances, it might have been considered a death by natural causes, but Gatthii Mutuku, the Kensington Premiere's manager, was acutely aware of the killing at the London Kensington Mayfair and was especially on alert because of it. First, he called Nairobi police, next Alan Cannon.

17

Cannon answered the cell that was inside his jacket pocket. "Hold a sec," he told Reilly. The two men were seated at a computer terminal in the London CCTV hub, where the entire city came into view through more than 55,000 cameras. London's pace played out in real time, 24/7, but could be rewound slower and frozen. With the help of Inspector Douglas Holloway, who managed the console, they screened the city's cameras following a young man as he casually strolled from the Kensington Royal, through meandering streets of Mayfair, and into Piccadilly. It was the same figure who had appeared on the hotel basement camera and carefully kept his head down to avoid any chance for facial recognition.

"He's good," Reilly said.

Holloway corrected him. "No, he's great. An expert. This guy had it down, including the locations of virtually every camera along the route—like he surveyed and photographed it or had full knowledge of our grid."

Reilly continued watching the replay. The subject ducked into a theater just minutes before curtain.

"He sure has a sense of humor," Holloway said.

"Why's that?" Reilly asked.

"The theater. Not just any London theater. St. Martin's." He backed up the footage to the entrance showing the marquee. "And not just any play. *The Mousetrap*."

Reilly instantly got it. *The Mousetrap*, Agatha Christie's classic murder mystery, which opened in 1952 and played continuously until the pandemic.

"Jesus. He's fucking with us," Reilly said. "He knew your cameras would pick him up. He wanted to have some fun. To play you. He likes games."

"Hell of a deadly game," Holloway added. "I'm willing to bet he left with a totally different identity."

At that moment Cannon returned to the computer bank, his face ashen. Reilly had seen the look before on the head of security. It was bad news. Cannon exhaled deeply. Without prompting he said, "Kenya." He held up two fingers.

Reilly shot him an inquisitive look.

"That was Mutuku."

Reilly had only recently promoted Gatthii Mutuku to GM in Nairobi. He was on the young side; thirty-four, but a rising star. Someone to be taken seriously.

"A second death."

"Oh God!" Reilly slid his hands from the computer desk and pushed back in his chair. Holloway froze the screen on the theater exterior.

"Discovered less than an hour ago. Police are on the scene."

"Do we know—?"

"Yes," Cannon continued. "Another big oil executive. Chinese."

"Shit!" Really blurted. "Cause?"

"Waiting for an autopsy. If we're lucky just a heart attack."

Reilly fixed an unmoving stare on Cannon. "Try *hard* attack. From that man." Reilly pointed to the still frame on the screen. "Second oil exec dead during an oil conference in one of our hotels? He was murdered."

* * *

Reilly and Cannon left the CCTV hub. The London investigation was in Inspector Holloway's hands. Now there were decisions to make about Nairobi. They hailed a Black Cab and quickly strategized in the back seat.

"Let's get down there. I'll check on the next flight out," Cannon said. He started texting his office, then switched to his Expedia app. "Quicker this way."

Reilly nodded but said nothing.

"You're thinking," Cannon noted as he clicked the prompts and entered Nairobi as the destination out of Heathrow.

"Yup."

Cannon was about to enter number of passengers in the correct field. He stopped.

"I know that look. You're not going."

"Not to Nairobi. That's all yours. I'm double jumping."

"To?"

"The next conference. I have an idea. But I'll need to run it by Shaw first."

* * *

"Boss," Reilly began on the phone from his room, "this time I'm getting to you before you call me."

Reilly explained what he had just learned from Cannon. "It's bigger than we imagined. I just don't know what *it* is yet." He reported that he felt there was enough to set off alarms. Like the ones he'd heard in service. Ones that ended badly if not listened to.

"Two oil execs dead. One a confirmed killing. I'm sure the other is going to turn out that way. Two for two at the regional oil conferences we're hosting, EJ. Two down, one to go."

"Beijing." Shaw stated.

"Which is where I'm going. Alan's off to Nairobi tonight."

"To do what? You don't know who the target is. It could be anyone."

"Not anyone. The person whose death will lead to a win for someone else. That's what the Crisis Committee is working on. As for the possible muscle behind the killings, we've come up with three, but really two: China and Russia."

"The third?"

"The U.S. But there are representatives from eleven other countries. They're all either government or private oil moguls or both. Big egos and big wallets."

Reilly heard Shaw breathe heavily over the phone, a sign that a question was coming. It did.

"Dan, could there be any direct connection to our hotels?"

It was a question that Reilly had considered. "Only insofar as we're hosting the events and it's where the VIPs are staying," Reilly replied. "I don't believe it's about us or our brand. That said, we should take a long and hard look at what we book and evaluate the risks more effectively."

"Thank you. And yes, we should look more closely at what we take on."

After hanging up with Shaw, Reilly made two new calls. The first to Chicago to ask COO Lou Tiano to check if any other oil-related sessions were scheduled at company properties—anywhere. The second to a very private number in Washington.

WASHINGTON, D.C.
U.S. STATE DEPARTMENT

"Elizabeth, if you haven't already caught this, it'll come across your desk soon. Another oil executive died at a conference. This one in Nairobi."

The Secretary of State had not heard it yet. But she texted out to CIA Director Watts while Dan Reilly continued his account from London.

"I'm worried about the next conference in Beijing. I'm going, and I need everything I can get on the participants."

"You said died. You didn't say killed," Elizabeth Matthews noted.

"We'll go with killed. An assassination in London, the second in Nairobi. Somebody's messing with oil futures. Somebody with much to gain."

"Take your pick of the top oil ministers or their country's representatives and everyone else who's got a stake in the market. Got any thoughts?"

"Not at this point," Reilly said, not giving away what the company's Crisis Committee was leaning toward.

Likewise, if Matthews had her own ideas, she also wasn't prepared to share them. Instead she asked Reilly when he expected to be in Beijing.

He gave her the time he expected to be checked in. "I sure could use an encrypted secure phone, though. You know how Chinese secret police love to listen in. And one other thing."

"Why does it feel like I'm your wife filling a shopping list?"

"Not wife, just the best secret shopper I know." It was a reference to people who go to stores and openly shop, but surreptitiously gather brand marketing information for their clients or their client's competitors.

"What is it?"

"I'll need an expert. Someone who can give me a crash course on who's who and what's what in oil and where it's all likely to go to shit." He paused. "Preferably in person."

"And where do you want all of this to show up?"

"Our hotel in Beijing." He told her which one.

Elizabeth Matthews exhaled deeply. Deeply enough to suggest Reilly was asking for a lot and that he'd owe her. "Let me see what I can do."

The next call was to Tiano who, within ten minutes and a call back, found out that a leading Chinese oil representative was on his way to DC to speak at Georgetown University. "It's the best I've got," the COO offered. "He's staying with us. Not a conference and probably not what you're looking for, but what the hell, he's an oil guy."

Reilly thanked Tiano and phoned his boss for the second time in thirty minutes.

"Thought we were through for the day," EJ Shaw said.

"Sorry, but I'm thinking we need to up security in the U.S., too."

Reilly heard Shaw clear his throat.

"That's not going to go over well with Snyder and finance."

"It'll go over better than bad PR," Reilly replied.

"Got a good reason, Dan?"

"Just a bad feeling. Can you get them on the phone? Let me make my case. Two minutes."

"All right, hang on."

Snyder was Chip Snyder, Reilly's domestic counterpart; president of Kensington Domestic Operations, a young executive with great potential and an undeniable sense of self-esteem.

Five minutes later, Snyder and Phyllis Coates, the VP of Finance, joined the call. Shaw also tied in Chris Collins.

"This is your conference, Dan." Shaw had explained that Reilly was calling in from London.

"Thanks, EJ. I appreciate everyone joining this call on no notice."

Silence. As Shaw said, this was Reilly's conference. They were waiting for him.

"Right to the point. We've had two murders on our properties— London and Nairobi. Both international. I'm off to Beijing where we're hosting another conference. I have every reason to believe there will be a new target there. I'm worried about an attempt in the U.S. Lou identified a potential target coming into D.C. I suggest you elevate the Kensington Capitol to Red Hotel status immediately."

"Dan, Chip here."

"Yes."

"I appreciate what you're saying, but as horrible as the attacks have been abroad in recent years, terrorists haven't gone after our properties at home."

"Right, and we're damned lucky," Reilly argued. "But I'm not talking about our properties being targeted. It's someone who might be booked into one of our properties."

"The Capitol has hundreds of guests who come and go daily," Snyder replied.

"Not all of them international oil executives, Chip."

"Look, Dan, I understand your problems. And I can't argue with your worry, but they're your problems."

Reilly bit his lip.

"Frankly, we haven't needed to establish anything near to what you've done and done extremely well."

Reilly heard the three knuckle raps on Shaw's oak conference table. His knock on wood.

"So, thank you for sharing your concern, Dan," Chip Snyder continued. "If we feel the need to adopt your program, I'll be sure to call you in to advise."

Reilly heard Snyder's voice go down an octave. He had made his point. He was finished. Reilly was not.

"Chip, with all due respect—"

Snyder interrupted rudely. "Dan, you've got your territory. I've got mine."

"Hold on, Chip," Shaw implored. "Let's keep this parked between the lanes. As long as I've known Dan, his instincts have been spot-on. And what he doesn't know, he trusts others to tell him. He's right. Add more security."

Chip Snyder nodded to EJ Shaw.

"Phyllis, keep me posted on costs," Shaw continued.

"Will do."

"Chris, notify our insurance carriers and let them know what we're doing and why. I think they'll be happy considering the news from London and Nairobi."

"Got it."

"And Chip, take a look at the steps to bring our D.C. hotels up to Red Hotel status."

"Yes, sir." Snyder then addressed the finance officer. "Phyllis, let me know what I can spend."

Reilly remained silent over the phone. Snyder's attitude troubled him. Without seeing Snyder he nonetheless sensed that his domestic counterpart was in no real rush to add the appropriate measures.

18

WASHINGTON, D.C.

Elizabeth Matthews sat in the corner of the back dining room of Old Ebbitt Grill. Old because it was. 1856 old. Washington's oldest saloon. The backroom because her security insisted on it. The backroom because she wanted privacy tonight with her table mate, U.S. Senator Mikayla Colonnello.

Colonnello had called the meeting, but she suspected that Matthews had an agenda all her own. She always did.

The two Beltway titans looked like they shopped at the same stores, which they did. Both wore dark blue business suits, *de rigueur* for D.C. Each wearing silk shirts and gold necklaces. Both brunettes, or at least in Matthews's case, still a natural brunette. What set Secretary Matthews's look apart was the brooch she chose. A mime face. Telling and whimsical.

They were deep in their conversation. If the walls could talk their discussion would fit right in with so many held at Old Ebbitt Grill over the years. A card at the table offered a reminder of the restaurant's storied history.

Many other famous statesmen, and naval and military heroes too numerous to mention here, have been guests of the house.

They'd dined on Old Ebbitt seasonal pan-seared fish specialties. Matthews had the rockfish; Colonnello, the Atlantic salmon.

By the time they moved onto coffee, they'd reached a compromise. Matthews would come before the committee to discuss the attacks on America's infrastructure, but only within limits. She would take questions on the specific events and whether there was any departmental awareness of the attacks. Beyond that, it was a matter for the FBI domestically.

"And if anyone asks about the State Department report that detailed the country's vulnerabilities, including the actual targets?" Colonnello asked.

"I will not be able to discuss it as a matter of national security."

"Deal. If it comes up once, just say that. A second time I will cut it off."

Now it was Matthews's turn. The conversation was nothing like the senator expected.

"Mikayla," she whispered, "25 is dead. I can't get a majority of the cabinet to consider it. Not even close. Precedent, fear, political blowback. Take your pick. Now here's my problem: I'm sure I'm on his hit list. I may not be the first to go. But I'm positive I won't be the last. The longer I stay, the longer I can hold things together."

Colonnello frowned. "Hold things together?"

"Battaglio thinks he has the upper hand over Gorshkov. Wrong. He was royally played." She leaned in closer. "He traded missiles in Venezuela for the sovereignty of Ukraine and Latvia when we had other options. Pierce and I warned him. NATO warned him. Even the CIA shrink warned him. He wouldn't listen, kicked me out of the session. Soon, Lithuania and Estonia will follow if we don't stop him. It sets Gorshkov up to grab more. Hell, Poland and Hungary are becoming more illiberal. They'll bow to Russia. And what will happen if Germany's nationalists keep gaining traction?"

Senator Colonnello's eyes widened. "I can call a hearing to—"

"No. At least not yet. If and when I've got more, then. In the meantime, keep your eyes open too, and be very careful who you talk to. Can't say I trust many of your colleagues."

19

EGYPT

At first it looked like another accident. Like the one that occurred March 2021 when the *Ever Given* ran aground in a storm. Though its hull was breached, the ship was set free after six days. But this time, there was no storm to drive the massive vessel to the water's edge. This time, it wasn't a container ship. This time it wasn't an accident.

The *Aristotle Euro VIII*, a Suezmax class ship, floated 230 feet above the water and sixty-one feet below, with only five feet of room to spare from grazing the bottom of the Suez Canal. The tanker, with a deadweight of 160,000 tons, had departed King Abdul Aziz Port in Saudi Arabia for Rotterdam, a 7,373 mile voyage covering thirty days at an average of 10 knots per hour.

Radio traffic between the captain and the Suez Canal Authority (SCA) at Ismailia was at first clinical, straightforward, by the book. Then an alert. "SCA, this is the *Aristotle Euro VIII* reporting CB4. I repeat, CB4," meaning *I require assistance*. The communication was followed by exact GPS coordinates.

"Receive you, *Aristotle Euro VIII*. Confirmed. State your situation."

The ship's fifty-three-year-old captain, Dimitris Constantine, restated the code, but at present there didn't appear to be immediate danger. "Indication of … hold!"

SCA owned and operated the Suez Canal. It monitored its use, collected tolls in multiple currencies, and transited more than 21,400 ships a year. According to its charter, the SCA is bound by the 1888 Convention of Constantinople, which grants access of the canal to all ships—commercial and war—even to belligerent parties. Considering CB4 was not an urgent call and the ship's divers were already evaluating how quickly *Aristotle Euro VIII* could be set on course by tugboats, there was optimism. Optimism disappeared forty-five minutes later with Constantine's second alert, "HX 2! I repeat, HX 2! I have received serious damage. Explosions. We are—"

The radio transmission abruptly cut out.

Four explosions, timed within ten seconds of one another, tore through the ship, sending flames outward and upward. The engine room evaporated. The bridge was engulfed in the inferno. The *Aristotle* listed toward the eastern shore. That put the sinking ship at risk of becoming a triple threat: shutting down the Suez Canal, creating an ecological disaster, and indefinitely driving up the cost of oil for countries around the world.

The ship's 160,000 tonnage got lighter by the second as crude oil spilled into the Suez Canal.

Ships in the immediate queue were ordered to anchor. Ships heading in from the south held in the Gulf of Suez, as did the vessels to the north in the Mediterranean. Between them was the 120 miles of the canal, including the wider Great Bitter Lake.

Within sixty minutes, seventeen ships were delayed. Two hours later, the number tripled. So far, no one was focused on the $400 million per hour economic impact the companies would bear. But they would be soon.

The Suez Canal was dead to all traffic. It would have taken weeks, likely months, before it could reopen had the next minutes played out differently.

North of the crippled tanker, near Ismailia, the Greek ship *Next Time Around* moved forward under the stars. It was loaded with containers stacked ten high by twenty-four rows along the width of the ship and twenty-two down the length.

Some of the crew of thirty-three had broken out bottles of their favored ouzo and were playing cards. Others watched movies or were sleeping.

Suddenly, four shoulder-fired missiles blasted through the night sky from along 23rd July Street, the road named for the 1952 Egyptian army revolt against the monarchy. But this was an act of terrorism, not revolution. The weapons were true to their targets. But for good measure, the team along the shore reloaded and fired four more volleys at the targeted containers. A massive fireball swept up, consuming the ship and all souls onboard. Fuel spread in all directions.

The ship took four hours to sink. It would take more than a year to remove the sunken containers. There would be no *Next Time Around*.

Along the shore, the two teams reassembled, ready to follow their exfiltration plans, go home, reunite with their families, and count their money. But that meant too many people to keep a secret. Mission commanders Dae-Jung Woo and Gyeong Song had specific orders that they promptly dispatched—a bullet to the head of each man, and another for good measure once they were down. Fast, efficient. Without guilt. It didn't matter that their bodies and the equipment would be recovered. These men didn't exist, and all their weaponry and tools had been purchased through the dark web.

The Suez was closed for business. Shipping company executives around the world didn't sleep that night. Neither did operatives at the world's leading intelligence agencies.

One of the first to get a call was the CIA's Bob Heath, whose desk was already cluttered with tips, rumors, and possible leads on the attacks against America and reports about North Koreans, a Congressional aide's collusion with a Russian spy, and a report written by Daniel J. Reilly.

He dialed Dan's number, not knowing where in the world he'd find him.

LONDON

With a long flight ahead of him, Reilly was resting in the backseat of his taxi. His eyes were closed. He was thinking. Thinking about Chip

Snyder's attitude and what he should say to Shaw. He didn't want to torpedo the guy, but he felt that much like the lessons learned on January 6, preparing for the worst was the most prudent approach. He decided to ask Shaw to include Alan Cannon in the mix. *Better that the message be reinforced by the firm's security chief, not him.*

He was about to call Shaw in Chicago and Cannon in Nairobi when his phone rang with a number he knew all too well.

"What's up, Bob?"

"We've got a problem. Where are you?"

"On my way to Heathrow. Flight to Beijing."

"Listen up. In a few minutes the news will break. It's big, and it's bad, and it's already been confirmed through ITAC, sat images, right down to eyewitnesses. Postings will likely even hit Facebook before we finish talking."

Reilly sat up, imagining the possibilities. He didn't have to think too hard.

"Dan, multiple ships have gone down in the Suez. Top, bottom, middle. Dead in the water."

"How the hell?"

"Blown up remotely, sabotaged, fucking torpedoes, MANPADs. We don't know. But it was a massive mission and by the looks of it, 100 percent successful."

Reilly clamped his eyes shut and considered the ramifications—the global ramifications. Sea trade through the Middle East to the Mediterranean and Europe immediately paralyzed. International businesses about to be crippled. Insurance brokers hours away from scrambling to avoid bankruptcy. And then there were the political ramifications. Winners and losers. Heath was speaking but Reilly was stuck on the words he'd left the Crisis Committee to consider: *Cui bono.* Who benefits?

"Dan, did you get that?"

"Sorry. What?"

"I asked if this isn't the end, only the beginning, where's next?"

"Jesus, Bob. More like this would upset the global economy for years."

"More like this feels inevitable. I want to know where the next strikes will be."

Reilly's mind raced.

"Okay. Obvious and less obvious. Most obvious, with the same impact on the Western hemisphere, the Panama Canal. We should clear ships out. Don't let any new ones in. Average transit time is eight-to-ten hours. I've heard of ships going through faster. But with some thirty ships between locks, it'll be a race. The main problem is it'll be impossible to search the ships, and if the attacks come from the shore, well then it's a lost cause. Of course, will anybody believe the threat at the top?"

"Believing and acting on it are two different things," Heath said.

"There have to be contingency plans," Reilly offered.

"You'd think. But we both know the answer to that. What else?"

"Freezing out the Suez Canal could just be part of the plan. They might want to make the Strait of Hormuz impassable as well. But that's riskier if we have muscle in the Persian Gulf and the Sea of Oman."

"We do. The 5th Fleet out of Bahrain. Where else?"

"Alaska," Reilly said. "The entrance or exit, however you look at it, to the Northern Sea Route is the Bering Strait. It's narrow and it's vulnerable and the only way to and from the Arctic to the Bering Sea and into the Pacific. If you want to stop Russia's tankers, I'd go there and the Danish Strait. That's key to linking the North Sea with the Baltic. Lots of Russian tankers on their way to Europe.

"Now to the less obvious choke points. The Turkish Strait of Bosporus, linking the Med to the Black Sea. Then the Bab el-Mandeb Strait in Northeast Africa. That's where vessels wait to cross into the canal. But it's unnecessary with the Suez down."

"You know all this?"

"It's why you called. Classes you never took in the Army, buddy. And deeper research when I was at State before they put me on the joint domestic study."

"More?" Heath asked.

"Oh yeah. In fact, on second thought, I'd move this up on the critical list. The Malaccan Strait between the Pacific and the Indian Ocean. It's a serious choke point for Eastern maritime shipping."

Another ding. Reilly pictured a long line of names on the email chain.

"You haven't asked me the most important question, Bob."

"Which is?"

"Whose plan? And who's carrying it out?"

"Aren't they one and the same?"

"Not necessarily."

20

MOSCOW

Nicolai Gorshkov walked in front of a bank of TV monitors at the far end of his Kremlin office. He alternated between monitors showing news in Russian on Russia 1, Channel One, and NTV and in English on CNN International and Sky News.

He turned up the audio on all the sets. He listened to a cacophony of urgent voices, male and female, from anchor desks and correspondents in the field, reporting on the terrorist attacks and history on the Canal. It excited him.

"… two ships reported sunk …"

"… originally constructed between 1859 and 1869 …"

"… an estimated 250 ships with nowhere to go from the Mediterranean to the Red and Arabian Seas …"

"… Opened November 17, 1869 …"

"… fifty-six stuck between the two choke points …"

"… effectively a 360 mile traffic jam …"

"… earliest known attempt to construct a canal dates back to the Sixth Dynasty of Egypt …"

"… 13% of maritime trade stalled indefinitely …"

"… 16th Century desire to connect trade routes between Constantinople and the Indian Ocean …"

"... international stock markets react quickly ..."

"... Napoleon ordered feasibility studies to dig a canal when he conquered Egypt in 1799 ..."

"... direct route between the North Atlantic and Northern Indian Oceans ..."

"... closed at the beginning of the Six Day War on June 5, 1967, and remained closed for eight years ..."

"... doubled capacity with new construction in 2014 ..."

"... mine sweeping operations after the Yom Kippur War in 1974 ..."

"... older narrower bypass channel unable to be used ..."

Nicolai Gorshkov stopped in front of the CNN broadcast, silenced all the other monitors with the remotes, and turned up the sound on the American anchor.

"And with the Suez shut down for perhaps years, the Northern Sea Route becomes all the more important."

He didn't have an audience with him in his office, but soon the whole world would be listening to what Russia had to say about oil routes.

WASHINGTON, D.C.
DIRKSEN SENATE OFFICE BUILDING

Goddamned ships, Moakley Davidson thought as he hardly paid attention to the news in his Senate office. *Can't they steer those things right?* He flipped to the business channels on his office TVs: CNBC and Fox Business. The markets were taking a deep dive with the ships that went down. First 8, 12, and then 20 percent. Then a temporary correction, but as more fear set in, the stock market tumbled 39 percent. A disaster for most investors, but not for Davidson. He reasoned this could actually be phenomenal for the oil reserves on his North Dakota property. The business was in a blind trust, but he imagined prices soaring and his wealth expanding expeditiously.

He switched back to CNN just as the anchor began reading over video that had come in via cell phones. "In other breaking news, we have new footage from outside a Nairobi, Kenya hotel where an oil minister was reported to have been killed. If confirmed, this would be the second murder of a high-level oil executive within a week."

Davidson remembered visiting Nairobi on a congressional tour. He couldn't wait to leave. He lifted his head and half-tuned in to the rest of the report. The screen switched to a shot of the Russian victim in London and a retelling of that story. The anchor concluded, "Both deaths occurred at Kensington Royal International Hotels. We've reached out to the corporation for comment. They released a statement saying that investigations were ongoing and that these incidences were unrelated to civilian travel."

The anchor teased the next block, and CNN broke for two minutes of commercials. Davidson turned away from the screen. Something began to percolate. *What was it?*

The sixty-three-year-old senator from North Dakota searched his memory. He turned a nagging thought around in his mind a few times. *The hotel. Yes, the hotel. Kensington.* That's what stuck. But there was something else. Beyond the hotel and the loyalty rewards. *What is it?* He couldn't quite place it.

"Tasha!" he shouted to one of his aides. "Why the hell do I know Kensington?"

The woman replied from the outer office where a number of his minions sat.

"What, sir?"

"Kensington. The fucking Kensington!"

The question, the tone, and the volume were impolite, but Tasha Samuels was used to it. She walked into his office. "Sorry, sir. What is it?"

"Kensington! You know. Like Marriott, Hyatt! The hotels."

"What about them, sir?"

"How do I know them? And I don't mean because I've slept in their beds."

"I don't know," she responded.

"Well, find out!"

The Howard University poli-sci graduate had been working her way up Capitol Hill for five years. Some good assignments, some not so good. Just four weeks into this job, Tasha Samuels was already aware that she was working in a *not-so-good one* now.

Dwight Phillips, a long-suffering aide whose desk backed up to Tasha's, whispered, "Check out the senator's subcommittee schedule. About eighteen months ago. There was an exchange that went viral. That might be what he's not remembering."

"Thanks," Samuels said.

"Wait!" Phillips said thinking back. "It was the Senate Appropriations Subcommittee on State, Foreign Operations and Related Programs. The one he's off now." He leaned and laughed uncomfortably. "You know, he hates foreigners."

Five minutes later, and without much more than a few Google entries, Samuels had the answer. She knocked on his door.

"Who is it?"

"Tasha. I think I have what you want."

"What is it?" he demanded.

Moakley Davidson was a brute, crude and misogynistic, but he wielded political power and was considered one of the most powerful men in the Senate. Davidson was an old-school politician who liked to look tough, especially when the cameras were on. That's exactly what Samuels saw when she found an archived televised C-SPAN hearing and a witness named Daniel J. Reilly, an executive for Kensington Royal Hotels. Reilly was squaring off with the senator and giving back everything he got and more. A grudge match that day. Apparently one that still might be going on.

"Sir," she said, "regarding the Kensington question, you chaired a hearing where an international executive from Kensington Royal testified. A Mr. Daniel Reilly. He sought wider access to intelligence on the pretext," she thought he'd like that word, "that it would help his company evaluate terrorist threats against American properties. You questioned him."

"I buried him!" Davidson interrupted dismissively.

That wasn't what she'd seen.

"Corporate jerk," Davidson continued. "First he thought he could lecture me, the chairman. Right, I remember him. Then in total disregard to order, he got up and left in the middle of the testimony. Goddamned insolent."

Samuels easily gathered from the video that Reilly left because he was informed that his company's hotel in Tokyo had just been bombed. He left because there was an emergency. Because it was his job.

"Is there anything else? Would you like to review the testimony? I can get it for you."

"No." Then he corrected himself. "Yes. There's something familiar about him. Can't put my finger on it. We have history from someplace."

"The hearing, sir."

"Jesus, are you listening to me?" he shouted. "History, sweetheart. That means history, not current events. Find out when and where."

Samuels's face didn't reveal her real feelings or disdain. On one hand, she was getting used to his rants. On the other, she wanted to understand what was so important and why Kensington set him off.

Samuels left the office. The graying senator, who had struck it rich when oil was discovered on his property, valued his holdings and his connections. Like the oil in his portfolio, some of the people were crude, others refined. But to a politician with an insatiable appetite for more—more money, more power, more influence—he needed them all. And anyone who stopped the flow was an enemy.

He recalled his encounter in the Kennedy Senate Hearing Room a year-and-a-half ago. Yes, he remembered Reilly. *The arrogant witness who wanted access to security information from his committee. No, not wanted, demanded. Access to intelligence like he was entitled. Like he was a sitting member of Congress and I was his lackey. In front of the rest of the committee. On fucking C-SPAN.*

Davidson believed he had shut Reilly down. *On TV no less. Asshole.* The Senator viewed his committee performance versus Reilly's through a hazy, egotistical lens. He didn't really remember that day clearly. Nor did he recall his first encounter with Reilly, then a United States Army intelligence officer assigned to him on a tour of Shindand Air Force Base in Afghanistan.

21

THE WHITE HOUSE

Ryan Battaglio was the last to arrive in the Situation Room located in the White House basement. The basement, not the subbasement. There were floors upon secret floors below. The members of the National Security Council had been reviewing intelligence for the last three hours.

Secretary of State Elizabeth Matthews had just finished her assessment when the president entered. Everyone stood and, according to protocol, said, "Mr. President," "Good morning, Mr. President," or some version of a greeting.

Battaglio sat at the head of the table closest to the door where Marine Guards were posted outside and Secret Service agents stood along the hallway. Clockwise around the table were his National Security Advisor Pierce Kimball, White House Chief of Staff Lou Simon, CIA Director Gerald Watts, Secretary Matthews, Homeland Security Secretary Deborah Sclar, Defense Secretary Vincent Collingsworth, Energy Secretary Phyllis McMillan, Chairman of the Joint Chiefs Admiral Rhett Grimm, and other senior members of the Joint Chiefs: Air Force General Leon Zumwalt (no relation to the Vietnam-era admiral), Army General Zarif Abdo, and Marine General Scott Williams. Standing by a map on a fifty-inch television screen was Major General Elias Worthington, head of Middle East operations for USCENTCOM, the United States

Central Command. It was of utmost importance to have Worthington present since USCENTCOM directs and enables military operations with allies and partners to ensure regional security in support of U.S. interests. And right now, the interests of the United States and countries from around the world were threatened at least economically.

"What do we have, general?" Battaglio asked Worthington.

"In a word, a mess. Two disabled ships in the busiest shipping lane in the world. They're going no place fast."

"Who's in charge?"

"The Suez Canal Authority. The Egyptians. No way can they handle this on their own."

"Are you suggesting we send American resources?"

"Sir, that would be your call, but yes. Absolutely, yes. The magnitude and the expense are overwhelming. We have to help, even if ships aren't sailing under American registry. It's our problem as much as everyone else's."

Elizabeth Matthews spoke next. "I agree, Mr. President. While this will take an international effort, we should be first in—before Gorshkov. We need to take the lead. We have more hours managing oil spills and shoreline cleanup than anyone."

She wasn't asserting any pride of accomplishment. But considering the Deepwater Horizon explosions in 2010, the *Exxon Valdez* in 1989, the *Argo Merchant* in 1976, Santa Barbara in 1969, and dozens of other disasters, the U.S. had experience that many other nations lacked.

"Congress won't be happy. Neither will voters," Battaglio countered.

"Mr. President, they're not going to be happy with long gas lines and higher prices either," Matthews replied. "It's a message you can manage on TV. The harder challenge will be managing the crisis."

"What if I talk with Gorshkov? He's going to be impacted, too."

"Less so, sir." This was CIA Director Watts' assessment. "They're less reliant on the route. Likewise for the Strait of Hormuz. Their pipelines cut through Siberia. They're feeding China now and that will increase with their newest pipeline and their Arctic shipping. Quite honestly, this improves his position."

"Still, a bilateral approach would save us billions."

"Yes, sir, but NATO nations would—"

"NATO doesn't strengthen my relationship with the Russians."

"With all due respect," Watts continued, "the world expects us to act."

"And that's just the problem, Mr. Director. Why us again?"

There were one hundred reasons, but the president had shut down the debate.

Battaglio abruptly stood up. "I'm going to put this on Congress's back. They'll have to come up with appropriate committees to explore options. In the meantime, next on my agenda is talking to Nicolai Gorshkov."

"I'll join you," Pierce Kimball said.

"Actually, that won't be necessary, Pierce. I'll handle it myself."

Kimball had just been dissed, and everyone knew it. It would only be a matter of time before he was replaced. The same was inevitable for most of the cabinet. *After that,* thought Matthews, *who knows what level of incompetence might walk through the door.*

The Secretary of State recalled a parable she'd heard at a Kenyon College graduation address for her sister's ceremony. It had been delivered by acclaimed author and English professor David Foster Wallace. The speech not only stayed with her, but it seemed more than applicable about her boss in this moment and well beyond. A fish story with a long tail.

"There are these two young fish swimming along," Wallace told the students and attendees. "And they happen to meet an older fish swimming the other way who nods at them and says, 'Morning boys. How's the water?' The two young fish swim on for a bit ignoring the question. Eventually one of them looks over at the other and goes, 'What the hell is water?'"

To Matthews's thinking, Battaglio didn't know what water is even though he was trying to stay afloat in it. And now someone was pouring huge amounts of oil into the mix.

The president was ready to leave but stopped when Major General Elias Worthington cleared his throat and said, "Sir, soon there will be a hundred ships holding off the coast of Africa. They'll be ripe for the picking by Yemeni pirates. To protect them we are prepared to direct the 5th and 6th Fleets off the coast of East Africa."

"All right."

At least that was something, Matthews thought.

Still standing, Battaglio looked around the room. Energy Secretary McMillan was busily making notes.

"Phyllis, do you have anything to contribute?" Battaglio asked.

"Yes, sir. This is sure to affect oil prices and oil futures."

"Short-term only."

"I think it will be far longer." She had a file full of stats at the ready that she patted. "Oil futures took an immediate fast jump up with the first reports. They'll go further down when the Japanese markets open. That decline will continue for at least the next five days. I suspect it won't level out until it drops by 400 percent. That would be greater than the historic drop in 2020 during the outset of the COVID-19 pandemic and the price war between Saudi Arabia and Russia. This is going to send a shock wave across all the markets. Mr. President, couple this with the murders of oil execs, and I can assure you that prices will be rising at the pump. Maybe as much as two dollars a gallon. The longer the cleanup goes on, the higher the prices will go."

"Thank you, Phyllis," he said without really responding to her specific points.

"Actually, there's more to consider. Oil futures are contracts that set a price for oil based on a set date. It's risky, but it traditionally pays off for investors because of the constant need. When a contract falls a dollar from 50 to 49, the seller gets a $1,000 credit, based on the $1 decline multiplied by the 1,000 barrels the contract covered. To cover potential losses, cash has to be held in equity accounts. There's an acceptable margin, depending upon the date of the contract. If losses exceed the available cash, speculators must deposit more to keep their futures position.

"As this goes on, investors will be forced to sell other assets at a loss, from stocks and bonds to real property. In other words, Mr. President, this could be the greatest challenge to markets since the 2008 recession. It needs attention, and it's needed now."

Matthews studied Battaglio throughout the Energy Secretary's warning. She could tell he was gritting his teeth behind his closed mouth. Thinking, processing, worrying.

"You've made your point, Phyllis, Now get me solutions by six. From each department. In the meantime, as I said, I have a phone call to make."

The president left. Matthews quickly joined him outside the Situation Room. If Battaglio was about to phone the person she suspected, he needed guidance.

"Excuse me, Mr. President. A moment."

He stopped.

"Yes."

"I must caution you on how you handle any conversations with President Gorshkov. He has oil reserves. He's sailing through the Arctic with relative ease. This just might be what Gorshkov wants."

"You're not suggesting—?"

"I'm suggesting you don't make that call. We have a great deal to unpack first. And quite honestly, at this hour we don't know anything more than what Wolf Blitzer is reading off his teleprompter. Wait for the options to come in that you requested. You have an experienced team. Let us do our work."

He thought for a long moment, appearing impatient to leave, then added, "Okay, then call in Ambassador Lukin for a nice little chat."

Dimitri Lukin was Gorshkov's U.S. Ambassador.

"Good idea, sir," she said.

The president turned to leave, then stopped. "Elizabeth, you are an enigma to me," he unexpectedly said.

She steeled herself for what was to come. It came hard and fast.

"You don't like me. You don't think I'm up for the job."

She said nothing.

"Sometimes I'm convinced you're conspiring behind my back. Other times, like now, your advice seems sincere and sound. Which Elizabeth Matthews am I talking to at this moment?"

Matthews took in a deep breath and without pausing said, "Mr. President, I serve you, and through you, the best interests of the United States. With that comes the responsibility to caution you against having any conversation that could have far-reaching political ramifications beyond the immediate financial ones. You would want nothing less from me."

Battaglio nodded. "Okay, continue your meeting. I'll wait for all the options to come in. I'm getting anxious."

An understatement Matthews thought, but she thanked the president. She'd bought time but that didn't take away her concern that Ryan Battaglio could make another terrible mistake or do nothing.

22

BEIJING, CHINA

Reilly was used to prying eyes when he worked his way through customs at Beijing Capital International Airport. Visible eyes and those that saw but remained unseen to him through one-way mirrors, in light fixtures, store window displays, mannequin eyes, let alone lapel cameras on secret police roaming the airport. He knew to smile, answer questions promptly when asked, and remain businesslike. Anything out of the ordinary would be flagged. Once flagged, he would likely be tagged and followed. He had been in and out of China often enough to understand the necessity of adhering to protocol. He had been in and out of China enough to recognize that authorities also took extra interest in American executives with hopes of learning something new from their encounters, especially those thinking they could anonymously enjoy some of the exciting sexual experiences offered through many hotels.

Reilly had successfully ended the sexual trade that had been operating in Kensington Royal's Beijing hotels. It had taken him two years to clean things up with one unintended consequence. *Guoanbu*, the Ministry of State Security, which used sex workers to compromise clients, kept Dan Reilly in its sights. For that reason, he didn't count on a quick pass through new customs control robots. As expected, he was directed to a manned kiosk by an officer.

He politely handed over his passport. The officer scanned it, allowing extra time for scrutiny up the line. Then he examined it, looked to see that the photograph matched the man he faced, and placed it on his counter.

"The nature of your visit, Mr. Reilly?"

The question had more than a suspicious tone. It bordered on accusatory. But Reilly offered a half smile to the uniformed officer, who was obviously waiting for approval from superiors.

"Business. I work for an American hotel company. I'm here to consult with my staff." He intentionally avoided mentioning the oil conference. *Less is best.*

The customs agent examined Reilly's passport again and nodded, more to the voice he heard in his ear than to Reilly.

Here come the next questions.

"Where are you staying?"

"The Kensington Grand Hotel in the Dongcheng District. It's on Wangfujing Avenue, relatively near the Forbidden City. As I said, I work for the company that runs the hotel."

"So this is a business trip. The nature of your business?"

Reilly paused. He'd already answered the question, but he continued as if he hadn't. "Meetings."

"What kind of meetings?"

No smile from Reilly now.

"Staff meetings. I'm sure you can see that I often come to Beijing."

The guard had the information on his screen but went to his next delaying question. "Length of stay?"

"Uncertain."

The guard frowned. He was used to asking specific questions and getting specific answers.

"I'm here for business meetings. If you need a number, type in ten. Based on this greeting, I'd be happy to make it less."

The customs agent put his finger to his ear. Obviously another incoming question being fed from a supervisor.

"You are a participant in a conference?"

All right, they've lined that up. The oil conference is on their radar.
"No, I am an executive for the company that has leased the hotel to a Chinese firm."

"You've been here before?"

Obviously. Whoever's in your ear knows full well. "As I already told you, yes."

"And the nature of that visit."

Reilly was getting annoyed now but fought the urge to show it. He smiled and repeated what he'd said. "Yes, sir. I am an executive of the hotel corporation. I've come to Beijing numerous times over the past six years. It's all on record."

The guard nodded. "Are you carrying more than 20,000 RMB; $5,000 U.S. in cash?"

Finally, back to routine queries.

"No."

"Do you intend to leave the People's Republic of China with currencies equal to or above 20,000 RMB, 5,000 US dollars?"

"No."

Then came the standard questions about alcohol, cameras, cigarettes, cigars, animals, plants, biological products, even human tissue.

Reilly politely answered no to each. He was finally cleared with the sound of his passport getting stamped.

"Thank you," he said.

The officer gave him a cold last stare, probably wishing he had been able to trip up the American. It would have meant a good mark on his record.

As Reilly exited, he shared his opinion too. He stepped up to an interactive computer stall with a device displaying a caricature of a customs officer and a choice of choosing four faces from a nasty expression to a semi-smile, a normal smile, and an enthusiastic grin. Reilly chose the nasty face. Anyone who watched him on the closed circuit monitors probably expected it.

NAIROBI, KENYA

Alan Cannon was into his second day in Nairobi. For the last hour he had been waiting, waiting in the lobby of the Kenyan Police Department on Harambee Avenue. From Cannon's experience, the building, called Vigilance House, was highly vulnerable to attack. Glass windows on every floor. Concrete showing stress and cracks. Just being inside made him nervous. Vigilance was definitely the wrong name.

"Hello," said a tall hulk in a loose-fitting suit and no tie.

Hello would have been fine thirty minutes ago. *I'm sorry* would have been appropriate now. But Alan Cannon merely smiled.

"I'm Detective Gatimu Kamau." The officer was dark and barrel-chested, and had a perfectly horizontal jaw line, broken nose, and scar that ran from his left cheek downward. All of it told a story of decades of police work; a history of violence. This man had no compunction mixing things up officially and likely unofficially—maybe more of the latter.

"Thank you for meeting me, detective." Cannon explained who he was, but he was certain his phone call to the police station had triggered a bio-check. "We had a death in our hotel."

"Yes. Unfortunate for your guests to be around."

He gave nothing in the first response.

"We believe it was a murder. I want to make certain your medical team is doing a full toxicology report."

"People die in hotels every day, Mr. Cannon."

"Not two oil executives just days apart in two cities during a conference."

"Perhaps that changes the odds," the detective laughed loudly.

"I believe Jayo Meng died from poison, either injected or ingested."

"Do you have a suspect?" Kamau asked.

"Do you, detective?" Cannon responded sharply.

Kamau laughed again. "You are a man who gets right to the point."

"When it comes to assassinations in my hotels, yes."

The Kenyan stood eye to eye with Cannon. He gave a slight nod, then said, "Come with me."

* * *

Reilly didn't expect anyone to pick him up, so he wasn't looking when a man fell into step a few feet behind him. Not unusual at the airport, but when his shadow mirrored his moves through the concourse, he made an unexpected sharp right into a Ferragamo store. It put him right in front of a display of sunglasses with an oval mirror on the counter. He picked up a pair, tried them on, but was really checking out the view over his shoulder. And there was his tail. The eye contact with Reilly in the mirror told him he was burned. He shrugged and peeled off.

"Not bad for a rookie." The voice came up beside him from a man who poked his head down to look at watches in the glass case.

Reilly chuckled. He recognized the voice: American, distinctive, deep, and authoritative. The last time he heard it was almost a year ago.

"I thought you were a good sailor. How'd you end up so far off course?"

"A mutual friend apparently gave me a bum map."

Reilly casually turned to the man and smiled.

"That same friend gave me something to give to you."

"Well, word does get around."

Former CIA agent Skip Lenczycki and Reilly hugged warmly like they did after they had run down a Russian assassin in Brussels.

"One problem," said the retired operative. "I'll need a room at the inn. Know anybody with influence?"

Reilly laughed. "I just might. Come on."

* * *

The preliminary autopsy results were on Kamau's desk. Preliminary, hardly final. The examination of Meng's body had taken only two hours. But it might be weeks before a conclusive toxicological report came in. Nonetheless, Cannon suspected that the results would prove one of three poisons. Cannon's money was on tetrodotoxin, harvested from the organs of puffer fish, the Japanese delicacy fugu. If consumed, the toxin can cause paralysis or death within six hours. His second possibility was ricin, made from castor beans. It caused respiratory and organ failure. Death within a few hours. Third was compound 1080, an odorless and tasteless animal poison that blocks cellular metabolism and leads to a quick, painful death. But since Meng died in his bed and had shown no symptoms before returning to his room Cannon considered compound 1080 less likely.

Cannon made other inferences about the death of the Chinese oil executive. Video and witnesses, including Meng's own security, confirmed that Meng had been engaged in chess matches in the lobby. Cannon reasoned that in a very public place, Meng's security would assuredly let their guard down as time passed. They would miss a casual move from a skilled killer.

The poisons Cannon had on his list were all water soluble. Or for that matter, liquor soluble. Meng had been drinking while playing. He suspected the poison was dropped into his drink while he was playing.

Kamau slid the report across the desk. "Cause of death: Congestive heart failure. Possible traces of a toxic substance. Confirmation will take more time."

"Mail me a copy." Cannon handed him a card and stood.

"That's it?"

"I can do the rest by myself, without waiting. Thank you, detective."

Cannon played chess himself. Not too badly. Back at the Kensington, he sat down to examine the CCTV camera footage and look for the moment the poison was dropped in. Meng's security said he had three drinks. The killer wouldn't do it on the first, and not knowing if Meng would finish a third, he'd slip it into the second glass as either a pack of powder or a fast-dissolving capsule. He was certain he wouldn't see Meng's opponent's face. He would have positioned himself carefully. But his hand? Cannon was certain he would spot the moment as he rolled through the closed circuit footage from the lobby cameras.

The man, identified as Baete De Smet, took his seat, laid out the board, and placed pieces on specific squares, apparently just a few moves away from checkmate. He didn't recognize the set-up, but he remembered a quotation his high school chess club teacher shared about strategy. He'd quoted Professor Thomas Huxley, the famed biologist who had written a timeless essay about education and observation in the mid-19th century. It resonated now more than ever:

The chessboard is the world, the pieces are the phenomena of the Universe, the rules of the game are what we call the laws of Nature, and the player on the other side is hidden from us.

The quote, the game board, and his recollections brought him right back to the observation Reilly had made in London. "He's fucking with us. He wanted to have some fun. He likes games."

BEIJING, CHINA

Skip Lenczycki had not lost a step in retirement and in the years since he also got his sea legs. He was in his late sixties and living the life in Port Elizabeth, Grenadines, running a not-so-profitable Caribbean business with his long-time girlfriend, Layla. Skip's Carib Cruises was more a front—not for the CIA, rather his escape from his work for Uncle Sam.

The years were historic, though not publishable. Joe Lenczycki, better known as Skip these days, had been a company standout for decades, earning praise from every agency director he served under. His posts covered the end of the Cold War and more recent hot spots from the Philippines to Slovenia, Bosnia, and Sierra Leone.

He was, in every way, the real deal. Tough, smart, and deadly. Brash and bold. Driven and fiercely loyal. He had a mildly sarcastic bent that he often led with. The combination had made him one of the most liked operatives at the CIA. He was authentic then and now may be just playing the part of a skipper. But he was happy.

He never gave up his stories for a lucrative publishing deal or cashed in on any consulting offers. He just gave up his ghosts and sailed into the sunset—except when he got a call from an old colleague, Bob Heath.

Heath had asked him to help a year earlier. A friend was likely to get himself in trouble. If someone watched his back, that trouble might be manageable. Lenczycki kissed Layla goodbye, flew to Brussels, and took up surveillance on Dan Reilly. Reilly didn't know it, but Heath's intuition had been right. And together Reilly's trouble died on the street. Another assignment off the books.

Lenczycki's phone rang again. The same man could use some help, though he didn't know it. "Are you up for it?" Heath asked, "Or has the salt air made you complacent?"

Now Lenczycki was walking out of the Beijing International with Dan Reilly. He had a secure phone to deliver and some practical advice.

"Our mutual buddy says hi, and he's a little worried that you're about to land in a sack of shit."

"And he feels I need a helping hand?"

"At least another pair of eyes," the ex-CIA operative laughed. "He'd be here himself, but he's gotten to like his Brooks Brothers suits. Me, I've always been a tan slacks or jeans kind of guy. So you got me."

"I've had worse," Reilly joked.

They hailed a cab and didn't talk about anything other than sports. Reilly was still a Red Sox fan. Skip Lenczycki, the Yankees. The cab driver got bored listening. He had nothing worthwhile to report to his superiors at *Guoanbu*.

* * *

Cannon downloaded every image of the Belgian chess player, having little doubt that he wasn't Belgian. He shared them with the Kensington Royal Crisis Committee assembled in Chicago via a Zoom conference call.

"We're looking for a very deft guy. Late-twenties to mid-forties but can read older. You know," he said, "right in the sweet spot for someone in the game. I suppose that would actually make him thirty-five or thirty-six." Cannon continued. "Speaks multiple languages and is damned good with his accents. Height? Depends if he's standing up straight. Weight variable, but I'd go for 180. About 5'11". Forget hair color. Meaningless given his ability to change it fast."

"Gorshkov had a guy that pretty well fits the profile," General BD Coons said from Texas. BD stood for Bruce Dale, but no one had called him that since elementary school.

"Right. Andre Miklos. Gone," Cannon replied. Reilly and an ex-CIA officer had seen to that.

"Prints?" Tom Reardon, the former FBI agent on the committee asked.

"Gloves in London. Anything he touched in the Kenyan lobby would have been wiped. But my guess is he also used something like cyanoacrylate on his fingers to obscure his fingerprints."

Tiano didn't understand the reference. Reardon explained by giving the over-the-counter product name. "Superglue. The substance fills in the furrows, the dips between ridges. It does reduce tactile functions. Too much can affect grip strength, but the benefits outnumber the negatives. Plus, the glue can be removed with acetone."

"Well, that's one for the books," the COO said.

"So, you want help ID'ing a subject who leaves no prints, looks different wherever he goes, and is an actor the likes of Sir Laurence Olivier or Gary Oldman—a chameleon in every role?"

"That's why I'm calling. Reilly believes he's going to strike again in Beijing. He's there ahead of the next oil ministry meeting."

"Profiling him, I'd say he's a freelancer," Klugo offered. "Military trained. Russian, British, possibly American. Maybe Chechen. Ruling out Asian, Middle Eastern, and sub-Saharan African. I can put the word out."

"You don't think he's a government guy?" Cannon asked.

"Not my top choice."

"Organized crime?"

"No. They use their own guys." Klugo thought for a moment. "Unless the mob has a reason for the hits."

"Don't think so," Cannon replied.

The conversation drifted into silence. Cannon looked at the Zoom wide shot of everyone around the table. He'd given them enough to start whittling down the possibilities. He focused on one man leaning back in his chair, thinking about past days.

"There is one uncommon denominator." Cannon had everyone's attention again. "He's really good at games."

Alan Cannon explained.

23

THE WHITE HOUSE

Battaglio read all the options—from DHS and the CIA, the secretaries of Energy, Commerce, Interior, Defense, and State. To a person they recommended that the president convene a conference with all the G7 nations—Canada, France, Germany, Italy, Japan, and the United Kingdom, the U.S. being the seventh. For a time, there had been eight, making the Group of Nations the G8, but after Russia annexed Crimea in 2014, its membership was suspended.

The goal of the conference would be to present a proposal to the fifteen members of OPEC to establish a six-month freeze on oil prices, prohibit the sale of oil futures, and provide global support to the Suez cleanup. It was a big plan, and it would take time. It wouldn't involve either Russia or China—neither of which was in OPEC—until an actual agreement was reached. Russia and China would then be brought into a third agreement. China, a minor producer, could be invited in to observe the discussions but not have a vote.

The approach seemed sound to Battaglio. He asked his speechwriters to prepare a statement that he would present during the daily White House press briefing, after which he'd take questions.

Matthews was relieved and felt she took the same relieved breath as the others in the Situation Room.

Three hours later, President Battaglio stood in the press room behind the familiar podium emblazoned with the White House seal. Always seen, but rarely focused upon, was the messaging within the symbol. The American bald eagle was front and center; in one talon the eagle clutched an olive branch, in the other, thirteen arrows. Above and behind the eagle, an arc of thirteen puffs of clouds and a constellation of thirteen stars, representing the original thirteen states. Encircling the eagle, stars for each of fifty states and these words: The Office of the President of the United States. It was impressive, leaving no doubt about the meaning of the olive branch and the thirteen arrows. You choose—peace or war, and choose wisely.

President Ryan Battaglio offered the olive branch to oil-producing nations, whether traditional friend or foe. He proposed that everyone work together for a solution to a transnational crisis. "Today, I've proposed to G7 and OPEC nations a freeze on all oil prices for six months, a suspension of trading, and the creation of an international aid fund and oil delivery system to help developing countries hit especially hard by any shortfalls resulting from the Suez blockage."

The pool camera zoomed in. Reporters jotted down notes. In the margins, some added observations that this was Battaglio's first real presidential moment. He was doing well. Elizabeth Matthews watched and recognized the same thing. She had helped guarantee his moment in the sun.

Questions came fast. Battaglio answered in pithy soundbites.

The time frame?—"I've already begun calling G7 leaders to implore them to act quickly."

President Gorshkov and Russia?—"Russia is not part of the immediate conversation."

Cost to the United States?—"We're working on those numbers."

Any leads on the attack?—"Our intelligence services are working with appropriate agencies in the other countries. I have nothing to report to you at this time and won't until we have proof."

The president was about to take another question when an aide approached and whispered in his ear. Battaglio gave an almost imperceptible nod and smiled as if all was good. But his next words left the press wondering.

"I'm sorry. That's going to do it for today. Thank you everyone."

An hour later, no one had to wonder.

24

THE STRAIT OF HORMUZ

The night skies were clear. The air was thick with sweltering heat. The water was calm at the southern entrance to the narrowing Strait of Hormuz four miles ahead. Thirty minutes later, the Japanese container ship *Toyotomi Hidekyoshi* smoothly sailed at 16 knots up into the narrow sea way. Smoothly until 0228 Iran Daylight Time. At that moment, a massive explosion ripped through the ship under the bow. Losing control, the cargo ship took a hard swing to port. The captain, trying to right the boat, countered with an equally hard turn to starboard. Another blast created a gaping hole aft. Suddenly, forward and aft, *Toyotomi Hidekyoshi* took on water at an inescapable rate.

* * *

The first reports were sketchy. A ship of unknown registry was adrift and sinking just shy of the Strait of Hormuz. Eyewitnesses onboard nearby ships reported via cellphones and ham radio. The situation got worse with each update. Sky News was the first to put the details together.

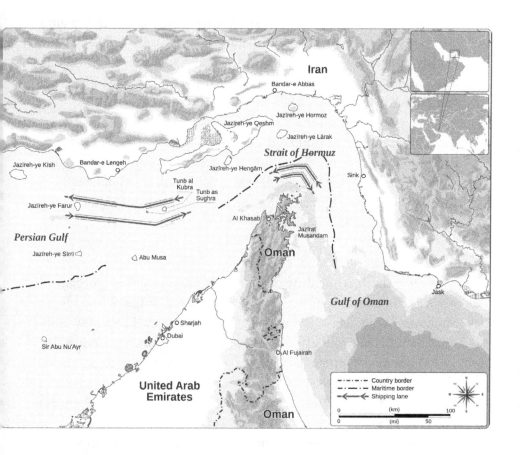

"Early this morning, a Japanese container ship sailing from the Gulf of Oman sank in the Strait of Hormuz. Though details are incomplete, the *Toyotomi Hidekyoshi* may have crossed international waters and hit a naval mine off the coast of Iran close to the island of Qeshm. Vessels of its size and registry can hold more than 17,000 shipping containers, including cars and trucks, food, and manufacturing supplies. We don't have word on survivors, but the ship typically carries twenty-two to twenty-five crew members. The *Toyotomi Hidekyoshi* was on a heading to the Port of Valencia, Italy. What does this mean for the markets? Let's find out with Sky News business reporter Sybil Lindenbaum."

With a map of the Strait of Hormuz sharing the screen, Lindenbaum warned that the global markets would further decline. "Tokyo has already dropped 16 percent on top of its previous losses following the attacks on the Suez Canal." She predicted the same for the European and New York exchanges when they opened.

And while the business news was terrible, the situation worsened when Iran's military command confirmed that *Toyotomi Hidekyoshi* had indeed crossed into its territorial waters. Ship captains who dared to venture off course knew the dangers: risking interception by Iranian patrol boats, hitting Iranian mines, or finding themselves on the wrong end of an Iranian sub's torpedoes.

THE WHITE HOUSE

"This isn't the first incident of its type," Admiral Grimm explained when the National Security Council reconvened in the White House Situation Room. Maps and satellite images were on the various monitors. "Iran has mined the bejesus out of their coastal waters. Couple that with submarine commanders who have fire authority, and the narrow channel becomes narrower and more harrowing."

"So which is it? Mine, torpedo, or explosion onboard?" President Battaglio asked.

"Based on preliminary sat images, it looks like the Japanese ship deviated from its path. If so, the fault lies with the captain."

"Stupid fucking jerk. It would be better if we could blame the Iranians."

"Sir," Grimm continued, "the Ayatollah has consistently warned that Iran will exercise its rights in the Strait, the Gulf of Oman, and the Persian Gulf. Captains know the risks but to save time they often try to jump ahead in line. Iran has been absolutely clear about deploying the IRGCN—"

"The what?" Battaglio demanded.

"The Iran Revolutionary Guard Corps Navy, sir. The country has consistently used its naval forces to protect its borders while terrorizing the maritime community. I'll put together a report on the history."

"How about starting right now."

"Certainly, Mr. President," Grimm said, recognizing he was really speaking to an audience of one. He explained, "The Strait of Hormuz is the channel that links the Persian Gulf with the Arabian Sea to the west and the Gulf of Oman to the southeast. The passage is ninety miles long and varies from twenty-one to fifty-two nautical miles wide."

Grimm stood and referred to the map on the TV monitor. "To the north, Iran. The south, the Arabian Peninsula. The Strait is vital to oil– and liquefied natural gas–producing countries in the region and buyers around the world. The strategic and economic development of Saudi Arabia, Iran, and the United Arab Emirates, as well as the overall stability of the Middle East, depends on safe and open passage through the Strait. Upwards of 21 million barrels are transported daily on as many as fourteen ships. Roughly one-third of all seaborne trade goes through the Strait of Hormuz. It is the most sensitive transportation choke point in the world for oil supplies, and it's especially critical near the islands of Hormuz, Larak, Hengam, and Qeshm, where the Japanese ship went down. It gets tight and risky in the area. Ship captains often turn off their transponders and alter their courses to avoid detection by the Iranians. Route changes are a breach of international convention. Without radio data transmitting vessel locations, ships that veer out of international waters and hug the coast look threatening to Iran, which has its fingers on multiple triggers. Those triggers are attached to conventional missiles and torpedoes. But the mines may get them first."

"And that's what happened," Battaglio surmised.

"Let's just say when that happens, a ship, no matter what flag it flies under, is asking for trouble."

"Okay, Iran took the ship down. What's Japan going to do about it?"

"I beg your pardon, Mr. President, but I didn't say that," Grimm replied sharply.

"That's what we should make of it."

"The facts don't support it."

"People need a villain. Iran's as good as we have," the president declared.

Grimm ignored Battaglio's assertion. "Mr. President, you asked what the Japanese are going to do. It's not a government problem. It's corporate. The owner of the vessel can lodge a formal complaint with the U.N. They can demand that survivors, held by Iran, be freed. They can sue for compensation for families of the dead and the company, but that's a long legal battle that requires an admission of guilt from Iran—which is unlikely."

"This is still going to drive up prices across the board. We'd do better to blame Iran for their unprovoked action." Battaglio paused. He looked around the room for support. He read none.

"Does anyone hear me? We're facing the biggest global economic crisis in memory. Shipping is fucked. If we're not going after Iran, then give me someone else crazy enough to do this. The boogeyman. That's what the country expects from me. I expect you to come up with them!"

Battaglio stood and stormed out of the Situation Room, putting a definite exclamation point on the end of the briefing. Before the room cleared, Matthews whispered to Pierce Kimball, "Hang for a sec?"

The National Security Advisor gave a slight nod. When they were alone, she said, "Question, Pierce. Any possibility this was Russia's play to make it look like Iran was responsible? A Russian torpedo takes out the Japanese ship, then Iran immediately does what's expected, denies involvement but grabs the survivors and throws them in prison. A ploy that plays into Battaglio's desire to turn Iran into the bad guy?"

"Not out of the realm of possibility, but this time, I'd say no. The evidence supports the cargo ship took a chance and paid the price. But I see where you're going. Two key water lanes suddenly out of commission? It makes Gorshkov's Northern Sea Route all the more valuable."

"Absolutely," Elizabeth Matthews replied. "All the way to China—a very oil-thirsty nation."

She thought for a long moment. Kimball waited.

"Okay, assuming the reports are confirmed, the sinking of the

Japanese tanker was a stupid mistake. But that still means Arab oil won't be moving anywhere quickly. A win for Mr. Gorshkov. Which is why you have to make the case against Russia, Pierce. Gorshkov had the motive and the means. Bring it to Battaglio."

"He won't act on anything. We both know that."

"Then the global economy pitches in Russia's favor. Irreversibly, for years," she said. "Try to explain it to him. If you don't, I will."

"Careful, Elizabeth. You're already treading on quicksand. Be careful where you step. From what I hear, Battaglio is watching your moves as much as you're watching his."

"And yours, Pierce."

* * *

"Get Moakley Davidson in here," the president barked to his secretary.

Lillian Westerman, another one of President Crowe's leftovers, replied, "Yes, sir. When would you like to meet with the senator?"

"This afternoon. Alone."

"Of course."

Westerman hadn't started looking for a new job yet. She had known and worked with President Alexander Crowe since his years in the Senate. She was loyal to him, which probably sealed her fate with President Battaglio. It would be hard at fifty-five to start again, but she had good references.

"That's right," she explained to Davidson's secretary when connected. "Right away."

Westerman hung up and confirmed the meeting with the president. "Twenty minutes, sir."

It didn't earn her a thank-you. But in the past few weeks she'd learned that Ryan Battaglio wasn't big on thank-yous.

25

WASHINTON, D.C.

DIRKSEN SENATE OFFICE BUILDING

Tasha Samuels was deep into Dan Reilly's bio, at least what was public. She pulled material from dozens of sources: interviews with travel reporters, including Peter Greenberg; a profile in *The Boston Business Journal* when he managed a property in Copley Square; a United Airlines magazine article when he reached ten million miles; and a survey piece on international travel leaders in *Condé Nast Traveler*.

Reilly's early years were interesting. According to a Boston University alumni magazine feature, he was raised in Boston by his mother, a 911 police operator. His father had been killed in action during his military service. While in college he worked as a part-time security guard at the Prudential Center and was shot during a robbery. His mother was on duty when the call came in. Police responded fast from the station less than a half-mile away on Berkeley Street. Reilly recovered quickly, continued his studies, went to Harvard, and then joined the army. What often came up was an award for valor he earned in Afghanistan. Reilly survived not one but two Taliban attacks. In the first, his Commando Select armored vehicle was fired upon. Exact details were unclear. There was no information on the second, but Captain Daniel J. Reilly's commendation indicated he had performed with distinction.

She reread the notes she'd made so far and stopped. *Interesting guy. Doesn't sound like the man Davidson described.*

Samuels dug further and found reports on Reilly rescuing survivors from the recent 14th Street Bridge bombing in Washington. She had seen the smoke and fire from her office. Another heroic moment for him, nothing like Davidson's brutal assessment.

This was going to take more effort and more coffee. As she poured, Senator Davidson blasted out of the office without a word about where he was going.

Back on her computer, Samuels downloaded an industry speech Reilly made announcing how seriously Kensington Royal Corporation took safety procedures. "Safety," he had told the crowd at a Boston Convention Center conference, "is the number-one priority for our guests." He cited how visible defensive measures in Mumbai discouraged terrorists from targeting the hotel. He explained the importance of working with intelligence agencies around the world to evaluate threats, and the importance of educating the staff: *if they see something, say something.* He even noted that he'd established a check-in protocol to remind guests to read the emergency procedures posted on every room door: where to go in case of a fire, when to avoid elevators, how to exit safely.

Reilly had also established a four-tiered color-coded system designed to rank threat levels, *RED* signifying the greatest threat to the hotel and guests. The initiative earned him a company promotion from vice president to president of the international division and an appearance on Capitol Hill, where he sparred with Moakley Davidson during a Senate hearing.

Samuels found that though Reilly's home base was Chicago, he had an apartment and a satellite office in Washington. He'd been married and divorced. No children.

This was her second day working on the report. There were still holes in Reilly's record; particularly his military service. For this, she called a contact at the Pentagon.

"Rhona, my turn. I can use your help."

Help meant information. Their relationship worked both ways. Unofficial and never revealing their sources. The Washington data shuffle.

"Kinda busy," Lieutenant Rhona Neill said. "What is it?

Samuels explained the hole she was trying to fill.

"Give me ninety." Neill called back in fifty. "Got something, but not a lot. Most of what I came up with has been redacted. I'll read what I can."

"Can you shoot me a copy?"

"You know how this works."

Samuels did. She'd just have to take notes and ask the right questions. "Confidential military shit?"

"More like political. After this, you're on your own."

Samuels' heart beat faster. She was excited to hear what her friend had. "Okay, ready."

"Paraphrased, no direct quotes. No dates. We never talked. Nothing to point back here."

"Agreed."

Neill spoke quickly. Samuels wrote as fast as possible.

"Captain Daniel Reilly, U.S. Army, accompanied a Congressional delegation to Afghanistan. Date removed. The group visited numerous locations, including the remote Shindand Airbase seventy-five miles from the Iranian border. The nearest town is seven miles away, Sabzwar City in Harat province. It was in the middle of the danger zone. The U.S. and NATO shared ops at the facility. Strategically," she said choosing her words carefully, "a perfect launching point for eyes on the ground to observe Iran."

"A usual stop for a Congressional tour?" Samuels asked.

"Possibly with intelligence clearance. Off the beaten path for most. And with that, I may have told you more than I should have."

Samuels believed it was an intentional slip. A suggestion for her to research who and when. She now knew where and had another parameter—people on intelligence committees.

"The U.S Air Force 838th Air Expeditionary Advisory Group operated out of Shindand, as did the U.S. Army. Hence your subject's presence. He was in Army Intelligence."

"Something happened there," Samuels concluded.

Neill said nothing.

"Any help on who made up the delegation?"

"A smart person could make an inference."

"Come on, who?" Samuels pressed. She only heard her friend's breathing. "Okay, I hope I haven't put you in a bad—"

Neill cut her off. "You haven't because we never spoke." With that, the line went dead.

Tasha Samuels spun around in her swivel chair. She hadn't checked before the call and was glad to see no one in the office was paying attention to her. Another cup of coffee later, she logged on to Capitol databases to search for committee member trips to Afghanistan over the last fifteen years. Hundreds of hits returned. Too broad. She needed to narrow it down to Reilly's duty. But she could only estimate that, since his military record was unspecific. After forty minutes she had his years which gave her a shorter list of Congressional tours. Nothing. More than nothing, twenty-two trips blacked out.

"Damn!" she said loud enough to be overheard.

"Everything okay?" a fellow aide asked.

"Fine. Mistyped."

Samuels thought for a moment. *Think. Think*, she said to herself. An idea came to her. Simple beyond belief, but she decided to try it anyway. Little did she know that this was the same road a *New York Times* reporter went down barely a month ago—a straightforward, open-source Google search. Samuels typed in the name of the base, the range of years, the words House of Representatives, and added one additional word to her inquiry: secret.

A lot of nothing appeared; 312 nothings. She added Reilly's name, likely a futile inclusion. It was. She removed it and tried another parameter. It came to her as she thought about Neill's last response, when she asked about the names of the Congressional delegation: "A smart person could make an inference."

"Of course! Moakley Davidson," she whispered. Tasha Samuels smiled to herself. She retyped the first search list and added one more term: Moakley Davidson.

Samuels didn't know how it worked, how Google could come up with responses so quickly. But in a fraction of a second, Google searched its index of more than 100 million gigabytes in dozens of datacenters in the U.S. and another forty-three around the world.

Samuel's inquiry went to a datacenter nearest to Washington. At the nanosecond she hit enter, the datacenter was overwhelmed with requests, so it was forwarded down the line, all at the speed of light. Within each datacenter, hundreds of computers are networked. The query was assigned to a master server that surveyed Google's web index. The results were returned and instantly organized, sorted, and sent back to Samuels. All still at the speed of light—186,000 miles per second.

And in that next second, Tasha Samuels said, "Shit!" She leaned back in her chair and exhaled heavily. A five-year old anonymous Quora question and answer loaded.

Query:

My brother served in Afghanistan. Looking for anyone who knows anything about an attack on a Congressional delegation at Shindand Airbase? Brother died. Can't get help.

Jackson Daniels, Omaha

Response:

I knew a Daniels killed there. Might be your bro. Patrick Daniels. A good guy. He'd do anything for anyone. He volunteered that night. The plan was for a midnight tour. Out and back for a photo op with the airbase behind them. Intel had warned against it, but a couple of the visiting yahoos from Washington insisted. They got their photo. We lost your brother and five others in an ambush. The photog was one of them. We were ordered to keep a lid on it. There are things I can't even say here. But it's no secret who wanted to go out that night. Fucking Maury Davison and some other asshole congressman I can't remember. May they rot in hell.

Anonymous

Samuels mouthed the name in the answer. "Maury Davison." But not Maury Davison. Anonymous had gotten the name wrong, which probably was why no one took any real notice of his posting before. Maury Davison for Moakley Davidson, an easy mistake for someone just overhearing a name. Equally interesting was "Some other asshole congressman." That, and the fact that Reilly was at Shindand accompanying a congressional delegation.

What did he know? What had he seen?

Samuels put the pieces together. Reilly's name rang a bell in Davidson's memory, but he didn't connect the man who testified before his committee with the Army officer who accompanied him and another member of Congress on their disastrous excursion.

No, Davidson didn't remember, but Tasha Samuels bet that Dan Reilly had never forgotten or forgiven him.

26

HAUGESUND, NORWAY

William Henry unlocked the door to his home. His stay would be short. He had another trip in a few days and preparations to make.

He'd left the heat low. It was cold. But he actually preferred it that way. Heat took the edge off. Heat made him too relaxed. He couldn't afford to be relaxed. Ever. Not at least until he retired. Then maybe.

He unpacked his newest overnight suitcase—he never moved from city to city using the same one. He showered, lit a fire in his fireplace, and returned to the latest Jack Reacher novel he'd picked up on a stopover at the Bonn Airport.

Of course, there wasn't any William Henry beyond this small one-bedroom house tucked into an isolated town along a fjord. No William Henry, any more than there had really been a Walter Grün in London, Father Timothy Eckhart travelling through the Chunnel to France, or Baete De Smet playing chess in Nairobi. Neither had he been Hoefsteder in Germany, Sautier in Martinique, or Salehi in Iran. But in Norway, being Norway, he had established himself as a quiet and polite travel writer who was always flitting in and out, often home only for a quick reboot. Now he wanted to rest and have a chance to research, which he considered the reason he stayed alive and invisible, and, if he allowed himself, a night with a pretty Haugesund maiden.

He already had a plan for his next assignment. It presented more challenges than the last two, but he was certain he had designed a plan that when perfectly executed would, he laughed to himself, lead to a perfect execution.

Of course, he had his favorite employers. He knew them. They never knew his true identity. They communicated via encrypted inquiries embedded in public online job search sites, including Angi, formerly Angie's List. After all, what better way to find a pro to do the work, though the assignments were far from the home and required very special tools.

He did have one contract stipulation. Employers who failed to live up to their financial obligations never had the opportunity to do so again. Not a Bulgarian president, a Cuban general, or an internet CEO.

When it came to his work, he preferred subtle approaches with a certain theatrical flair, which most recently he had put to good use in London and Nairobi.

He was proficient with handguns from around the world, poisons as evidenced in Nairobi, even bombs, though he sought to minimize collateral damage, civilian deaths. Arson was not his favorite. Too many things could go wrong. Strangulation only if he could overpower the victim by surprise. He'd seen how hard desperate people could fight. It was rarely good, too fraught with problems. A knife or box cutter, preferred by other assassins, was never his choice. Escaping in blood-splattered clothes invariably brought attention from eyewitnesses, and he liked to remain invisible. Sniper rifles always felt good in his hands. The science of it fascinated him. Wind, barometric pressure, angles, location, and distance offered complex puzzles that he delighted in solving. Also, a long gun also gave him the best chance to walk away cleanly. Walk, never run. Never draw attention to himself. Sometimes he even stayed around, a witness rather than a perpetrator.

He had no politics. He paid no taxes. He had no roots left. No one to visit. No family alive. No friends.

He had been a soldier. He used to salute his country's flag. Now he killed for many, but with no allegiance to any. In a twisted way, he believed his actions served a greater good. He eliminated rivals, which may have prevented wars. He took out crime bosses who would likely evade government prosecution. He changed equations in political and economic problems.

Killing. Not a bad way to earn a living.

Police, government spy agencies, or military forces weren't his most feared enemies. People with their cell phones were. Likewise mounted surveillance cameras. He was particularly careful at airports, where he avoided being in the background of selfies or caught face-on by CCTV lenses.

Whatever name he went by, he considered himself the best—the most careful.

27

THE WHITE HOUSE

Pierce Kimball arrived at his West Wing office the next morning only to discover his secretary wasn't in and his door locked.

"Miriam," he called out.

No response. He stepped out in the hall and called again. Nothing. A usually friendly White House aide walked by. This time she avoided eye contact.

Kimball returned to his secretary's outer office. Her desk hadn't been touched. It was as neat as it had been when she left the night before, stacked with files for Kimball to review.

He was about to dial the president's secretary when he heard his name called.

"Mr. Kimball?" the voice came from behind him. Monotone. Serious.

Kimball looked up.

"Yes?"

He was facing a member of the Presidential Protective Division (PPD), the Secret Service agents charged with close protection of the president.

"Sir, we've been instructed to escort you from the White House." The agent held an envelope.

Dumbfounded, Kimball barely uttered, "What?"

"This will explain." He handed the sixty-eight-year-old career dip-lomat the envelope.

Kimball opened it, though he surmised what it contained.

"May I see the president?" he asked.

"Sir, the president has requested that I escort you to the exit." Sorry was not part of the statement.

"My personal belongings? Photographs?"

"What is yours will be returned in due course."

"My laptop?"

"What is yours will be returned," the Secret Service agent repeated. "Now I'll take your White House pass."

"Who?"

"Who what, sir?"

"Who's the lucky winner of this goddamned job?"

"Congressman Roger Whitfield, sir. He's waiting with the president until you're—"

"Out, agent. Until I'm out."

With that, Pierce Kimball abruptly left his job in the Battaglio White House. He had been a holdover from President Alexander Crowe's administration and more than half-expected that he would have been asked to resign soon anyway. Soon came sooner than he thought.

*　*　*

"Mr. President," Moakley Davidson said after being led into the Oval Office. He had been there at least thirty times before. This was his first visit since Ryan Battaglio became president. His own ambition told him he deserved to sit at the desk Battaglio was at. He would be a far better president. Far, far better. But that didn't show on his face—only allegiance and the outward desire to please. "Look where our years together in Congress and the Senate brought you, Mr. President." Davidson almost said *Ryan* but caught himself. "My God, the Oval Office. Leader of the free world. I'm proud of you."

Battaglio liked what he heard. In fact, it played into the reason he had summoned Davidson. The president slowly pushed his chair back, stood, and walked around the Resolute Desk. Davidson saw it as a performance. He offered his hand. Battaglio took it.

"Sit, sit, Moakley. We have much to talk about."

Battaglio settled into a high-back leather chair with some historic distinction he didn't know. Davidson sat on the couch opposite him.

"If I knew what you wanted to discuss, I would have prepared."

"Not necessary. Just conversation between two old friends," Battaglio said. "Care for a scotch?"

"Thank you, Mr. President. A little too early."

"Come now, Moakley, it's cocktail hour someplace in the world."

"Well then—"

Battaglio attended to the drink. He hid a smile from Davidson as he poured and served. They clinked.

Moakley Davidson hated walking into any meeting without preparation. He should have asked Battaglio's secretary what the visit was about. He would remember the next time. Now he sipped and waited for the president to get to it—whatever *it* was. He racked his brain for something he might have done wrong. *Of course,* he thought, *he's pissed I didn't call to congratulate him after he officially became president.*

"Moakley, I'll be blunt," Battaglio began.

That's it. Payback time. Davidson steeled himself for what was coming. *The bastard wants to extract an ounce of blood.*

* * *

Across Washington in the Harry S Truman Building, generally referred to as Foggy Bottom, Secretary of State Elizabeth Matthews sat with Secretary of the Interior Bradley W. Snavely. The door to her office was closed.

"Elizabeth, I'm probably the furthest thing from a political player. I'm an old forester. I cut down trees. I'm not the one to knock down the government."

"Then I'm sure you know the answer to this, Brad. When's the best time to plant a tree?"

Snavely still had the build of a logger—tall and beefy with thick arms and thicker muscles that required special tailoring on his suits. Matthews knew he was very much like his official title: Interior, not exterior. He laughed at Matthews's question.

"The best time to plant a tree? Twenty-years ago."

Matthews nodded. "Yes," she replied. "And the second best time is right now. The seeds we plant today will affect the future timber of the nation."

Snavely sighed. "From where I sit, it's an awfully big ask."

"I know. The biggest."

"I understand your concern. But I haven't seen what you've seen, Elizabeth."

"Yet," she said. "I'm just hoping that when you do, it won't be too late."

Another sigh.

"Look Brad, Gorshkov steamrolled Battaglio."

"President Battaglio," he said invoking his title.

"President Battaglio." Matthews gave him that. "But because of President Battaglio's acquiescence, the map of Europe is changing. He's on his way to rebuilding the former Soviet satellite bloc. He's not finished. But as members of the Cabinet there is something we can do."

Bradley Snavely creased his brow. He was well aware of what she wasn't directly stating.

"There's more," Matthews continued. "Gorshkov's interests extend well beyond Europe. He wants land. He needs Europe's breadbasket just as Hitler and Stalin sought. But he's also moving fast in Asia. Not to take over China—that's impossible. But keeping Beijing dependent on Russian oil is well within his grasp."

She fixed her eyes on Snavely. "Oil, Brad. Oil *is* a natural resource that flows right through your department. You can't avoid it."

The Interior Secretary was feeling increasingly uncomfortable, cornered. Matthews recognized she may have pushed too hard.

"Brad, I can't tell you how much Gorshkov will risk in order to achieve his goals. But he has a plan, and it's moving forward. Without trying to prevent it, we will be complicit in allowing Gorshkov to return Russia to superpower status, possibly destabilize the West and eviscerate NATO, and definitely control the oil market."

She paused for a breath. She still wasn't cracking Snavely's reluctance. He needed to understand what the consequences would be if Ryan Battaglio remained in office.

Bradley Snavely wasn't Battaglio's man. None of the Cabinet members were. Elizabeth Matthews decided to appeal to his patriotism.

"I need you to consider the country, Mr. Secretary."

He said nothing.

"Above all else, Brad."

He said nothing.

"Watch the elections in Ukraine and Latvia. Then ask yourself what Battaglio will do?"

Bradley Snavely looked around her office: At the photographs with world leaders. At the framed photograph of her father, a former state attorney general and ambassador to Germany. At the State Department seal behind her. He should have noticed her pin handcrafted by a Santa Fe artist—a wide-eyed owl perched on a branch. As always, she wore her brooches with real forethought.

"Thank you, Elizabeth. You've given me a great deal to think about."

In her mind, she didn't give him enough.

Snavely left without committing to a position. This was how her conversations went with three other Cabinet members. She had eleven to go—fifteen members in all, including herself. She had to be very careful. Any one of them could turn against her. After her talks with the Secretaries of Health and Human Services, Commerce, and Agriculture she thought she still had time to pull a majority of members together. It would take eight: eight of the fifteen could invoke the 25th Amendment and remove Ryan Battaglio from the presidency. Without a vice president, that would send Speaker of the House Sean Allphin to the Oval Office. A good man: perhaps not the best, but far better than Battaglio.

Elizabeth Matthews leaned back in her chair and strategized who she'd contact next. *Yes,* she thought, *she still had time.* Then her phone rang. It was Pierce Kimball.

"Elizabeth, I'm out. I'm calling to wish you good luck. You'll need it."

28

WASHINGTON, D.C.

Protocol typically required the Russian ambassador to meet in the White House. But Elizabeth Matthews had a different strategy. She would go to Dimitri Lukin's office at 2650 Wisconsin Avenue, NW. There, her meeting would be recorded. She knew it, and Lukin would be a fool not to know she knew and fully intended for her words to get directly to Moscow. Nicolai Gorshkov's English was good enough that he wouldn't need the transcript. She figured he'd be listening before she even got back to the White House.

"Madame Secretary, so nice of you to come here for a change," Lukin said, greeting her in his office.

Lukin was standing when she entered his office, which was appointed with the Russian Federation flag, a national map, and framed photographs of Gorshkov, Russian missiles, tanks, and planes. The differences from the Soviet Era when the embassy opened in 1984 were minor. They amounted to the color of the flag, the persona of the dictator, the updated military hardware, and the size of the map. Today the map of Russian territory was much smaller. Gorshkov was working on changing that.

The ambassador was six-five, bald, but with bushy eyebrows. He was military fit and university savvy. Tough and smart. He wore a dark blue suit, white shirt, and red tie. A scar ran off the corner of his left eye, an inch toward his ear. Plastic surgery could have made it virtually invisible, but Lukin wore it like a badge of honor. She assumed there was a story behind it—a story that probably went back to his army career.

"Mr. Ambassador, thank you for seeing me on short notice."

He led her to a seat at a small round table set in the corner, likely well-wired for audio and video. In the center, a dark blue vase held low cut flowers.

"Coffee or water?"

"No thank you, Dimitri," she said switching to his first name. "I'd like to get right to it."

"Please do. To what do I owe this honor?"

She had decided to lead with the breaking news.

"As I'm sure you are, we're troubled by the incidents in the Persian Gulf and the Suez Canal. Global markets reacted swiftly. The president needs assurance that the Russian Federation has had no hand in these actions."

Lukin gritted his teeth. It pulled his scar tighter. "Excuse me, Madame Secretary, but if you're suggesting we are responsible, you are completely wrong. The two incidents, as you call them, are completely separate. The second falls on the Islamic Republic of Iran. The first is still under review."

"We view—"

"I'm not finished," Lukin demanded. The ambassador had deftly avoided answering Matthews's question and turned the conversation on a dime—the equivalent of about ten rubles. "You failed to mention the murder of a highly regarded Russian oil executive in London in one of your American-owned hotels. This has us deeply troubled. And since there are questions you pose of us, I seek assurance that you will apprize us of everything that comes from the investigation of that terrible murder."

"You have that assurance."

"Good, because it hasn't happened yet."

"And vice versa, Mr. Ambassador. However, back to my question.

The United States would be greatly disturbed to discover any Russian fingerprints on the actions in the Strait of Hormuz."

"An insult."

"The container ship was sunk in international waters, Mr. Ambassador."

Lukin leaned in across the table. "Heading out of its established lane toward land. A threatening move to the Islamic Republic of Iran."

Enough for the recording on that point, Matthews determined. Now her second volley.

"I'd like to address the Northern Sea Route and the toll you've attempted to collect for transit."

"Madame Secretary—" he was back to formalities. "The waters are ours."

"Mr. Ambassador. Same point, different waters. *Some* of the NSR is within your navigational boundaries. Not *all*. Furthermore, Russia has no right to require transit fees or escorts in waters that are clearly international."

"Russian icebreakers—"

Matthews powered on. "The Northern Sea Route is becoming more navigable because of the rising temperatures in the Arctic. Your icebreakers contribute to safer passage. So do ships under American registry as well as ships from Canada, Finland, Sweden, Denmark, Norway, Estonia, Latvia. I can go on. The point is, the route is not yours, Mr. Ambassador."

"It is the shortest, safest way between Russia's east and west. That gives the NSR high strategic value to be protected and monitored. Moreover, it is incumbent that we safeguard our oil reserves in the seas from attack. My country views that as a priority, made all the more clear today given how transit is curtailed in the Suez Canal and the Strait of Hormuz. Your introductory point today, Madame Secretary."

"We are not looking to prevent transit," Lukin continued, "but our national interests depend upon guaranteeing the security of the region. The NSR cuts shipping time in half from the Suez. Now that the canal is shut down for an indeterminate time, the Arctic route is essential to the Russian Federation's economic survival."

"Does that include flyovers that taunt NATO flights? Russian subs pinging ours. It's a deadly game of catch and release. One of these days, somebody's going to get hurt."

"Elizabeth," he said in a cheery voice, much more informally, "you sound like a cold warrior. The days are warmer."

"As noted, so are the waters, which makes our conversation very timely, Dimitri."

"Is there a message you want to formally communicate to President Gorshkov?"

She had been doing that since she stepped into his bugged room.

"Yes. Your elections come and go and yet your presidents tend to stay for life. The same can be said for China. In the U.S., the White House is like a dormitory with temporary occupants. But don't take that as weakness. We are who we are because of the people who stick around. We have memories that go way back. Don't base your judgments on one particular man sitting at one particularly historic desk."

Elizabeth Matthews made sure she delivered her last line into the vase in the middle of the table.

29

MOSCOW

THE KREMLIN

The Russian president was a better talker than a listener. But today he had settled into his deep leather chair, puffing a Havana cigar, smiling broadly, and happy with what he was hearing.

"The Suez will be out of commission for six months," reported the oligarch Markov Kudorff. "And God and the Ayatollah's mines, strictly by coincidence and the Japanese tanker captain's stupidity, worked in our favor. And now, oil futures are shaking up the world's stock exchanges even faster than I expected."

"And we're not finished," Gorshkov boasted. "I'm going to revise my schedule on taking Muldova. And get me a report on how our efforts inside Finland and Sweden are going. We have a window before they fall to NATO. They are key to our further control of the Northern Sea Route." He focused on his new chief spy, FSB head General Valery Rotenberg. "But first, the Latvia vote."

"The numbers will be in our favor."

"Are you certain?"

"With a quarter of a million Russian nationals now voting thanks to the way you maneuvered Battaglio in Stockholm, we will win. Ballots over bullets, Mr. President, with bots thrown in for good measure."

Rotenberg punctuated his assessment adding, "Your masterful negotiating victory."

Across the conference table, General Ivan Zalinski, Commander of the Southern Military District, stiffened. "Mr. President, would you welcome a word of caution despite the optimistic picture Colonel Rotenberg paints?"

"Certainly. Speak freely."

Rotenberg nearly choked on the president's words.

"Thank you. The goal is to secure our borders in a manner we have not seen since the end of the Soviet era."

Gorshkov nodded.

"Doing so gives us economic stability and renewed influence in global affairs unlike anything we have ever seen."

Another nod.

"However, in my estimation, we must plan better this time. Upgrade our armored units, bolster our gasoline and food supply lines, and prepare our troops better. We must—"

Zalinski stopped suddenly, regretting his last point. "Excuse me, Mr. President. That was out of order. No disrespect intended."

"None taken," Gorshkov lied, smiling at his general while deciding Zalinski would be a short-lived commander. He turned to General Arkady Bolonguv. "Arkady, your assessments of our troops and equipment?"

"In my estimation, Mr. President," the general said, taking more care than his fellow general, "we are ready and awaiting your orders. In so far as Latvia is concerned, the 7th Guards Airborne Division is set to deploy. Meanwhile, the plainclothes 'influencers' are in place. I should add they have been most effective."

Gorshkov smiled. The so-called influencers were trained troops in civilian clothes: young singles and couples posing as married, making friends in bars, taking up jobs in the cities and throughout the country. Slipping into all aspects of government and civilian life. Changing the political structure from within, and gaining access to all levels of corporate offices, educational institutions, and Saeima, the country's legislative body. It was a page of out Gorshkov's old Cold War playbook with a few updates.

After some additional details, Gorshkov excused everyone except Colonel Rotenberg. He waited for the room to empty, poured a vodka for his FSB chief, and pointedly asked, "Has the cat found a mouse yet?"

"From our intelligence, he really wants to blame Iran, but his advisors have told him not to."

"Then maybe we should give Mr. Battaglio more reason."

30

OFF THE COAST OF NEW ENGLAND

"XO, sonar track now two-four, bearing zero-four-zero. Range twenty-seven hundred."

Executive Officer Ricky Moore repeated the tracking and shot his Commanding Officer, Commander Andrew Policano, a raised eyebrow.

Sonar control onboard the USS *Hartford* had been tracking the Russian sub in the North Atlantic for the past five days. The sonar crew of fourteen traded off every eight hours with half always on watch, rotating shifts between port and starboard stations. The target had steadily moved south after emerging from the Arctic Sea. The *Hartford* stayed with it except for nineteen harrowing hours when the *Admiral Kashira* disappeared within the New England Seamounts.

One hundred million years ago, these now submerged mountains were above sea level. But as the North American continent drifted west, the volcanic range cooled and sank. The peaks are now more than a half-mile below the surface, and for a submariner they offer endless possibilities.

"Target speed, two-three knots," reported the chief sonar operator on duty, Lieutenant Marcus James.

Speed was an important way of tracking. The *Admiral Kashira*—the most capable attack submarine in the Russian fleet—was quiet in relative terms at 35 knots. Below 20, it was virtually silent. Two-three knots was the closest it had come to going invisible.

"What's he up to, Mr. James?" the *Hartford* CO asked.

"Back to hugging the ridges closely, sir. We could lose him again with one fast jink."

"Just stay on him."

"Aye aye, sir."

The sonar signal was reacquired, and with it came a new firing solution in the fire control tracking party computers. Even in peacetime, this was an exhausting and intense game of undersea hide-and-seek, and peacetime could change in a second with the distinctive sound of torpedo tubes flooding or missiles tubes opening.

Thirty-seven minutes later, the sonar watch reported the Russian nosed down. "Five degrees down angle. Speed, two-zero knots. He's trying to shake us again."

The ocean is full of noise. Everything provides a distraction in the shallows: wind and rain above, below the surface biological activity, including whales, and rising and falling geography. Deep oceans have channels that trap noise, allowing it to travel for hundreds of miles. In Arctic waters, ice caps and snow melts create vertical sound reflectors, physical sonic mirrors that throw hunters off. But for a submariner who knows he's being hunted, the best place to hide is silently on the bottom or behind a mountain.

Sound is actually energy that moves through mediums—air and water. It travels from a source in waves that radiate out in all directions. The waves have both a wavelength, a frequency, and an amplitude, or energy level. Sonar detects these waves. Sonar operators read them.

The principal source of a submarine's noise comes from its propulsion system. But sound can also radiate through the water from a toilet seat being slammed, a hammer hit against the hull, or other unintentional sounds. Captain Andrew Policano of the USS *Hartford* knew that the *Admiral Kashira* was designed with a low acoustic profile. As a nuclear sub, it was cooled without pumps, a major source of noise in a diesel ship. Also, its outer layer was composed of tiles that reduced interior transmission of sound and incoming echoes from active pinging sonar. The *Hartford* was using passive sonar, which emits no signal and keeps the hunter silently in pursuit.

Ninety-minutes later, things suddenly changed again.

"Sonar reports signal lost."

"Roger. Signal lost."

"Find him, Mr. James."

"Aye aye, sir."

But he didn't.

*　*　*

Another Russian Yasen-class guided missile submarine, the *Severodinsk*, had given the U.S. Navy command ulcers a few years earlier when it evaded detection for weeks. Policano's concern was heightened, considering how Russia was turning the Northern Sea Route into its private ocean freeway, and heightened further with the still-unexplained sinking of the Japanese container ship in the Strait of Hormuz. That concern was also felt when Policano raised the antenna and updated 2nd Fleet Command that his prey had disappeared. Minutes later, word reached COMUSFLTFORCOM, the U.S Fleet Forces Command in the Pentagon. From the Pentagon, alarms rang in the White House.

Newly appointed National Security Advisor Roger Whitfield failed to understand the complexity, based on his predisposition toward what he considered the Pentagon's historic alarmist reactions. Consequently, he sat on the warning.

But there were other ways information bubbled up. COMUSFLTFORCOM also reported to the CIA.

"Will you take a call from Director Watts?" Elizabeth Matthews's secretary asked.

It was her first call of the day, 6:05 a.m.

"Good morning, Gerald, what's up?"

"Head start before the today's PDB."

"Topic?"

"A Russian killer sub is missing again off New England. 13,800 tons and 390 feet of nothing. It's the *Admiral Kashira*. All things considered, it's probably just a game."

"Any chance it's a rogue captain?"

""Doubtful," the CIA Director posited. "Captain Boris Sidorov is one of Russia's most experienced commanders."

"What happened and why tell me? I have trouble finding the soap in the bathtub," Matthews joked.

"Given everything else going on, it seemed like there may be a negotiated side to this. Now or later."

"Did we vary from normal procedure?" she asked.

"Not at all. The Russians took a fast dive, made some wild Crazy Ivans, jinked behind a ridge. Poof."

Crazy Ivan was a term born after an incident between a Soviet nuclear submarine and the USS *Tautog* in 1970 in the Sea Of Okhotsk near Russia's Kamchatka base. The American sub was following the Russian when suddenly it executed frequent sharp undersea course reversals, including 90 and 180 degree turns. The *Tautog* crew gave the maneuver a name. It stuck.

"Who was on him?"

"Andrew Policano. Seasoned commander of *Hartford*. An old Annapolis buddy of mine. He's used to the drill and the chase. It goes on all the time. Except—"

"Yeh right. Except. How does the Pentagon rate the threat?"

"Under present circumstances, highly suspect."

"Prickling hairs on your neck suspect?" she asked.

"Every hair and every East Coast harbor suspect."

"Jesus." *Could what happened in the Strait of Hormuz come to homeland waters? Of course it could,* Matthews reasoned.

"We'll give POTUS the full picture this morning, starting with the basic fact that this Russian sub is a real war machine and its commander is a pro."

He shared Commander Sidorov's bio. "Decorated officer with

a distinguished career, loyal and obedient. According to the limited psych intel available, he's not someone to go off the reservation. He's true-blue to Gorshkov, promoted by him and photographed with him multiple times. Most recently, he was spotted going into the Kremlin just before shipping out from the Northern Fleet's base in Severomorsk. Satellite photos show *Admiral Kashira* had been in port long enough to get fully loaded."

"Which includes?"

"More ways to close down strategic Atlantic ports and hit every major city from the East Coast all the way to Dallas and Denver. Oh, and protect himself in the process. His supersonic Kalibr and Biryuza land attack and anti-ship missiles, launchable through its torpedo tubes, have a range of 300 nautical miles. And for long range attacks, *Admiral Kashira* carries nuclear-attack cruise missiles."

Matthews let everything settle in. She weighed frightening possibilities. Under ordinary circumstances, this could merely be an exercise. As Watts had said, the usual hide and seek. She thought cat and mouse worked better. But considering the other naval actions in the past weeks, she couldn't excuse the fear about what the next target might be.

"Gerald, how many tankers are just offshore, close enough to port to shut us down and create chaos?" she asked.

"No idea. Probably hundreds. Department of Energy could pull that up; I'll call it in."

"And Homeland Security. Multiple attacks at East Coast oil ports would be devastating. We need a full assessment. Better circle Roger Whitfield in."

The line went quiet.

"Gerald?" she asked, thinking she'd dropped the call.

"I'm here. I talked to Whitfleld just before you. He had the report before me and sat on it. The Pentagon called him. Didn't think it was important."

Matthews sighed heavily. "And Battaglio threw out Kimball for this guy?"

"Some pick for National Security Advisor. He pleaded with me not to bring that up in the meeting."

"Will you?"

"Not today. It's a hand to play later."

"Write it down, Gerald."

"Already have."

Both of them knew there would be a time. That's how things worked in Washington.

31

BEIJING

Reilly booked Lenczycki into a room next to his on the eighth floor of the posh Kensington Grand. Safe, but this would not be the place for discrete conversations. Better on the street. Best in the U.S. Embassy. Right now, the two men walked along Wangfujing Avenue, taking a perfectly normal stroll after a long flight.

"The phone's encrypted?" Reilly tapped his new acquisition in his sport coat breast pocket.

"Jesus, you're sounding more and more like a spook. That's what they tell me. It works like a normal cell phone. Just make sure you put the code in before you dial. Otherwise—"

"Otherwise I might as well be shouting in a crowd."

"Bingo."

"And the code?"

"Yes. You'll love it. The date of your divorce from Pam. Eight digits. Heath figured you'd never forget the date."

Reilly grinned. "Like one of the two best days in a boat owner's life."

Lenczycki knew the joke, but it wasn't his story. He loved buying, and he had no intention of selling. He believed sailing *No Frills,* his forty-foot Bavaria yacht, had added back the decades to his life that the CIA had taken from him. And yet, here he was again, doing the company's business. A favor.

They walked past high-end stores that you'd see along the Champs-Élysées, Rodeo Drive, 6th Avenue, the Forum Shops at Caesar's Palace, and the Venetian in Macau. Lenczycki wasn't buying for his beach bum girlfriend Layla, and Reilly had no one on his list. So they just traded pleasantries while every so often glancing to check for tails.

"You know how I described my trip to see you to Layla?"

"Wouldn't even venture a guess," Reilly replied.

"I butchered a quote from an author that fairly well nails you."

"Shakespeare? Hemingway?"

Lenczycki laughed, "Not even close. Former U.S. Army Lieutenant Colonel Theodore Geisel."

Reilly raised an eyebrow.

"Dr. Seuss, my friend and his poem, 'Oh the Places You'll Go.' You're willing to go to the streets that aren't marked and peer through the windows not lit."

Reilly smiled. "Never took you as a children's book kind of guy."

"See, you never know what you'll get from a former CIA operative. Observations come in all manner of speaking, including Dr. Seuss. Geisel dug into what makes us tick—the inner psychology of people, which he turned into training films during World War II. There's a lot to gather from his work. Even considering the way I slaughtered his poem, I think it pretty much describes you."

Reilly stopped and looked at the not-so-ex spy. "Am I that easy to read?"

"Yes and no. It helps that I got a chance to look at your Army record."

"Which is not public."

"Neither is your State Department work. By the way, nice research on our homeland weaknesses. Shame that it fell into enemy hands."

"Jesus," Reilly replied. "Is nothing secret?"

"Not if you know the right people."

Reilly nodded and laughed. Passersby had to work around them.

"Which, by the way, apparently you do, too. And I have something for you from one of those other people."

He produced a dozen folded pages from his leather jacket. "A woman named Elizabeth said you wanted these."

* * *

That night, while Reilly read the briefs on the oil executives and ministers scheduled for the Beijing conference, Elizabeth Matthews looked at a list she kept locked in her desk. It had the names of all her fellow cabinet members and two columns to the side: a plus sign atop one, a minus sign on the other. She had no plusses marked and four minuses. She hadn't given any of her colleagues a good enough or even relatively good reason to come to her side of the political equation. A feeling wasn't enough. But to a man and woman on the cabinet, they were not going to join in her battle. It was hers, not theirs. Besides, they felt they could contain Battaglio more from the inside. In retrospect, they shared her point of view that putting Battaglio on the ticket had been the party's mistake. He'd brought in Southern votes and under President Crowe, he'd remained marginalized. But now he was the Commander-in-Chief. Though Battaglio didn't know or suspect, it had been the work of Nicolai Gorshkov through a North Korean operative.

After the call from Pierce Kimball, it was apparent that Battaglio would soon replace them all if only to prevent Crowe's leftovers from invoking the 25th Amendment.

32

THE WHITE HOUSE

The key stakeholders met in the Oval Office. Like most days, the participants didn't know *everything* that was in the President's Daily Brief until they walked in. Gerald Watts cleared his throat and began.

"Mr. President, new developments overnight give us great concern."

President Battaglio leaned his chin on the clenched knuckles of his right hand with his elbow anchored on the Resolute Desk.

"Oh?"

"A Russian nuclear submarine, the *Admiral Kashira*, disappeared off the Massachusetts coast at 0217 Atlantic time. The USS *Hartford* had been on its tail since it emerged from northern waters." Watts kept it simple. "As an exercise, it was pretty normal. We hunt them. They hide from us. Sometimes vice versa."

"Why does this have you so concerned?"

"The order of things: Russia's icebreakers tearing through the Arctic, the Suez attack, and the Strait of Hormuz shut down, presumably by mistake, yet a timely accident. The deaths of two international executives. All in quick succession. All with oil in common."

"To the point, Gerald."

Watts wanted to shift his glance to Matthews, but he held on the president.

"The commander of *Admiral Kashira* could launch an attack on one or more oil tankers near or within American ports. It's within terribly lethal striking distance. Even worse, the sub is capable of launching first-strike nuclear attacks on more than half of the United States."

Battaglio straightened. "Come now, Mr. Director. *Could?* Of course it could. But tell me when the Russian Federation, or the Soviet Union before it, ever attacked the United States of America."

"Mr. President, Russia has consistently used cyber and microwave technology to attack America's infrastructure. We also believe that the attacks on the 14th Street Bridge in Washington, the Lincoln Tunnel in New York, and St. Louis' Stan Musial Bridge were all Kremlin-inspired, as was the attempt to knock out Hoover Dam."

"Now you add *believe* to *could.* The President is not moved," Battaglio said, employing the third person. "As I see it, the only thing you've brought me this morning is the fact that we lost a Russian sub in the middle of the fucking Atlantic Ocean. What the hell kind of Navy are we running?"

Defense Secretary Vincent Collingsworth interrupted. "Sir, with all due respect, we have the best navy in the world. But this submarine is super stealthy. Furthermore, to Director Watts' point, it was not in the middle of the Atlantic. It may be well within torpedo firing range of Boston, Portsmouth, Portland, and perhaps by now, New York and New Jersey."

"Find the goddamned boat, and all your worry will go away!" Battaglio declared. "What's next on the agenda?"

"Sir," Watts continued, "we're not ready to move on. It's imperative that the National Security Council meet on this matter."

The president said nothing.

The NSC is chaired by the President of the United States. Its regular members are the Vice President; the Secretaries of State, Treasury, Defense, Energy, and Homeland Security; the Attorney General; the country's representative to the United Nations; the Chief of Staff; and the Chairman of the Joint Chiefs. Also invited is the president's counsel, among others.

"We'll coordinate with your schedule. We should meet today."

The CIA Director had openly challenged the President of the United States. Everyone sat stone cold, waiting for Battaglio's response.

Ryan Battaglio ended the awkward silence with a smile. "Certainly. Let's set it for one." Then his smile disappeared. "Hopefully, you'll have a substantive update by then. Brief Roger on everything beforehand."

The new National Security Advisor traded an uncomfortable look with Watts.

"Anything else?"

"Everything's in the PDB," the CIA Director said.

"Well then, I have an important announcement to make."

In President Crowe's administration, Elizabeth Matthews would have known what was coming. So would some of the others in the room. She didn't. They didn't.

"Since I assumed power ..."

Matthews shuddered at the use of the word *power. Office* would have sufficed. Power was true, but much more Machiavellian.

"... the nation has not had a Number Two. A Vice President. Should something happen to me ..."

Now Matthews felt Battaglio's stare—old and hard, judgmental and intentional.

"... the seat of government would shift to the other political party with the ascension of the Speaker of the House. I cannot let that possibility remain unresolved. Therefore, today I will be submitting my choice for Vice President of the United States to the Senate."

He paused, proud of the drama he had created in the room.

"I expect the Senate to confirm a fellow member quickly and with little debate."

Battaglio looked at each of the constituents. He read their anticipation.

"I see I have your attention."

Nods in the affirmative.

"I'll make the announcement during the press briefing. You are not—and I repeat, *not*—to leak this to anyone prior to my statement. I expect you to support my choice and work with the new Vice President, bringing him up to speed on our challenges."

More nods, but with pursed lips and silent guesses.

"Good. I'd like him to join the NSC meeting this afternoon. And don't worry, he already has security clearance."

Who? Matthews thought. She ran through the possibilities: senators on the appropriate committees; an ally; a friend. In the time it took the president to continue she'd come up with four names. Three decent choices. She completely missed Battaglio's selection.

33

Moakley Davidson breezed into his office with a broad smile. He even said, "Good morning," which threw off his staff members. They looked at one another confused. Though they didn't know it yet, that confusion would be cleared up shortly.

"Senator," Tasha Samuels said, "I've got that summary you asked for." She held a folder, now twice as thick as before he left the previous day.

"What summary?" Davidson asked as he sat at his desk looking happier than she'd ever seen him.

"On Reilly."

"Who?"

"Dan Reilly, the hotel executive who testified last year. You asked me—"

"Right, right." Remembering, he reverted to his dismissive nature. "Leave it."

"I think I should go over it with you, sir. There's something sensitive."

"Can't it wait?"

"Of course, *but*." She gave *but* greater emphasis than *of course*. She saw that even Davidson recognized the difference.

"All right, Bullet points, then leave it."

"Yes, Senator."

She sat opposite him, opened the file, and started at the top. At the same time he rudely turned to his computer and opened his email.

"Reilly was raised in Boston. Single mother. Father killed in—"

"Cut to the chase, Tasha."

"Certainly. Some law enforcement in his background. Special Army training, served four years, most of it apparently hush-hush. Not much public."

"Right, then he moved into a cushy hotel job." He returned to his showdown with Reilly. "A fucking desk jockey."

"Sir, just the opposite. He's the type of guy who definitely doesn't lead with his feet on the desk."

"Good for him. Look, Ms. Samuels, I've got a busy day ahead so if you don't—"

"I do, Senator. I found something about his military record. He served in Afghanistan. Saw fire twice. I think you'll be interested in one of those times." Samuels was careful not to reveal how the information came to her.

Moakley Davidson swiveled in his chair. The last line had triggered something. He peered over his glasses. "Go on."

"You were there."

She held a sheet of paper with her notes typed up.

"Part of a congressional delegation. You and—"

"Give that to me," he suddenly barked.

She handed over the report. He riffled through the limited account. Samuels watched. His eyes narrowed. He seemed to be reading between the lines into what wasn't there more than what was. She saw his eyes go to the bottom of the page, and he shuddered.

"Who's your source?"

"Just research, Senator."

"Who?" he demanded.

She hesitated. "I—"

"You think about that answer. You work for me. You're not a reporter. You have no source to protect."

She nodded but didn't fill in the blank.

"What else did he tell you?"

Good. He, not her. She thought she could make up a name if pressed further.

"Just what I included, Senator." Of course, she wondered what was so important it had been redacted, especially given his abrupt reaction. "Would you like me to follow up?"

"No," Davidson said sharply. "No. That will be all."

"Yes, sir."

Samuels stood and clutched the full file.

"Ms. Samuels."

"Yes."

"The file."

"Right."

"And all of your written notes, printouts; everything."

"Certainly, Senator." She intentionally omitted the extract from Quora.

"You know it's nothing," he added in such a way that begged all the questions she had asked herself.

Tasha Samuels smiled politely and left the file on the corner of Davidson's desk. She caught him opening it and running his finger across each word. Moakley Davidson was completely interested in something he described as nothing.

"One more thing," Davidson called out before Samuels reached the door.

She turned obediently and straightened. He liked when his staff stood at attention.

"Delete your file and emails." He smiled. "National security."

Samuels cocked her head to the side. Not in any sense a challenge but a prompt. She was looking for a reason. She considered it doubtful she'd actually hear one.

"Certainly," she said again. Samuels relaxed her shoulders and turned.

Now a new thought. Reilly had touched a sensitive nerve. She just didn't know what it was. Finding out might not be the best idea.

* * *

Samuels waited until Davidson was called to the Senate floor for a vote. Then she got Reilly's cell numbers from the Congressional aide who had booked him for Davidson's hearing. This allowed her to bypass Reilly's office and call him directly. She wasn't sure what she would even ask, but she was drawn to him like a moth to a flame.

BEIJING

Reilly was in the Beijing general manager's office reviewing the conference schedule when his personal cell phone rang. Area code 202, but a number that wasn't in his directory.

"Excuse me," he said to Yong Tong. "Hello."

"Mr. Reilly? Daniel Reilly?"

"Yes, who's this?"

"Mr. Reilly, my name is Tasha Samuels. I work on the Hill. Am I getting you at a bad time?"

"Actually, Ms. Samuels, you *have* reached me at a bad time. I have a good deal going on." He didn't say what or where.

"I understand and I won't keep you long. I'd just like to see if you can help me on some research regarding Senator Moakley Davidson."

Reilly remained silent. There was no question yet, so an answer wasn't required.

"About Shindand Air Base and a congressional visit." She gave the approximate date.

"Who did you say you were?"

"Tasha Samuels."

"And from where?"

She had intentionally left out the critical information. Now she would have to tell him.

WASHINGTON, D.C.

At the same time Samuels was carefully phrasing her response to Reilly, President Ryan Battaglio walked to the podium at the White House briefing with no warning. Even his press secretary, Ellen Calmas was taken by surprise.

"Ellen," he whispered, "I'd like a few minutes at the microphone."

She breathed in and quickly stated, "Ladies and gentlemen, the President of the United States."

"Thank you, Ellen." She stepped aside. "Thank you everyone. Sorry for the disruption, but I figured this was the best place to make some news."

His comment brought the laughter he expected. Now they'd pay attention. Real attention.

"As you know, this administration has been operating at half strength. That's not good for the nation. That's not a good signal to the world. Today I propose to correct that. America needs a stable White House, strong and committed to face any crisis that may arise. *Any* crisis that surely will arise. I'd like to say the Founding Fathers envisioned the situation we are in. I'm talking about what happens when the office of Vice President is open. Actually, they didn't. It wasn't until the ratification of the 25th Amendment in 1967 that the procedure was codified. It is the president's job to select a nominee. That nominee is presented to the men and women in Congress, and by a majority of votes in both the House and the Senate, the nominee is confirmed and sworn in.

"Prior to the 25th Amendment, a vacancy could be left unfilled. Historic examples include Lyndon Johnson's ascension to the presidency. There was no vice president in place until the following election.

"Well, enough history. You can look up the rest for your stories. Now to current events."

Members of the press corps laughed. Pencils and pens were ready. For weeks anchors, columnists and pundits had speculated who Battaglio would appoint. The names ranged from talking head idols on the cable news channels to members of the cabinet, generals, and admirals. The Oval Office had given no hint, but today the country would have the answer, and nobody would see it coming.

"It is in my honor to offer into nomination a great American who has proudly served this country with distinction. A patriot who served eight terms in the House of Representatives. Through his tenure, he has earned respect on both sides of the aisle."

Battaglio saw the wheels turning. Everyone in the press corps, right down to the most senior members, was trying to figure out who he had selected.

"As a United States Representative he fought with unbridled energy against the fiercest lobbyists and special interest groups on behalf of his district and state, and beyond those boundaries, for the people of our great nation."

Not a clue there, Battaglio thought. *Time to peel another layer off.*

"Even with all he could accomplish in the House, he understood that the Senate offered greater opportunity—an opportunity to help all Americans. To further voting rights. To provide for equal pay for women. To strengthen our military. To make our streets safer. To repair our outdated infrastructure. And so for ten years he has distinguished himself in the Senate, where I consider him a friend and an ally."

Battaglio saw some nods. He had narrowed it down to no more than three men. No women.

"And now, as President, I have called on him to accept his most important job ever. To be my Vice President. To be your Vice President."

He felt their palpable anticipation. It was time to reveal his appointment.

"Ladies and gentlemen of the press, to you and to the American people," Battaglio said, looking directly into the camera, "today I am submitting to Congress, for immediate confirmation, United States Senator—"

* * *

"Moakley Davidson," Tasha Samuels told Dan Reilly. "I work for Senator Davidson."

Reilly whispered the name. "Davidson."

"Yes. You testified before his committee a year ago. Requesting—"

"Oh, I remember. I cut it short."

"Yes, the Tokyo bombing."

"If you're inviting me to another of his hearings, I'm busy. I'll be busy anytime you ask. Unless subpoenaed. And then I won't be particularly friendly."

"No sir. Like I said, I'm calling about a Congressional visit to Shindand Air Force Base."

"I work for a hotel company. You should be talking to someone with bars and stripes."

"Mr. Reilly, you were there."

Reilly said nothing.

"You were there."

"I was at a lot of places."

"Something happened. Something significant."

More silence from Reilly.

"Mr. Reilly, I'm not calling on the Senator's behalf. He assigned me to do some serious digging on you. I gave him what I could find. Now I'm curious about what I couldn't. He asked me to stop, but I'm intrigued by your eminent career."

"Meaning?"

"What happened there? The historic report is full of redactions."

"It's Ms. Samuels?"

"Yes."

"Ms. Samuels, I really can't help you."

"But there was a posting on the internet. I can read it to you. It references a tour gone wrong at Shindand involving a Congressional delegation. From the pieces I've put together, you were there. So was Davidson, though it got his name wrong."

"Ms. Samuels, this is not a good time. In fact, I don't expect we'll have a good time to chat. Goodbye."

With that, he hung up.

"Problem?" the Kensington general manager asked.

"Cobwebs," Reilly replied looking well beyond Yong. "Sticky old cobwebs. Let's get back to work."

34

SHINDAND AIR FORCE BASE, AFGHANISTAN

TWELVE YEARS EARLIER

The patrol rolled out at 1415. Four armored vehicles in the lead. A Humvee with the two dignitaries and their armed escorts next, followed by two more armored vehicles. The expedition rolled down the all-weather asphalt road, part of Highway 1, the national ring road. Command in the second vehicle was on the radio with the base. There were whispers of what a bad idea this was. There had been recent intercepts indicating new Taliban fighters were digging in along the road. But the two U.S. congressmen on their first tour of Afghanistan insisted on meeting with a tribal leader in the hills, six miles southwest outside of Sabzwar.

One of the people particularly worried was U.S. Army Captain Daniel Reilly. He tried to convince the delegation to cancel. The route was not safe, the leader was not trustworthy, and even with an Apache attack helicopter overhead, he couldn't guarantee their safety.

He had already been in one firefight because of an ill-advised journey that should have been cancelled. It resulted in an attack in which twelve servicemen were killed. Reilly survived by hiding among the rocks, his body over one of the injured, Captain Robert Heath. He blamed a general's bad decision for that attack. And now, just weeks from his ticket out, these two congressmen were putting him in another hot spot all for the sake of a photo op.

A thirty-minute trip up. An hour in the hills. A quicker ride back. "What could go wrong?" Congressman Moakley Davidson had asked Reilly.

"Everything, sir. You are putting yourselves and your troops at risk."

"We didn't fly all the way to this hellhole to just eat at the base mess. I've cleared this up through your command. We're going." His companion, another congressman, remained silent, less sure of what was right, but nonetheless believing they could campaign on the public relations to come from the trip.

"With all due respect, sir—"

"With all due respect, Captain, make sure the photographer has enough film."

Reilly smiled. No need to correct the congressman, but they were shooting digital these days.

Davidson didn't know who Reilly was or what unit he worked with. He didn't care. Reilly tried one more time to put the kibosh on the expedition. It was unnecessary and more importantly, dangerous. He took his intelligence to the base commander, who listened and threw up his hands.

"I know, I know. They've made a big deal out of this. Just do it. You'll have air support."

"Sure, for retaliation after the fact. For rescue, make sure Sixty-Eight Whiskey is tagging along." He wasn't joking. Reilly definitely wanted Army medics at the ready on-ground and in the air.

"Quick in and out, Captain. Eyes on you all the way."

Reilly acknowledged the support but knew that drones wouldn't see landmines. "Sir," he said trying one more time, "I strongly recommend …"

The major interrupted. "We're through, Captain Reilly. We treat them well, and we get what we need."

"Assuming that we survive."

"Well, you and your team just make that happen."

The drones lifted off and the caravan rolled out. Eyes watched the road, front and the sides. They covered the distance in just over twenty minutes. Nine minutes at high speed along Highway 1, the remainder winding up a dirt road into the hills.

Infantrymen and women armed with M4 carbines, M249 squad automatic weapons, and M240L medium machine guns quickly disembarked and provided a 360-degree view with the congressmen's vehicle at the center. After getting an all-clear from above, Reilly opened the rear door. The congressmen got out and took in the surroundings: mud huts, shoeless children running by, and members of the tribe, all armed and watching with suspicion. One man walked forward. He identified himself as Sergeant Akbarkhan, though he wore simple native clothes, a *khet partug, perahan wa* turban, and sandals.

"Welcome," he said in passable English. "Please take these." He gave them each burkas. "Colonel Kabir will see you." Reilly knew that most Afghans do not have family names. The members of Congress didn't know or, if they did, they didn't care. "Follow me, please."

The congressmen started walking. Reilly held them up. "Troops first." He nodded to four young U.S. soldiers to step forward. "Now you. Then your aides." There were two, one for each of the congressmen. Reilly fell in behind them, then four more infantrymen. They walked up a winding path, around ramshackle structures, past the smell of food on a stove, around garbage of all description in open cans. The congressmen covered their faces with the burkas they'd been given. It helped. It also hid their disgust. Davidson whispered to his colleague, a representative from Wisconsin. "Let's make this quick." It earned him a definite nod in the affirmative.

The congressmen were each greeted with a handshake by Colonel Kabir, a man with a battle-hardened look and torn camouflage to match. "*Salam alaikum.*" He placed his hand over his heart. "Peace be upon you."

"*Wa-Alaikum salam,*" they returned just as politely. It was the response they had been instructed to provide.

Kabir continued in perfectly articulated English, "I welcome you to my humble home."

It was a home unlike any they had ever been in. Rugs on the dirt floor, stone walls with photographs of bearded men. Ancestors or contemporaries? It was impossible for them to tell given how time was frozen in this hut, in this country. They were disgusted by the scent of food they couldn't imagine eating and unnerved by the guards with automatic weapons flanking the colonel and in every corner of the room. Still, Kabir's courteousness was marked with a smile. "You have shown great courage venturing to see me. For that, I thank you."

The two congressmen nodded.

"I wish you to carry back my appreciation ..."

The Americans smiled and were ready for a quick photo and a fast retreat.

"... and a warning," Kabir said. His smile disappeared. His eyes narrowed. He brought his body to his full height, hidden until now by the way he stood, rising to a commanding presence. He lowered his voice.

"There is talk of withdrawal. There is talk of the end of funding for our fight. There is talk of America turning a blind eye to the Afghan people. This is talk that burns our ears, that frightens our families, that threatens our lives. We have seen the result of your policy in the Republic of Iraq, showing no regard for the lives of the people you abandoned. We have seen how your nation cancelled your treaty with the Islamic Republic of Iran. We have witnessed your willingness to support extreme regimes if it is to the benefit of your economy, even at the expense of others' freedom. This talk comes from your hallowed halls of your Capitol. Neither I, nor my countrymen, need to have spies within the chambers. It is reported on your news networks and in your newspapers. It is evident by the votes you propose and the votes you take. So my warning is given with no disrespect, yet let it be very clear as you leave. Beware of the devil you will unleash with a hasty decision. Beware that devil knows no borders and has no politics. Beware that the devil sees a void and fills it with death. Beware that America will become, employing the original medieval Latin, *advocatus diaboli*."

The congressmen didn't understand the term.

"In plain English. If you pursue this course, America will become the true devil's advocate, and you, Representative Moakley Davidson, and you, Representative Ryan Battaglio, will wear his mark."

The two members of Congress got the quick exit they sought. But there were no photographs that afternoon from the meeting, no visual record of Kabir's admonition. There were, however, enemy soldiers waiting for them along the road on their return trip to Shindand.

35

WASHINGTON, D.C.

U.S. STATE DEPARTMENT

PRESENT DAY

There was nothing unusual about having lunch together. Two Cabinet secretaries dining to discuss whatever they had in common to discuss, Secretary of State Matthews and Secretary of Health and Human Services Myra Gutin. It was on both of their public calendars. Public as far as insiders in their own departments would know. Beyond that, private. It lined up with their usual luncheons every five or six weeks, sometimes at Secretary Gutin's office, other times at State.

The Jefferson State Reception Room was one of forty-two principal rooms available to Elizabeth Matthews. The rooms contained some of America's outstanding museum pieces and decorative objects related to the country's history.

A table was set for two. Sterling silver was placed atop white linen napkins, which sat atop a white tablecloth. Signature State Department china was at each setting, only to be replaced when the pre-plated grilled Alaskan salmon, a beet salad, and julienned potatoes arrived.

Matthews favored this setting because of her appreciation of Jefferson. His words spoke to her through the ages. Today she was thinking about a passage he wrote to Abigail Adams from Paris on February 22, 1787, in answer to her letter which had included papers he wanted. "The spirit of resistance to government," he wrote, "is so valuable on certain occasions that I wish it be always kept alive." Though he was referring to France's political issues, the quotation rang true to her. He continued, "I like a little rebellion now and then. It is like a storm in the atmosphere."

Matthews was indeed stirring the political winds. Ill or ill-begotten, she believed it was necessary. Now she hoped she could convince Gutin.

At first, they talked about little things as a ten-foot statue of Thomas Jefferson loomed over them from a display to Matthews's right, Gutin's left. They were about the same age, both lawyers, both steeped in Beltway experience and intrigue. Both soon to be unemployed.

"What will you do next, Myra?" Matthews asked.

She laughed. "Maybe a teaching position. GW or American. I've lectured there."

"A book?"

Gutin laughed good-naturedly. "No one's interested in what the HHS secretary might write. So, no book deal. You, on the other hand, have real stories to tell."

Matthews glanced at Jefferson. It was time to get to the point. "Maybe the biggest story is yet to be told."

"Elizabeth?" The statement caught her off guard. "What story?"

"Battaglio." She turned back to Gutin. "What he'll do to the country."

"Elizabeth, if you're planning or even hinting at trying to remove him, I can't be part of it. While I don't expect to be around long, you have no basis."

"I do, Myra." With that, Matthews pushed aside her plate and made her case.

Gutin sat emotionless for fifteen minutes. She listened to the arguments Matthews had given others: How Battaglio had caved to Nicolai Gorshkov's demands during a recent Stockholm conference and willingly traded elections in Ukraine and likely the Baltic States for a deal that removed North Korean missiles from Venezuela. How NATO was dissed. How the attacks in the U.S. weren't even addressed.

"He's still feeling his oats," Gutin said. "He's not my favorite, but he's what we've got. It's his administration now. He gets to govern the way he sees fit, whether or not we're to be part of it."

"Which Battaglio is intent on doing!"

"Which the Constitution allows."

They were sparring more than arguing, but the tempo and the heat had definitely increased.

"We don't have much time, Myra. The Senate will assuredly confirm Moakley Davidson as Veep. Then America will have the two most inept politicians at the top."

"May I remind you, Crowe accepted Battaglio as his running mate?"

"Sure, with pressure from the party. Actually, an ultimatum. Take him or risk losing the election. It was a huge mistake."

"Then the voters get to decide again in a couple of years."

Matthews fixed her eyes on Gutin. "We can't afford to wait."

"Then give me a real reason. I haven't heard one to hang the 25th Amendment on yet."

"Battaglio's in Gorshkov's pocket."

"Just because he gave in, as you said, in Stockholm, doesn't mean—"

"What if there is? What if he is colluding with Gorshkov?"

"If he is, bring it to the Justice Department. By the time they deal with it, I'll be long gone from the White House, correcting papers from graduate students at GW."

36

The pouring rain was going to help. So was the hour. The medical offices were closed for appointments. The cleaning staff had finished.

Moakley Davidson picked the D.C. medical building on 18th St. NW not out of convenience but something far more tactical. The underground garage still lacked cameras to capture license plate numbers on entry. There would be no record of his visits.

This was where he arranged to meet Sherwood Baker. 1:30 a.m. Far right corner of P3.

Davidson arrived early and waited. He expected Baker to be on time. He usually was for these meetings. He leaked stories to Baker. They produced breaking news in *The Hill*. In turn, Baker fed him tidbits. Often a reporter could get more inside information than even a United States senator.

Moakley Davidson heard the car's tires screeching on the spiral ramp before he saw it. He waited. Baker backed up next to Davidson so that they faced driver-to-driver. This way they could talk to each other without getting out of their vehicles.

The reporter rolled down his window first and waited for Davidson to do the same. "Good evening, Senator. Thought you'd be out celebrating tonight, not lurking in the shadows."

"Soon enough."

"I'm looking forward to having a friend in high places."

"We won't be able to meet like this, of course," Davidson stated.

"No, I don't suppose we will. But there's always a way. So, what can I do for you tonight?"

Davidson reached in his pocket and handed an envelope through his window. The reporter took it and quickly scanned the contents. A name, some background, and what he wanted. "Pretty straightforward. Shouldn't be too hard," he said.

"Good. It'll help me and a friend."

Baker smiled. "That friend must be very special."

"He is."

"Someone who lives in a big white house?"

The senator ignored the question.

"How much of a priority?" Baker asked this to begin gauging whether this would be a favor or something more valuable.

"Significant. Time-sensitive. I consider the subject to be a potential political liability. Get me everything you can on him."

"Generally time-sensitive, or time-sensitive under the present circumstances? Present circumstances being your nomination for Vice President?" Baker asked pointedly.

"Mr. Baker, let me make this very clear. If you're not interested, just hand the envelope back. You're not the only one I can go to."

Baker read the comment as a threat to his access, access he was going to enjoy all the more after Davidson's confirmation.

"Hey, just asking. No need to go shopping. But any hint what you are looking for in particular?"

"Something that would help me," Davidson said. He then added, "It will be to your benefit."

Baker flashed on his high school Latin class. There was a term for that. He just couldn't remember what it was.

37

AS ELIZABETH MATTHEWS RESTED her head on her pillow for her typical five hours of nightly sleep, she was resigned to the fact that she didn't have the Cabinet's votes. Not a majority of eight. Not even one other person who had the political will to publicly take on Ryan Battaglio. She was a coach without a team.

So now what? she thought through the first precious hour of her always limited sleep period. She was certain to be replaced. Should she fight to stay? Should she show some loyalty, keep Battaglio from shooting himself in the foot, and prevent the yet unimaginable—whatever that might be—from becoming reality?

Suck it up, Matthews. You can do more from the inside.

Of course, she recognized her willingness to stay wouldn't guarantee anything. Battaglio was a wild card, possibly a useful idiot in the Russian president's mind. With Pierce Kimball gone, it was all the more important that she stay and be seen as an ally, a voice of reason to present alternate points of view, while at the same time gathering information, intelligence for another day.

She needed her own allies, trusted confidants, reliable old friends in government, those on the outside, and even someone with a foot in both. At the top of the list, Daniel Reilly.

Hour two and still not asleep, Elizabeth Matthews called him.

Thirteen hours forward, 1410 hours, 2:10 p.m. in Beijing, Reilly answered on his regular phone. It was a personal cell number he recognized; he knew not to mention any names or talk about specifics.

"Hey there. Did I catch you at a bad time?"

"Not at all. Thanks for the care package." Lenczycki and the oil ministers' biographies were the care package.

"You're welcome. I thought you'd like to know I've had a change of heart on the management restructuring plan we talked about."

Reilly immediately understood. Her plan to invoke the 25th Amendment, to boot out Battaglio, was off. He was actually relieved.

"The best thing I can do is make this whole business work," she said.

For anyone listening, and assuredly someone might be, the call, whether heard now or replayed later, was simply between two colleagues who were having a work discussion. It might even be about the hotel business.

"Frankly, I think you're making the right decision."

"Glad you agree, but I would like to talk to you about the overall market when you can."

"Of course," Reilly replied. *Market? Commercial market with China? Job market? Does Elizabeth think Battaglio is going to fire her soon?* All those thoughts and one more. Yet, no matter what Battaglio did to her, Reilly would never bet against Elizabeth Matthews.

"Meaning?"

"Just how to work things without disrupting the system," she replied.

Good. She was going to cool things down, win favor with Battaglio.

"Well, good thinking. I take it we can wait to talk until I get back in the States?"

"Absolutely. Just wanted you to know my thinking. No rush," Matthews paused. "I think."

She felt he understood, though Elizabeth Matthews didn't know what her own standing was. She'd given up on her original plan. Now she was going to play the good soldier and see if she could buy breathing room to consider her next move.

Meanwhile, Reilly wondered whether it was time for him to share something he had never told her.

38

SHINDAND AIR FORCE BASE, AFGHANISTAN

TWELVE YEARS EARLIER

Dan Reilly had been here before. A bad Afghan road on a bad day. An American convoy that shouldn't have, by all accounts, been out. A Taliban force waiting for them to pass.

The drones didn't see it coming. Neither did spotters in the lead mine-resistant Oshkosh L-ATV. But Reilly felt if it was going to come, it would be somewhere below the mountain home of Colonel Kabir's forces and the midpoint to Shindand. He was right.

The first IED, the improvised explosive device, did not take out the L-ATV, but the blast immediately stopped the caravan for fear of rolling over another. Five soldiers jumped out of their vehicles, ready to provide cover for the delegation. Overhead, live images from one of two circling Predator drones gave them eyes on the ground targets.

From nearby mounds on either side of the caravan they saw two Taliban teams rising up.

"3 o'clock and 10 o'clock," shouted the spotter. That was a second before the enemy at the 3 o'clock fired a rocket-propelled grenade (RPG). The first missed the congressmen's vehicle but connected solidly with the following vehicle. A second hit precisely where the American soldiers had exited. Davidson and Battaglio felt the concussion and heat of the blast sweeping over them. They were twenty-five yards ahead of the explosion.

"Go, go, go!" Reilly yelled to the driver. At the same time he threw his body across the two congressmen. "Don't move until I tell you to!"

He smelled their fear. It was more than just sweat in the heat of battle. It was their false bravado burning up; panic reigniting the deepest prehistoric impulses. It was the sickening smell of political lies.

"Get me out of here!" Battaglio screamed.

Reilly was acutely aware that he said *me,* not *us.*

The drones did their job. The enemy was neutralized with two Hellfire missiles. The caravan drivers did theirs, speeding toward Shindand. Halfway to the base, they had cover from an Apache attack helicopter. The paramedics that Reilly had requested only had to do cleanup. Because of the congressmen's insistence on making the trip, five American servicemen would be returning to the United States in body bags.

At 2340 hours Davidson and Battaglio were hurried onto an outgoing USAF C-40 Clipper, the military transport version of Boeing's commercial 737-700C. They had requested another night in Hong Kong before heading back to Washington. Request denied.

Dan Reilly hoped he'd never see either of them again.

39

BEIJING

PRESENT DAY

Reilly and Lenczycki walked the streets around the hotel without much worry. They were in full view of the city's CCTV cameras, and to the most discerning eyes they were nothing but boring. They talked about old days, and new and future plans. The more time Reilly spent with Skip Lenczycki, the more he liked him. He was genuine and devoted to his country and friends.

Lenczycki told him how the Army targeted him when he was an Eagle Scout the way a top star quarterback is wooed by a Big Ten school. That is to say, the United States Army working on behalf of the Central Intelligence Agency. A colonel came to talk to his parents and laid out a plan: a full ride at West Point with a focus on international studies and languages. Then, promotion to a higher rank than those graduates who had not been Eagle Scouts. Higher rank equaled higher pay, more responsibility, more opportunity.

Lenczycki explained how he was mentored. But he was also aware he was being watched and evaluated. Watched through binoculars and evaluated as he proved his grit and demonstrated his leadership ability. After three years in the Army, he was formally recruited by the CIA, which he would later learn had been footing the bill from the beginning.

"I went through intel training in the Army, too," Reilly offered. "The Army's Intelligence and Command Center and NETCOM."

Lenczycki knew it well. The U.S. Army Network Enterprise Technology Command in Fort Huachuca, Arizona. "And from there, you were assigned to the Presidio, where you learned Farsi and Russian and some Mandarin."

"Jesus, Skip, is there anything about me you don't know?"

"Very little," Lenczycki said, laughing the questions off.

Reilly had a sudden realization. "You've never really left. The Caribbean fishing business is just a cover. You're still on the payroll. That's why you're here."

"Wrong. I came of my own volition. As strange as it sounds, I like you. And there are others who do, too. So, like it or not, we've got your six."

Reilly smiled. It was a relief to know that his back was covered. "I suppose by extension that means I have to have yours as well?"

"That's the way it works."

"You think I'm in over my head?" Reilly asked Lenczycki.

"Swimming in the deep end, my friend, with weights on your legs. What do you really know about the spy business?"

It was an interesting question. A little from his military career, but mostly as an analyst, an observer, and a critic of bad decisions that only got him burnt when he reported them. He shared intel with Bob Heath at the CIA. He had a direct line to Elizabeth Matthews. Of course, he relied on good information to keep his hotels safe, but what did he really know?

"Not much."

Skip Lenczycki laughed. "For someone who doesn't, you've got the right instincts."

But not enough experience, Reilly thought but didn't say, recalling his run at the FBI's Hogan's Alley. "Thanks."

The fairly recently retired CIA operative launched into a colorful history of the trade. "You know, in one form or another, spies have been around for as long as there've been secrets. And that was well before the first recorded evidence, a carved table in the court of Babylonian King Hammurabi. About 1800 BCE. In 500 BCE, Sun Tzu wrote *The Art of War* with the basics of espionage and strategy that hold true for today.

"Queen Elizabeth had her spy ring in the 1500s with Sir Francis Walsingham lurking in the shadows. And the need for spies certainly didn't escape George Washington during the Revolutionary War."

Lenczycki shared how, during the Civil War, Union forces launched hydrogen balloons with spotters. From high up, they could report on Confederate troop strength and send intelligence to the ground via long telegraph lines. The war also saw the formation of the Bureau of Military Information, the first American intelligence agency.

"Of course there are the top players on the collectable cards. Queen of them all was Mata Hari, a German, executed by the French." Other names came up, many surprising to Reilly. Baseball player Moe Berg, British novelist Grahame Greene, children's author Roald Dahl, jazz singer Josephine Baker. "And don't forget chef Julia Child."

"No way."

"Totally true. She worked with the OSS as a research assistant to William Donovan, the head of the unit. Then she transitioned into the Emergency Sea Rescue Equipment Section, where she helped create a chemical shark repellent, and from 1944 to 1945 had assignments in Ceylon and China trafficking top secret documents."

Reilly was completely engaged and let Lenczycki fly through the history of the OSS morphing into the CIA, Truman creating the National Security Council, the arrests and executions of Julius and Ethel Rosenberg, the launching of the Corona spy satellite in 1959, right through U-2 flights over Russia, and recent ones that confirmed Reilly's ground-spotting North Korean missiles in Venezuela.

He tiptoed through more contemporary espionage leaks to the Russians and Chinese via naïve and inexperienced government employees and even public pronouncements by recent administrations that put allies at the disadvantage. Each episode put American intelligence officers at risk. It's especially a problem when political figures with no experience in intelligence operations are elevated to positions of immense power. They love to talk. But loose lips still sink ships.

The current president, Ryan Battaglio, came to Reilly's mind. But he kept his thoughts to himself.

They had walked five miles and covered almost four thousand years of history. Amazing history that, Reilly recognized, will never end, especially evident when they stood under a CCTV camera leading back into their hotel.

"It's a dangerous business, Reilly. All the more dangerous for someone working in daylight and not in the shadows. You should think long and hard about what you're doing. About your bifurcated existence. Your hotel job is dangerous enough. Sure you're up for both?"

Reilly wondered whether this was a warning from Heath to stand down. Or did EJ Shaw somehow get to Lenczycki. *No,* he reasoned. *Neither.* He was getting it from a trained operative who claimed he had no horse in the race anymore, but really did. The Company was still in his blood.

40

WASHINGTON, D.C.

Identifications worked perfectly. Half a payment cleared, proper arrangements made, and a package had been left at a monthly self-storage rental
facility in, of all places, Kensington, Maryland. *Purely a coincidence,* an
attractive Middle Eastern woman thought as she recovered the box with
the key that was left for her in an envelope at an Amazon locker in a
Bethesda, Maryland 7-11.

It was no coincidence. It was an inside joke, a game understood
by only one person. The man who had left the device for Dominique
Dhafari. The man who had set up all the proper arrangements. A man,
now in China, taking steps toward his next kill.

Dhafari was from the holy city of Najaf, Iraq, the daughter of a café
owner. She studied in Syria at Damascus University, where her high
grades and extraordinary athletic ability and gymnastic skills garnered
the attention of the military intelligence directorate. Dhafari was offered
a graduate school scholarship at the Military College of Administrative
Affairs in Masyaf. Her studies were anything but administrative. She
had special classes that prepared her in special ways, all exciting to the
young woman who recognized she was being groomed for more than
a career in business.

After Masyaf, she received additional training in Russia at the revived

Andropov Institute, where she learned and excelled in spy craft. After finishing, she returned to Syria and took a job in counterintelligence. Her assignments were varied and often came with a degree of physicality and very nice paydays. The money made life easier for her parents in Iraq.

Her current mission took her to the American capital city. She traveled under a falsified UAE passport, telling U.S. Immigration and Customs Enforcement officials at Dulles International Airport that she had teaching interviews at Georgetown and George Washington universities and the College of William and Mary, whoever they were. Each would check out if anyone cared to seek confirmation. Proof that no one had was her complete operational freedom in Washington.

Dominique Dhafari was a proven resource, one who could be trusted to complete an assignment. She was instructed never to question an operation, just execute it. She should have today.

Dhafari was also a natural beauty. Five-four, slim, with long-black eyebrows and shoulder-length black hair. She had an engaging smile with lily-white teeth. Her dark brown, almost black eyes looked like they could charm any suitor. A useful tool, given her unique training. Today, however, she would rely on other talents.

The key worked in the storage, and she was in and out in under eight minutes. She placed the unmarked box, roughly the size of a toaster, in her backpack and put it in her trunk. Dhafari then programmed the GPS for the drive into Washington and the newly opened Kensington Royal Metro Hotel. At the valet, she took the claim ticket. That was the last she thought about the car. She would never return it to Hertz.

She checked in and allowed a bellman to help her with her two suitcases while she held onto her backpack. Nothing unusual. Casual and friendly. Employees were told if they see something, say something. The friendly woman traveling under the name Andrea Bashir gave neither the front desk nor the bellman any reason for concern.

Reaching the room, she tipped the bellman a five, kicked off her shoes, and flopped onto the bed. She had six hours to rest. Then she'd get to work.

BEIJING

Dr. Yibing Cheng waited for Reilly in the hotel lobby. She'd studied his photo. She would pick him out. She was good at retaining information. Her specialty was oil. Facts and figures on barrels and tonnage, market percentages, government ministries, corporations and their CEOs, lobbyists, conservationists, and the people she never wanted to meet in a dark alley. The influencers and enforcers.

Until three years ago, she'd strictly been on the academic tenure track, teaching and researching in MIT's Joint Program on the Science and Policy of Global Change. She was well published with two books and hundreds of citations. The program drilled deep into the natural and social sciences, providing analytical studies on how the environment, the economy, and human nature intersect. Her papers focused on the impact of ever-evolving geopolitical strategies linked to fossil fuels. In other words, she was a predictor of future trends and how the fate of the world is intrinsically tied to the flow of oil and gas.

Not surprisingly, her research brought her wide attention—not only in academic circles, but squarely in the center of America's think tanks. From there, it was an easy jump to being hired on as a government consultant. The U.S. Department of Energy secretary liked what she had to say. The State Department liked it even more. State needed more critical thinking in the area of global warming. Yibing Cheng had the credentials, the personality, and the character to stand head-to-head with government officials and billionaire businessmen and women.

Now Elizabeth Matthews asked Dr. Cheng to be Daniel Reilly's teacher. She gave her a round trip ticket DC-to-Beijing and a specific duty: "Bring him up to speed and leave. He attracts trouble. You don't want to be around him for too long." It sounded like Matthews had a history with him. Dr. Cheng was intrigued.

She spotted Reilly when he entered the hotel lobby. He didn't especially look like the kind of man who would attract trouble. The same couldn't be said for the man walking with him.

"Mr. Reilly?"

He stopped short and turned, on guard. Ever since a man in a Paris hotel lobby was shot after being incorrectly identified as Reilly, he was on alert for people suddenly calling out his name and approaching him.

"Yes," he said tentatively to the tall, attractive Asian woman carrying a stylish light brown leather attaché case. He judged her to be mid-thirties.

The man with Reilly stepped between them.

"Excuse me. I'm Dr. Yibing Cheng," she said peering around Lenczycki. "A mutual friend said you asked for someone to help you a little with, shall we say, character studies before the upcoming conference here. Seems you have some concerns."

Reilly nodded, not yet relieved. He studied her confident eyes. They looked sincere. The thin-framed glasses added an academic quality. That would be about right. She wore a fashionable black business suit with a navy blue blouse and low heels. Reilly didn't know what they were called, and if she told him, he probably wouldn't remember. But he would remember her engaging smile and friendly voice.

"Yes," He offered his hand. "Nice to meet you. This is my friend Skip. He's … protective."

"Hello, Skip," she said. "Looks like I approached a little too fast. I'm sorry."

"No harm, no foul," Reilly said. "Recent history makes approaches like this a bit dubious. That's why the caution."

Cheng didn't know what the issue was but Matthews's counsel came to mind. *He attracts trouble. You don't want to be around him for too long.*

"Sorry," she said again.

"All fine," Reilly offered. He asked if she was checked in. She was.

"Let me know if you need anything."

"I think you're the man in need today. I'm ready to get started if you are."

Matthews had texted Reilly to look for a Dr. Cheng. She hadn't indicated a female Dr. Cheng.

They proceeded to Reilly's suite, where he ordered wine and appetizers to get through the afternoon to dinner. While he was on the phone, she looked at Reilly's preparatory work: Photos of the conference participants from their registration portfolios were mounted on poster boards. In all, there were representatives from nine southeast Asian Pacific Rim countries and a Canadian observer. Most were government ministers, but there were a few executives from private oil companies. She had background on each and was prepared to discuss them individually.

From left to right on the top row, Cyrus Bloomfield of the Australian Petroleum Production & Exploration Association; Hunter Clark from New Zealand Petroleum & Mines; Seung Han, CEO of KNOC, the Korea National Oil Corporation. The next row down, Bianh Phan, the chief executive of PetroVietnam; Neelem Giri from India's Ministry of Petroleum and Natural Gas; Ponleu Phy, Cambodia's president of MME, the Ministry of Mines and Energy. Filling out the bottom row, Omar Mahr, Chief Marketing Officer in the Pakistan Ministry of Energy; Thailand's Ministry of Oil head, Boon-Mee Tan; the Canada BP executive Haoran Shih; and the Chinese host, Shen Ma, Chairman of the National Energy Commission.

"Interesting," she said.

"Especially if you consider that in a few days, one of them may be dead."

Cheng froze. She'd been briefed about the assignment, warned about Reilly. But his stark statement suddenly catapulted her into a world of danger she'd never experienced.

She tried to hide her fear. It was impossible. Her legs shook and she shot Reilly a look of despair.

"It's all right, Dr. Cheng. You can do it. And I need you. Take a deep breath and let's get to work."

She closed her eyes, cleared her head, and straightened. "I'm okay." Opening her eyes she examined the photographs and the biographies. "Only nine? I read fifteen were coming."

"Six pulled out after Nairobi" Reilly explained.

"Apparently uncomfortable with the notion that they might get killed," Skip Lenczycki added, completely humorlessly.

Cheng ignored the comment and quietly asked, "Where would you like to start?"

"An overview," Reilly proposed. "Let's sit and talk in general terms."

They gathered in the living room suite around a coffee table. Reilly sat in one cushy easy chair, Cheng in another to his left. Lenczycki stood and looked out the window. Always on watch.

"Can I assume that our friend has explained my concern," he said without offering Matthews's name. He hoped she had but didn't want to take the chance of stating her name, even though his suite was swept for bugs the day before Reilly arrived. Those that had been found when they acquired the hotel eight months ago had been removed. But that didn't prevent Chinese Secret Police from checking in as tourists and installing new, more stealthy devices, room after room. In fact they did. By day, but mostly by night.

Cheng removed files from her case, each meticulously labeled and color coded. A different color for each subject, individual, and country. But before opening any of the individual files, she pulled a single top sheet.

"Up to now, I've worked on my assumptions. It would help if you'd tell me what—"

Reilly spread his arms apart, palms up. Lenczycki continued to look at the street below and the high rise hotel across the street.

"Okay. Let me know if I give you too much or too little."

Reilly tipped his head slightly.

"I'll go slowly, but there's a lot to understand. You might want to take notes."

"No notes," Lenczycki said, his back to them as he saw new arrivals enter below.

She didn't flinch. Cheng was used to requests like that. "No problem. But before I get going, I can be much more productive if I knew what you were looking for."

Briefing, Reilly thought. Dr. Cheng was used to the drill, but probably not the full picture. Not yet.

"Fair enough," he began. "You're going to tell us who's most likely to be killed, starting in three days. Together we'll figure out why, and then we're going to stop it."

* * *

Some sixteen hours after Matthieu Lefebvre comfortably departed Los Angeles, he stepped into the summer smog that engulfed Beijing. He was just another of the thousands of passengers at Liberty Airport who were happy to be stretching his legs. He looked like he needed to stretch more than many others. To Chinese eyes, he appeared to be typically American, though he was French by birth, possibly fifty pounds over-weight for his age, which, according to his passport, was sixty-three. He was not particularly interesting to the authorities. He didn't fit any profiles. Lefebvre was just another weary traveler to let in. The customs officers expected his stay would be as humdrum as he looked; unless of course, he went to one of the hotels that provided extra services. Then he'd be picked up on surveillance cameras. Then there might be more to make of Matthieu Lefebvre.

To flight attendants on the way over, he was the ideal passenger. He wanted nothing. He was polite and he kept his head in his book until after dinner. The flight attendant in business class saw what he was reading—a spy thriller. She laughed to herself. The bookish middle-aged man with oversized tortoise-shell glasses couldn't be further from the hero in the novel.

On that point, and only that point, the American Airlines flight attendant was right. He was no hero. Then again, Lefebvre wasn't his name. And though he had explained he was going to China on a trip that he and his wife had planned but never took because she had died the previous year, he had other business to conduct, more in keeping with the novel he was reading.

After claiming his bag and passing through all the security stops, Lefebvre was directed to the cab line. He spoke English slowly and asked to be taken to the Kensington. His driver answered, "Yes, sir."

That was the end of the discussion. Lefebvre closed his eyes and to the cabbie looked like he fell into a deep sleep for the rest of the way. The driver dropped him off fifty minutes later with nothing to report to the Secret Police.

Lefebvre checked in. His basic room was ready. Basic was better. He didn't want anyone coming with amenities—*compliments of the management.*

Thirty minutes later, Lefebvre went out to get working on the next part of his plan. He left with only a backpack and his fake ID.

WASHINGTON, D.C.

Halfway around the world, Dominique Dhafari awoke. She went to the bathroom, brushed her teeth, and returned to the bedroom. She put her rolling suitcase on the bed and removed the contents: Turtleneck, tights, socks, and gloves—all black. She'd also brought Black Diamond Shadow Climbing shoes, a sport harness, and specially designed clamps.

These were the tools of buildering, the art of climbing an urban structure. In this case, the Kensington where she was staying.

Dhafari only had to ascend seven floors from where she was, round the northeast corner, and secure the package in her backpack—a self-contained explosive device.

At 2:45 a.m., still in her bra and panties from sleeping, she dropped to the floor, did 200 sit-ups and 50 push-ups. It was a fraction of her daily training. Now it was strictly for her head space. Fifteen minutes later she showered. At 3:40 she was fully dressed. At 3:48 she wired the bomb to a fully charged burner cellphone. She had the number.

At 3:52 she jimmied the window wide enough to exit with the full backpack and reenter with it empty. The woman known as Dominique Dhafari smiled to herself as she took hold of the first crevice with her right hand. She was in her element—thriving between the cracks.

Those cracks, places for fingers to grip and toes to get footing, reached higher than most Washington Buildings. In metro DC, height was restricted to 130 feet. Beyond downtown they could be built taller. The new Kensington Hotel stood fourteen stories high. Dhafari's target was at the top on the penthouse floor.

She'd decided to climb floor-to-floor first, the hard part, though it wasn't difficult for her. She made her way straight up, clear of windows in eleven minutes. The building cooperated—no slippery pipes, no crumbling concrete. The façade was well-maintained. *Good for the owner,* she thought. *Good for me. Thank you.*

The cloudy dry night also served her well. Another *thank you.* But that wouldn't have stopped her. She had only one night. She'd scaled buildings in the rain with no difficulty. Snow and wind were different; they presented real challenges. Tonight was an easy, almost effortless climb.

Next, she worked her way across the hotel, quietly passing below windows. She heard a variety of sounds: love-making, TV news channels, a few movies, and snoring. No one heard her. She rounded the corner and eased herself up to her target's window and peered in. Fortune was on her side. The bedroom curtain was open. A man was asleep, and the undrawn curtain made her task more likely to turn into a complete success.

Dhafari attached a clamp to the crevice just above the window. In the clamp, she clipped a carabiner, with a rope that was secured around her. This gave her free movement and the ability to work. Should the man wake, she had two options: slip down below sight or simply shoot him. However, her handler wanted the mission to go as planned. She removed the device from her backpack. It was affixed to a three-inch mechanical suction cup that she now secured to the window.

BEIJING

Reilly was dead serious. Cheng recognized that by the tone of his response. Again she thought, *he attracts trouble. You don't want to be around him for too long.* She pushed past the thought and got to the work she was sent to cover.

First a flyover. "Oil imports," she began. "Buyers and sellers. Haves and have nots. The haves jockey for the top slot. Saudi Arabia, Russia, and even the U.S. Then Iraq, Canada …"

"Canada's up there?" Reilly asked.

"They certainly are. Holding at number four, with the most drilling in Alberta, then Saskatchewan, plus reserves off Newfoundland."

"Who knew?"

"I did," Cheng replied.

It was an effective reply. She was there to teach, Reilly to learn. He got it. "Point taken, Dr. Cheng."

She smiled. The room was hers.

"Continuing, United Arab Emirates, Iran, Kuwait, Nigeria, and Kazakhstan. Venezuela in better political times. Recently, with a spike in shale production, we surpassed the Saudis, jumping ahead of Russia."

"Which undoubtedly pissed off Gorshkov."

"You're getting ahead of me, Mr. Reilly."

"Sorry."

"It's expected that we'll drop back to second place, but that still usurps Russia's position. And why is that important? Because," she said, not really inviting an answer, "oil is Russia's top export. More than 5.2 million bpd (barrels per day) of crude oil go out the door along with 2.4-plus bpd of petroleum products. Overall, they manage more than 11.5 percent of the global oil exports. Europe guzzles up most of it. But that's not the most important fact. It's who else they sell to."

A few questions were forming in Reilly's mind. But it was not time to ask them yet. Not until the teacher invited them.

"The annual value of all this in American currency is north of 130 billion. Not surprisingly, any threat to that number represents a threat to Gorshkov. And he's all about growing his business. He adds more Russian refineries every year. And thanks to global warming, if thanks are in order, more offshore reserves to the north have become accessible, as well as open and clear Arctic shipping routes. This, of course, gives Russia more opportunity to transport product to Asia, supplementing its new pipelines south into China.

"What does this mean?" Another rhetorical question. "Russia has become China's largest oil supplier. Imports amount to nearly 1.5 million barrels a day. That's a 4 percent increase over last year, which was an increase over the prior year. And next year, when the latest China-bound valve is turned on, that market share will grow.

"U.S. supplies to China have fallen by 80 percent. Eight-zero. Chalk it up to escalating trade tensions. But even more important is how much of the Chinese market share Iran lost. A few years ago, Iran's average was 764,000 bpd. Today, it's 260,000 barrels per day. Russia is outdelivering Saudi Arabia now, too. They're down 25 percent from a year ago. But all of this is temporary. The earth is going to run out of oil. In 1999, the American Petroleum Institute predicted that day would come between 2062 and 2094. But seven years later, the Cambridge Energy Research Associates estimated the date was off because there's actually more oil down there than anyone previously thought.

"That means that there are millions of barrels yet to be discovered, pumped, and processed. More to burn off into the atmosphere. More climate change.

"Bottom line, we won't run out of fossil fuels in our lifetime, but we can't promise the same for our great-grandchildren's world.

"There's money to be made now, but not forever. When you think about it, oil really will have a short run. The Chinese first discovered it in 600 BCE and transported it through bamboo pipes. Pennsylvania oil began flowing in 1859. The modern age began in the early 1900s and helped fuel World War I. So from the time of the automobile and the airplane until the likely last drop, maybe 200 years, 250 tops.

"Gentlemen, what's the expression? Make hay while the sun shines?"

"Close. Modern alchemy. Turning oil into gold," Reilly offered.

Lenczycki finally crossed to the couch. "Back to the markets. You glossed over Russia's other markets."

"Before I do that, care to tell me who you are? Who you really are? I never got anything beyond your name."

"Just a guy."

"I know a lot of guys. There's nothing *just* about you," Cheng observed.

"I run a fishing boat rental business in the Caribbean."

"The Caribbean is pretty far from here. And I'm close to leaving if I don't get a straight answer." She addressed Reilly. "Does he work for you?"

"He was invited. Like you."

"Do I have to play 21 Questions?"

"Dr. Cheng," Lenczycki said as he stood, "I'm a consultant." He put a finger to his lips, instructing her not to speak. He walked around the room and moved a picture frame aside on the wall. "I cover different areas than you." Then he picked up the landline phone, held it, and looked under it.

She got it and nodded.

"I'm able to figure out some things. You, others. Our job is to help Reilly. He's on a tight schedule, so back to my question. Russia's other principal markets?"

She put her folder down. She knew the information cold. It was also a matter of public record. "As I said, China's at the top. Country-by-country, the Netherlands second, followed by Germany, the Republic of Korea, then back to Europe, its principal market, with Belarus, Italy, Poland, and Finland. Then Japan."

"What will the new pipeline mean?"

"There are two questions to ask. What will the new pipeline mean, and what will Russia's new icebreakers through the Arctic mean for sales in Asia? The answer is everything. They can undercut Middle Eastern prices, monopolize the market, boost Russia's economy, fund its military, and give Gorshkov the resources to tighten his grip throughout Eastern Europe."

"The long game," the former spy said.

Reilly concluded, "That gets considerably shorter."

"But we're not here to talk about Russia," Dr. Cheng said.

Reilly lowered his eyes. *Aren't we?* he thought.

Cheng continued without any awareness of Reilly's reaction.

"Since you could have covered this by logging onto Google, I suspect you have more to drill down on."

"Perfect way to describe it. Yes, Dr. Cheng," Reilly said. "Two international oil conferences this month, two murders. Both in Kensington Hotels. This is the third meeting. I'm convinced there will be a third murder. Here. This hotel. This conference."

She gasped and thought for the third time, *He attracts trouble. You don't want to be around him for too long.*

WASHINGTON, D.C.

Dominique Dhafari gave the sleeping man one last look. She didn't know him, but it wouldn't have mattered if she had. She'd killed people she'd gotten close to, worked with, even slept with. All she needed to do now was turn on the phone's power, return to her room, dial the burner's number, and wait just long enough that she wouldn't be the first to hit the nearby stairwell. Being first could draw suspicion and flag her later on CCTV cameras, but joining the panicked guests in the mad dash to safety would allow her to blend in.

But that didn't happen. The instant she turned on the power, she went to the same place as the man sleeping—or perhaps someplace different.

41

BEIJING

"You're going to help us figure out who's the target," Reilly said, repeating Cheng's word play.

At precisely that moment, there was a knock on the door. Cheng automatically returned her top sheet to the file. She stood, straightened her dress, and paced. Pacing was good, considering what Reilly had just said. Lenczycki automatically took up a position to the side of the door frame.

Reilly didn't have to ask who was at the door. A monitor beside the doorframe showed him—a woman wearing hotel colors pushing a food cart with an assortment of delights and bottles of wine. One red, one white.

"It's okay. Snacks," he said.

Reilly let the woman in. It took two minutes to lay everything out and pour the wine. There was no check for Reilly to sign, but he handed her 2.7 yen, roughly the equivalent of twenty-five US dollars. Reilly served his team. They made small talk for five minutes, then Reilly called an end to it. "We may want those minutes back in a few days."

Cheng understood. Lenczycki did one of the things he did best. He returned to the window and watched.

"Given the turn the conversation took, there's more to consider."

Reilly had no pre-conceived notions. "The floor is all yours."

"Then up to the 40,000 foot view to look down at the whole globe, starting with Saudi Arabia. Oil outpaces everything in their economy—more than 135 billion in U.S. dollars. They sell the most right here to China. But they don't top Russian sales. Every dollar that goes to Russia is a dollar the Saudis don't get, and vice versa."

Skip Lenczycki said from the window, "Worthy of going to war over, doctor?"

"Worthy of staking ground," she replied.

"Or sand," Reilly said.

"And water," the ex-CIA operative added. "The Gulf of Hormuz. The attack this month."

This brought the room to a stop.

"And where does the U.S. stand in the mix?" Reilly asked.

"We'd like to have a bigger bite of the apple. Our top markets are Mexico and China. Japan, South Korea, and Brazil follow. So sure, we'd like to sell more to China, but the trouble is we're not right next door. Shipping takes more time. Same problem for Saudi Arabia and its neighbors. But Russia is on top with a straight shot down and a route that is not subject to Middle East tensions on land or sea."

"Back to the question. Worthy of waging war?"

"No need. But anytime Arabian oil becomes more costly, as it is now, Russia benefits. And as I said, Gorshkov will put the money to good use. More money fuels his ability to seize more land across Europe."

This exchange took Reilly back to Chicago. Who benefits: *cui bono*? Russia benefits.

"Then Russia attacks," Reilly declared. "And we—"Lenczycki answered for the room. "We do—," he mouthed the next word silently, *nothing*.

The facts underscored his assertion. Russia had taken Crimea and now was on the verge of controlling all of Ukraine. Next, a not-so-polite door knock on the Baltic States.

"If you really think about it, it's a perfect strategy. There are also the other oil-producing countries he could gobble up. They're small, but they'd bring more revenue in."

"What countries?" Reilly asked.

"Kazakhstan for one. There's a significant Russian population there. Another, Tatarstan. The majority supports Russian rule. Both have ample oil and would get Russia even more back into the Empire business. As they say, 'Watch this space.'"

"Is there any limit to his expansionism, Dr. Cheng?"

"Well if you're asking whether Gorshkov will be as foolish as Hitler, the answer is still to come. Consider this. Had Hitler stopped where France met the Atlantic, declared victory, and sought peace with Great Britain and the United States, he might have held Europe. Remember the Battle for France was from May to June, 1940. That was more than six months *before* Pearl Harbor.

"Hitler had an off ramp then. He didn't take it. And instead of sending 50 percent of his troops to Russia, he could have built an empire to the west far bigger and wealthier than anything he would get trying to take the Soviet Union. Strategically, he should have made the Mediterranean his own private lake, conquering the Middle East, moving south from Libya and Egypt to all of Africa. If he'd maintained Germany's alliance with Russia, Stalin could have acquired Iran, while everything to the west would be Germany's. The next step would have been to incite India to declare its freedom from Great Britain and form an alliance with Hitler.

"Remember, the U.S. was ill-equipped to wage war after Japan's attack. Now, play out a scenario where Germany offers the United States aid to fight Japan, allied with the Soviet Union. England would eventually seek peace, unable to defend its holdings in Africa and Asia on its own."

"But none of it played out that way," Lenczycki said.

"Not one bit, but it could have if Hitler had not made stupid decisions. South instead of East and an early declaration of victory. If he'd done that, Germany would have redrawn the map and become the superpower."

Reilly shook his head. "There's a lot of *ifs* to this version of alternate history. And as my mother used to say, 'If she had wheels, she'd be a wagon.'"

Everyone shared a much-needed laugh following the horrifying possibilities.

"Now for the real lesson this alternate history, as you noted, tells us."

Lenczycki and Reilly were ready.

"There is no limit to Gorshkov's lust for world building. To ignore that fact we risk greater peril than we saw in Ukraine. He's shrewd. He's a megalomaniac. He's a brutal killer feeling nothing for his victims. He takes want he wants. The only thing he needs to take more is capital."

"And the Chinese oil market is his solution," Reilly said.

"Precisely."

Reilly leaned back in his seat. He hadn't taken a bite of food or sip of his wine since Cheng began her history seminar. He had an idea where to start.

42

This time, Sherwood Baker was at the medical building rendezvous before Moakley Davidson. The senator pulled up next to him and rolled down his dark-tinted window. He looked past the reporter and around the general area.

"Good evening, Senator."

"No titles. No names."

"Oh, right. I wouldn't want to sully your reputation just as you move up the ladder."

"You called. Tell me what the fuck you found. Then this will be the last time. Like you said, I'm moving up."

The Hill reporter smiled. "Loose pieces. A bit of a jigsaw puzzle, but if I put it all together, it might reveal an interesting picture."

Davidson said nothing.

"It's still forming, but I see two men," Baker continued.

Davidson gripped the steering wheel with both hands.

"But here's my dilemma," the reporter said coldly. "I could get a Pulitzer if I did some serious due diligence."

"A dilemma has two horns," Davidson said coldly. "What's the second?"

"You could find a way for me to consider taking an early retirement.

A big oil guy like you has enormous resources. That's one story I've never written."

There was an unsaid *but* at the end of the sentence. Baker laughed. Davidson didn't.

"When I break it down, it's a pretty easy dilemma to solve. You get the file, and I get a condo in South Beach, work on my tan, and maybe teach a journalism ethics course."

Davidson looked into Baker's car. He saw nothing. "Let me see what you have."

"First, I'd like to know what direction you're leaning." He didn't hold back, adding, "Mr. presumptive Vice President."

Davidson blew out an angry breath and shook his head. "All right, forget what I said before. I'll feed you stories from inside! You'll be my go-to guy."

"I already have sources in the White House," Baker replied. "I'm thinking Pulitzer and a big raise or a condo on the beach before the Atlantic gets too high."

"What do you have?" Davidson was insistent.

"It's such an easy choice for you to make."

"Jesus, Baker. We have history."

"History is overrated. I'm looking toward the future."

Davidson loosened his grip and slowly smiled. "Well, change is good. Looking forward to my own. But I don't see you in Miami. You're more of a Chicago guy. The Cubs, pizza, and beer."

"You could be right. Maybe a combo. Chicago in the summer, Miami Beach in the winter."

He removed a sealed manila envelope from between his seat and the door and brought it up chest level, but no further.

Moakley Davidson hated being manipulated. Not in business. Not in Congress. Certainly not now as his own future looked remarkably bright. When people tried to play him, he doubled down and found ways to raise the stakes. Sometimes those stakes created life decisions for the people who crossed him.

A thought flashed before him. He slowly slid back the lid of the compartment between the two front seats. His fingers grazed the barrel of his Heckler & Koch 9mm P30 pistol and ended on the grip. He had a concealed carry license, though it wasn't allowed on the floor of the Senate. But here—here and now—he could take care of matters himself.

"I don't recall hearing a definitive answer, Senator."

"A hint of what you uncovered."

"First, we talk about my retirement. My guess is that's going to be the choice once you read what I turned up."

"Okay. What do you have in mind? Bitcoins? Stock? Cash? Of course, I can't write you a check."

"Of course," the reporter acknowledged.

"There are ways to make this work. Through various holdings. I have many at arm's length."

"I suspect you do. Those could make an interesting part of my Pulitzer story."

Davidson glanced at the folder again as his right hand inched away from his gun. "Actually, I can make this work," realizing he needed to understand more of what the reporter had found. What was worth so much to this man? "We skipped over a question. How much is that retirement fund?"

"I thought you would never ask. Two million. And yes, as difficult as it will be, cash. I don't want to take a chance with any market volatility."

"You're making this very difficult. Especially not knowing—"

"I can give you two headlines."

Davidson eased his right hand back to his lap.

"The man you're interested in was an Army intelligence officer when two young congressmen were on a junket in Afghanistan."

"Not good enough for season tickets to the Cubs," Davidson said.

"Perhaps, but did you know that later that man became a State Department researcher?"

"One of my first-year aides has more than you do! Goodbye."

Baker came back with, "Really? Did that aide tell you that he wrote a secret paper that correctly predicted all of the terrorist attacks against the bridges and tunnels, including the 14th Street Bridge right here in town?"

Davidson said nothing.

"And somehow, I don't know how, it found its way into the hands of terrorists. Did he leak it? That would be an interesting thread to tug on. A good way to discredit him."

"You can confirm this?" Davidson asked.

"So far, for the sake of this discussion, it's hearsay. But I can say *here*." He waved the file.

Davidson nodded. "You said two headlines."

"Yes, I did, Senator." He patted the file. "Macau. Twelve years ago, just after the junket to Afghanistan. The same two members of Congress were accompanied by the same Army officer. While they were there, an unpleasant incident occurred with one of them. From what I found from a source, it could ruin one, maybe two careers."

Davidson tensed, his fingers still on the pistol.

"Shall I go on?"

"How much do you know?"

"Enough to lead me to other Chinese sources. I hear there are photos. I have a few pieces, not the entire story. But I'm a damned good reporter, and it wouldn't take too much to unravel the rest. There is more, isn't there Senator?"

Baker was playing his best hand. "I do think it is Pulitzer worthy. Who knows, I might become a regular on *Meet the Press*. Come to think of it, in the long run, it might be worth more than the two million to keep me off TV." He slid the file back between the seat and the door. "The price is two and a half."

"Cash. Two million. Two days."

"The last counter was two and a half."

"Fuck you. Two and a half. I'll make the arrangements. You bring the file. You turn over everything. No coming back in a year ... or ever. You announce your retirement before the transfer. That way I will have your commitment."

The reported gloated. "I accept."

Davidson stared directly at Baker; the slits of his eyes narrowed with an unmistakable cold, heartless expression. "Listen to me. Listen carefully. If you violate the terms, I would not be able to guarantee the safety of people close to you, though I hear they're not so close. If I'm not mistaken, since your divorce they've been living in Minneapolis with their mother. In another year, your oldest will be in college; the twins, a few years behind. Undoubtedly all with hopes and dreams that I'm certain you want to see fulfilled."

Now Baker was seized with the realization he had overplayed his hand. He bellowed, "I said I fucking accept!"

"Good. We'll meet one more time. Then never again. You won't call me. You won't email. You will never contact me."

"Agreed."

"You'll bring everything in your car, including any computers you worked on. You'll certainly be able to buy replacements." For good measure, Davidson added, "Cash."

Baker nodded.

Davidson eased his fingers off his Heckler & Koch, closed the map compartment, and drove off. As he exited the unsupervised medical parking lot, he thought about how he could make this problem go away.

43

THE EXPLOSION in the corner suite blew a nine-foot hole through the building, sending debris hurtling down to 14th Street NW. Inside, the blast tore through the bedroom, instantly incinerating anything flammable—wood, carpet, skin. The heat melted all the glass—the mirrors, light bulbs, and liquor bottles. The impact continued through the hallway wall, where the dead man's personal security had been posted. They had no time to react and nowhere to go.

The flames spread across the hotel hall to three other rooms where five guests received burns, cuts, and abrasions. They all survived.

Fire alarms boomed. Sprinklers cut in. Prerecorded announcements blared through the system-wide PA. "Proceed to the nearest stairwell. Walk down in an orderly manner. Do not take the elevators." It repeated every eight seconds.

The explosion rocked the fourteenth floor. Most hook and ladder trucks in the U.S. can extend an aerial ladder from 75 to 105 feet; typically no higher than seven-to-eight stories. Specialty trucks can reach upwards of 125 feet, maybe to the twelfth floor. The firefighters had twenty feet more to go. That meant that getting to the fire above the reach of the ladder required using the stairs.

Within eleven minutes, the DCFD had the three ladder trucks out, five engines, and two battalion chiefs. Thirty firefighters entered the building with turnouts (fire-resistive clothing) and breathing apparatus.

The fast ascent team ran up the stairs. They hooked up hoses to the hotel's internal standpipes on the fourteenth floor. The twelfth floor became their staging area. A lieutenant rushed to check the Kensington's ventilation, sprinkler, and smoke control systems. Another was posted in the lobby to direct firefighters in and hotel guests out.

The hotel's defensive measures all worked and exceeded district codes. The fire was contained to the northeast corner.

The bomb maker, not a particular fan of mass murder, had a job to do—insure that the principal target was taken out, along with the assassin assigned to the job. That was an unfortunate loss but insisted upon in the contract terms. Any secondary targets should be limited to bodyguards and staff. They were.

News, especially given the identity of the victim, would travel fast to Beijing where the bomb maker, preparing for another hit, would hear about it. Another deposit in his retirement fund.

* * *

Kensington had a preestablished phone tree. The general manager of the DC Kensington Hotel called the president of domestic operations in Chicago, Chip Snyder. The call woke him up. Snyder phoned CEO EJ Shaw, another wake up. After Shaw, Snyder reached legal head Chris Collins, security chief Alan Cannon, and PR VP Lois Duvall. The only one awake within this group was Cannon who was seven hours ahead in Nairobi, Kenya and about to board a plane for his first leg to Beijing to catch up with Reilly.

"Shit, Snyder!" Cannon exclaimed.

"I know, I know."

"Not good enough. You were warned. Did you implement anything?"

"I doubled up the lobby security."

Cannon let out an exasperated breath that he was sure Snyder felt on the back of his neck all the way in Chicago.

"I'm changing my flight to DC. I'll text you the details. In the meantime, get down there."

"Already booked," Snyder said with audible resignation. He feared his job was on the line, but maybe he could hold things together, if—

Before he could think things out, Cannon dictated the immediate steps he needed to take.

"One, call Tiano. He'll put this front and center of the Crisis Committee. They'll work with DC police. You listen to them. Two, implement all of the Red Hotel protocols. If you don't know them, they're on the company server. You do realize that if you had the dogs on site, they might have sniffed out the bombs."

"Yeh."

"Three. Wait 15 minutes, then call Reilly in Beijing. He'll be up to speed because I'm going to get him first." Cannon expected a response. He didn't get one. "Four, I strongly suggest you practice what you're going to say, Snyder. This is on you."

* * *

Reilly answered on the sixth ring.

"Dan."

"Hey Alan. On your way?"

"Change of plans."

Reilly heard an unmistakable serious beginning to a cold conversation that was only going to get colder.

Reilly excused himself from Yibing and Skip. "Sorry, my office. Have to take this."

He walked into the bedroom of his junior suite and pointedly asked, "Another?"

"Yes, but not at a conference. Worse."

Reilly closed the door, leaving his team to wonder. The former CIA agent had an inkling. The consultant had none. "Go on."

"Just like you said, the Kensington Capital."

"Christ Almighty! Did Synder—"

"No. He's calling you in a few."

Reilly voice flattened. No expression. Just a prompt. "Go on."

"An explosion, 14th floor northwest corner. From the description, it blew inward from outside."

"Fatalities?"

"Three confirmed." Cannon swallowed hard. "Two bodyguards in the hall."

Bodyguards. Reilly saw the scene clearly. "The third, a Chinese national. An oil executive or minister?"

"We don't know yet. But you're probably right."

"Snyder," Reilly said again.

"Even Snyder might not have been able to prevent it. Could have been a MANPAD fired from another building. But ... hold a sec. Getting a text."

Cannon read it silently first, then gave Reilly the summary.

"All right, police found the remains of someone who landed on the street ... in parts. Burned beyond recognition."

"A jumper?"

"Wait. More coming in. Not a jumper. Victim had scaling belt and hooks."

"The bomber," Reilly declared. "Climbed the building, planted the bomb, but it went off too early."

"Looks that way," Cannon replied. "Ingenious. Would have taken an athletic guy and training."

"They're around."

They ended the call after Reilly agreed it was best for Alan Cannon to go to DC.

"Problem?" Lenczycki asked when Reilly re-emerged.

"Big one."

Before he could explain, his phone rang again. This time Chip Snyder. "I'll be back."

Reilly answered. Snyder launched into an apology. Reilly stopped him.

"You better hope there were no other civilian fatalities," he said.

It was enough of a judgment for now.

"Alan went through the latest. We're thinking the guy blown out was the bomber."

"Really?"

"Really. Force of the explosion that took out the suite sent him flying. Any idea of the target?"

"Yes," Snyder said. "Just got it from the front desk." He paused, nervous about what he was about to say.

"And?"

"According to the reservation, he's Lee Kang."

"An oil minister?"

"A shipping magnate in D.C. for trade talks."

"And let me guess. His ships are tankers, and the tankers aren't filled with milk."

"I don't know," Snyder said softly.

"You also didn't know he was in the hotel."

"No. No I didn't."

Reilly hung up thinking they had a new kind of threat assessment to add to the playbook. Anyone playing Spider-Man.

44

BEIJING

Reilly gave Yibing and Skip the news. He told them to keep working while he made a round of calls to Chicago and the District of Columbia. The first was to Elizabeth Matthews in Washington. He'd keep it short and far beyond sweet.

"Hello," she answered.

"Madame Secretary, it's Reilly in Beijing."

The Secretary of State instantly felt the urgency in Reilly's voice.

"Dan, what time is it there?" she asked.

The question confirmed Reilly's suspicion that he'd woken her up.

"I'll put it this way, I have sun and you don't."

She laughed.

Once Reilly explained why he called, there was no more laughing. It had been less than 45 minutes since the explosion. Matthews was surprised she hadn't gotten a call.

The conversation was short. Matthews was already up and pulling clothes together. They hung up, but Reilly's bottom line message to her stuck.

"Elizabeth, it looks like my problem is also now yours."

* * *

When Reilly returned to the living room and explained what had occurred in Washington, it only underscored the urgency more. At that moment, there was an insistent knock at the door. Not like the gentle knock of housekeeping in the morning or the food delivery they'd had. This was the knock of authority.

Lenczycki stood abruptly. "Expecting anyone?"

"No," Reilly said.

Once again, the ex-CIA officer took up a position to the side of the door.

Another knock. This time it came with a booming voice. "Mr. Reilly. Chinese People's Armed Police. Open, please."

The *please* was not to be confused with a cordial request.

Reilly shot a look at Lenczycki, then to Cheng. "It's okay. Based on the last call, I expected it was only a matter of time. This was quicker than I imagined."

"What about—?" Cheng motioned to the photographs.

"No secrets there. He'll probably have the same ones. Keep them up."

Reilly crossed to the door and forced a smile not knowing what was to come. Upon opening it he offered, "Yes?"

"I'm Colonel Huang Zhang."

He produced his ID. They quickly sized one another up, police officer to hotel executive. And yet, on another level, Chinese intelligence officer to whatever Reilly proved to be.

Reilly remained blocking the entrance. The officer was shorter than Reilly by a few inches. His jet black hair was cut to military length. He was thin, but not so much as to be considered skinny. He had piercing dark eyes that had likely seen, and likely directed, many horrors. He wore a black suit, white shirt, and blue tie. Reilly took Zhang to be roughly his age or no more than a few years older. The policeman didn't bow.

"I'm sorry to disturb you." He wasn't. "But an urgent matter has come up."

He peered around Reilly, sizing up the woman and focusing harder on the man. This was Zhang's play. Reilly remained silent.

"You are Daniel Reilly, with the Kensington Royal Hotel organization."

"I am." Titles mattered in China. He added, "President of the International Division."

"And you have come to Beijing because of your concern that another attack will occur?"

"I have." Reilly corrected himself because introductions were sure to come. "We have."

"Well, I have been asked to work with you."

"We haven't requested help at this point."

"No, you haven't," came the sharp reply. "Nonetheless, I am here. It appears we share the same concern. The safety of delegates to the conference. But it is too late for a countryman of mine who was, within the hour, murdered in your Washington hotel. That should explain the urgency my supervisors felt sending me, Mr. Reilly." He stretched out the *Mister* to more than three times its length. "You must realize there is reason for everyone to cooperate." For good measure and with a half-smile the police officer added, "As a guest of The People's Republic of China."

"Of course," Reilly said.

Zhang smiled. "I should tell you, *Huang* means Happy. My associates say I do not live up to my name."

Reilly couldn't help but laugh. The Chinese man frowned. "You'll have to excuse me, Colonel Zhang, but I think you've been watching too many Clint Eastwood movies."

Zhang's expression lightened. He chuckled.

Reilly gestured with his right hand to enter. Zhang told two officers who had accompanied him something that Reilly assumed was assurance he would be okay or to stand guard. Then he finally bowed to Reilly.

"Thank you, Mr. Reilly." With that he stepped into the room.

Reilly offered Zhang water. He accepted.

Zhang glanced at the photographs mounted on the poster board and noted all of the names.

"I'll be direct, Mr. Reilly. We are taking over security for the upcoming conference."

He walked directly to the board and removed the photo in the lower right corner. He put it at the very top. Center. It was the Chinese delegate; the host. "Specifically, the well-being of Mr. Shen Ma, the honorable Chairman of the People's Republic of China's National Energy Commission. To the point, my government does not believe you can guarantee his safety."

Reilly showed no reaction.

"It appears you are trying to determine who may be next."

"Not just who," Reilly interrupted. "Why. One delegate has been targeted at each meeting. The death of your shipping executive in Washington may be related."

"And America will answer for his death."

Lenczycki stiffened. Zhang felt it. "Care to introduce me to your colleagues?"

"Dr. Yibing Cheng, an economics expert." Reilly didn't go deeper into her biography. Zhang would do that all on his own. Now he needed to be more obtuse with Lenczycki. "And a friend of mine, a law enforcement advisor, Skip Lenczycki." Reilly intentionally avoided giving Zhang the ex-CIA operative's real first name.

"Skip, an unusual name."

"It works for me, Lenczycki."

"Ah, people's roles are becoming more recognizable. Management," he tipped his head to Reilly. "Muscle," noting Lenczycki. "And Dr. Cheng's purpose? Perhaps intelligence?"

Reilly wanted to quickly invalidate the opinion. "She's a college professor, an expert in petroleum history and politics. She's helping us work through the questions."

"I am only interested in Mr. Ma, but if you share your suspicions, we might find, as your Mr. Clint Eastwood might say, 'a two-way street.'"

"Mutual cooperation, in the interest of friendship," Reilly offered.

"We don't need to be friends. Mr. *Lensweeki* doesn't look like someone who's looking for friends." No one corrected his pronunciation. "And I'm sure Dr. Cheng doesn't want to have to remain in China longer than she would consider necessary."

Zhang smiled a gangster's smile.

"We'd be pleased to cooperate, Colonel Zhang." Reilly said. "The two-way street would be in everyone's best interests."

Under the circumstances, best interests were also best practices. Reilly knew what Zhang was from the moment he opened the door—a spy. A spy with a badge. The Chinese People's Armed Forces (PAP) is a highly trained armed defense force of 1.1 million-plus, with more than mere law enforcement duties. The PAP is charged with managing domestic defense throughout China with ultimate jurisdiction over acts of sabotage and terrorism and, to the problem at hand, protecting national security. Chairman Ma's life was definitely an issue of national security, and the Kensington Hotel was considered a potential terrorist target.

"As you and your officers will see, we are currently in the process of elevating the hotel to our highest defense posture; a category Red. Over the next 24 hours you will see bollards up in front. There will be restrictions on parking, deliveries, and even entering the grounds without identification. No one except guests will be permitted on the elevators, and even then, they will have to produce proper identification and working room keys. We will have additional security posted throughout the hotel. Anyone unaffiliated with the oil conference will not be allowed on the conference room floor."

"I expect you will give us the names of all the guests."

Reilly smiled. "I suspect you already have them, Colonel."

Zhang ignored the comment; instead he said, "There will be an additional room booking. Someone who currently doesn't have a reservation."

"Oh?"

"Me."

Reilly smiled. "Please allow me to comp your stay."

Zhang didn't understand the term.

"You will be my company's guest—no charges. Should you require additional rooms—"

"My men are already here."

"Chinese efficiency," Reilly said. "I don't suppose you'll let me know who they are."

"No, I won't be doing that. As for their rooms—" he said playfully and somewhat out of character.

"Yes?"

"You won't need to comp them."

45

Sherwood Baker sat at his desk, contemplating the next chapter in his life. Two-point-five million, invested on top of his newspaper 401K. *A good killing*, he thought. No more daily deadlines. Martinis and cigars on the balcony. He'd help with his kids' college, travel, and maybe even teach. Then another realization hit him. He had made a good deal with a bad man. *A very bad man.* He tapped his fingers on his desk. He would have to trust him.

An hour later, Baker, still completing his work, answered his desk phone.

"Baker. Hello."

No caller ID displayed.

"Mr. Baker, I 'm calling on behalf of a mutual friend who is arranging for your retirement."

The reporter looked around the newsroom. Everyone was busy with their own calls, writing, re-writing. No one cared what he was doing any more than he cared about theirs. "Go on."

"Write down this address on a single sheet of paper. Nothing under it. Do not make a copy or give the address to anyone. Do you understand?"

"Yes," Baker said tentatively. This was more intrigue than he anticipated.

"You will see that it is a parking lot overlooking the river. You are to arrive precisely at 2 a.m. Drive to the far southeast corner. Step out of your car and wait on the passenger side. Within two minutes a black BMW with Maryland plates will meet you. Then you will give him the package, your computers, and any additional notes. You will be given a suitcase. It will have precisely what was agreed upon. Once the exchange is completed, you will stay, and the courier will leave. Do you understand?"

"Yes."

"This will also be the last contact you will have with the individual your business is with. There will be no phone calls, emails, or letters. No intermediaries, no writing, no memoirs, no copies."

Davidson's warning, but colder.

"Yes," Baker said again.

"Two a.m."

The line went dead.

Sherwood Baker typed a short letter and sent it to a shared printer. It hit the tray just as he walked up. Baker returned to his desk, inserted the paper into an envelope, addressed it, dropped it in the mailroom, and left. His resignation. He sighed. The end of a long writing career. No Pulitzer, but a great pay day. He replayed the conversation in his head as he disconnected his laptop and walked out with the package.

He followed the instructions and arrived right on time—not a minute earlier or later. This was one deadline he was not going to miss. He got out of his car, waited on the passenger side as ordered. Thirty seconds later he saw headlights veer off the road and drive into the parking lot. The car came closer: a black BMW with Maryland plates just as he had been told. His heart raced. The BMW pulled up next to him. The driver rolled down his window. Baker looked in and said, "Hello," not knowing what else to do. "I'm—"

The driver, wearing all-black clothing, sunglasses even at night, and gloves, held up a finger to his lips and shook his head. There would be no conversation over the exchange. He saw the package in Baker's left hand and a shoulder bag in his right, and he pointed to each.

"Yes, yes. It's all here. Printouts, the computer, thumb drives, and a backup drive." He handed everything to the driver through the window.

The driver examined the contents and put them on the passenger seat. Next he smiled but didn't get out to complete the exchange.

"Wait, you've got something for me," the now retired reporter said.

The driver nodded, raised his finger again indicating for him to wait a moment. He opened the glove compartment between the two front seats. In the few seconds it took for Baker to imagine how $2.5 million would fit inside such a small compartment, the driver removed a single black item with his right hand, swept it across his lap, raised it, and shot Sherwood Baker between the eyes. A double tap; the second shot following precisely through the hole of the first.

46

REILLY STUDIED THE BOARDS with Yibing Cheng at his side. They were nowhere closer as the sun set than earlier in the day. They were also only two days away from the delegates arriving.

"Any one of them could be the target," Cheng said.

"No. It is Chairman Shen Ma," Zhang insisted. "I have made plans that he will appear only via video conference."

Skip Lenczycki laughed aloud.

"What makes you laugh, Mr. *Lewsanshi*?" he said, still not getting the name right.

"You could have shared that as soon as you came. Not a bad decision, though. This whole conference should have been moved to Zoom. But if you really believe he's the target and not going to show up, then why is it so important for you to stick around?"

"To observe," Zhang said, sounding every bit the policeman/spy.

"No, to see if we're any better than you at figuring this shit out."

Zhang laughed. "You never said what kind of law enforcement you were in."

"No," Lenczycki replied quite humorously. "No I didn't." He figured Zhang would get to the task as soon as he left for the night.

"Now, let's focus," Reilly said, as much for a diversion as a point of order. "Help me. I think we're missing a common denominator."

"It's oil," Yibing Cheng stated.

"Yes, but what *specifically* about oil?"

"Each imports."

"From where?"

Cheng went through the list again. "Primarily, the Middle East, Russia, the U.S."

"Okay. Now by percentages."

Zhang stood and crossed closer to the photographs. "Of course, we are the biggest. The Russian Federation is fulfilling our needs quite nicely. Best prices. Best of neighbors."

"They could benefit all the more by being your only supplier."

"It is not for me to say," Zhang noted.

"But if Russia were your only supplier?"

Zhang shrugged his shoulders. Dr. Cheng answered. "Arab oil would take a hit. So would American exports."

"Correct, and would that be a good trade decision?" Reilly asked.

Another shrug.

"Colonel Zhang, we have an expression in America. You shouldn't put all your eggs in one basket."

Zhang understood. He was familiar with a Chinese quote that spoke to the same notion. *The little bunny should have three holes to hide from the enemy.* Reilly was opening his mind to a larger strategy.

* * *

A half-hour later they broke for the evening. Colonel Zhang left first, then Skip Lenczycki. Yibing Cheng lingered.

"Have to check in. They're holding my room. The bell captain is holding my suitcases."

"I'm sorry, I never asked. Let me see if I can get you an upgrade."

Reilly called the front desk, provided Cheng's claim check number for her bags, and asked the assistant manager to meet them with the suitcases at the new accommodations.

When they got there, Cheng was immediately impressed. It was better than Reilly's junior suite. The door opened to a foyer that led to a magnificent living room. Off to the right, an equally exquisite bedroom and an immense bathroom with a Jacuzzi tub.

"My goodness," she said. "Do I get the extra loyalty points that go along with this?"

Reilly laughed. "I'll see what I can do."

It was in that moment that Dan Reilly completely focused on Cheng's beauty. The brunette had striking green eyes, which especially sparkled as she smiled. Her long neckline was accentuated with a string of freshwater pearls. The smart black business suit with a kelly-green silk blouse brought everything together. And everything was looking very good to Reilly. Even the fact that she had neither an engagement nor wedding ring.

"What do you say we continue our conversation over dinner?" he blurted like a schoolboy summoning up courage.

She answered without hesitation. "That would be very nice." Cheng peered into his eyes with *everything was looking good to her, too* approval.

"Good. Say nine?"

"Perfect. Where?"

"Bianyifang. A 600-year-old restaurant, but they have new food every night," he joked. "The restaurant is renowned for its Peking duck, uniquely cooked in a closed oven that gives it an especially crispy skin and a perfect blending of sweet and sour flavors."

Yibing Cheng raised an eyebrow. "From the Ming dynasty."

"Yes," he replied, knowing he shouldn't be impressed. "You've been there."

"I have, and it's a perfect choice for a business meal."

A business meal, he thought with some disappointment. "Of course, Dr. Cheng. Business."

Dinner definitely started out that way. Over cocktails, more discussion about the current global oil economy and Cheng's assessment of oil politics in the near future. "Seventy years ago, governments should have recognized that fossil fuels are finite. Drain resources long enough, and those resources will run out. We've been charting the depletion through a mathematical curve known as Hubbert's peak theory."

She explained that the research actually came from the inside, from Shell Oil geologist and geophysicist M. King Hubbert. Hubbert published his hypothesis in 1956, noting that discovery and extraction of new petroleum sources would lead to a peak in a bell shaped curve, but that curve would not keep going up and the world would run out.

"He also predicted that if the world burned all its known sources without reducing carbon dioxide emissions in the atmosphere, we'd continue to heat up the planet and use up our carbon budget."

"And we're over budget?"

"Yes. We should leave two-thirds of the known oil reserves in the ground to meet our global climate targets. The changing weather patterns, the impact on growing seasons, the rising seas are evidence of the carbon budget deficit."

She shook her head. "There's still no unified global strategy, let alone national agreement, considering the tribalism in America's politics. The Arctic ice will continue to melt, Russia will pump more oil to fuel its economy, China will consume more, and the U.S. firms will fight to keep up. Meanwhile, what happens when the wells go dry in the Middle East and no new economic resources are brought to the already unstable region? That's when we'll see wars over water rather than oil as those countries find ways to reinvent themselves."

"Is there any hope?" Reilly asked.

"Without enlightened leadership around the globe? The U.S., Russia, and—"

She was about to say China when the waiter interrupted. Reilly ordered the Peking duck.

"You will be most pleased," the waiter said as he eased away, never turning his back to them.

When it was clear to talk again, Reilly said, "What do you say we stop talking shop for a while, Dr. Cheng?"

She smiled her perfect smile. "It's Yibing. Yi for short." She reached across the table to shake his hand. "May I call you Daniel?"

"Of course. Or Dan." He took her hand.

"You strike me as a Daniel."

"Then Daniel it is for as long as you like." He couldn't believe he actually said that. "I'm sorry. I didn't mean to be so forward."

Their touch lingered, a link between business and wherever the rest of the conversation was going to go. To her thinking, *dangerous or not.*

Reilly withdrew first and fumbled for a new comment. "I don't believe you were born fully formed as Dr. Cheng. What came before the PhD?"

Yibing laughed. He hadn't heard a woman laugh for too long.

"Quite right. Lots before and a whole lot after. I was born in Tianjin, China along the Bohai coast."

"Know it well. We're looking at a property there. Big city, growing fast."

"Third largest. My mother taught economics at the university, the first modern college in China. Kind of natural that I went into the same field."

"Father?"

"He died when I was young. We were told it was a military training exercise."

"And you don't believe it?"

She looked around. "Of course I do," she lied.

"Brothers or sisters?"

She laughed her laugh again.

"Come now. Not allowed. One child per family back then. Besides, it takes a contribution from a male donor and, as I said, my father was—"

She lowered her eyes. Reilly wondered whether she had come to China to find out more about her father's death. It would be hard to impossible to ever find out.

"You emigrated to the U.S.?"

"Yes, with my mother when I was eleven. We had a cousin we'd never seen in Irvine, California. We never got further than there. It took two years, but she got a teaching job at UC Irvine. My high school test scores eventually got me into an accelerated math program. That led to enrollment in the college where my mother taught, gratefully tuition free. I earned my PhD at MIT. Pretty smooth running after that. Then a few think tanks that didn't especially take to my thinking." A smirk. "They were wrong and discovered it too late. Some consulting jobs and an invitation from Washington."

Reilly didn't need to be told who that was. He also recognized that Yibing was being careful about what she said over concern about the likely presence of hidden microphones in the restaurant.

"And where is Dan Reilly from, or did he pop out of the womb as a hotel executive?"

"Far from it." Reilly ran through his life and resume with equal awareness of how much he wanted to say publicly. How his mother worked on a 911 desk in Boston, and how his father had died. General things about his military service. Nothing about the State Department. He suspected that Elizabeth Matthews had also kept that out of her introduction to him. "And I landed this gig. Enough millions of miles on United Airlines that they named a plane for me."

"No way!" she exclaimed.

It never failed to get a reaction. "Way. I have a photo back at the office. It was only for a while. Loyalty builder. Then it was painted over and someone else got to brag."

"Love to see the photograph."

Reilly smiled and wondered, *Was this all going somewhere?* Her next question suggested it certainly might be.

"No time for relationships?" she asked without warning.

Reilly didn't answer immediately.

"I'm sorry," Cheng said sensing her faux pas. "Bad breakup?"

"In a manner of speaking."

Reilly's thoughts went to a memorial service in London, when he stood in the back of the church, said a silent goodbye to Marnie Babbitt, and left out that chapter of his life.

"Ultimately geographically undesirable," he said about the Russian sleeper spy. "And you? Anyone in your life?"

She chuckled. "Wannabees along the way. What's the old country song? "*Heartbreaks by the Numbers?*" There was sadness in her voice as she added, "But who's counting." Cheng looked away, then forced a smile. "Maybe we'd do better by sticking to business."

"Actually," he said disagreeing, "I'm glad we're not. Let's finish dinner and take in the town."

"Maybe another night," Yibing said. "It's been a long day. I'm fading, and we've got a lot to go through tomorrow."

"You're right."

Now Reilly reached across the table. She took his hand and touched his fingertips lightly. It was exactly what Reilly had hoped she'd do.

47

WASHINGTON, D.C.

"What the hell is going on?"

"Still getting details from Metropolitan Police and the FBI," Roger Whitfield, the newly appointed National Security Advisor, told President Ryan Battaglio.

"Come on Whitfield, get on top of things."

Whitfield shrugged. He'd only been on the job a few days and didn't even know where his bathroom was or who to call in an emergency. Until a few days ago he was a congressman from Mississippi, an old friend of Battaglio's from the House, and a member of the Foreign Relations committee known for theatrical grandstanding and little else. Battaglio tapped him as Pierce Kimball's replacement because he valued loyalty as the primary qualification. But so far, he hadn't even had enough minutes in the Oval Office to sit and take in the austere environment. It was *enter, stand, listen.* As a fifty-six-year-old, nine-term congressman with a personal problem, he wondered if he should have discussed this job with his wife before taking it. Better yet, his girlfriend.

"I'll find out," Whitfield sheepishly said.

"Damn straight you will!" Battaglio shouted. "Tell the fucking Chinese ambassador I've got this under control."

Whitfield resisted letting out a deep breath. Instead, he took one, inflating his chest. He felt it would make him look more in control. "Yes, sir. Of course, Mr. President."

"You do that. And on your way out, tell my secretary to get me a ham sandwich from the kitchen. I'm starved."

* * *

"We're all on?" Elizabeth Matthews asked.

"Watts here."

"McCafferty."

The trio consisted of the CIA and FBI directors and Elizabeth Matthews.

"Good. What do we have at this hour?"

"Nothing to work with but burned body parts," offered from the FBI. "Uncertain age, but adult. Blown off the building. Not much left, but we were able to recover climbing gear. Forensics is doing what it can. Messy job. Meanwhile we're working inside to find out who was on the outside."

"Do we have anything that ties the killer to the executions abroad?" Matthews asked.

"No, but yes," McCafferty continued.

"There was certainly enough time for the assassin to make it to Washington and make it a hat trick. I mean we're looking at a very adept individual. Multitalented. I think this is our man."

Matthews sighed. If true it would take a heavy load off Dan Reilly's shoulders. She texted him the news using the cryptonym they established for the assassin. "Poss good news. Alpha may be down."

"Considering no one saw anyone start ground up, we're working the possibility our climber had checked in ahead of time, exited through a room window, went up or down, and placed the bomb."

"Then took his own life?" Watts asked. "That's completely out of character given the profile our in-house shrink's been working up."

"Could have been a mistake," Matthews offered. "Bad timer, Reese?"

"Highly possible."

"Or," the CIA Director proposed, "he was expecting to detonate from a remote location, but the device was jerry-rigged to explode once set. Not his idea. A little parting gift from above."

"And who's above?" Matthews asked.

"For that, Elizabeth, we have to look beyond the three assassinations. Put the attack in the Strait of Hormuz in the equation. Somebody who's interested in creating big time chaos."

"The Ayatollah," McCafferty offered. "Iran?"

CIA Director Watts disagreed. "On the fence. Iran gains nothing by intentionally slowing down traffic in the Strait. The sinking could have been simply an ill-timed stupid decision."

"You don't really think that?" McCafferty asked.

"Well, no. Back to the Chinese shipping exec. We have to advise the president," Watts said. "He's due to meet with the Chinese ambassador this afternoon."

"What do you recommend?" Matthews asked.

"Denial. The Chinese unequivocally need to hear we're not behind it," the CIA director maintained. "Reese, give Battaglio talking points on where you are with the investigation. Better yet, tell him you need to be in the meeting with him. Otherwise he'll fumble."

"I should be there too," Matthews added. "Meanwhile, any chatter in channels you're monitoring, Gerald?"

"Nothing to report. But we're on it."

"Jesus, I wish Kimball was still in the White House. Hey, Gerald, how about quietly bringing him in to help you?" Matthews proposed.

"Not sure he'd do it, all things considered. But then again, he might enjoy the notion of subterfuge behind POTUS' back. A fuck you very much."

"Good," she said. "Meanwhile, Reese, call the president. Let him know our thinking. You and I should be there. Gerald, best the CIA stays in the background."

"That's where we're most comfortable, Elizabeth."

* * *

President Ryan Battaglio flashed a wide smile; inappropriate for the meeting. "Good afternoon, Ambassador Gao." He had Whitfield's scant notes and Matthews and McCafferty for backup.

Gao walked in with two of his delegation. They didn't have "Good afternoon" faces on.

"Mr. President, let us get right to the issue."

"Of course. Please be seated. You know Secretary of State Matthews."

Gao bowed. "Madame Secretary."

"Ambassador," she replied.

"And FBI Director Reese McCafferty. His bureau is handling the investigation."

Gao bowed again. McCafferty nodded.

The three Chinese walked to the couch opposite two leather chairs. Gao sat first, followed by his two aides: one to his left, the other to his right. Next, Battaglio took a single leather chair to their side while Matthews and McCafferty sat across from the Chinese. Battaglio offered tea. Gao declined for them.

"Mr. Ambassador, thank you for coming."

"We have more to discuss than *thank you's*, Mr. President."

"Yes, we do." He looked to McCafferty and Matthews to take over as they had discussed. But it was too soon. The plan was for the FBI Director to cover the investigation; the Secretary of State to talk diplomacy. That would leave room for Battaglio to be, Matthews nearly choked on the word, "presidential."

"You have much to apologize for, Mr. President," Ambassador Gao continued. "That is one of the reasons I am here. There are others. The People's Republic of China insists on being fully informed on all aspects of the investigation. Director McCafferty, I will be sending a team to your office. We expect complete cooperation."

Matthews quickly surmised the meeting with the diplomat was going to be anything but diplomatic. Time for McCafferty to speak up. She touched her right knee. A cue.

"Ambassador Gao, please convey to your government that America's law enforcement agencies are committed to identify the perpetrator of this heinous crime. However, this is a matter for American law enforcement."

Gao frowned and repeated his demands. "With complete cooperation and full disclosure."

Battaglio remained silent. Matthews's turn.

"Mr. Ambassador, if the situation were reversed, would you allow U.S. investigators in? I don't believe so."

"Secretary Matthews, at this very moment we are cooperating with an American hotel executive in Beijing. Perhaps you know him," Gao said. "Mr. Daniel Reilly."

Battaglio stiffened at hearing the name. *Reilly... again?*

"Cooperation and disclosure. We are doing it right now. Perhaps we should stop. Or you should begin."

Their control over the meeting was quickly eroding. Elizabeth Matthews didn't know, but she hid her surprise. McCafferty jumped back in.

"Mr. Ambassador, the assassin was a woman. We are attempting to identify her through forensic analysis. Given her unique skills, we strongly believe she was responsible for the other killings in London and Nairobi."

Matthews silently wondered how strong those skills were considering she blew herself up in the process. McCafferty came to that point next.

"The bomb exploded early, taking her life as well as Chairman Wu. So to your point, your investigators will be welcome at the FBI."

"Thank you, Director McCafferty."

"As observers."

Gao pursed his lips and turned to Ryan Battaglio, dissatisfied. "I expect—no, President Yáo expects more than platitudes. A Chinese oil official was assassinated in an American hotel, in your nation's capital, mere blocks from where we sit. It was not the first in this particular hotel chain. Perhaps it will not be the last."

President Battaglio blanched. Reilly was definitely becoming an important name.

McCafferty drew Gao's attention away from the president. "Ambassador Gao, if there is a connection among the killings, I can assure you we will find it. Right now, we're looking for evidence that would tie the assassin to all three attacks."

"And what have you found, Director McCafferty?"

"Our teams are working with authorities in London and Nairobi, as well as Washington Metro Police. It is too early to formulate a hypothesis."

Ryan Battaglio cleared his throat. "Ambassador Gao, I will instruct the FBI to share whatever they find. I hope you consider this a good beginning."

"A beginning, Mr. President. We also seek cooperation from all of your intelligence agencies, not simply your FBI."

"Of course," Battaglio said without thinking. "Elizabeth, you'll speak to Director Watts today." He turned to the Chinese Ambassador. "He's the head of the Central Intelligence Agency."

Gao didn't need to be told that.

"And Mr. Ambassador, my new National Security Advisor, Roger Whitfield, will be your direct contact. I will instruct him to share information openly with whomever you post."

Matthews shivered inwardly and hid her true reaction with a simple blink. This was turning into another Stockholm, where Battaglio gave in to the Russian president. McCafferty had given general information. Now Battaglio was giving away the farm. Again.

* * *

Following the meeting and the less-than-cordial exit of the Chinese Ambassador, the president excused McCafferty and held over Elizabeth Matthews. He returned to his desk and indicated she should sit. He looked quite proud of himself; gloating. "Well, that went better than expected."

Matthews had the opposite opinion.

"Elizabeth, we need to blame someone. Let's lay this on the Iranians.

I'm sure you and your pals can come up with reasons."

"Mr. President," she ventured, "ever since I took this job, I've been guided by a basic principle. You can't let a bad assumption lie to you."

"Secretary Matthews, you and your alphabet agencies find the evidence to fit the crime and assess the blame!" Battaglio stood, a move that instantly said a number of things. The meeting was over, and she may have gone too far.

Matthews knew she could do more good from within. Her attempt to round up enough cabinet votes to remove Battaglio through invoking the 25th Amendment had failed. Now she had to win back his confidence.

"I understand sir. We'll work as quickly as possible, and in the meantime, I'll back channel with the Chinese."

"You surprise me, Elizabeth. Here I thought you were conspiring against me again."

She swallowed hard. "There is work to be done, Mr. President. Together."

"Well then, Madame Secretary, get back to work."

On her way out she saw Senator Moakley Davidson, the Vice President-designate, waiting to enter.

A bank of television sets was turned on in the outer office: CNN, MSNBC, FOX, and network affiliate stations WRC, WJAL, WUSA, and WTTG. The cable nets were engaged in roundtable discussions, all the locals carrying morning talk shows except one. The sound was down on the WRC monitor as a news story cut in. A photograph instantly caught Moakley's attention. He stepped forward to the screen and turned up the volume.

"Senator," Lillian Westerman said, "the president is ready to see you."

He waved her away and watched the anchor lead to a live shot.

"Right, Ginger. As you noted, just minutes ago the identity of the victim was released, *Hill* reporter Sherwood Baker. He was discovered at dawn by a jogger in the North River Parking lot in McLean. Paramedics pronounced Mr. Baker dead. Earlier I spoke with McLean Police Chief Chas Martin."

The station rolled the previously recorded video. "Chief Martin, given ongoing criticism of the press and targeting of specific reporters, do you have any information whether the killing of Sherwood Baker is a single occurrence or part of a larger threat?"

The chief, in blues and standing tall, responded with commanding authority. "We have no information other than the cause of death. Mr. Baker was killed at approximately 12:30 last night. He was shot twice in the head. Beyond that, we have no further information."

"Are there any cameras in the lot?" It was a natural follow-up.

"I have no comment."

"Can you surmise that Sherwood Baker had gone to the parking lot for a meeting? To rendezvous with a possible contact, perhaps a source who decided to kill him?"

"We're investigating all possibilities."

"Could that include a sexual encounter?"

"I have no comment."

The report went live again to reporter Chuck Austin. "Since I spoke with Chief Martin earlier this morning, I've learned that the FBI is also investigating."

The anchor asked, "What about D.C. Metro Police?"

"Ginger, the incident occurred outside their jurisdiction. But should anything lead to his work for *The Hill*, that would change."

"Thank you, Chuck. Let us know when you have more." The station morning news anchor next read a tag off the teleprompter. "Meanwhile, *Hill* editor Gale Ann Wolman told NBC4 news that she discovered a letter of resignation from Sherwood Baker. She's since turned it over to authorities. In other news—"

Moakley Davidson hid his smile from the president's secretary and the departing Secretary of State. He was quite pleased. The contract killer, a mercenary, never knew who he worked for and by now was already halfway to Brazil.

Davidson entered the Oval Office. President Battaglio enthusiastically shook his hand. "Moakley, welcome."

"Good morning, Mr. President." He closed the door behind him. "Thank you for seeing me. We have to talk."

"Of course. Look at us. This place is ours, Moakley. Did you ever imagine?"

"Every day," Davidson beamed. He didn't admit that his real dream was he'd be president, not Battaglio. How Battaglio ever got on the ticket was still beyond him.

"We're going to get a lot done together. We'll start with executive actions." He nodded to a stack of papers on his desk to sign. "Meanwhile, no problem whipping together confirmation votes?"

"Oh, there will be few assholes who will abstain. People I've pissed off. But the chair will speed it through. For the sake of correctness, it'll go two days. We've got it pretty well worked out." Davidson dropped his voice, "Except if—" He turned to the door just to make sure it was closed, then continued in a whisper, "Ryan, there is someone who could become trouble."

Battaglio's eyes narrowed. He gave Davidson a piercing look. "Who?"

"His name is Reilly, Dan Reilly."

"Who the fuck is he, and why could he give you trouble?"

"Not just me—us. He's in the private sector now. We met him years ago at Shindand Air Force Base."

Battaglio remembered. "Christ! That Army spook. So what? The Pentagon redacted details on the trip. You don't think I checked? The past is dead and buried."

That confirmed what Tasha Samuels had told Davidson. "That part, yes," Davidson continued. "But he was in Macau."

Battaglio stood and paced silently. He paced behind his desk, balled up his fists, and rested them on the top. "Bullshit. Nothing's ever come up. We took some R&R days that's all."

Davidson paced around the Oval Office, picking up lamps and vases, moving picture frames.

"Don't be paranoid. If you're looking for microphones or cameras, there are none."

"Good. Then we can talk about what really happened during our R&R?"

"Jesus, Moakley. We put that to rest years ago."

"Well, I had an investigator dig into Reilly. He was also in Macau. That means he may also know about us there."

Now Ryan Battaglio paused. "He's never said anything?"

"No. He testified before my committee last year and showed no recollection of me. I certainly had forgotten who he was."

"What was he there for?"

"Hotel crap. He wanted more intelligence information."

"Why the hell would he need that?"

"He runs an international operation. Feels he's entitled. Asshole then, asshole now."

"And you think now that we're together he might—"

"Let's just say I'm worried enough to bring it up."

"What the fuck do you want me to do? Send a team to take him out?"

"I think we should consider all options. National security."

"Jesus, Moakley. There's no record."

"There may be," Davidson said.

This stunned Battaglio. "How do you know?"

"If my investigator began to put things together, maybe it's time we make sure the rest of the past stays dead and buried."

PART TWO

RISK/REWARD

48

SHINDAND AIR FORCE BASE, AFGHANISTAN

TWELVE YEARS EARLIER

"Reilly!"

The shout had an unmistakable ring to it. Not so much an order, but a warning.

"Yes?" Captain Daniel J. Reilly responded from his desk, three down from where a corporal sat after putting the phone call he'd taken on hold. "What's up?"

"INSCOM, sir," the young man replied.

"Okay, I'll take it."

"Sir."

Reilly distinctly heard another warning in the corporal's tone.

"It's not a friendly call. Major Upton Williams, sir. Sounds 'meaner than a junkyard dog,'" he said quoting from the Jim Croce song.

Reilly worked for, reported and answered to INSCOM, the United States Army Intelligence and Security Command. The agency is a joint operation of the Army and the National Security Agency with the mission of collecting and disseminating intelligence to the field. Reilly was on both the receiving and delivering end. He got updates that affected battlefield decisions and provided daily updates that were evaluated at the INSCOM headquarters at Fort Belvoir, Virginia.

He had scheduled calls with command. The next was on the calendar. This was unexpected. He picked up his line. "Cpt. Reilly here."

"Reilly," Williams began without any pleasantry, "where the hell are those congressmen?"

"Sir?" Reilly replied.

"You heard me, Captain. Where the fuck are those two United States congressmen who were your responsibility?"

"Sir, they flew out to Hickam on a transport thirty-six hours ago. It's in a report I filed."

"I read your goddammed report. They stopped in Kadena AFB."

"Sure. That was their refueling stop."

"Well, Reilly, they did more than stop. They redirected to Hong Kong."

"Jesus," Reilly declared. "I had no idea."

"And that is something we'll talk about later. Your job now is to find why the hell two members of the United States Congress went AWOL. And where they are."

"Sir, they aren't military; they can set their own agenda."

"Well, their offices are on our asses. And since you presumably have intelligence, it's time to show some. Find them, Lieutenant Reilly."

"Captain, sir."

"For now."

Reilly hung up. *Jesus,* he thought. *They'd been trouble at Shindand. Bodies were going back home because of them. Now they were into God knows what in Hong Kong.*

"Corporal," he asked, "what do we have on the ground that can get me to Hong Kong?"

"Sir?"

"Immediately."

49

"Mr. Reilly—"

EJ Shaw never addressed Reilly so formally. *Son,* yes. *Daniel,* often. But never *Mr. Reilly.* "Explain exactly why we're in the middle of this?"

Right now, security wasn't as much an issue as honesty. "Multiple reasons, sir," Reilly said over his room phone. "We won the bid for the global oil conferences. In the future, we should put such decisions to the Crisis Committee and play out the possible ramifications. But there may be another factor."

"Which is?"

"A vendetta." Now he chose his words more carefully. "For Stockholm."

"I don't understand."

"The bombing."

"We weren't responsible," Shaw declared. "Insurance signed off on—"

"No, we weren't responsible, but other people may have placed blame at our doorstep."

"Is this related to what we discussed in my office?"

"Perhaps." That was the limit to how far Reilly was prepared to go. His single word response was answered with long silence.

"Dan," Shaw finally responded, "I said a year. Maybe we should revisit that time frame."

Reilly suddenly felt backed into a corner. This was his own doing. Now he had to work his way through the rest of the conversation without lying and without saying anything that could compromise him on an open line.

"Boss, there are other companies that put people up for the night. We just happen to have beds in virtually every hot spot on the planet. That makes us more vulnerable than the competition. But I believe we're also better prepared to defend against attacks."

"Recent history excepted, Dan."

There was no arguing that point. "After I get back, I'll work up a memo that reassesses our risks. Without a doubt, the threats we've been facing are different because the enemy is different. Not just a team of terrorists with a bomb-laden truck crashing into the bollards. Unknowingly, we've welcomed assassins as guests, given them rooms with a view, chocolates on their pillows, and what they want the most—opportunity. It's time to add enhanced facial recognition, run real-time background checks, and tie into as many open and closed databases as allowed." He stopped short of saying there were ways of tapping into those that aren't allowed.

"I'm confused," Shaw countered. "Based on the remains recovered at the Washington attack, the FBI is leaning toward a woman behind all the oil executive murders."

"And I think they're wrong. No disrespect for women assassins," he said lightly, "but for my money, the bomber's death was intended to throw us off and give the more dangerous killer more freedom to hunt. A game which he—and I do mean *he*—is very, very good at, and is actually having fun in the process."

WASHINGTON, D.C.

A few blocks from the White House, Tasha Samuels leaned back in her chair, shaken by the morning news that led the online editions of the *Washington Post*, *Washington Times*, and Sherwood Baker's own newspaper, *The Hill*, as well as all the local broadcast outlets.

Washington reporter, 45. Virginia parking lot. Apparent robbery. Police investigating.

The facts were the same across all platforms. Nothing was really known. No witnesses. No motive. Sherwood Baker was Moakley Davidson's inside contact at *The Hill*. Samuels had her own. She called a game-night buddy of her husband's, Reuben Estevez.

"Rube, Tasha. Got a sec?"

Estevez did. He quickly explained that everyone was confused, especially since Baker had surprisingly resigned hours before he was killed. "When you think about that, it raises all sorts of questions," he said.

"Got any answers?"

"For you or for your boss?"

"This one's for me."

"I'll keep you posted."

* * *

Moakley Davidson returned to his office swinging his briefcase. He breezed by Tasha Samuels and everyone else on his staff. Their "hellos" to the senator were dismissed with a wave of his hand. This didn't deter Samuels from following him.

He put his briefcase on his desk and began unloading the contents, but stopped short when he saw her.

"Sir, do you have a moment?"

"Not really."

"It's about Sherwood Baker. The news—"

"What about it?"

"I'm wondering what we should say if the FBI calls."

Davidson lifted his head and glared at his aide. "Why would they do that?"

"You'd just talked to him."

"I talk to hundreds of people."

"Of course, sir. But Mr. Baker was killed, and I thought—"

"What? What do you think, Ms. Samuels?" he interrupted.

The question and tone threw her. "Nothing, I just thought you might want to tell them—"

Another interruption. "I have nothing to say. He was a source. It's too bad what happened. Shit happens."

Heartless. Then again, it was nothing new.

"You have work to share?" he asked with unblinking eyes.

"In a few minutes—the daily summaries."

"And they're on your desk?"

"Yes sir."

"And your desk is not in here."

She nodded. "No sir."

"Then I suggest you go and find it."

Samuels backed away, hating her boss just a little bit more today.

That evening over dinner with her husband at Grillfish near Dupont Circle, Samuels quietly opened up about her last few days, specifically today when she talked to Senator Davidson about the reporter who was killed. "He was awful."

"I don't understand," Jamil replied.

"The reporter was a contact, a source. He leaked things to Baker. Baker gave him things in return. It was fairly well known around the office, but no one really talked about it."

"What else is new? Politicians use the press, the press uses them."

"Of course, but this felt different. He was completely dismissive. And the way he looked at me? It was ice cold and accusatory."

"About?"

She swirled her glass of wine. "About why I was even asking. Hell, the reporter's dead."

"That doesn't mean he knows anything."

"But the timing," she said. "It was right after Davidson had me do research on this guy."

"Wait, what guy? The reporter?"

"A hotel executive who had appeared before one of his senate hearings." She leaned in and whispered, "I didn't tell him everything. But what I did, got him really pissed off."

"Like what?"

"That he knew him personally."

"You said he was at a hearing."

"It was more than that. Something about the past. Something Davidson didn't want anyone to know anything about."

"Tash, I think you're all wound up. One thing doesn't have anything to do with the other."

"But if it does? And right after I gave Davidson what I had, he called the reporter."

"How many times have I told you to get out of there?" Jamil said.

"Since day one."

"And how many days has it been?"

"I lost count."

"Then do it. Tomorrow. Walk right in and give your resignation."

Resignation. It reminded Samuels of her conversation with her contact at *The Hill.* She decided not to share that with her husband.

She brought her shoulders in tight. "Not tomorrow. Soon."

* * *

Tasha and Jamil Samuels were like many D.C. couples. They both worked in the District but in distinct spheres. They weren't supposed to talk about any issues that might be deemed sensitive or secret. But like many D.C. couples, sometimes they did. In fact, when people in the know did talk to one another, things had a better chance of working. When they don't, terrible things happen, like 9/11, January 6, or further back, the Japanese attack on Pearl Harbor. Jamil Samuels didn't consider what Tasha shared as anything equal to those ignominious dates. But it stuck with him. He decided to pass along her worry and let others determine its value.

Early the next morning, Jamil met with his direct supervisor at the FBI, the associate deputy director. Above her was the executive assistant director, the associate executive assistant director, the assistant director, the deputy assistant director, and at the top, Director McCafferty.

Samuels had to identify his source to give credence to the report. But he wasn't sure if the report itself had any merit. After all, he was an IT specialist, not a field agent.

"It's probably nothing," he began.

Coming from an engineer whose job was to root out problems in an ever-worsening world of cyberattacks, employing the phrase *probably nothing* was like waving a red flag in the Indianapolis 500. It gets attention.

Associate Deputy Director Rachel Richardson peered over her reading glasses, prompting Samuels to continue.

"It's not an IT issue. My wife is very disturbed by the death of *The Hill* reporter."

"So?"

"Her boss used him to leak stories. They talked often, right up until the day before he was killed."

"That's not unusual. They all have their sources. The place leaks like a sieve." She closed her eyes ready to dismiss him. "Jamil—"

"Director Richardson, my wife is worried. And I feel she's scared. She thinks it may have had something to do with the research she'd been asked to do."

"What kind of research?" the Deputy Director asked sharply.

"A man. Someone who apparently had a run in with Davidson years ago when he was a congressman."

"Apparently?"

"I don't know. That's what she said. But it's someone he's suddenly concerned about. She dug into it. A friend at the Pentagon helped. *Apparently*—"

"There's that word again," Richardson said.

"I'm sorry. From what Tasha said, the Pentagon file is sealed. But the little she got was enough to rile up Davidson and dismiss her. Right after, she heard him call the reporter. And now—"

"Jamil, it's what goes on 24/7. Political ass-covering. It's an applied science on the Hill."

"But it doesn't always end up with a reporter dead in the middle of the night at a deserted parking lot right after resigning."

Richardson tilted her head and thought. "You said she was checking on some guy. Who?"

"A former Army officer. He works for a hotel company now, even testified a year ago in a Davidson intelligence hearing. His name is Reilly, Dan Reilly."

The name didn't mean anything to Richardson, but it put her at a crossroad that many law enforcement officers approached. Consider or ignore. *Consider* meant more work. Higher level conversations and paperwork. *Ignore*, the easier road to go down, begins with *Thank you* and a dismissal to get back to work. Everything Jamil Samuels had brought to her attention in the past had bolstered cyber defenses within the Bureau and led to effective counterintelligence reprisals; all secret; all handled by other visible and invisible agencies within the intelligence community. His reputation was solid.

Richardson made a decision. "Tell me more about your wife's research."

"I want to keep her out of this if possible," Jamil replied. "Given her job, her relationship to—"

"Let's just see what there is to all of this before the bureau makes any promises."

Jamil Samuels understood and shared what remembered. When he finished, Rachel Richardson called the executive assistant director. Two hours later it hit Director McCafferty's desk. McCafferty phoned Elizabeth Matthews across town. The name Dan Reilly was one they both knew for a whole variety of reasons.

50

The ring on the phone threw Reilly. It wasn't his regular sound, and it didn't come from his regular phone. It hit him on the fourth ring. It took another three rings before he turned on the nightlight. No one to reach over. He had decided to take it slow with Yibing. If she was disappointed, she hadn't shown it.

Reilly recovered the secure sat phone and answered. He offered a tired, tentative "Hello."

"Hello," came a distinctive woman's response. "Sounds like I woke you this time."

"Yup. What's the latest?" he asked.

"Nothing new on the bombing. But I have a heads up for you," Elizabeth Matthews said.

"Oh?"

Matthews cleared her throat. It wasn't just important. It was awkward, uncomfortable. Better to be discussed in person, not a half a world away.

"Your name has come up tangentially in regard to a case the FBI is beginning to look into."

"Not again," Reilly replied.

"Different this time. Not related to your report on the infrastructure."

"Then what?"

"There was a murder in Virginia. A reporter, Sherwood Baker."

"Never heard of him."

"No reason to. He wrote for *The Hill*. But he was a source for Senator Moakley Davidson."

"All right, stop," Reilly said. "This is getting weird."

"Why?"

"Because I got a call from a staffer of Davidson's the other day."

"Was her name Tasha Samuels?"

Reilly paused. The conversation with Samuels came back to him. "Yes."

"Well, at least you've confirmed one part of the story."

Reilly remembered more of the phone call. *The woman said she was doing research which led to him. No,* he thought. *She didn't say research, she said she was doing some serious digging on him for Moakley Davidson. She mentioned Shindand Air Base and the congressional visit. She had the approximate date. And she asked, "What happened there?"*

"Elizabeth, what's this got to do with the reporter's death?"

"Maybe nothing. Then again, is there anything you can tell me?"

Reilly remembered hanging up on Samuels, now realizing he should have tried to learn more.

"Dan?" Matthews said through the silence. "Anything—"

"Not on an open line."

* * *

Reilly found Lenczycki in the hotel bar, nursing a scotch and watching a soccer game on an international sports channel. He took the open seat next to him. "Who's playing?"

"Barcelona and Milan."

"Got a favorite?"

"Since I don't know anything about either, I'm rooting for the food. Going with the Italians."

Just then Milan scored.

"Eh," the former CIA officer sighed. "Wanna join me?"

"Rather take a walk."

Reilly didn't need to explain. Lenczycki understood. Reilly needed another conversation without nearby ears or microphones.

Reilly signed the bill and they left, walking briskly away from crowds.

"Need your help, Skip."

Lenczycki automatically scanned for anyone nearby. In one of the world's most crowded cities, they were alone. Without looking directly at Reilly, he said, "At your service. What do you need?"

"What you do."

"This isn't the easiest city for me to do that."

"I know," Reilly replied, also avoiding eye contact.

"Any hints?"

"I've got someone back home very curious about me. Apparently, memory kicked in about an incident that he would prefer I forget. And if there's one person, there's likely two who might view me as a long-term liability."

"And these people have the means to make that happen?"

"Means, yes. Desire, I can't say. I've just been warned."

"Any idea what jogged their memory?"

"I'm afraid I do."

51

HONG KONG

TWELVE YEARS EARLIER

Second-term Congressman Ryan Battaglio's plane touched down in Hong Kong. After Afghanistan he was grateful to be alive. He blamed Army Intelligence and a few grunts for the fuck-up; certainly not himself or his colleague Moakley Davidson. Now both would put the experience behind them, forget the explosions, the gunshots, and their heart-pounding fear. He didn't remember if he had screamed. No, he couldn't have—not Ryan Battaglio, not the rising politico and go-to cable news soundbite star. He was the brave one. It had to be Moakley. *Definitely Moakley. Moakley Davidson was the screamer.* But now in Hong Kong, and on a trip over to Macau, he'd be the screamer—for a whole other reason.

"We're going to have a good time. No handlers, nobody watching, three days off the grid."

The plan was hatched over beers at the base in Shindand before they went out to visit the tribal chief. "We'll take the transport to Hong Kong and disappear for a few nights in Macau. Gambling, five-star dining, checking out the sites—assuming we ever got out of our bedrooms," Battaglio schemed.

Now off the plane, they ferried across the harbor; a sixty-minute voyage, past expensive new leisure crafts and decades-old Chinese junks. From present to past and back again. Onshore they picked up a cab for the short drive to the Macau Venetian Resort. The luxury hotel is the twin of the Las Vegas destination, but bigger, far bigger. Thirty-nine stories, three thousand rooms. It's the largest hotel in Asia and, by floor area—10,500,000 square feet—the seventh-largest building in the world. But it was full for the night and without invoking their actual identities, they had to move on. Finding an acceptable backup they checked in, agreed to meet in the casino for a few hours of gambling, and then find more fun.

Davidson's game was poker. Battaglio played blackjack. He was good in Atlantic City, his hometown. But here, the cards came so fast he couldn't keep up with the dealer. So after losing the equivalent of $300, Battaglio caught up with Davidson and told him that he was going for a walk and would see him later.

Later wouldn't be for another three days.

* * *

Reilly landed at Hong Kong International Airport hours later. The Air Force transport taxied to the private jet charter terminal. Inside he phoned command.

"Your job is to find them," Major Upton Williams said. "They went AWOL, missed their flight out of Hong Kong. They called their congressional staffs and explained that after their harrowing experience in Afghanistan they called an audible and decided to take some R&R. Beyond that, we've got nothing but two missing members of Congress. So, soldier," Williams demanded, "where would you take off to if you went to Hong Kong?"

"I am in Hong Kong, sir. And if I were them, I'd hop a ferry to Macau and not let anyone know who I am."

"Well then, you do the same. Make yourself invisible, son, and get these misbehaving sons of bitches back home."

Reilly changed in an airport bathroom. His uniform went into his suitcase, civvies came out. He asked for the fastest way to Macau, faster than waiting for a ferry.

"Charter helicopter," the twenty-three-year old generically uniformed attendant replied. "But by the time you book it, you'd probably be there by ferry." She checked a schedule. "The next one leaves in twenty minutes, direct from Skypier, arriving in Macau outer harbor about an hour later. We can shuttle you there."

On the way over, Reilly figured that any member of the United States Congress eager for anonymity would have enough pull to keep their names off the books at Macau's big hotels. Cash would do nicely at the desk. After all, cash bought all sorts of things out in the open and even more in the shadows.

Reilly concluded that Battaglio and Davidson would go large: extravagant, opulent, full service. That immediately narrowed the possibilities down to the Morpheus, the Ritz Carlton, the St. Regis, the Venetian Macao, Sofitel, Sheraton, MGM, Grand Hyatt, Marriott, and the Four Seasons. *Where to start?*

Battaglio hit Reilly as a showboat. Davidson seemed to be the also-ran of the duo, a self-aggrandizing bloviate. *God bless America. Quite a pair.*

He hit the Westin first. Reilly didn't expect they'd be using their own names, so he showed photographs to the staff at check-in, the bartenders, and hostesses with a tip, obvious to the touch, underneath the pictures. Nothing. The same with the concierge. He waited in the lobby, strolled through the casinos including the high-roller rooms, and hung out across the street at the park. If he really thought about the numbers, the odds were against him. Macau is the gambling capital of the world, with the highest-grossing gaming revenue anywhere. Gambling, legal in the city since the mid-1800s when Macau was under Portuguese rule, accounts for more than 50 percent of its economy. With nearly fifty casinos within the 12.7 square miles, Reilly could have been looking for a needle in a haystack. But he stuck with his plan: brand names, big hotels along Cotai Strip, which linked the islands of Coloane and Taipa.

He went from one property to another, speeding up the process as he ran out of cash. Each search produced nothing. He may have figured wrong. *What if they went for less ritzy hotels?*

Reilly realized that the more places he'd show up, the more likely he'd earn serious attention from Chinese authorities. That wouldn't be good. The idea was to locate the two congressmen and get them out as fast as possible, without embarrassment.

After having no luck with five hotels, Reilly went with another option. He had the name and number of a man known to Army intelligence for his side business, leftover from the Portuguese rule and still very profitable. The man had the resources to do his leg work, make the calls, and find out what bed or beds Battaglio and Davidson might be in.

The man was available to him only by phone. The information would cost money and possibly a favor at a later date. He'd heard that other intelligence officers had tracked down soldiers who'd gone AWOL in Macau through this resource. Now it was his best bet in the Las Vegas of Asia.

"Mr. Ey Wing Li, please," Reilly said from a phone in the Grand Hyatt.

"He's not in," an Asian male voice curtly said.

"Please tell Mr. Wing Li that his rich uncle is calling. I'm visiting from Washington."

There was a pause and then a request to hold. It lasted for two minutes. "I'll put you through now."

"You have one minute, I suggest you don't wait a second," said the gruff voice on the other end of the line.

Reilly had heard serious prompts before. From generals, from Secret Service agents, from dignitaries, and from neighborhood bullies. But no one ever sounded as formidable as Ey Wing Li. He was business tough, gangster tough.

Ey Wing Li was, for lack of a better word, a fixer. He fixed things for the Wu family—the William Wu family, to be specific. A family not to be crossed. A family that had a long memory.

The Wu's owned five hotels in Hong Kong and three in Macau.

They kept a tight grip on their holdings, which included young women in their employ from the mainland and Vietnam. Ey Wing Li was the man who took care of things openly and in dark alleys—with words and, when words weren't enough, with other means at his disposal. Reilly assumed that the Chinese Secret Police looked the other way when Wing Li was in the disposal business. And for that favor he likely shared information that might be of interest to the government.

Reilly considered it risky to contact Ey Wing Li directly, but he needed help.

"I'm looking for two prominent Americans, Mr. Wing Li. They departed from their established itinerary after visiting a military base where I serve. We've tracked them to Macau, but once here, they've slipped through the cracks. Maybe they're taking in a show or two, or a spending a few nights at the tables. Maybe, but unlikely. I think there's also the possibility they had other plans that might bring them into your line of business. I thought you might be able to use your resources. Given all that Macau has to offer," Reilly chose his next words carefully, "perhaps there's the chance your associates may have spent some time with one or both of them. Though you and I have never spoken before, I have been told that you have helped others in my situation." He dropped his voice wrapping up his pitch. "I can assure you your assistance will be rewarded."

Reilly paused. He felt he had ten or fifteen seconds left, but he'd laid out his offer; everything but the money.

After silence filled out his minute Reilly heard a deep chuckle.

"Well, I'd say you have a problem. Congressmen?"

"Yes."

"Two of them?"

"Two."

"Checked in under assumed names."

"Most likely."

Another throaty chuckle. "You really do have a problem."

"The reason for my call, Mr. Wing Li."

"I didn't get their names."

"I didn't give them to you."

"How do you expect me to find them?" the Chinese asked.

"I understand you have the means."

Wing Li laughed harder, "I do indeed. Let me see what I can come up with. Tell your rich uncle that I appreciate his business."

"I will," Reilly replied.

"Good. Call back at 6 p.m. Don't make any dinner plans."

The line went dead before Captain Reilly, United States Army, could say, "Thank you."

Precisely at 6 p.m. from his modest room at the Metropole, Reilly phoned again as instructed.

"I was asked to call Mr. Wing Li regarding dinner." Again, he didn't volunteer his name.

"Write this down," the receptionist, assistant, or whoever answered the phone said.

"Ready."

"At 2000 hours go outside, turn right and walk."

"I'm staying at—"

The line went dead, and Reilly suddenly had a very bad feeling.

With two hours to spare, he showered, changed, and put his feet up to rest. At 7:50, he took the elevator down, hitting the street precisely on time. He turned right on *da Avenida dos Jogos da Ásia Oriental* and began walking. With no further instructions, he continued. He hadn't given the name of his hotel, but apparently Wing Li had the wherewithal to find him. And if he could locate him, he'd probably be able to track down two partying Americans.

The thought evaporated as Reilly cocked his ears to the sound of a slow-moving vehicle behind him. He didn't stop to look; instead he picked up his pace. The car did the same. He dared a quick glance to the left as if he was going to cross the street. A black van was definitely following him. Reilly calculated his options. Duck into a storefront, run, or stand his ground. Circumstances suddenly removed those options.

The vehicle sped up, screeched to a stop. The side door slid open beside Reilly.

"Get in, Mr. Reilly." The voice was insistent. The accent pronounced. "Mr. Wing Li is waiting."

Reilly stood. "Tell me where to meet him. I'll take a cab."

"We'll save you the money."

"I'd rather—"

"He's waiting. He doesn't like being kept waiting."

Reilly stepped forward, considering how much he disliked Davidson and Battaglio.

Beyond the initial order to get in, Wing Li's men remained silent. But the fact that he wasn't hooded told him the destination was likely public. He also suspected this was Wing Li's way to guarantee no U.S. Army or government operatives would get there first—wherever *there* was.

Twelve minutes later he found out as the van pulled up to the Macallan Whisky Bar & Lounge on Macao Estrada da Baia de Nossa Senhora da Esperanca.

"Go. Tell the girl in front to seat you at Mr. Wing Li's regular table. Then wait."

He exited the van without another word. Inside, he identified himself to a beautiful young woman who spoke perfect English.

"Yes, Captain Reilly. You are the first in your party."

Party. Reilly thought it had so many meanings. Friendly and dangerous, and in Macau and other cities around the world, sexual by the hour.

He was led to a corner seat in the back of the stylish bar. It left the out-facing position, which he would have preferred, for Wing Li.

Two minutes later, three huge men entered. One remained at the door, the other walked half the distance to Reilly. The third thundered through the bar. Reilly saw him and stood. Ey Wing Li was everything his voice suggested. WWE solid, muscles bulging, a block of a man.

"Captain Reilly," he said. Simultaneously he snapped his fingers over his shoulder to an unseen bartender.

"Mr. Wing Li, thank you for your willingness to meet."

"I like to see who I'm working with. Please sit."

Reilly had been careful not to give his name. Wing Li had it anyway. It required the natural follow-up.

"I suppose I shouldn't be surprised that you know who I am."

"It's my business to remain informed. Although intelligence is a noun, I consider it an active verb. Given your military assignment, I suspect you do as well. That's what brings us together."

"You're right, Mr. Wing Li," Reilly replied nodding. For an enforcer and possibly a sex trafficker, he actually found Ey Wing Li quite likeable.

"My friends call me Sammy." He laughed broadly. "We shall see how this goes, Captain. But first we shall enjoy some pours. You'll forgive me if I don't treat you to the thirty-year Macallan. A bottle goes for 1500 US. Macallan 18 should be fine. Unless, of course, you want me to add it to the fee."

"I'm fine with 18," Reilly said just as two preordered Macallan-etched glasses appeared.

Their conversation covered multiple topics over the first pour. Best universities in America. This question was all about where Wing Li's high-school age daughter should apply. Wing Li's newest investment position, Bitcoins. America's prolonged engagement in Afghanistan. Whether the British monarchy would last another generation; and the 1990 art theft from the Isabella Stewart Gardner Museum in Boston. On that last topic, Reilly thought Wing Li might actually know the whereabouts of some of the thirteen stolen masterpieces. But he surely didn't ask.

Reilly did his best to contribute as they moved onto their second glass, but it was evident that Wing Li was adept at holding court.

"Well now, to your problem," the Chinese said. His tone changed. His eyes narrowed. "I have located the hotel where the men you seek have stayed."

Reilly was aghast.

"Of course, you're wondering why I waited to tell you."

"It is front of mind."

"First I must understand who I am dealing with. Someone whose motives are questionable, or someone worth helping. A user, a taker, or a man I can trust. I have studied you as we spoke to understand the man who lives behind his inquiring eyes. However, as much as I have faith in my own observations, I had you checked out. Not difficult considering my sources." He laughed. "Please don't ask how."

Reilly didn't.

"I learned your name and rank, your service record, your degrees from Boston University and Harvard. And though your training is somewhat obscured, certain individuals have assured me that you are an honorable man. More honorable than the two you seek, despite the elected offices they hold."

Reilly said nothing. Nothing was needed. Wing Li was in a talking mood.

"I said I located their hotel. That is only partially true. They checked into the Lisboa Hotel. Your Congressman Davidson has eaten well, gambled, lost a little, won a lot, and generally behaved himself. That is to say, he took advantage of some of the extras, and though not a perfect gentleman, he performed well, paid without arguing, and tipped appropriately. At this moment he is sleeping at the hotel. My men are at his door. They will wake him in six hours and accompany him to a safe house. He will be frightened and embarrassed enough to comply. Congressman Battaglio is another matter. He was seen leaving the hotel with an escort. Neither he, nor the young woman, has returned. I find that troubling."

Reilly's nostrils flared. "Christ!"

Ey Wing Li anticipated the response. "We will find him, Captain. Or at least we better before my friends in Guoanbu do."

Reilly knew the organization by its more formal name, MSS or Ministry of State Security—China's secret police.

"Captain Reilly, Mr. Battaglio's behavior is most disturbing. Beyond the level of acceptable," he laughed, "even by my standards."

"I understand. How can I help?"

"Nothing yet. But once we have Mr. Battaglio, we will make sure he is cleaned up and presentable. We'll escort them to Hong Kong airport. You should have assignees accept delivery. It will be best if they do not engage them in any conversation. Discretion matters in circumstances like this. Don't you agree, Captain Reilly?"

"I do."

"It will be best that they never return."

"I will pass that along. Do you have any idea where Mr. Battaglio might be?"

"Given what he's interested in, it comes down to 40,000 Macau hotel rooms. Rest assured, we have ways. We'll come up with him hopefully before he gets himself into any trouble."

The we, Reilly reasoned was the Wu Family and all the places their tentacles reached through the city.

"Now is there anything else I can do for you tonight? Perhaps you'd like—"

Reilly laughed, suspecting what he was offering. "No, Mr. Wing Li. Thank you nonetheless, but no."

"Are you sure?" Wing Li proceeded to offer Reilly the opportunity to "test drive" some of the women in the Wu stable. He considered it an honorable, age-old profession.

Reilly argued with the term honorable. *Women had been kidnapped and brought in from small Chinese towns. How honorable a life do they have? When does their usefulness end?*

"Captain, forgive me if I've offended."

"No offense taken."

The evening ended with a handshake and a promise. "I have a feeling this will not be our last conversation, Daniel. You can expect my call."

52

Later, two of the highest level government officials walked along the Washington Mall accompanied by armed staff ahead, behind, and to either side. Unseen, other agents of the FBI and the members of the Diplomatic Security Service covered them from a wider perimeter.

"It's a bit off the wall, Elizabeth," FBI Director Reese McCafferty said.

The Secretary of State lazily watched the passersby as if she were simply having a casual stroll with a friend. This friend was more focused on her.

"We got a tip. We're quietly looking into it."

"Involving my department?"

"No," McCafferty replied.

She looked straight ahead and kept walking. No immediate need to turn the conversation into a Q&A. McCafferty had come to talk, or perhaps to warn her.

"First, this remains confidential."

"No one listens to me these days."

"They will. We have an anonymous source who must remain anonymous. But this individual ..." He said neither male nor female, which suggested the source was female, "works on the Hill and is worried that research dug up for a member of Congress may have contributed to the death of Sherwood Baker. Like I said, it's probably unrelated, but this particular person's spouse works in the Bureau, so right now we're treating it like family."

Matthews didn't connect the dots yet. An anonymous tipster. A member of Congress. That narrowed it down to 100 Senators, 435 voting members of the House of Representatives, and five non-voting delegates, plus one commissioner. Five-hundred-forty one with no hints. Each had staff.

"What's the woman sharing?"

"I didn't say woman."

"You did in a manner of speaking."

"I really can't confirm," McCafferty said.

"I understand, but what did she say?"

* * *

BEIJING

Matthieu Lefebvre smiled to the doorman and nodded to the three Chinese military guards and their bomb-sniffing dogs as he reentered the Kensington Hotel.

"Nice walk today?"

"Yes, thank you," Lefebvre said with a heavy accent. The seventy-three-year-old Frenchman had been conducting self-guided walking tours through Beijing's streets for two days. He photographed the typical historical sites and often went off the beaten path, taking pictures of street vendors and old Chinese women rocking in chairs, looking out of their apartment windows the way generations before them had.

Matthieu Lefebvre was a primary school teacher who had retired in Moustiers-Sainte-Marie, France, a tiny mountain town frozen in time in the Provence-Alpes-Côte d'Azur region of southeastern France. Since he traveled a great deal, he had no real friends there, but neighbors and shop keepers could vouch for him.

Lefebvre liked to relax in the hotel bar after his walks and look through the day's photographs. He always sat alone at a table, sipped a 2020 Fonseca port and smiled at other guests, but rarely talked to them. He was like thousands of other tourists who visited Beijing on their own with one exception. The places he visited and the streets that he walked were the same places and streets where Haoran Shih, an expatriate Chinese, was likely to go on his time off from his oil conference.

Lefebvre knew because Facebook had told him. So had Instagram postings. So much was public—his actual footprints and all those that were digital.

Shih was a vice-president of BP Canada, headquartered in Calgary. Senior, respected, knowledgeable. He was known as a shrewd dealmaker and brilliant strategist. His family had emigrated from Beijing to Toronto when he was six. He eventually moved to Calgary, where he'd been working for nine years. Company business brought him to China at least one a year. Each time he conducted his own personal pilgrimage to his family's roots, walking where they walked, eating where they ate, and looking at the timeless things they saw.

Hotel security teams were making no effort to remain concealed at the hotel. They openly patrolled the lobby, required room keys, studied faces against picture IDs at the elevators, and examined guests' passports at check-in. Uniformed military carried QBZ-95/Type-95 automatic rifles, variants of the Russian designed AK-47. Chinese Secret Police were no less secret. They all seemed cut from the same mold—tall, rock-hard chiseled bodies, constantly roving cold eyes, and hands never more than two inches from their service pistols under their tailored jacket flaps.

And there was another level of security—Haoran Shih's own detail. Two rotating teams, one always walking with him, the other behind. They watched him while he ate, guarded his suite from the hall, and stood vigil outside his bedroom door while he slept.

The routine was repeated by every other delegate at the final regional conference. But Matthieu Lefebvre was only interested in Shih.

Lefebvre was in no rush. Shih was going to be tied to his meetings for the next three days. The hotel was locked down. Everyone with a badge was waiting for him. Yet here he was, watching Haoran Shih walk across the lobby, security in tow. An easy target. Not such an easy escape. But this wasn't where he would act.

There was one other thing that Lefebvre would do to ensure that everything would go according to plan. His and no one else's. That was his rule. Nicolai Gorshkov never challenged him on it.

* * *

"Elizabeth," McCafferty said, "you know what they say about a butterfly flapping its wings and affecting the weather halfway around the world?"

"It's a metaphor."

"Often quoted."

"Reese, to the point. Am I the subject of an inquiry?"

"Not an inquiry and not you. A butterfly flapping its wings in Beijing. She was researching—"

"I know," she admitted. "Reilly. He knows, too."

* * *

Reilly joined representatives of all the security forces in the Zhou boardroom. The area had been declared safe after an electronic sweep for listening devices and dogs sniffing for bombs. They sat down to discuss the preparation surrounded by classical artwork on the walls depicting the Zhou dynasty, China's longest-lasting empire, and its eight centuries of achievement. Individual pieces celebrated the codification of writing, advances in coinage and monetary systems, and the birth of Confucianism, Taoism, and Mohism.

There were paintings of the greatest Chinese poets and philosophers, Confucius and Tao Qian, among them, and the great military strategist Sun-Tzu, whose *The Art of War* remains a manual at war colleges around the world. Reilly had studied Sun-Tzu at Fort Huachuca, Arizona. He'd taken many of the lessons from the Army to the private sector. One principle, "To know your enemy, you must become your enemy." He used this conducting international business negotiations and even maneuvering through internal politics. Another of Sun-Tzu's tenets especially resonated as he tried to outthink the assassin: "Strategy without tactics is the slowest route to victory. Tactics without strategy is the noise before defeat."

What's the killer's strategy? And what are his tactics?

Strategy was easier—infiltrate, kill, exfiltrate. His tactics were evident by now—blend in, use disguises, and create opportunity.

In a very short time Reilly had developed respect for the assassin. He didn't consider him to be an ideologue. Not like the assassin he fought in Brussels. Not indoctrinated like the sleeper spy who enticed him to bed. Not like the apolitical terrorists who used his State Department blueprint to bomb America's bridges and tunnels.

This time Reilly felt he was dealing with an artist. An actor. A chameleon. A killer who enjoyed his work and viewed each death as a creative challenge; never repeating himself. He was trained by someone's military, fluent in multiple languages, adept at makeup. That would have meant he likely had high school or college work in theater. So, each assignment was a role to play.

But thinking back on London and Nairobi there was another factor. The assassin took sheer delight in gamesmanship.

"We need to cancel," Reilly told Colonel Zhang.

"Not an acceptable solution," the Chinese colonel replied. "My orders are to capture and question. Oil is vital to our economy. Whoever is trying to manipulate the market must be stopped. I've been charged with stopping him."

"And if he succeeds, you fail?"

"It will be all our failures."

The conversation got no better over the next hour.

* * *

The Beijing Oil Conference convened. Visible security on every floor and with each of the delegates took some worry away. Some, not all. There were so many ways to make trouble. A drone attack through a picture window, an explosive device planted in a suite by a prior guest, a rocket fired from another high-rise.

Reilly concluded that it was impossible to defend against every kind of attack. Based on the previous conference assassinations, if and when another came, it would be attempted from the inside and in person. Poison laced in a delicious appetizer, a brush-by and pinprick with a deadly toxin, or another twenty ways he could detail. All relatively quick and easy. The fact of the matter was he didn't know. Zhang didn't know. Only the killer knew, and he could very well be checked in right next door.

* * *

Matthieu Lefebvre boarded the elevator up to the rooftop bar. It offered a great view of old and new Beijing. A city of more than 21 million. A business capital where communism and capitalism converged. Where people are free to walk anywhere, but not free to roam everywhere on the internet. A leading center for science, technology, education, research, and culture. Beijing is one of the oldest cities in the world, but its modern industries also make it one of the globe's most polluted.

Metropolitan Beijing also has the longest and busiest urban subway system in the world. Yet even though it's monitored with thousands of cameras, a skilled magician could disappear in plain sight. That's what Matthieu Lefebvre, a Frenchman only for a few more days, had planned. But at this moment he was content to relax, have a cocktail and a selection of dim sum appetizers, and watch the oil executive from Canada three tables away. His habit was to drink through the sunset, tonight hardly visible through the smog.

Twenty-three floors below the rooftop deck, Reilly was back to staring at the wall of photographs in his suite with Yibing and Skip Lenczycki, and back to the question still unanswered. "What are the common denominators?" he asked.

"All high-level executives," Yibing offered.

"What else?"

She spread out the twelve executive bios on Reilly's dining room table. "Okay, it's easy to get lost in ink. So we're going to read these aloud, one at a time." Cheng passed them out; each of them with four. "Listen for anything special that jumps out—education, age, past jobs. Anything that might trigger a commonality with either the mission or the other victims."

One-by-one they read. One-by-one nothing came up.

"Nice try," the former CIA operative said. "Now what?"

At a loss for what to do next, they sat on the couch, looking straight ahead at the dozen names and photographs opposite them. Ten minutes. Twenty minutes. Reilly seemed focused on one particular headshot. He stood and walked to the photo and studied the image, then returned to the table and highlighted the potential victims' names.

"What?" Cheng tilted her head, inquisitively.

"The assassin likes games. He can't just murder. He has to find the fun in it, the sport. Killing is the easy part. He's a pro. Probably easily bored at this point. So he finds a way to entertain himself. London cameras lost him when he ducked into the theater presenting *The Mousetrap*. He killed over a chess game. And there's something else that's gnawing at me. Can't put my finger on it yet." He slammed his right fist into his left palm. "Dammit!"

"Take your time, Dan."

"It's not there. But my point is, if we can spot anything that looks, seems, sounds, or smells like a game or amusement, we might ID the killer."

"You think like a policeman," Cheng noted.

"Just trying to think out of the box."

"Why do I feel like there's more than what meets the eye?" She held her gaze. "Could be because of the woman we have in common."

Reilly shrugged off the comment. "Hey, back to work. We're not trying to figure out my identity."

"Right, but one other question. If we figure out the target, what are you going to do?" She paused a beat. "No, what are you capable of doing?"

"If that happens, and I hope it does, Colonel Zhang better be there."

They broke for the evening. Reilly offered to take everyone to dinner. Lenczycki declined. "Thanks, but dinner and a movie in my room."

Reilly smiled. "Right." He actually thought the last thing Lenczycki would do was retire to his room. More likely, he'd do what he'd done in Europe, what Bob Heath asked him to do in Beijing—keep an eye on him. He was probably somewhere nearby when he had dinner with Sammy, his old acquaintance from Macau.

"Dr. Cheng? What about you?" Reilly asked.

"Sure. Give me a few minutes."

*   *   *

As Reilly sat at one of the hotel bars, a memory engulfed him from years back. Two congressmen. A pair he had long thought had only been a nuisance. A pair who had risen in the American political system, men who—

Before he completed the thought, Yibing casually stepped up to Reilly. She watched him circle the rim of his tumbler with his finger.

"Lost in thought?" she asked.

Reilly looked to his right, amazed that he had been so preoccupied that he hadn't seen her slip in. "Sorry. Yes. Processing some things."

He now fully focused on her. Yi, he liked the sound of that, wore a black cocktail dress and a red silk blouse with a freshwater pearl necklace. Striking. Beautiful.

"This was your idea. When do you plan on arriving?" she joked.

"I'm here."

"I don't know, you were pretty far away."

"You're right. Try twelve years."

"Some hot *femme fatale* who still haunts you?"

"Not a woman. But it's a nightmare, and it's not going to go away unless—" He went silent and returned to the place twelve years ago—to Macau.

Yi caught the bartender's attention and ordered a Vesper, a drink that originated in the Bond book *Casino Royale*, then became the real thing—a mixture of gin, vodka and dry vermouth or *Lillet Blanc*.

This brought Reilly back to the present and the striking beauty beside him. "Guess what?"

"What?" she asked.

"I'm off the plane now, out of the cab, and I've unpacked the old baggage I brought to the bar. I'm happy to be here with you, Dr. Cheng."

"Well then, Mr. Reilly. Let's make a night of it."

What started at the lobby bar continued on the rooftop deck before sunset with another round and appetizers. Electricity was passing between them. They were both thinking the same thing but hadn't yet verbalized their intentions. When the waitress asked if they'd like anything else, Yibing volunteered, "Yes, we'll have the oysters."

They sat side-by-side. They quietly saw the sun go down along with twenty other couples and a few lone souls. Reilly recognized the British Petroleum executive from Canada and his security. The others included an older man reading a thin paperback with what looked like Galileo on the cover, some single women, possibly working girls, and Zhang's men patrolling with their weapons.

It was hard for Reilly to leave work behind, but when Yi smiled all other thoughts disappeared. They joked and talked about growing up. They swapped stories about their pasts. Reilly shared some of his more recent experiences: how important it was to understand local culture in managing his operations. How he negotiated with a Mexican cartel after a hurricane to get his guests to safety. How he had discovered a bomb in a Brussels hotel florist shop cooler. How he had stolen a bus in Kyiv to get seventy people to a remote airport.

"All part of a normal day's work?" she asked.

"Thankfully not every day."

"What kind of training prepares you for all this?"

"A graduate degree in life," Reilly noted. "Management classes helped, but only up to a point. They didn't cover real-world experiences in a danger-filled world. My military training filled more in. But I've had to figure out most of it along the way. Hell, maybe I'll write my own business book someday."

Reilly asked Yi if she'd ever been in any harrowing situations. Some of this was to read her expressions and probe her background. These days, people he came in contact with were increasingly more than they appeared. He really hoped Yibing Cheng was the real article.

"I've pretty well lived life with my head in my books or facing the computer screen. Kind of nerdy but compared to you, safe and comfortable. I get to think the unthinkable. You get to experience it. Exciting."

"I could do for a little less excitement."

"Well, this is the closest I've ever come to any real adventure."

That brought them back to work.

Yi asked, "Any clue to what you were trying to put together before?"

"Nothing. It's a word. It's a name. I just don't know."

"It'll come to you."

"I wish." Then he thought. "Wait! What did you ask me?"

"What do you mean?"

"What did you ask me a moment ago?'

"Anything come to you?"

"No. The exact words."

She thought. "Any clue to what you were—"

"Clue!"

"Right, any clue."

Reilly leaned across the table and kissed Yi on the lips. A soft kiss. A thank you.

"That was nice. Mind telling me what the kiss was for?"

"Mr. Green."

"And that means?"

"Green. In German, Grün. Grün was the name of the assassin used in London."

"Which means?"

"Grün, Green. You gave it to me when you said 'clue.' Like in the board game. Mr. Green. It works right in with the assassin's signature. He's so confident he's willing to play games. It's probably going to show up on more murders than just what we're dealing with. But right now,

I'm only interested in one that hasn't happened."

Yi slipped her bare foot out of her heels, inched her toes across the floor, found Reilly's right foot and gently caressed it. More electricity flowed. Reilly let out a little low hum. She smiled.

"You realize there are games we can play, too," she offered seductively.

* * *

First a stop in the general manager's office. Yibing hoped it would be quick.

Reilly told Yong Tong to check the reservations of guests that had the names White, Green, Plum, and Scarlet. Then he added Mario from Mario Bros., Perseus from *Call of Duty*.

"Translate them into French, English, Italian, Russian, German, Japanese, and Chinese."

"I don't understand, Mr. Reilly," Tong said, oblivious to what else was going on.

"Probably nothing, but maybe the assassin is getting too full of himself and we can nail him by his ego. I also want to know anyone who's playing chess, mahjong, video games, or board games."

"Okay, it'll take a while. I can't do this on my own."

"Put as many people on it as necessary. Maybe we'll get lucky."

Yi laughed a little too loudly at the remark. Reilly realized what he'd said and flashed Yi an embarrassed look. As soon as they were out the door they laughed, hooked arms, and headed for the elevator bank all the more excited.

Reilly pressed the button. Anticipation turned every second into a minute. Finally the door opened and they entered, ready to be alone.

"Pardon, monsieur, mademoiselle," said an older Frenchman sticking his arm in as the doors were about to close. He stepped in. *"Merci."*

He was slightly out of breath, especially from wearing a KN95 face-mask. He had a backpack over one shoulder and held a shopping bag in another. Reilly had seen him coming and going. Slow and hunched. Indistinctive, bland, and grey.

"Of course," Yi said.

Reilly asked, "What floor?"

"Rooftop. An aperitif before bed. What you call a nightcap?"

Reilly pressed the button. The elevator started up.

"You look like a happy couple." His accent was completely understandable.

Yi glanced at Dan and smiled. "We're associates."

"Ah, *excusez-moi.* An old man's eyes."

"That's okay." Reilly smiled and studied the Frenchman. *His eyes.* They seemed younger than his look and colder than his demeanor.

"Our floor, Dan?"

Reilly snapped back. He'd pressed the Frenchman's floor, not his. Now they were past it.

"We'll catch it on the way down."

Silence.

Reilly traded another look. The passenger smiled and while humming lightly brought his shopping bag up to chest level and rummaged through papers and wrapping. He appeared to settle on something and raised his arm slightly. Reilly stiffened. She read his alert and reached for his hand. He withdrew it. She frowned, turned to the man, then back to Reilly, who appeared ready to coil and strike—at someone forty years older.

"Care for a Chinese almond cookie?" the man said.

"Ah, no thank you," Yi said politely.

"You, monsieur?"

Reilly shook his head and said nothing.

"Then I shall enjoy them all and exercise them off."

"Excuse me for asking," Reilly said, "but I work with the hotel. Is there anything I can help you with, Monsieur—?"

"*Je suis Lefebvre.* That's kind of you, but no."

Now Lefebvre turned the question around. "Mister—?

"Reilly."

"Very good, Mr. Reilly. I shall remember, perhaps another time."

Reilly nodded. And with no more questions they stood in silence until they got to the top.

The door opened; Lefebvre left. With a wave over his shoulder he said, "*Au revoir.*"

As they descended, Yibing asked, "What was all that about?"

"I don't know. I think I'm all wound up."

"Well, in that case, let me unwind you." She pressed the button and pressed her lips onto his.

53

ATLANTIC OCEAN

298 MILES EAST OF RHODE ISLAND

"Nothing, Captain."

It was the same report hour after hour for the past three days. Sonar aboard the USS *Hartford* had not reacquired the *Admiral Kashira*. None of the other ships of the 2nd Fleet above and below the surface had succeeded either.

COMUSFLTCOM's crisscrossing grid, spanning roughly 900 miles from Portland, Maine to Charleston, North Carolina and 30-to-300 miles off the U.S. coast should have produced some contact. But it hadn't.

"She's got to be lying low, sir," James proposed. "May I speak freely, sir?"

"Go, Mr. James."

"My two cents—we made a mistake. We should have stayed on point. I believe *Admiral Kashira* never moved from where we first lost her."

Commander Andrew Policano chewed on the notion. He had an experienced team on headphones, but no one better than James. If he was right, they had to backtrack. They could do it slowly with less noise or quickly but risk giving away their location to any other Russian subs lurking in the grid. The difference in time? Maybe the delta between locating the *Admiral Kashira* before it struck and missing the opportunity to prevent an attack. Given Policano's read of the current geopolitical situation, he feared the Russian was on mission and had gone silent in preparation for firing and running.

Policano crossed to the nautical chart. He reviewed the present position of the other ships in the 2nd Fleet and made a fast calculation. The computer would provide a more accurate one. But on first glance, from where they were to where they needed to go, it would take just under twelve hours. A half day. An eternity. But the *Hartford* had the best chance of getting back to where they had lost contact than anyone. He placed an X at the spot, quickly plotted the route, and called out orders.

"Steer course two four five. Bearing zero-zero five."

The helmsman repeated the order.

"Speed three-zero knots."

"Speed three-zero knots. Aye."

"Planesman, six-five feet.

The order was confirmed. The USS *Hartford* was on a fast rendezvous course.

Policano crossed to Marcel James. He put his hand on the young man's shoulder.

"I hope I'm right, sir," James admitted.

"Just keep best ears on it, son."

James had two hours left on his shift, then eight hours rest. That meant he'd be back on post two hours before reaching their destination.

When it was his shift change, he closed his eyes and cleared his mind. He had to sleep, and he had to be ready. James had family in East Boston. East Boston was home to the city's major oil ports. However, the more vulnerable and strategic target was thirteen miles from the shore in Massachusetts Bay—the new Northeast Gateway deepwater port. The port contains a submerged dual turret-loading buoy system and a sixteen-mile pipeline that connects to an existing subsea pipeline. Through it flows natural gas that's distributed throughout the Northeast.

* * *

The men under Boris Sidorov's command had remained quiet for fifteen hours. They had practiced for up to seventy-two hours but were prepared to continue for as long as it took. The standing order—no shoes, no talking, no hard objects in their hands, no flushing. No active sonar. Only hand signals and written communications. The ocean was an echo chamber, and there was no sound coming from *Admiral Kashira* lying on a flat ridge tucked into the New England Seamounts 250 meters below the surface, 180 miles due east of Cape Cod, with a straight shot into the heart of America's economy.

Sidorov had an eight-hour window of time in which to operate. According to Kremlin plans, it included the scheduled mission with *Karim Khan,* a submarine from another country; an example of hands across the waters, or in this case under.

The *Karim Khan* headed due west. Its crew of forty-two souls were excited. They had been told all their training would come to bear. Perhaps they'd even get to test the sub's complement of ballistic missiles and torpedoes.

The sub was built by North Korea and sold to the navy of the Islamic Republic of Iran. Though not a nuclear-powered sub, the Gorae-class sub remained a threat wherever it sailed.

Soon, though neither the captain nor his loyal men onboard knew, the *Karim Khan* was on its way to becoming a sacrificial lamb. Captain Sidorov of the *Admiral Kashira* considered it almost biblical.

54

Ey Wing Li, Sammy to his American associates, was led into the president's office in the traditional red-tiered Chinese building within the Zhongnanhai complex west of the Forbidden City. This is the central headquarters of the Chinese Communist Party and the State Council. It is protected in ways that the public, foreign dignitaries, and even members of the Chinese hierarchy don't know. The beneficiary of this protection was Yichén Yáo, president of China.

Yáo ruled the world's largest population, commanded the globe's biggest navy, and presided over the earth's major manufacturing nation. With an economy about to overtake the United States as number one, modern China is considered the world's factory. Its output also makes it earth's worst polluter.

President Yáo oversaw every aspect of China's huge economic success and its immense problems. He inherited both and was determined to keep one going and solve the others. Solving included quashing dissent and exerting complete control over his people and returning China to its long and historic prominence. And there was another issue on his agenda. Now that Hong Kong was falling into line, Yáo was strategizing on when global politics and America's weakness would intersect and provide China with the window to move on Taiwan.

All in good time, he thought. And that good time would be coming soon.

As he ascended the government ranks Yáo met and befriended Ey Wing Li, Sammy to those who knew him the best. He had risen from being a local Macau fixer to a businessman who knew how to twist arms and break legs, to an enforcer with a long memory for anyone who got in his way … or worse, hurt him. Sammy kept detailed lists of the favors and aid he'd granted over the years. He converted many of those favors into the support Yáo needed to consolidate power. Sammy was offered a high-ranking position in the government, which he turned down.

"Too many ways to disappoint. And we both know how that ends," he only half-joked at the time. He proposed that he remain on the outside. "But keep me on speed dial. I can do for you what I've always done. Fix things."

55

DAN REILLY ANSWERED his room phone on the third ring.

"Hello," Reilly whispered hoping not to disturb Yibing lying beside him.

"*Nǐ hǎo*. Hello."

The woman's voice on the line was warm and friendly. Young, but authoritative. Unmistakably Chinese.

"Is this Mr. Reilly?"

"Yes, it is."

Reilly waited. This was an unsolicited call.

"One moment, Mr. Reilly."

Chinese music on hold filled the next two minutes, during which time Reilly put on a robe and went to the other living room. Then a deep booming voice came on the line.

"Daniel, Daniel, Daniel. You can't tell an old friend when you're back in town?"

Reilly instantly recognized the caller. "What an unpleasant time to call."

The voice laughed. "Yes, this hour can be. A surprise to hear you were in Beijing."

Reilly figured it was no surprise. Little occurred in Beijing these days without Sammy, Ey Wing Li, knowing.

"How long has it been, Dan?"

"Five years since we acquired the Diplomat Hotel from you here. Twelve since Macau."

"Far too long for people who share history." Sammy's tone suddenly changed. Darkened. "Daniel, some of that history has become more relevant than ever."

Sammy's comment suggested that this was going to be a business call more than anything else.

"Let me take you out for an early breakfast."

"I'd be honored. I'm actually busy for a few more days—"

"I understand, but we have things we must talk about."

Must. It was unspecific yet suggesting urgency. Maybe Sammy had information. Maybe Sammy needed his help.

"Okay. Same type of pickup?"

"Why would I change after all these years?"

56

REILLY SLEPT SOUNDLY for three hours after Sammy's call. As the early morning light sneaked around the edges of his curtains, he rolled over to spoon with Yi. Early in the night, they had played every game she'd come up with and some of his. Now, before he left for his breakfast he craved more.

"Good morning," he said as he softly kissed the back of her neck.

Yi stirred in the best of all ways. "Mmmmm."

She rolled over. Her toes touched his. She welcomed his caress and answered it in kind. Soon they were intertwined again.

An hour and a shower later they dressed and talked playfully like the lovers they were.

"Too fast?" he asked.

"Mr. Reilly, I believe I was the instigator."

"As a matter of fact—"

She smiled, then closed her eyes and turned her head to the side. "Don't feel as if you have to carry this on."

Reilly squeezed her hand. "What if I want to?"

She still looked away.

"Yi, this doesn't have to be one night." He smiled and squeezed again. "One wonderful night."

Yibing Cheng opened her eyes and gave Reilly a warm smile.

"Very wonderful." She laughed. "Most memorable, too."

"Enough to last, or can we schedule time to see one another in Washington? If you'd prefer, we can take it slow once we're back in the real world."

"Ask me out to dinner when we get there. But I do believe we have another night before you leave," Yi offered seductively.

Reilly nodded.

Reilly had explained that he was being picked up to meet a friend. Yibing said that she'd take the time to get caught up on her email and report in.

"Do you report everything to Secretary Matthews?" he asked with some embarrassment.

"Not everything," she slyly replied. "Unless you want me to tell her how good you are in—"

"Ah, that's not necessary," Reilly interrupted. "She—"

"Oh?" Yi said picking up on how quickly he stopped.

"Nothing. Nothing at all."

* * *

Sammy's driver was waiting for Reilly in front of the hotel. Like years ago, he didn't learn a thing from the driver, not even where they were going. But arriving at a classic, centuries-old Ming Dynasty building overlooking Beijing did not disappoint.

"Mr. Wing Li will meet you inside. His aides will direct you."

The associates looked a weight class above an NFL linebacker. They pointed with hefty arms that wouldn't easily fold across their chests.

Reilly entered an open, airy restaurant called TRB Forbidden City. Inside, a hostess led Reilly to a private room where two more hefty guards barred the door.

"Dan Reilly. I'm expected."

They knocked on the door, announced Reilly in Mandarin, got approval to open, and allowed him in. Sammy was seated at a large table for two in a private room that provided for his ample girth. He was likely to remain seated until the last of the food was digested. Reilly approached. The big man straightened. Reilly bowed.

"Time has treated you well," Sammy said warmly. "What is your expression? Fit as a fiddle?"

Reilly replied in kind. "As are you." It was an obvious lie. Sammy had gone bald and gained at least a good thirty or more pounds. As if that's ever good.

"I read about you all the time, Dan. Newspapers, business journals. Often I wonder if there's more left between the lines."

"I watch what I say."

"And then there was a particularly interesting faceoff you had during one of those television congressional hearings with an old friend. A friend who seems to be moving up in life thanks to some twists and turns in your country's politics."

"Every day has its surprises," Reilly said.

"And you have had your own—most recently in Europe. You see, I do keep track of you."

Reilly smiled.

"Ah, but I embarrass you. We all have our secrets. But I think we can agree, we've both done well."

"We have," Reilly said without real comment.

A thin waiter came to the table and bowed. Sammy ordered the eggs Benedict for both of them.

"You will love the food as much as the view of the Forbidden City. It's sinful. The asparagus is especially crunchy, and the hollandaise sauce is perfect"

Undoubtedly, Sammy had enjoyed more than his share in prior visits.

Over mimosas they talked about family—mostly Sammy's. He boasted about his daughter who had earned her undergraduate degree at Harvard and a PhD in economics at Stanford—both Reilly's recommendation from years ago. "She's back here now and works for China Construction Bank, though she performs little errands for me. All respectable. And you, my friend, any children?"

"No. Divorced and most recently I fell into a relationship that went bad."

He explained that behind bad was the fact that the woman he had fallen in love with lived a double life. One for England, where she lived and worked, and another for the actual country she was from and died in its service.

"My, my, Dan. You of all people fell into an executive honey trap."

"Head over heels with blinders on."

"Did you leave all your training at the foot of the bed?"

Reilly drew in a breath. "At first. Then when I thought there was time to turn things around, there wasn't."

"Nasty business. I'm sorry," Sammy said quite sincerely. He used that turn in the conversation to segue into his reason for calling Reilly. "Daniel, I believe it's time to bring up the past."

"Oh?" Reilly tentatively asked.

"Present events necessitate it for certain people I'm associated with and ultimately a relationship you have as well."

The swift change in Sammy's tone blindsided Reilly. He pushed his plate to the side leaving room for him to fold his arms on the table.

The past instantly took him back to what brought them together in the first place. Two American congressmen: one, now United States President, the other about to become Vice President. And with that, his mind raced to the call from Elizabeth Matthews and back to the extremely unusual phone call from Davidson's aide.

Now, he thought the day would come with its own surprises. Sammy didn't disappoint.

* * *

Elizabeth Matthews answered her phone. Reilly explained that he needed to talk to her discreetly—immediately. That meant he didn't even trust the satellite phone.

"Give me an hour," Elizabeth Matthews said. "I'll clear you at the Embassy. We'll move this over to the SCIF."

SCIF was the Sensitive Compartmented Information Facility, a secure room used by intelligence services to prevent eavesdropping.

"Thank you." He hung up without a hint of the subject, but Reilly was certain that Matthews understood the seriousness. He only requested use of a SCIF when it was absolutely necessary.

Exactly one hour later, a U.S. Marine manning one of numerous desks within the modern building, scanned Reilly's ID into a reader. "One moment, sir." A prompt immediately appeared on his computer: approval to proceed.

"Straight through security, sir. You'll be met by an officer and taken to Mr. Ellsworth's office. He's the—"

Reilly completed the sentence. "*Chargé d'affaires.*"

Not everyone off the street met with Ellsworth. The Marine lieutenant wondered why this man could. He wouldn't find out.

"Mr. Reilly, good to see you again," Whit Ellsworth said as he thrust out his hand. The six-foot-six retired Army major was enjoying what he considered his back nine, still in the service of his country. "I suppose this is about the oil conference. Any way I can help?" It was a sincere offer, but one that begged for more.

"Just here to drop a dime. Long distance, Whit."

Reilly had last seen Ellsworth at a Chinese government function booked at the Kensington. He only knew Dan Reilly as a hotel executive. The personal call from the Secretary of State surprised him. The fact that she had cleared him to use a SCIF was unusual. But he wasn't going to learn why from Reilly.

"I'll get you right in. If you have time, stop by before you leave. I'll fill you in on business here."

Reilly thanked Ellsworth, but he asked for a raincheck. The last thing he wanted to do was get pumped by a diplomat.

Ellsworth led Reilly to a well-guarded room. He signed a register before opening the door, sat Reilly down, and was surprised a second time. The hotel executive showed complete familiarity with the equipment.

"You've done this before," he said.

"I have."

"Okay. And make sure you block out some time for us next trip."

"Will do."

Ellsworth left Reilly to his work—whatever that was. He'd make his own calls back to Langley. Maybe someone there would know.

* * *

Elizabeth Matthews, 6,942 miles away in her SCIF, was ready for the call. She picked up the secure phone on the second ring. "Hello."

"Hello," he said.

"Hello. Suffice it to say, you have my interest. News on the killer?"

"No," he replied.

"Well then, what? The meter's running."

Reilly cleared his throat. He held the phone tightly and leaned in further from the door even though no one outside could hear him.

"I'll need to see you as soon as I get back."

"Sounds urgent."

"It is."

Elizabeth Matthews listened intently. She took no notes but remembered everything. At first the story seemed impossible. But the more she considered it, the impossible became all the more plausible.

She'd pressed Reilly on the reliability of his source.

"Completely."

"Evidence? We've got nothing without it."

Reilly's voice dropped on the secure phone. "He claims he has it."

"And what's it cost us?"

"A change in dance partners."

"Does he know you're calling me?"

"Yes."

"And he expects I can do this? Hell, I'm hanging on with a thread. I don't have that power."

"He—" he corrected himself, "*they* believe you do."

* * *

Matthews had other troubles on her scope. Trouble that had been on the sonar scope of the USS *Hartford* and was now off. The missing Russian killer sub. Trouble with how Battaglio's new National Security Advisor had not grasped the significance of the rogue ship. Trouble that the president was likely to dismiss the threat out of hand.

She hadn't shared any of this with Dan Reilly. She couldn't. She wouldn't. Yet, with what he told her, she saw a possible way through the complicated morass.

Matthews had calls to make. First, FBI Director Reese McCafferty. Next, her friend and chair of the Senate Judiciary Committee, Mikayla Colonnello. She made notes for each of the calls, deciding what she would share: just enough to get them ready for the coming storm.

57

BEIJING

The conference ended at five. One by one, the delegates, eager to leave, checked out. Colonel Zhang believed his enhanced surveillance and highly visible teams had thwarted any plan. Back at the hotel, Reilly was relieved. He notified EJ Shaw and Kensington Security Chief Alan Cannon on a conference call.

"Good work, Daniel," Shaw offered, "Wrap up, congratulate your staff, and come back home. I'll see you in Chicago."

"All booked. Scheduled out tomorrow, late morning."

Reilly thought about his nighttime plans with Yibing. He counted on making up for lost sleep on the plane the next day.

"Dan?" Cannon chimed in from Nairobi where he was still working with investigators.

"Yeah, Alan?"

"One thing." He sounded serious. "A word of caution, Dan. Hell, more than caution. I'm waving a big fat red flag. We've gone over every second of video of this guy and every square inch of his room and what he touched. Nothing for facial recognition, no fingerprints. He's a forensics magician. He knew where all the cameras were, and hell, he didn't even sleep in his room; just made it appear like he did. I've never seen or heard of a killer more adept at disguises and then poof! He walked around in plain sight, and nobody could really describe him. You may think you're out of the woods. I don't buy it. He's not finished."

* * *

Reilly met with the general manager and Colonel Zhang in Yong Tong's office. "We can't let up yet," he said. "Eyes on everyone still with us."

Zhang agreed.

"But it sure looks like we dodged the bullet so far," the hotel general manager offered. He looked relieved and was grateful for all the visible and invisible help.

"I've always hated that phrase," Reilly replied. He flashed on his recent FBI training when he not only didn't dodge the bullet, he didn't see it coming. *How long ago was that?* he thought. *A week? It feels like a year.*

"Any last-minute changes to the checkout schedule?" the GM asked.

Reilly and the Chinese agent had a detailed spreadsheet, recently updated based on flight changes. "The Canadian, Haoran Shih, will be the last out. He's staying through tonight, out tomorrow. Other than him, everyone will be out by late afternoon on evening flights home. They'll be under our care until they're on the plane."

"According to our profile on Shih, he holds dual citizenship," Reilly said. "What's he got planned?"

Zhang knew. "Family visits in the area. No surprises from my point of view. We're ready to peel back."

Reilly didn't agree. "My team is worried that until the last guy is out, we face the possibility of a hit."

"Mr. Reilly, the conference is over. We've done our job. More than I can say your authorities did in Washington."

Reilly bristled at the criticism but chose not to engage. He and Zhang had developed an even-handed working relationship. No need to blow it over one pointed comment. Nonetheless, he wanted to keep tabs on Shih.

"Let's just not drop our guard on Haoran Shih when he's in the hotel," Reilly said again.

"Our guys have been working overtime since we went Red. They need a break, Dan," said Yong Tong.

"After Shih's out!"

"May need some outside hires."

"No."

Zhang offered a solution. "Tell me what hours you can't cover. I'll assign a few men."

"Thank you," Reilly said, moving Zhang back onto the good list. But he still was concerned enough to ask his GM to get Shih's schedule.

"Of course, we'll need it anyway. But don't worry."

From his military service, through his State Department assignment, right through his work for Kensington, Dan Reilly had developed a set of rules: understand and respect local hires who can empower employees, hold to core beliefs, and lead. Leading meant worrying about the things other people aren't worrying about.

Until Haoran Shih was out the door and on the airplane, Reilly was going to worry.

58

HAORAN SHIH HAD CHECKED all the boxes on his to-do list. He'd visited his mother's first cousin and the family's ancient burial plot, and picked up gifts for his wife, kids, and associates. During the conference the security made him feel safer. Now Shih was happy to see his handlers loosen their grip. Instead of three, he had one. Instead of feeling like he was a visiting president, he began shifting back to a sense of normalcy. And his normal routine included rooftop drinks at sunset. This, his last night.

The open deck, which covered much of the fifty-first floor, included a fifty-foot pool; two bars; tables for two, four, six and eight; a full kitchen and staff dressed in short skirts and multicolored print blouses. Needless to say, all women.

Shih sat at a glass cocktail table for two and ordered a Jameson and avocado toast. His sole security planted himself at the bar some twenty-five feet away. From his position, he could watch Shih and see who came and went from the rooftop.

The Canadian British Petroleum executive was on his second drink when Reilly got off the elevator and surveyed the deck. There were four in the pool, three kids and one parent, and another dozen or so people scattered around the various tables. Some catching the sunset, others absorbed in conversation. It was quiet compared to what it would be like a few hours later when the after-dinner and dating crowd moved in.

Reilly spotted the security officer. He was one of the hotel's men.

They nodded to one another. He looked alert, but Reilly figured that after the past few days, he was also tired.

* * *

Matthieu Lefebvre was also a familiar patron to the roof-top waitresses. Familiar, yet at the same time relatively indistinguishable. A 15 percent tipper, precisely. No more, no less. Lefebvre wore drab colors, a loose-fitting grey sweater covering a white shirt, khakis, grey socks, and old black sneakers. He casually leafed through a magazine. Like many in China, he wore latex gloves and a KN95 medical mask, which he lifted as he nibbled cheese and crackers and sipped a ginger ale. The mask served to cover his features without drawing attention. The gloves meant he wouldn't leave fingerprints. Beside him, lay a large backpack and a shopping bag from his day's explorations.

Though he was polite to the staff, he didn't engage anyone in pro-longed conversation, though at sunset he enjoyed sidling up to the edge of the deck and taking in the sights.

Lefebvre heard heavier footsteps than the waitress behind him. But he didn't turn to look until the sound of the steps trailed off. Lefebvre casually lowered the magazine he was reading, peered over his shoulder, and noted that it was the American hotel executive. He was always prowling. Always observing. Always asking questions. Always looking further. Lefebvre also spotted the hotel security officer at the bar. He looked tired. His reactions would be slower. That was good.

After circling the deck once, the American took a seat at a table for four. At a table that big, he'd be getting company soon. That was also good. More people would add to the confusion.

A few minutes later, an Asian woman got off the elevator and looked around. Lefebvre figured she was also an employee, and so was the next person with her: an older, rugged, sun-tanned man. She pointed to the American, and they both joined him.

Lefebvre dropped his gaze and returned to his reading. It was an American publication, *Flying*.

* * *

"What are we drinking?" Skip Lenczycki asked.

"Whatever it is, my treat." Reilly stood to greet his friends. A handshake for the former CIA agent. A kiss on both cheeks for Yibing. She smiled and winked.

"You think they make a piña colada up here?" the former CIA officer asked.

Reilly laughed. Skip was going for one of his island drinks. He was definitely ready to get back to the Caribbean and his boat. Reilly appreciated Bob Heath sending him as backup. He had done his job. As soon as the last delegate was on the plane, Lenczycki would be on another.

They settled for prosecco and replayed the events of the last few days. Reilly kept Shih in view. He was on the phone. Animated and waiting for the sun to set. His regular drill according to reports from security.

Reilly put the question to the table. "Did anything hit you? Anyone?"

"No. And probably due to the presence of Zhang's men and the hotels," Lenczycki offered. "Nice work all around. Almost a vacation on the company's tab." Almost. The company being the CIA. Almost, because the retired spy had done far more than Reilly knew. He had called in his own resources. Extra eyes and extra muscle. Coming and going. Drinking and dining. Photographing and observing. A man and a woman no one ever expected, as much to watch Reilly's back as to prevent another assassination. He'd released them, and now Skip Lenczycki was ready for the drink he'd passed up since arriving.

"When are you heading back?" Lenczycki asked Yibing.

"A few more days." She dared a quick look to her right. "Haven't had any time to act like a tourist. Dan's offered to take me around."

"Lots to see," Reilly added.

Lenczycki smiled. "I'm sure you two will have a great time."

It was clear by his answer that the old spy had not lost a step. He either recognized the signs, read their looks, or had heard them.

Another ten minutes, and the sun would be setting. Patrons were beginning to line up against the four-foot high fence. Just beyond it, a mere six inches, a clear plastic barrier two feet higher was bolted to the deck. Beyond that, a sheer drop to the street below.

"Shih's last sunset." Yibing noted that the oil executive stood and moved up to the barrier. "Do you think he ever saw himself as a target?"

"Was he?" Reilly wondered. He glanced across the deck. Where there had been maybe twenty, there were now fifty or more. Two additional waitresses were now serving customers. Drinks were flowing.

Reilly focused for a moment on the bland tourist he'd seen a few times around the hotel—Matthieu Lefebvre. Lefebvre was probably the least interesting person at the hotel, but that didn't stop Reilly from confirming his identity. Retired teacher. Widower. A guy likely putting another checkmark in a box on his bucket list. He was also an avid reader. Today it was a magazine. From six tables away Reilly saw a featured photograph of small plane. *Interesting read,* he thought. *Maybe the next adventure on his list.*

"What's next for you, Skip?" Yibing asked, not really knowing what had come before.

"Got my boat. Got my girl."

"Your sweetie agree with that order?"

"Layla? She prefers it that way." Lenczycki laughed. "Believe me, my boat is much more demanding." For a moment he was lost in the reverie. He sighed deeply.

Reilly recognized where he went. Where Lenczycki had lived almost every day since he retired from the CIA—in the glow of the sun, with the warmth of the Caribbean, and in the arms of a wonderful woman. He lived far from the troubles of the world—except when Reilly or one of Reilly's friends like Bob Heath called.

"What about you, Reilly?" the skipper posed. "What's next?"

"Back to Chicago. Regroup and debrief our Crisis Committee. And, given Nicolai Gorshkov's machinations, wondering where the next shoe will fall.

"Take your pick: the Baltic, Poland, Tajikistan, Finland. He's just getting started. Oh, and I've got a return date at the FBI's Hogan's Alley."

The spy laughed. "Dead man walking."

"Hoping not next time."

"What are you two talking about?"

"Reilly knows I'm going home so I won't be there to watch his six."

"His what?"

"Watch his sorry corporate ass. His six. It means that I've got his back."

"It's a saying fighter pilots came up with during World War I," Reilly added. "Picture yourself flying behind another airplane. Looking at it as a clock, the lead plane is at the twelve o'clock position. You're at six o'clock. Six o'clock is watching your back. Transfer it to the battlefield or the street, it has the same meaning. Skip was covering me."

"Becoming a full time job," Lenczycki said.

Yibing frowned.

"He didn't tell you about Brussels?"

She looked at Reilly. "No."

"Okay, okay. Enough," Reilly said. "Skip was in the right place at the right time, and yes," he faced his friend, "thankfully you did save my sorry corporate ass."

With that, Skip offered everyone a toast, "To better times."

* * *

Haoran Shih had his spot up at the barrier. Others crowded in to catch the sunset. Matthieu Lefebvre rose from his seat. He slung his backpack over his shoulder, slipped his arms through the straps, and fastened an attached belt around his stomach. He picked up his shopping bag and maneuvered directly behind the Canadian oil man.

"Like to join them?" Yibing asked.

"You two go. Couldn't possibly compare to what I get to see every evening," Lenczycki offered.

"Come on, Dan." She grabbed their drinks and sauntered toward the crowd.

"Okay."

As Reilly walked up, he noticed the bland man and his backpack. He laughed to himself. Looked like Lefebvre was about to parachute off, right in keeping with his reading.

Reilly stood next to Yibing. She took his arms and wrapped them around her waist and pushed up against him. Feeling his warmth, his breathing, and his excitement at being so close.

Everything seemed to unfold in slow motion. The sun dissolving from yellow to orange, to red; the horizon swallowing up the day's light. It was all so perfect, as if nature knew exactly how to please: a production staged every evening, weather permitting, around the world. Orderly and magnificent. The sight drew cheers and applause, and couples kissed, perhaps hoping the last of magic hour would spread magic over them.

Yi and Reilly's kiss lasted longer than most. It was deep and passionate—something he hadn't done in public for a long time. But it felt liberating now. He stepped back and took Yibing in with a look he never thought he'd have for a woman again. Reilly was starting to lean in for a second kiss, when a flash of light caught his eye—a reflection off a long piece of metal still sweeping out of a shopping bag. A restaurant knife or spoon?

"What?" she asked.

Reilly didn't hear her; he was focused on the shiny object. It had a tapered tube about eight inches long and a handle. It wasn't a knife or spoon. It was in the hands of a man. The guest he dubbed Bland Man.

"Jesus!" he exclaimed.

Lenczycki jumped up protectively. His eyes went from Reilly to where Reilly was looking and suddenly going.

Reilly pushed people aside. The tapered tube was still rising.

"No!" Skip Lenczycki shouted. "Reilly don't!"

No one heard him over the three fast shots, a quarter of a second apart, from Matthieu Lefebvre's Diablo, a powerful 12 gauge pistol. Reilly was ten feet away. The ex-CIA operative, steps closer. The blast went wide of Shih. *A miracle,* Reilly thought. *An impossible to miss shot. Or, he missed on purpose.*

The plexiglass barrier shattered.

Guests shrieked and scattered.

"Stop!" Lenczycki shouted. He cut in front of Reilly, pulled out his Sig Sauer from under his sports coat, and yelled an order. "Drop the gun!"

Lefebvre turned, pivoted, and fired first at the tall man rushing toward him. He caught him center mass. Skip Lenczycki dropped to his knees. His gun fell directly in front of Reilly.

Yibing screamed. Reilly picked up the gun. But before he could aim and shoot, the man with the backpack, the most boring man Reilly had seen in China, shoved Haoran Shih past where the plexiglass had been and dove off the building with him in front.

Reilly raced to the edge, and against the glow in the horizon he saw a parachute unfurl, catch the wind, and deftly steer away while the Canadian BP oil executive lay dead on the ground.

59

A YOUNG DOCTOR who had been working on drinking his date to bed rushed to Lenczycki's aid. "*Jiákè!*" he roared in Mandarin. "Jacket!" An older man handed him his. The doctor bunched up the fabric and pressed it against the chest wound. A bartender called downstairs to hotel security. Waitresses, not trained for the crisis, still had the sense to move people away from the edge. All of this in the first twenty seconds, all while Bland Man sailed directly to the subway entrance that would, in a matter of minutes, connect him to the world's largest subway system.

Reilly ran back to his compatriot. "What can I do?" he asked the doctor.

"Stay back," the physician said in stilted English.

"Will he—?"

"Let me work."

Reilly helped Yibing up. She was crying. He walked her away and held her tightly. She tried to speak. The only word that came out was, "Why?"

Reilly knew why. The assassin had waited until the conference was over. Not because he couldn't have acted earlier. This was his plan. The magazine, a leave-behind, the killer's game.

"Wait here," he told Yibing marching her to a table.

"Okay, but why, Dan?"

"Just wait."

Reilly went to Bland Man's table. *Fingerprints,* he thought, *on the magazine.* But there wouldn't be any. He remembered, but did not question, that the assassin wore latex gloves.

"I should have seen it," he said to himself. "Fucking should have seen it."

He looked back toward Skip Lenczycki just as the doctor slipped the borrowed jacket across his face. Reilly would be calling Layla tonight.

* * *

After settling Yibing in her room, Reilly met Colonel Zhang in the lobby. The colonel's team immediately closed down the street and put tape around the crime scene. Spectators were not permitted to get close to where Shih had crushed the roof of a tan SAIC Motors sedan. But people looking out from their rooms on the west side of the hotel had a view of the fall, the impact, and a parachute gently floating down.

"We got this wrong, Reilly," Zhang said walking the perimeter.

"Very wrong. I saw it all. We tried to stop, and Lenczycki—"

"I'm sorry. I heard," the Chinese said compassionately. "We'll need your statement and Yibing Cheng's."

"She's in her room. Whenever you're ready."

They walked silently. Reilly looked up to the top of the Kensington and tried to imagine what Shih's thoughts were as he fell to his death. His wife? His family? Or simply the end of all things?

Five seconds. Reilly flashed on what those thoughts would be for him. *His ex-wife, Pam? His job? Marnie Babbitt? Yibing Cheng? Five seconds. Regrets or some twisted form of ultimate exhilaration?*

He hadn't gone there himself since he was under fire in Afghanistan. But now five seconds seemed far too short a time to put a life in perspective, and the assassin had robbed Skip Lenczycki of even those brief moments.

"Shit!" Reilly said returning to the present. "Have you closed down the subway? That's where he sailed to."

"Yes. We have witnesses, and there are cameras. We have the largest police force in the world here. We will find him."

"You won't." Reilly reminded Zhang how quickly the killer changed appearances in London and disappeared in the theater. "Remember, he's a chameleon, Colonel. A master of disguise, adept at the quick change and blending in. And he's a planner. He had an escape route, probably more than one, and multiple identities he could assume. So far, he's evaded facial recognition and investigators in London and Nairobi. Believe me, whether he's a man, a woman, or a barking dog, he's gone."

Reilly added one other point. "Oh, we're even now."

Zhang frowned.

"Beijing and Washington. You were no more successful preventing the assassination here than they were in Washington."

Zhang cut him a dismissive laugh. "Not so very equal, my friend. There will still be amends for your government to make. Now let's see if your chameleon left any droppings. First, did he stay right under our noses in your hotel?"

"Checking now."

It didn't take long. Enough staff had seen Matthieu Lefebvre checking in, entering and exiting his fourth-floor room, talking to the staff—everything a normal guest would do. Everything to appear normal—the opposite of someone trying to appear suspicious.

Once Lefebvre's room was confirmed, Zhang brought two bomb-sniffing dogs along with their handlers and armed agents. Reilly and the hotel general manager were the last to enter. Zhang's gloved men dusted for fingerprints, took photographs, and examined every item in the room. They checked for hair in the sink and shower and remnants of tissue or toilet paper—anything that might contain DNA. There was nothing. Lefebvre had even taken the sheets, pillows, bedspread, and the TV remote. More than a chameleon, he was an invisible man. And by now, quite possibly posing as a woman.

* * *

Madame Juliette d'Arnaud returned to her room in the Peking Yard Boutique Hotel, set in a 400-year-old courtyard across the city. A young man politely helped the seventy-three-year-old French tourist at the front door as she struggled with food bags from a nearby market along Dongsibei Street. She'd been away since early morning. Inside, the front desk clerk smiled to the French woman, walked around his desk, and held open the rickety elevator for her. D'Arnaud replied with the only word she'd said aloud in the hotel, *"Xiè xiè."* Thank you.

She intended on staying two more days, venturing out for small neighborhood excursions. After that, her itinerary was to take a train to Shanghai where she would become a *he* again and tour another few days.

60

NICOLAI GORSHKOV had never sat for a psychologist and had no intentions of ever starting. Any Russian shrink who had tried to diagnosis him in print had a sudden and permanent heartache. Biographers in the West constantly speculated about his state of mind and sold books based on their scholarly opinions. Doctors in America's intelligence agencies had their own analysis. Gorshkov was everything his most recent predecessors were and more, driven by a deep-rooted, life-long view of himself at the center of the political world. *Psychology Today*'s applied term for the condition, and it is a condition, is the "Hubris Syndrome." Gorshkov checked every box.

His personality and his willingness to tickle any international tiger gave agency shrinks greater respect for the lengths he would go to get his way. Every year they reevaluated and updated their assessments and briefed America's command, from the president on down. The latest was the scariest.

The Hubris Syndrome overlapped three key and disturbing markers. Gorshkov was diagnosed with narcissistic, antisocial, and histrionic personality disorders. These were manifest by distinct symptoms.

Gorshkov viewed the world as a place for his self-glorification with the power and authority to follow through. This gave him a messianic mission to act without accountability to anyone or anything but history itself. The symptoms were manifest in his contempt for others, especially people he considered inferior and those who criticized him or advised him in a manner that he disagreed with. Outwardly, he actively chose opportunities to enhance his personal image with exaggerated pride. He ignored personal failures, blaming others for any misstep. All of this put him out of touch with the real world and yet closer to destroying it.

Gorshkov's earliest memories were of a Marxist-Leninist world: Khrushchev's and Brezhnev's. He was a statist, believing people served the state rather than the other way around. The Cold War shaped his contemptuous opinion of the West. And according to intelligence experts, contempt festering over a long period of time had made Gorshkov blind to risk. Above all else, he was an egocentric, unpredictable despot, willing to go after targets big and small, nations and individuals.

Ukraine was one, the Baltic States another. He sought all of China's oil market, control of the Northern Sea Route, destabilization of the American political system and its economy, and one other thing—revenge.

Power lives in the darkest regions of the Hubris Syndrome. The attacks at the Kensington hotels in London and Nairobi and Beijing were strategic moves in a complex scheme. His ultimate success depended on allies and enemies alike not knowing what his next move was going to be. He was playing Iran, which was taking the blame for the attacks in the Strait of Hormuz. The death of an operative in Washington would be an important element to focus blame. Soon an American autopsy would determine the bomber was an Iranian woman. More subterfuge. More layers of deceit to protect Russia. More reason to continue sanctions against Iran and its oil.

And yet, Iran needed Russia's aid. It needed military support. It needed to advance its submarine fleet and its ability to stand up to the infidels. Of course, Gorshkov was there as a true ally. What better way to underscore that than a joint exercise in international waters off the New England coast? They would take a practice run at the Northeast Gateway deepwater terminal east of Boston Harbor. The purpose was to show America's Navy that it did not own the Atlantic. Together, their submarine fleets could challenge Western dominance, further dilute U.S. military operations, and create more chaos whenever they wanted.

Weeks earlier the captains of the *Admiral Kashira* and *Karim Khan* had met, talked, and heartily shook hands to their success at Severomorsk, the Russian submarine base along the Kola Peninsula. There, they reviewed plans, timing, and the absolute need for silent running. The operation would be conducted without radio communication; everything would proceed like clockwork right up to the test firing of the new generation of torpedoes by the Iranians. Then the submarines would slowly slip away along the undersea mountain range. No harm, no foul. Just an exercise. A show of goodwill between two nations against a common enemy and a blueprint for a possible future attack.

That was the plan. But there was more to it.

61

General Valery Rotenberg, Gorshkov's newly elevated senior FSB officer, nervously knocked on his president's door: the messenger with the bad news. Many others in his position, one quite recently, had left with a broad smile from Gorshkov and thanks for their years of service. He also had a big fat target on his back. Of course, the news was not entirely his fault, but blame-shifting was not an acceptable excuse.

"Enter." Gorshkov held up a finger for Rotenberg to wait. "Yes, yes. Do it." He put the phone on the cradle without a goodbye. "Now let me guess. Latvia," he said.

The general forced himself to maintain eye contact. "Mr. President." *Stay on point,* he told himself. *And the facts.* "Yes. The numbers are not with us."

"You're the second to tell me." He motioned to the telephone. "You should have been the first."

"Sir," the new advisor acknowledged.

"It's the problem with herding sheep. Dogs can do it only up to a point. But put a bear into the field, those sheep will go where they're supposed to."

Rotenberg nodded, not understanding. Gorshkov noted his expression.

"We tried the nice way, Valery. Now we release the bear."

WASHINGTON, D.C.

Battaglio's press secretary took the question from *Newsweek* reporter Toni Donina.

"A comment on the Latvia election? Early results show a rejection of Russian control."

"President Battaglio supports the will of the Latvian people and their national interests. President Gorshkov gave us assurance in Stockholm that there would be a free and open election. That has happened. When the final results are in, President Battaglio will phone the new president and extend his thanks to President Gorshkov."

* * *

Senator Mikayla Colonnello watched the news with Secretary Matthews in the State Department executive dining room. "That's one for the win column."

"For now," Matthews said.

"Then why don't you sound happier? And eat your breakfast."

Matthews had been pushing her omelet with her fork without taking a bite.

"Gorshkov hates losing. This is a loss. He won't stop."

"And go back on what he told the president?"

"It was a lie then and it's a lie now. Nicolai Gorshkov wants all of the Baltic, eventually including Finland and Sweden. Like Ukraine, he's out to redraw the map of Eastern Europe. We might as well call it Battaglio's folly."

"NATO?" Colonnello said.

"Will do nothing without the U.S. And the U.S. will do nothing so long as Ryan Battaglio is president."

BEIJING

Morning came all too quickly for Dan Reilly. He didn't want to fully wake up. Waking up meant getting to the airport, taking a sixteen-hour flight, getting back to his office—make that his offices in Chicago and DC. Waking up meant saying goodbye.

The second night with Yibing was better than the first, without the first night's nervousness and awkwardness. The second night brought patience and tenderness, knowledge of each other's bodies, and the desire to please. But there was something else: a primal urge they both craved after the killings on the hotel roof. A friend and a stranger—both should be alive today. Reilly felt responsible. Alan Cannon had warned him. Red flags. Flags unseen.

Morning light was the intruder. It ignored what he really wanted. Soon the alarm would chime in as its accomplice.

Yi and Reilly showered together as they had the day before, but this time it lacked the playfulness. The clock had joined the conspiracy.

Room service helped replenish them. But they both avoided talking about the obvious until Yibing broached the subject.

"You can't blame yourself, Dan. Skip was a trained operative. Even he didn't see it coming."

Reilly said nothing.

"The assassin wasn't going to be denied. He had a mission and an escape plan. He was also prepared to kill to accomplish both. You can't take it personally."

"Personally!" Reilly raised his voice. "Of course I take it personally."

Yibing leaned back.

"It's my job to take threats seriously." Reilly softened. "And I didn't."

Now Yibing chose not to speak.

"Yes, he was intent on what he was going to do. But I should have done more. We closed our eyes too soon, partly because Washington said game over when they ID'd the bomber as a woman. The game wasn't over."

He lowered his head. She saw his tears and reached across the table to hold his hands.

"What now?" she asked.

"Colonel Zhang takes over again. His team examines all the local CCTV footage from the landing point, and they conduct a city-wide search—which won't succeed. Not today, not tomorrow, not ever. The assassin undoubtedly changed his identity in seconds with whatever he carried on his jump. Hell, we were on the elevator with him. We talked."

Yibing rose, walked behind Reilly, wrapped her arms around him.

"He was playing with you, darling."

"I should have …" He stopped. *Darling* registered. Reilly hadn't been called darling by anyone in a long, long time. Not even Marnie Babbitt. If she had, he'd forgotten.

"And the magazine. The dullest-looking man in the hotel reading a magazine about flying. Then his backpack? His parachute? Yi, I missed all the clues, and they were right in front of me. Now he's in the wind."

"Let the Chinese police deal with it now."

Reilly bowed his head. *I should have seen it.*

Downstairs Reilly met up with Colonel Zhang, who told him his officers were tracking down eleven different subjects that showed up on the video recordings. Reilly was certain none would turn out positive.

Outside the hotel Reilly and Yi embraced. They'd said goodbye with kisses upstairs in private.

"Dinner in Washington, Mr. Reilly?"

"Dinner, Dr. Cheng." He sighed and held onto her. "And breakfast."

He felt her nod, then they separated. Yibing returned to the hotel; Reilly signaled he was ready for a cab.

One strolling suitcase. That's all he had brought to Beijing, all he was leaving with—with the exception of a bag full of sadness and regrets.

"Airport, Mr. Reilly?"

Almost everyone on the staff knew him by sight.

"Thank you. Yes."

The bell captain, dressed in a grey suit, tie, and crisp white shirt, flagged a cab. But before it stopped, a Chinese-made black SUV cut in front and rolled to a stop right in front of Reilly. The cabbie yelled in Mandarin. So did the staffer. The driver of the SUV rolled down the window.

"Mr. Reilly, please get in." The invitation was pleasant, yet insistent.

"Actually, I'll take the taxi as planned."

"No need for a taxi."

"I said I'll take the taxi," Reilly repeated. He thrust his arm up.

"Mr. Wing Li requests your presence."

Reilly stiffened but remained polite. "While it would be my honor to see Mr. Wing Li again, please tell him I have a plane to catch."

"Mr. Wing Li has graciously taken the opportunity to change your flight to later. You are to come with me."

With that the driver pressed a button on the dashboard and the tail gate opened. The bell captain understood two things. First, when Sammy Wing Li gave an order, you took it. Second, he should put the suitcase in the SUV without asking any questions.

Reilly tipped him well, got in the backseat, and drove off. He was certain their conversation was over. No more words until they arrived at wherever they were going.

The ride was smooth and not too long. The destination, the public gardens along the Summer Palace. The driver stopped, exited, and opened the door for Reilly, who went to the back to retrieve his bag.

"Mr. Reilly, I will be here until you and Mr. Wing Li have concluded business. I will watch your luggage. It will be safe with me."

Of that, Reilly had no doubt. He did wonder what was in store for him.

Reilly had visited the massive gardens in the past as a tourist. Today he felt more like a hostage.

"Which way?"

The driver pointed straight ahead. "You will find your way."

He did. Every hundred yards he was met by another of Sammy's men who directed him to the next turn. Five men. Some five hundred yards at his typical rate. He calculated the distance in meters. Almost the same, maybe 450 or 460. He remembered that the U.S. had come very close to adopting the metric system, then abandoned the proposal at the eleventh hour. The eleventh hour. His mind went to where that term originated. There were various meanings. In the 19th century, the typical workday was from six in the morning to six in the evening. The last hour, sometimes feeling the longest, was the eleventh. But growing up he'd heard it had a biblical origin. A parable from Matthew referred to a long workday in a vineyard in which even the late laborers were paid. He wondered if this was his eleventh hour.

Ahead, Sammy sat on a park bench overlooking the lake that took up more than three-quarters of the ancient gardens. He was alone, but men were visibly posted in three directions forming an equilateral triangle of defense. *Why?* he wondered.

He approached the businessman he had met years ago in Macau. Then a fixer and an entrepreneur, today, Reilly was certain, a government operative.

"Sit, sit, my friend."

Reilly obliged, keeping two of the points of the triangle in sight.

"You appear nervous. I shouldn't make you nervous. We have history, and today we shall go back to the beginning."

Reilly said nothing. Sammy noted Reilly's fixation on his men.

"My men. They worry you? Relax. They are here to make sure we have an uninterrupted conversation."

"About?" It was Reilly's first word.

Sammy laughed. "The past, the present, and the future."

"I try to live in the present, Sammy. It's where everything happens."

"Not everything. The present exists because of all that has happened."

Reilly turned toward his friend. "If this is a philosophy lesson, forget it. I have a plane to catch."

"Consider it a combination of history and current events. Yours, your country's. Mine as well, all intertwined from the day we met."

Reilly checked his watch. Wing Li noted his impatience.

"Please. There are many flights. I have you booked on them all."

It was clear to Reilly that he wasn't going anywhere for now, so he relaxed into the park bench, ready to listen.

"We have two issues to discuss. You shall be our messenger."

"Oh? I've never liked the sound of that."

"Doesn't it depend upon how successful one is in the art of convincing?"

"More whether the intended audience wants to hear it. Who am I supposed to convince?"

"People you know. People you can get to. And those people that can get to you that you don't know."

"You certainly love your Chinese riddles," Reilly replied.

"Solving riddles has long been important to our people," Sammy said. His mood chilled as he continued. "And they can be deadly serious."

"Including to a messenger. Time for specificity," Reilly said tapping the face on his watch.

"Of course. My apologies. You are a man who always sees the straight line between two points."

Reilly nodded.

"The two points are Beijing and Washington."

"Stop. You want to make a business deal on a hotel. I'm your guy. Politics, no."

"Then think of this as business."

"What kind of business?"

"In the matter of the first issue, oil."

"Sammy, like I said, wrong business."

"Really? Haven't you been hosting oil conferences around the globe?"

"Yes, and apparently not so successfully."

Reilly looked out at the boats floating lazily on the lake. A tranquil sight. Right now, that was an activity he'd rather be doing.

"None of it was your fault, Dan."

Reilly looked down.

"But tell me what you think the purpose of the assassinations has been?" Sammy asked.

"To discredit the market," he said, head still lowered. "To create instability. To drive out competitors and prices up. To create greater profit."

"And the attacks in the Suez Canal?"

"More of the same."

"Who?"

"Not my area of expertise."

"Venture a guess."

"A nation with power and means. Iran."

"Iran. Interesting. You mean they were willing to destroy their own tankers and routes through the Arabian Sea and the Suez Canal? How's that help?"

This was a question he should have asked Yibing. *Why didn't he?* He was solely focused on identifying the next target, not the reason someone wanted to take him out.

"Don't think me impertinent to correct you, my friend, but I must," Sammy said softly and with complete seriousness.

"Go on."

"Think more globally. A nation that could benefit even if one of their own oil executives had been killed and their ships were waylaid between ports."

"China did this?"

"No, no, no. China is a target, but not in the manner that would appear obvious."

Reilly didn't follow.

"There is a nation that has positioned itself to be the principal supplier of oil and gas to the People's Republic of China. With a monopoly, its coffers will be filled for generations. And that money would, in turn, finance its other goals in Europe and elsewhere."

"Russia," Reilly whispered.

"Correct," Sammy replied. "The answer to one riddle. A monopoly. Competitors frozen out of the China market with a long-term deal at the highest fees. Billions of gallons flowing through new pipelines and transported on board ships through warming Arctic waters—Russia's waters. An obvious deal when you think about it. With the other major shipping lanes shut down, it's a perfect scenario for Russia. We get what we need; Russia gets what it needs and wants. But you see, we have no leverage. No negotiating power."

Reilly let it all settle in. All of it. It had started with the death of the Russian oil oligarch. A calculated move. A meaningless loss in the greater scheme of things. Then the killing of the Japanese executive in Nairobi, the explosion in D.C., and now the death of the Canadian. An oil shell game to obscure attention from the perpetrator and the purpose designed to tighten the screws on China. *Yes,* he thought, *it was possible. After all, aren't possibilities what I'm supposed to see that others don't?*

"Is Gorshkov acting alone?" Reilly asked.

"Now that's a very interesting question. One I don't have the answer to, only speculation. Perhaps it's all tied to the attacks on your own bridges and tunnels. Your intelligence agencies have their suspicions. They've even briefed the president. So far, he hasn't acted on the information, which has only added to the chaos that lies at our feet today."

Reilly blanched. *How did Sammy have such insight into American intelligence and what Battaglio was and was not willing to do?*

Sammy read the look. "Oh, don't be so surprised, Daniel. Just as you have worked your way up, so have I. And I learn things, just as you do, and we don't talk about how or where."

"Alone?" Reilly asked again about Russia.

"An outlier by any standards."

"Venezuela?"

"No, though keep your eye on what happens there."

"Back to Iran," Reilly proposed.

"Too risky to try on its own. But likely complicit."

"North Korea!"

Sammy smiled. "Not a country to be trusted. But it, like the others you mentioned, still largely inefficient and bumbling. However, pay attention to their submarine fleet."

Sammy was back to his riddles. The answer was suddenly obvious.

"Not any of them individually. All of them collectively, and Gorshkov is the puppet master," Reilly declared.

"One could come to that conclusion. The question is, would that person take that deduction to people who would be most interested?"

Another riddle, Reilly saw the answer. *People who would be most interested did not include Ryan Battaglio.*

"Like I said, Sammy, you have the wrong guy. There's nothing I can do."

"But there is. You will be our emissary."

"An emissary no one will believe."

"The emissary with a proposition to consider."

"Whose?"

"On a small scale, mine. Your friend."

"And the larger?" Reilly asked.

Sammy smiled. "Those of far greater consequence than me." He laughed. "Of course, no names."

"I have a plane to catch," Reilly said impatiently.

"And you will take off, but with a message. My government proposes an increase in oil imports from the United States. Significant increases. An opportunity that doesn't come along every day. What do you say, *hands across the water?* This will stabilize the market rather than desta- bilize it. It will give us room to deal with Russia and not so subtly let President Gorshkov know we know what he's up to and will not allow him to hold us up to his terms."

"Sammy, like I said, I'm just not your guy."

"But you are. You are a businessman. This is business. And before you board your flight, you will have our opening proposal to present. It is the opening." Sammy looked to his sides and whispered, "There may be room to negotiate."

"You're using me!" Reilly shot back.

"I'm trusting you."

"There's no precedent for me taking any diplomatic offer to the U.S."

"Oh, sure there is. You're familiar with your own Cuban Missile Crisis?"

"Yes."

"Did you know that your President Kennedy relied on an ABC News reporter to serve as his go-between to Russia? His work likely prevented war."

"No," Reilly admitted.

"Quite true. The reporter, sworn to secrecy for years, communicated a solution that gave Nikita Khrushchev a way to pull Russian missiles out of Cuba in exchange for the removal of America's nuclear arsenal in Turkey. His name was John Scali. You, Daniel Reilly, shall be our emissary."

"I can't. I have no authority."

"You don't need authority. You need the proposal. And you'll have it."

"No," Reilly said with no sign of giving in.

"There's an old Chinese expression, Dan."

"Of course there is."

Sammy laughed.

"A folk tale. There was a street entertainer who earned an ample living with his dancing monkey. All was fine until the day the monkey decided not to dance. No dancing meant no money for the street performer. What did he do?"

"I suspect you're going to tell me."

"He bought a live chicken and killed it in front of the monkey."

Reilly got it. "And the monkey started dancing again."

"Very good. Kill the chicken to scare the monkey."

Reilly took it in but failed to see the meaning.

"My friend, Russia has been killing the chicken to scare the monkey. The monkey is the PRC, the People's Republic of China."

Reilly's eyes widened. He began to see the possibilities. *Intimidation and diversion. Pure trickery. Gorshkov was driving China toward believing that no one else's oil was safe.*

"I see you're thinking," Sammy noted. "That's good."

Barely above a whisper, Reilly said, "You have no reason to put your trust in me. Besides, my government isn't exactly cozy with yours these days. Our president—"

Sammy rested his hand on Reilly's arm. "Your president. Yes, that brings me to the second issue that also has global ramifications. This one, even more difficult than the first."

62

REILLY'S BODY TIGHTENED. He had no idea what bomb Sammy was about to drop next.

"Remember our first encounter? Of course, you do," Sammy answered before Reilly. "But what do you really remember? Let's see if our recollections match."

Reilly relaxed and looked out over the park to the families now with two children, a forlorn elderly woman on a bench, probably the same bench she and her husband had sat together on for years, and a young artist painting a landscape he hoped would sell and provide him with enough money for dinner.

He closed his eyes to the present and called up the past. The images and his emotions began to form: Relief that the two contemptible congressmen were finally out of his sight, then word that they hadn't made their connecting flight to DC. The order to go to Hong Kong; the boat ride to Macau; meeting Sammy for the first time, then the second. Getting the two worst representatives of the American government he'd ever met back to Washington, D.C.

He filled in between the shades of grey in his memory. He focused on the details he remembered and wondered about the things he was never told—about the first one who went off the rails but was located quicker than the other. And that other had remained at large for days, then was found, hooded, spirited to the airport, and unceremoniously put on the transport with his companion. None of the details of the *how and where* had been explained. Back twelve years ago, it was a story about two terrible Americans. Now they were about to be joined at the hip again in the White House.

"I remember," Reilly said. "But I don't know what actually went down."

"I spared you then."

"And?"

"No longer. I will entrust you with an item that's important to my government and will be of interest to some in yours."

"Some?" Reilly asked.

"Some who will be able to use the information for good while principals will deny it until they see and hear what I will be leaving in your care."

"Sammy, if it's video, you know as well as I do that it's easy to impeach. Deep fakes are everywhere on the internet, fucking up political campaigns and people's lives. Kids are making them on their laptops. I'm sure your Chinese technical wizards are light-years ahead of them. But in terms of evidence, deep fakes are easy to challenge."

Reilly had referred to the doctored videos that seemed real but were in fact computer-generated videos that create a false narrative, putting new words into people's mouths—generally celebrities and politicians. The result was something that looks absolutely real but that's 100 percent false.

"True. Video isn't enough. Neither are photographs or audio. But a confession is much harder when it is signed and dated with witnesses."

Still not knowing what the subject was, Reilly noted, "If you're talking about confessions under duress, drug- or alcohol-induced, or coerced, forget it."

"You will be the judge of whether to move forward with it."

"With what?"

"You'll see soon."

"I never took you as a man who dangled bait, Sammy. Break necks? Yes.

Make people disappear? Probably. But getting me to bite off a long line?"

"It is a failing of mine. But I am a good storyteller, and I suppose it's time for my story."

"My plane, Sammy." Reilly stood. "You can email me."

Simultaneously, Sammy grabbed his arm and pulled him down. Reilly slipped through the grip. The three Chinese guards moved closer.

"Please, Mr. Dan. We are friends. Sit." Sammy waved his men back. "Listen to my story, then decide. Indulge me."

Reilly locked on his companion's eyes. A blink or a look away would say more than he wanted, and he didn't want to give Sammy anything.

"You have friends in high places," Sammy said bluntly.

Reilly kept focused. *Was Sammy really fishing, or did he know about his extracurricular activities?*

"You also have enemies in higher places."

Reilly exhaled. He steeled himself for what was to come. He sat again and gave Sammy all he had—a time limit. "Ten minutes."

Sammy Wing Li smiled broadly. "I think you'll ask for more time once I get into the details. You might even consider it a gift."

At five minutes in, Reilly stopped paying attention to the time.

63

"IMPOSSIBLE!" REILLY DECLARED. "And if it were true, why only now?"

"Because now it's critical. Now is the time to expose the crime."

"The American people won't believe it."

"The American people won't have to," Sammy replied. "Just one man. He will believe it because he was there. The photographs, the video, the audio, his signature on a sheet of paper will convince him." The Chinese fixer fixed a smile on Reilly. "And you will show it to him."

"No. I'm not your agent for blackmail."

"An agent for change, my friend. For the betterment of your country."

"Find someone else. Why not go to the U.S. Ambassador?"

"Because he cannot be trusted."

"The Secretary of State?" Reilly tentatively offered.

"That, my friend is what you can do for us. You see, the first proposition I discussed with you is related to the second. The first cannot be accomplished without acting upon the second."

"And when it's questioned for authenticity and why it's not photoshopped propaganda or a deep fake created by your graphic artists?"

"You prove that it is authentic. You explain others are after it. My home was broken into, and the longer I keep it, the more I am at risk."

"Not good enough," Reilly replied.

"Then you will tell them you were there."

MACAO
TWELVE YEARS AGO

Sammy Wing Li's driver took U.S. Army Captain Reilly beyond the area where the grand hotels stood. By the fifth turn, he realized he wasn't heading to the airport water shuttle.

"Hey! Wrong way."

"Not wrong way. Way to see Mr. Sammy. Then you catch plane. I wait and take you to the airport."

"No, airport now," Captain Reilly argued.

"Dahengqin Island now. Then airport."

And that's the way it was, across the bridge to an area Reilly hadn't seen. It was developed and commercial, but not to the level of the two-square miles of reclaimed land from Seac Pai Bay known as Cotai. They came to a stop at the Zhuhai Hengqin Bay Nightowl Inn, where the prices were a fraction of those of the ritzy hotels and the sheets weren't washed as often. It wouldn't have been a hotel he'd choose.

"You meet Mr. Sammy inside. Go now."

Reilly got out of the car, not fearing for his life, but uncertain what to expect from this fixer, who always seemed to know more than he said. Once in the lobby, he was directed to a hallway by a very young and very beautiful woman. She lowered her eyes as he passed. *Fifteen or sixteen.* He knew what she did.

He passed five closed doors on either side of the hall before coming to one that was open. A refrigerator-sized man stood in the entrance. He stopped Reilly. Reilly peered around him, not a simple task.

Sammy saw him. "Come in." There was no warmth in his voice.

Reilly looked inside. The last thing he wanted to do was enter.

He'd witnessed horrible things in Afghanistan, escaped from them, then dreamt about them. This was different. This was worse. Not a war zone, but a hotel room. Not a combatant, but a young girl, like the one in the lobby who had lowered her eyes—less out of deference, more because she knew what he was about to see.

"Oh my God, Sammy. What? Why?"

"To remember. One day we may need to revisit this time and place. Now my driver will take you to the airport."

BEIJING

PRESENT DAY

Reilly remembered as if it were yesterday. The arms and legs of the girl tied to the four bed posts. The strangulation marks around her neck. Her pupils wide with fear. Her mouth agape. Reilly remembered. Then other things came to him. Personal items scattered on the floor, items he'd forgotten. For twelve years, Reilly didn't know why Sammy had brought him to the hotel. A stop along the way to scare him? To suggest that he was in a Chinese triad or the secret police?"

"Who are you, Sammy?" Reilly asked.

"Someone who doesn't forget. Someone who trusts you to right a wrong. Someone who is asking for justice from a friend."

"I don't understand."

"You will."

Reilly looked for an envelope, a package, something that contained whatever Sammy was alluding to.

"Not here," Sammy said. "You will have it before you leave. But a word of caution. There are others who want this as much as I want you to have it."

"You make it sound like what you have is the only copy," Reilly said.

"It is. What I didn't tell you is that it's personal. The girl."

Reilly sighed heavily. There was only one girl Sammy could be talking about. "The girl in the room?"

"Yes, Daniel Reilly, Captain Daniel Reilly. She was out with friends. She was not a prostitute. She was a good girl. She was my sister's daughter, my niece. Just fourteen, a child. Taken, used, and murdered."

"Why didn't you do something then?"

"I was forbidden. We were building bridges. I couldn't take down the foundation."

"And people know what you have kept?"

"Some in my government have suspected it. Such suspicions can be transmitted to others who seek to use the information or bury it. And for that reason, I cannot trust anyone here. But I can trust you."

Reilly glanced at Sammy's three men. *Were they to be trusted or not?* It didn't matter. Sammy hadn't brought whatever it was he had.

"How will you get it to me?"

Sammy held a finger to his lips.

"There are individuals, many individuals in my government with questionable loyalties tied to their hidden bank accounts. Money talks louder than nationalism. We've gotten very good at capitalism for a communist state, and I'm well aware that people are willing to sell out for the right price. Those I've discovered who have crossed me have paid a very different price. But vermin breed fast. Kill one, there's another one ready to crawl into the space. Democracy, dictatorship—it's all the same."

Sammy rubbed his knuckles again. Knuckles of a boxer without gloves. Reilly now focused on how rough they were, nearly scraped to the bone. Sammy's eyes narrowed. "Very recently, an aide in my organization showed extraordinary interest in an association I had with a certain American businessman."

He stopped and stared at Reilly.

Reilly shivered.

"Curious as it was," Sammy continued, "I explained that we were friends who had bonded years ago and conducted mutually beneficial transactions since. She was less interested in those and more in our history, which made me quite willing to engage her in what she really wanted to know. That was her mistake. Though her voice was steady, her eyes betrayed her. Disloyalty is always evident in the eyes. I encouraged her with a little lie to explain the truth." He clenched his fists. "I told her she'd live if she answered my questions. She finally opened up, and now I'm looking for someone to take over her job."

Reilly fixed on Sammy's eyes. There was no betrayal in them. "For that you killed her?"

"No, for that she died. There is a distinction. And before she departed this mortal coil she, shall I say, volunteered that she had been offered a substantial sum to learn more about the events in Macau years ago."

"To learn?"

"To learn what I showed you before you left Macau. To steal what I kept as my own and never shared with you. She came well prepared. A syringe, a nasty little pistol, and a knife. All the things that demonstrated that she had sold out. Even at the end, she couldn't tell me who had paid her. Sadly, I believe that's true."

"Nothing happened except two asshole American congressmen went on a binge."

"So far as what I allowed you to see. But there was more. And yes, she was in the right place to find it, but she was an amateur." Sammy's voice lowered an octave, "Daniel, an amateur. The next time they'll send a professional, which is why it is time for me to open my vault to you."

Reilly said nothing.

"What I held onto through the years is the thing that powerful people would pay a great deal of money to have. Some to exploit, others to bury. Blackmail or suppression? Valuable either way. It is also information that will restore balance."

* * *

It happened like this. Madame Juliette d'Arnaud was typing on her hotel's guest computer, checking out restaurant reviews in *DàZhòngDiǎnPing*, China's equivalent of Yelp. The service simply translated as *masses of people to comment*. However, the information in a coded text was intended for only one person.

It read like a review, but it was a job inquiry—a specific kind of job that required a change of plans. It offered a trip to Washington and a very short window to coordinate multiple assets. A target's name was concealed in a coded menu along with a must-have dish.

As she sat at the keyboard in full view of the hotel clerk, Madame d'Arnaud typed her reply; a thank you for the information and the offer:

$750,000. He could make that work. But he had to make quick airline arrangements. He mused that the only real negative of his work was that he could never collect on all the airline frequent flier miles.

64

"Office or the Sit Room?' asked Chairman of the Joint Chiefs Admiral Rhett Grimm over the phone.

"Oval Office," White House Chief of Staff Lou Simon replied. "Be succinct. You know how he likes it. Short sentences; few adjectives; no personal observations unless invited. No editorializing."

"Copy that," Grimm replied.

Simon wasn't sure how much more he could take from this new president. By week two, he'd felt beaten up. And he was tired of telling career officers, diplomats, and experts how to act in front of Battaglio. *Just a little bit more,* he consoled himself. Then he'd leave, wait the appropriate amount of time—a month or two—and move over to cable TV as a commentator and say the many things he couldn't now. *Soon, not yet.*

"And the president said don't start with, 'The Russians are coming, the Russians are coming,' Admiral."

"Christ, Lou. I've got a briefing from the 2nd Fleet. I can't say they're coming, but the fucking Ivan is still missing! That should raise a few eyebrows."

"Take him through the steps. I'll prompt you with questions if he has none."

"He won't have any. You know that. I know that."

"Step by step," Simon repeated. "And if it's about money—"

"It's about the defense of the country, for Christ's sake! And yes, that might cost a few more dollars," Admiral Grimm fumed.

"Step by step. We'll get him there."

The Chairman of the Joint Chiefs tapped his fingers on his desk. He breathed in and out to get his heart rate down. Then he continued. "You realize after the attacks in the Strait and the Suez, this round of hide-and-seek smells like either really bad timing or a calculated move."

"I do and he's heard that. Best recommendation is not to go over the same ground."

"Water, Lou! The Atlantic, a big fucking ocean."

"Take your time. We'll get him there."

Living up to his name, Admiral Grimm wasn't so sure.

Before hanging up, Chief of Staff Simon elicited a promise from the Admiral that he would hold his tongue. He'd be civil. But he wondered if Grimm would be as rudely booted from the administration as Pierce Kimball had been. And would he himself also be following the Admiral in the growing list of ex-administration employees and advisors? Inevitably yes. So far, he felt safe. Occasionally Battaglio even listened to him when he suggested that he pump the brakes; slow down, give people their due, and weigh decisions carefully.

Simon had inserted himself between the few Cabinet members who conspired for a 25th Amendment coup. Now that Battaglio had begun to install loyalists, that option was evaporating, much to his relief. Simon believed it would have been more destructive than productive.

His guiding beliefs, which admittedly were harder to follow by the day—show respect for the office and the institution, defer to tradition and faith in the system, and on a personal level, lead Ryan Battaglio through his own missteps. That was his overarching reason for not walking out the West Wing door. As unpredictable and ineffectual as the president was, Simon believed Moakley Davidson would make a far worse chief executive if he ever succeeded Battaglio. A bully with a pulpit and a commander who was more likely to act like a tribal chief.

* * *

"Mr. President," Simon said while Admiral Grimm waited in the outer office, "the Chairman is ready. I spoke with him for a few minutes. He really is concerned. Recommend we see what he has, sir."

"Okay, got it. But if I tap my pen three times that's it. You remind me to get to my phone call."

Simon knew there was no scheduled call.

"Yes, Mr. President. What if I throw out some hard questions and see what he comes up with?"

"Fine, fine. I like that. But the pen will be in my hand."

A moment later, Grimm was in for the briefing. "Mr. President, thank you for seeing me."

"Lou tells me you have something relevant."

Those weren't Simon's exact words. Battaglio knew that. He was just being snide.

"Yes, Mr. President. The Joint Chiefs are unanimous with their assessment. We have lost a Russian submarine, a nuclear attack submarine, at the worst possible time. It could it be another exercise. They've done it before, and we've lost them before. However, never with so many geopolitical flashpoints firing at the same time."

"Really, Admiral? No one's firing at us," the president said twirling his pen.

"No, sir. But until we reacquire the *Admiral Kashira*, we have to be prepared for a worst-case scenario. At this moment, the USS *Hartford* has changed course and is circling back to where it lost contact."

"Why?" Simon asked, knowing the answer.

"Belief that they never moved from their hiding spot. They're just lying low. And if that's the case, we have to ask ourselves why?"

"All right, I'll sing along." Battaglio said. "Why?"

"Routinely it's not unusual. They do it. We do it. But never so close to the New England coast. That's what concerns us. That and another thing."

His pen was about to come down again. He stopped and looked at the Admiral with a crinkled brow.

"The weight of the attacks in the Middle East, Russia's strong arming in the Northern Sea Route, and their move into Ukraine sets up an ideal time for President Gorshkov to test our resolve. Sir, *your* resolve. We're spread thin around the globe. If they challenge us, we will have to act."

Battaglio tapped his pen once, then again. He was about to tap it a third time but stopped.

"Admiral, let me be clear. You may carry this message back to the Joint Chiefs," the president stipulated. "I will pick the battles, and I don't believe our battle is with Russia. I'm more worried about the Chinese, the North Koreans, and the Iranians."

Grimm clenched his teeth but hid it. The president was asking him to make a misstep, say the wrong thing, show disregard for command and, in the process, give him reason for a curt dismissal.

"Mr. President," Grimm said in a way that suggested how he really felt about his Commander-in-Chief, "I'd like to walk you through the situation."

Walk, not teach. Explain, not lecture. Lou Simon relaxed. Admiral Grimm had taken his advice to heart. As Grimm pulled out cardboard cards from his attaché case, Battaglio slipped the pen in his pocket.

"Go on," Battaglio said.

"Thank you."

Admiral Grimm set up the cards on a small tripod art stand to face Battaglio. "These are charts that show launch time of missiles and torpedoes to the closest offshore oil facilities within 250 miles of the Russian sub. If this isn't a test, the time from launch to target is …"

President Battaglio stopped listening. He decided as soon as Grimm was out he'd call his friend Gorshkov and the whole thing would be settled.

65

"RYAN, so good to hear from you again. I trust you are well," Gorshkov said in somewhat halting English. He could do better, but he used this as a smoke screen, suggesting when necessary that he didn't understand everything that was said.

"I am, Nicolai. I wish I could say everything here was good. Members of my National Defense Council are very concerned that one of your submarines has disappeared. I'm getting alarms and alerts. They're worried that a commander has gone rogue."

"Oh? If that's true, I share your concern. I have not heard of a problem. When you say disappeared, what do you mean?"

"Our 2nd Fleet lost contact in the North Atlantic."

Battaglio had no idea that the Russian president was holding back laughing.

"Has your Navy identified the submarine?"

"Yes, it's *Admiral Kashira*. I think I pronounced it correctly."

"Ah, I know it. One of our newer boats. Will you hold, Ryan? I'll just make a call to my people."

Gorshkov put his phone on hold, crossed the office to his credenza, poured himself a vodka, took it back to his desk, sat and drank for three minutes before he finally picked up the line again.

"Good news, Ryan. All is fine. *Admiral Kashira* is in warm waters in the South Pacific," he lied. "I surely appreciate your concern. I hope this helps."

"It will. I think some of our folks are a little on edge given the terrorist attacks."

"I hear similar reports, especially from our shipping executives. The assassinations and sinking ships can fray anyone's nerves." Gorshkov took another long sip. "Is there anything else, my friend?"

"No, thank you. I'll let the Pentagon know."

"Good. And remember, our line of communication is always open."

The call ended. Ryan Battaglio was satisfied that his Navy had gotten it wrong. Nicolai Gorshkov had a hearty laugh and a second pour. His useful idiot was proving himself on both counts.

66

PANAMA CANAL

One day later everyone up and down the chain of command would be saying it was preventable. There were signs, warnings. An observer on land noted a ship moving a bit too fast. A port radar tech had recorded the increased speed but failed to notify operations. Satellite monitoring provided real-time intel to the NSA, but no one responded in time.

All the training, all the regulations, all the insistence on following protocol—all were ignored. Multiple governments, multiple agencies. Tomorrow they'd be called before superiors, looking for lawyers, preparing statements, and stepping away from their duties. Tomorrow the global stock market would take a dive. Tomorrow, Russia's ability to deliver oil would become more important than ever. Tonight, it happened within minutes.

* * *

The three North Koreans left their day jobs as a hotel cook, an Uber driver, and a dock warehouse worker to commandeer a harbor pilot boat. They killed the captain and crew and crossed the harbor for the 900-foot cargo ship *Adagio*. Alongside, looking completely official in uniforms, they boarded, announced the need to inspect the ship, split up, and proceeded to their predetermined targets: the bridge, the engine room, and the lower holds. Their duties were specific.

#1 Kill the captain and everyone on the bridge. Set course toward a tanker a quarter mile ahead and set the speed to five knots faster than allowed. It was not enough to immediately send clear warnings, but fast enough that slowing down in time with tugboats would be impossible.

#2 Disable the engine, which came easily by placing a time bomb after the crew was eliminated.

#3 Start fires below with Class 4 flammable solids that would spread quickly throughout the ship and engulf the 4,560 twenty-foot long containers top side.

Everything proceeded as planned, with no casualties among the terrorists.

On impact with the fully loaded tanker *Harmony Gold*, two things occurred. The collision fractured the tanker's hull plates below the waterline, and fire leaped across from *Adagio*. *Harmony Gold's* cargo of the liquified natural gas leaked out from its refrigerated aluminum compartments, hit the air that was hundreds of degrees warmer, and ignited into a firestorm, incinerating everything flammable and melting the ship's metal frame. The Panama Canal, like the Suez, was immediately, and for the foreseeable future, shuttered.

On shore, the North Koreans reunited with their control, a Russian FSB agent, to celebrate their success. They met at a seedy Panama City bar and drank until their clashing toasts left more margaritas on the table than in their glasses. After two hours, the three operatives stumbled out to the alley, where their commander called them together for one last group hug and a bullet to each of their brains. Only the third man, the warehouse worker, was briefly aware of his impending death.

The Russian spy left their bodies where they'd fallen, placing family photos in their wallets for Panamanian police to find. In short order, American intelligence agents working in Panama would connect the photos to locations in Pyonyang, the capital of North Korea. It was Gorshkov's catnip for his cat in the White House, the mouse to chase after if Battaglio had the courage.

The entire effort would have been a tactical success had it not been for one unexpected game changer. *Adagio* was supposed to have collided with a ship of American registry. But *Harmony Gold* had moved up in the queue. The tanker was managed by a Chinese conglomerate, a matter made worse because the fire spread to Margarita Island Port, one of two Panama Canal ports now managed by the Chinese. The shock wave was felt all the way to Beijing.

THE WHITE HOUSE

The usual suspects assembled in the Situation Room. The situation was dire.

"What are we looking at?" the president asked.

Admiral Grimm slowly rose and walked around the conference table to the front of the room, opposite from the president. He presented satellite and ground photos from Panama. He had bad news with every sentence. Even Battaglio understood.

"What can we do?" he asked with definite desperation. "Who do we go after?"

"Well, we know one thing," Secretary of State Elizabeth Matthews said. "It's not China."

"Why are you so damned sure of that?"

"Because the port was theirs."

The principal stakeholders at the table looked down. No one wanted to be staring at the president at this moment. They knew something Battaglio apparently didn't—the deal in 2018 that allowed Chinese corporations to buy into the Panama Canal.

BEIJING

Dan Reilly was more than ready to head home. Well, nearly ready. The best part of his stay in Beijing was meeting Yibing Cheng and the days and nights they had together. The worst? Everything else. The thing that happened and the things he'd now have to deal with.

He settled into his first class seat, wishing he could put it in full recline, just close his eyes, and sleep all the way. That would all come after at least a scotch and appetizers.

This wasn't the original flight he'd booked, or the second, third, fourth, or fifth Sammy had held seats on. This was the tenth one that would get him back to Washington, though through Amsterdam.

"Ladies and gentlemen, I'm sorry we're experiencing a short ground delay," the pilot reported over the PA system.

What now? Reilly wondered.

The pilot had an answer for him and everyone else on board.

"Traffic's a bit busy this time of day. We'll have you in the air as soon as possible."

"Any idea how long?" Reilly politely asked the Chinese flight attendant.

"I don't know, sir. Shouldn't be more than a few more minutes. In the meantime, may I get you a cocktail?"

Twenty minutes later and well into his drink, Reilly watched as a beautiful woman walked onto the plane. She spoke with the senior attendant and was directed down the aisle. She stopped by 3A.

"Mr. Reilly?"

"Yes."

"Mr. Dan Reilly?"

"Yes."

She examined a photograph of Reilly and was satisfied. "My name is Junrui. I was asked to see you before you took off," she said sweetly.

"Someone with enough power to control departures?"

"He is able to call in favors now and then, Mr. Dan."

The woman removed a thick parcel from a bag slung over her shoulder. Given the sensitivity of the material Reilly assumed she had, he was surprised she'd carried it onboard in such a cavalier manner. He now wondered if he was being used as a tool for the Chinese government for some greater goal.

"As promised by Mr. Sammy."

Reilly didn't immediately reach for the package. Taking it would be owning it. Owning it would mean he'd have to see it through—all the way through. All the way didn't mean lateral. It reached to the pinnacle. And the pinnacle was where the fall could be deadly.

"I'm sorry," she said. "But you must."

"You came alone? I would have thought—"

She smiled and looked to Reilly's right. "Oh no. I'm rarely allowed to go anywhere without security."

The woman looked back toward the open door. She exchanged eye contact with a very large man who would undoubtedly put the plane over its takeoff weight. But he wasn't there to fly. He was the beast behind the beauty.

"So you mustn't worry about me. But please take care of yourself."

The envelope was inches away. Reilly regarded the woman's manner and appearance. *A rare beauty. Smart. One of Sammy's consorts?* He imagined what might happen to her if he didn't accept the delivery. Sammy was surely capable of the most unspeakable acts in service of all the masters he served.

"Thank you," he finally said. He took the envelope. "Do I need to sign for it?"

"Oh no. It's all being recorded." She gestured to a brooch over her heart: a snake with a tiny glass eye staring directly ahead. A camera eye.

"Wait. Why does Sammy trust you above all others?"

"A question from a worthy man on a noble mission demands an honest answer. He is my father. My cousin's name was Ting. Her name means enduring. You will meet her again shortly." She patted the envelope. "You will be doing her memory an honor. Make it right, Mr. Daniel."

PART THREE

ALL IN

67

BEIJING

Reilly smiled inwardly. Ey Wing Li—Sammy—had more influence than he ever imagined. Now Reilly would have to see how much he had in the United States. He clutched the envelope, thinking he couldn't take the chance to sleep. He put the drink aside and requested a black coffee.

Three hours into the flight, somewhere over central China, Reilly opened the larger envelope and removed its inner contents. More envelopes, smaller. In them, 8x11s; ten black-and-white photographs and fifteen more in color. He examined them slowly, painfully. The black-and-white photos, wide shots and close-ups, were graphic enough; the color photographs were even harder to look at. They showed unimaginable images he had tried to forget. Now he couldn't. He knew the name of the young girl brutally murdered. He knew her uncle.

He slipped the pictures back in the envelope and opened another. In this one, a single sheet of paper, handwritten in Chinese and English. He presumed the English was a translation. It was dated and signed by two people. One of the names was Ey Wing Li. The other, an American, explained all the questions he hadn't asked Sammy but he'd come to realize.

Reilly took out his cell phone and shot a series of photographs of the American's signature. Next, he checked for Wi-Fi. No signal. *Damn*, he thought. Now it might be hours before he could text the image with a simple question mark out to Bob Heath. Once it was delivered, he was certain his CIA friend would figure out his request. He was also certain the signature was authentic.

The single page went back into its envelope. An even smaller envelope contained a thumb drive. Reilly assumed this was the most explosive evidence—perhaps live action of what the pictures depicted. Death. Video and audio of what the sheet of paper affirmed, with a face and voice to go with it.

Reilly didn't have a laptop. He wasn't certain if he had one he'd even want to watch. But he had to. He had to know what was on the drive.

He unbuckled his safety belt, stood in the aisle, and saw what he needed at 6B. A laptop on a lap, a sleeping girl next to her mother. He casually walked to the row, spotted the port that would take his thumb drive, and softly asked the mother, "Okay if I borrowed your girl's computer for a few minutes? I have one thing to check."

The mother was uncertain.

"Just a couple of minutes. Not really going anywhere."

The mother looked at Reilly, then her daughter.

"It's important. Honestly."

She gently lifted the computer from her sleeping daughter's lap.

"The password is Dua Lipa."

Reilly frowned.

"The English singer? Karla loves her." The mom spelled the name.

"Thank you," he said. "I'll be right back."

He'd seen enough after five minutes. The murder scene, the questioning. Denials, crying, apologies, and the confession.

He extracted the thumb drive and closed the computer down.

"Get your work done?"

"It's just starting. Thank you."

Reilly returned to his seat. He tucked the envelope under his shirt behind his back. He adjusted his seat into a partial recline, closed his eyes, and willed himself to see Yibing's face instead of Sammy Wing Li's dead niece. Fortunately he fell asleep until the plane was fifty minutes out of Amsterdam.

On the ground, Reilly went through customs without having to explain much more than he was a hotel executive on his way back to America. The officer was not interested in the envelope he carried along with an *International New York Times* he brought off the plane.

Reilly found his way to the United VIP lounge, where he texted Heath and grazed on the buffet selections. A minute later, he received a text. *Roger-tango.* Heath confirmed he understood. Ninety-two minutes into his three-hour layover and his third cup of black coffee, another text. *Real deal.*

Reilly went to the bathroom and tucked the envelope under his shirt again. He washed his face and stared long and hard into the mirror. How would he be viewed? *Traitor? Conspirator? Patriot?* Sammy wanted him to deliver the package. What did he say? *"You have friends in high places"* and that "the information would restore the balance."

Traitor, conspirator, or patriot, he was on the way to Washington with dynamite.

* * *

As Reilly flew the friendly skies, an Iranian killer sub was on course in the Atlantic. The days had been whittled down to a few hours. Captain Ali Shirvani was pleased with how well his crew had performed. They would all be honored as heroes of the Islamic Republic of Iran, decorated for their service to the new alliance between their nation and the Russian Federation.

His orders were clear: No communication. Stay below 120 meters. Follow the directive without question. Count on the *Admiral Kashira* to be at the rendezvous coordinates just as they had trained.

Shirvani ordered the next timed course change, precisely to the minute. The next turn, in another eighty-seven minutes. The captain smiled. In addition to the accolades his men would receive, Shirvani, fifty-five, was ready to spend the rest of his life on solid ground, with a promotion and an incentive: a side deal sealed with a handshake from the Russian commander, and money. Change of life money, deposited into a Swiss bank account. Shirvani assumed it was for a job well done, which he would do.

* * *

The USS *Hartford* was on its last wide turn to the New England Seamounts where Cmdr. Andrew Policano was convinced the *Admiral Kashira* was hiding—hiding and waiting. *Waiting for what?* That was a question typically above his pay grade, except for now. He considered Ivan's actions suspicious and threatening. He radioed as much to 2nd Fleet Command before going quiet. He hoped he had conveyed the danger with all due urgency. The message was received loud and clear as high up as the Joint Chiefs: locate the *Admiral Kashira* and seriously fuck up his plans. Whatever the hell they were.

* * *

Reilly phoned Elizabeth Matthews once he was in the town car that Brenda had arranged to get him from Dulles into D.C. His plan was to meet outside her office and put the package right in her hands. *Hers and no one else's.* She didn't know it was coming, but he couldn't discount the chance that someone else might. Someone who could have spies within the Chinese government or relationships in the U.S. Someone who had a great deal to gain, or someone who had a great deal to lose.

"Secretary Matthews, please. Dan Reilly calling," he told the Secretary of State's assistant.

"I'm sorry, Mr. Reilly, but she's in a session."

"Tell her it's urgent." To underscore his point he added, "I'll hold."

"Please hold."

He assumed that the assistant was instructed never to ignore anyone using the word *urgent*. Three minutes later, a somewhat out of breath Elizabeth Matthews picked up the phone.

"Dan, what is it?"

"I need to see you."

"I've got a full day—"

"In ninety minutes. I'm on my way in from the airport. We'll take a stroll."

"I can't. I'm due in the Situation Room in fifteen. Got some things to deal with," she said without any emotion. Then, more warmly she said, "Sorry for what happened to your friend."

"Right. Thanks."

"Look, go home, rest for a few hours. I'll call you when I get a breather."

The last place he wanted to go was the obvious—his Georgetown condo. However, he didn't tell her. "Call me as soon as you're through," he said.

"Got any topic sentence for me?" Matthews asked.

"Just call."

Reilly hung up without saying goodbye. He was sure she'd get the message. But she was also giving him one: *the Situation Room.* There was a situation.

*　*　*

There are natural ways submarines can slip into invisibility. Seasonal weather phenomena impact sound propagation. Changing wind-driven waves and temperature gradients throughout the day affect acoustic signatures. Mountain ranges create perfect hiding places.

Since the main source of noise from a submarine comes from its engines and the propeller blades, anti-submarine warfare (ASW) is all about listening and evaluating data—listening for the nearly undetectable through passive and active sonar and acoustic sensors, using technology to detect tiny disturbances to the Earth's magnetic field that are caused by submarine hulls.

Policano relied on his computers, but with all the advances available, he relied on something else even more—his crew.

"Contact, Mr. James?"

"If she's there, she's sitting quiet, where we last had her. No crew sounds, no blades."

"Keep your best ear." Policano said, happy Marcel James was back at his watch.

"Yes sir," James responded. James closed his eyes, listened, and pictured *Admiral Kashira* lying low. He also thought about the leisure boats sailing off the coast of New England, swimmers from Maine to Cape Cod, and his relatives in Boston. An attack on the submerged offshore oil intake facilities as well as on the storage tanks along Boston harbor would be devastating, leaving thousands dead and the coast rendered useless. *Best ears,* James thought.

"Captain?" he asked, holding his right hand to his ear to keep the cans in place.

"Yes?"

Marcel James turned his head to the left and slid the earpiece back. "Permission to speak freely?"

"Go ahead, son."

"Quite out of order."

Policano nodded consent.

"It's a hunch, sir. A feeling."

A feeling. Policano had been harboring his for days.

"Feelings matter, Mr. James. Go ahead."

At Annapolis, Andrew Policano had written a paper on hunches that earned him a C from a disagreeable professor, but that grade never dissuaded him from acknowledging the importance of hunches. Knowledge and expertise were essential; however, not every situation can be wrapped in an experiential bow. Many situations aren't completely readable. He maintained that unprejudiced thinking can often identify gaps in knowledge, and a hunch, based on that experience, can frame important decision-making—lifesaving decision-making. He read stories about Marines who instinctively knew where IEDs were buried and Army drivers who avoided roadside bombs because they sensed trash wasn't thrown randomly but for a very real purpose. And Navy commanders who suddenly altered course to avoid mines because of the way dolphins were swimming.

A grade of C for his paper. He'd forgotten the name of the instructor. He never gave up believing he was right. Now Marcel James was asking him to consider a feeling.

"Lives have been saved on feelings, Mr. James. Go ahead."

"Just a feeling, you understand."

Policano put his arm on the young black man's shoulder.

"Let's have it."

The petty officer locked eyes with his commander, who was twice his age. "Sir ..."

"Yes."

"Something's not right."

68

WASHINGTON, D.C.

Reilly produced his credit card and ID and passed them to the Kensington Capital Hotel desk clerk. He deliberately did not identify himself as a Kensington employee or use a Kensington Rewards card. Less was best, though he would call down to the general manager once he was settled in.

"We're limited on room choices, Mr. Reilly," the young woman said, reading his name off his Illinois driver's license. "We're in the middle of renovations. Two of the elevator banks are also being repaired. You may see workers coming and going." She smiled a normal smile and didn't provide any other information. No need to scare the guy from Chicago.

Reilly nodded. He didn't ask about the scaffolding on the side and corner of the fourteenth floor or why some of the elevators were out.

"I can put you on the twelfth floor," she said.

"Actually, seven or below." It was his preference based on his awareness of how high most hook-and-ladder equipment reached.

"Well, let's see."

As the desk clerk checked her computer, Reilly casually unbuttoned his sports jacket and adjusted it slightly until he felt the package securely tucked in against the small of his back. He turned and surveyed the lobby. The bar was open; guests were chatting across low, round tables and milling about. He figured the Kensington Capital was booking at half capacity or less because of the attack—which obviously wasn't part of the staff's welcome speech.

"How's fifth floor? I can upgrade you to a junior suite."

"That'll be nice," Reilly said. "One night."

She returned to the computer and completed the check-in. A minute later she returned his identification and gave him two room keys. Two was typical.

"Do you need any help with your bag?"

"No, thank you. I'm set."

Reilly wasn't about to let anyone separate him from his luggage or accompany him. The more isolated he remained, the better. He'd shave and shower and wait for Elizabeth Matthews's phone call. Then he'd get rid of the goddamned gift Sammy had given him.

* * *

The gavel came down. It was time to start the hearing. The Sergeant of Arms asked Senator Moakley Davidson to stand, raise his right hand, and take the oath. Davidson finished with a proud and rousing, "So help me God." He was one step closer to becoming Vice President of the United States.

Davidson sat opposite fellow senators who had mostly softball questions for what was described as a merely *pro forma* confirmation hearing. He was anything but loved, but not loathed enough to derail his ascension.

Senator Walter Littlefield, the chairman of the committee and an acknowledged lion of the Senate, began. "Welcome, Senator. I believe we all know you well." They didn't. "I think we can agree as a committee that you have distinguished yourself through your career in Congress in an unimpeachable manner" He hadn't. "We're not here to look under every rock or to besmirch your character and reputation." They should. "However, we have our duty to fulfill before you assume your new office. Please answer honestly and fully." He wouldn't. "Now let's begin. I understand you have an opening statement."

"Thank you, Senator Littlefield. I do."

Moakley Davidson wore a black pin-striped three-piece suit, white shirt, red tie, and the all-but-mandatory American flag pin. He waxed philosophic, recounted his humble formative years growing up on a North Dakota ranch, and shared his early dream to serve the good people of his state in the nation's capital. His first step was a run for the local school board. From there, county supervisor, the state legislature, the House, and then the Senate. He smiled when he spoke of his children and ignored the ugly divorce from his wife. He declared himself a religious man, a patriot, and a dedicated public servant. He skipped over the political muscle he exerted to ruin competitors, his misbehavior on Congressional tours abroad—Macau was one of many—and the recent murder of a *Hill* reporter.

"To my friends in the Senate on both sides of the aisle, and to Americans everywhere, I pledge to honor and uphold the Constitution of the United States and bring every fiber in my body to the job as your Vice President. My experience becomes your assurance that I will tirelessly work with President Battaglio, the beloved Senate that I will preside over, and the entire nation I will serve every day on your behalf. Now, I understand you have some questions. I'll be happy to answer them."

One by one, senators went through their opening remarks and congratulations. Davidson was familiar with questions from his party and had been assured that there'd be little objection to his nomination. When prompted, he talked about the oil discovered on his ranch thirty years ago, the deals he made, and whether his holdings were indeed in a blind trust. He assured the committee he was not in big oil's pocket. There were lobbyists, none scheduled to testify, who would have disagreed.

Davidson discussed the multiple bills he had introduced over the years that were signed by both Republican and Democrat presidents. He failed to discuss the legislation he had heartlessly blocked.

He chronicled his record on civil rights. He sidestepped a follow-up about his lack of concern for Native American concerns in his home state.

To Senator Moakley Davidson's mind, the first two hours were going very well. President Ryan Battaglio, watching at the White House, had the same impression. He told his new National Security advisor that soon they'd be one step closer to rebuilding the senior staff from the vice president, through the Cabinet, down to Pentagon leadership and even his communications staff. Then he would begin working on his reelection, which would be all but guaranteed with Davidson on the ticket.

* * *

Pilots were rerouting ships in the Panama Canal while engineers argued over conflicting computer models for the best immediate approach for repairing the damaged port, recovering the containers that had toppled overboard, and backing out the ship. The crime scene was under the jurisdiction of the Panama Canal Authority, but within twelve hours the Pentagon put Major General Rufus T. Holmes from the United States Southern Command (USSOUTHCOM) on the ground. The command is responsible for all U.S. military activities south of Mexico, through Central and South America, the Caribbean, thirteen island nations, and U.S. territories. Holmes arrived with a team from the Army Corps of Engineers. He quickly surmised that the Panamanians were ill-equipped to handle cleanup within an acceptable time frame. He reported his initial finding to USSOUTHCOM. The message was quickly communicated to the White House Situation Room.

* * *

"What's it going to take?" Defense Secretary Vincent Collingsworth asked.

"To repair?" Admiral Grimm asked. "The Army Corps is assessing now. But securing and protecting the canal, boots on the ground?" He gave an estimated recommendation for 3,000 troops.

"The president will need to sign off," Chief of Staff Lou Simon said. "And I'm not sure he'll be inclined to commit that many."

Collingsworth, frustrated, looked left to right, up and down the table. "Why the hell isn't the National Security Advisor here?"

"He's with POTUS," Simon noted. "Following the Veep confirmation hearing."

The room fell silent. Matthews took a deep breath and stated what was probably on everyone's mind.

"Look, many of us may be gone in a month. Department by department, we're going to be minimalized, squeezed out, or summarily fired. It won't be pretty, and the country will be all the worse for it. But at this moment, we are sitting members of the United States government with a duty to fulfill."

She addressed the Chairman of the Joint Chiefs. "Admiral, do you have the authority to redirect American forces for the purpose of an exercise?"

He smiled. "For an exercise, yes."

"Good."

Next, Matthews turned to the Secretary of Homeland Security, Deborah Sclar. "Deb, we have a valued submarine commander who believes there's a Russian killer sub at our doorstep. That suggests we should do something to bar the door."

Now Sclar smiled.

The Situation Room was finally dealing with the situation.

69

OFF THE COAST OF NEW ENGLAND

"Speed to ten knots," ordered Commander Policano as he traced the course he set on the chart.

"Speed ten knots," replied the helmsman.

"Steady as she goes."

Eight minutes later, sonar called out, ""Coming to target in 600 yards."

"Roger that, Mr. James.

"Slow to two knots, Mr. Chanko."

"Aye, sir," the helmsman replied. "Slow to two knots."

Twelve minutes later came the order, "All stop."

"Sit tight everyone." Policano's request went down the line. The crew of the USS *Hartford* knew the drill: shoes off, no speaking, limited movement.

"Anything, Mr. James?"

"If *Admiral Kashira* is there, sir, she's less than 500 feet away."

"And if she's not?" Policano asked.

"Then I'm convinced someone else is."

* * *

Admiral Kashira was actually thirty-three miles due north, sitting silently. Most of the crew were in their bunks, sleeping or reading as they had been for the last three days. Captain Boris Sidorov looked at his Breitling watch, a personal gift from President Nicolai Gorshkov. He had successfully outwitted the American Navy. Soon there would be chaos, and he would return home. Mission completed.

70

WASHINGTON, D.C.

After a thirty-minute break, more questions for Davidson. The junior senator from Massachusetts, not a fan, pressed him on his finances. He recycled a variation of his stock answer. "My businesses are in a blind trust. I hope their positions are improving, but it is a blind trust, Senator. And while my sight is 20-20, I don't peek."

The final follow-up was put to bed with, "I'm sorry, Senator I've answered that. If you have another question for me—?"

He didn't. It was time for Chairman Littlefield to move onto another senator, but he was caught listening to his aide. He talked with his hand over the microphone so the conversation wouldn't be picked up for the room or the coverage. "What?"

"A note sir."

"Not now," Senator Littlefield told his Senate aide Carlos Deleon.

"Sir." Deleon was insistent.

Littlefield raised his fingers above his left shoulder and took the folded paper without looking away from the proceedings. He put it on his desk, opened it, and read. Once, then twice.

A potential witness with a serious charge.

After the second pass, he gaveled for a break.

"Senator Davidson, let's give ourselves another breather. Say fifteen minutes?"

Davidson smiled. "Certainly." He'd seen Littlefield read the paper and figured it was something personal.

"I ask everyone to wait a moment until Senator Davidson has a chance to clear the room before rising." Littlefield stood. His aide was a few steps behind him. "Really Carlos?"

"I wouldn't have interrupted except—"

"Who is this witness?"

"A woman who works on the Hill."

"Oh God," Littlefield said. "Not another—"

"No, someone else. I know her. She's responsible, married. A Harvard grad. She's worked with Davidson for a short time, but she has something. Please, listen to her, Senator."

Littlefield nodded. "She better get right to the point."

Littlefield and Deleon made the one minute walk to an office off the Kennedy Hearing Room. He spent ten minutes with the woman, then one minute back and a minute to settle in. All within the fifteen minutes he allotted.

"All right Miss, in the history of confirmation hearings to fill the vacancy of the office of Vice President of the United States, I've never known of a junior Congressional aide, no disrespect intended ..."

"None taken, sir."

"... to stop the process dead in its tracks. Believe me, in preparation for today's session, I did my homework. And either you're going to make the history books, or I'll make bloody sure you'll be a punch line on the late-night talkers. You better have a good explanation. Now who the hell are you?"

"My name is Tasha Samuels." She swallowed hard. "I actually work for Senator Davidson."

"You work for the United States of America, Ms. Samuels."

She quickly gathered her thoughts. "Yes, sir, and I recognize this is highly out of order."

"Highly. But since you've put the committee and the country on hold, you alone have my ear for," he checked his watch, "nine minutes and thirty seconds. I suggest you use your remaining time wisely."

"Mr. Chairman—" She took in a long breath, closed then opened her eyes, and was transformed, stronger, determined. "You can't confirm Davidson."

* * *

Nobody sat while Samuels spoke. She had her notes but didn't refer to them. She went through the timeline one point at a time. She presented facts, not opinion, in a completely organized, though abridged manner. At four minutes, she stopped and stared at Littlefield.

She had hoped for a positive reaction. He gave her nothing. Nothing for sixty excruciating seconds, during which she foresaw the end of her short Capitol Hill career and more importantly, her husband's.

"I'm sorry I bothered you," Samuels said, breaking the silence. She lowered her shoulders. "I thought I'd give you enough to at least ask me a few questions. I hadn't considered what it would do to your reputation if you challenged a Senate colleague about to become vice president."

She did an about face and began walking away.

Littlefield laughed. She stopped and turned.

"What's so funny?"

"With friends like Davidson, who needs enemies? Come back, Ms. Samuels. Now about those questions—"

* * *

Each Senator was allowed three rounds of questions. Davidson had agreed to the format and believed by the end of the day Moakley Davidson would clear the committee. The full Senate would take up the vote the next day. They were almost finished with the second round. Littlefield chaired the hearing efficiently, without any hint as to what Tasha Samuels had told him. He was buying time. Samuels had made her argument, but he needed more than just the word of an aide whose testimony could be quickly impeached.

"Evidence, Ms. Samuels," Littlefield had told her in the outer office. "You have very few hours to prove your case. And considering you're starting so late, I don't place much hope in your success. Take Carlos with you. Maybe between the two of you, you can pull off a miracle—assuming a miracle is there to be found. Give me enough to put the confirmation on hold, and I'll buy you another twenty-four hours, with help." He left them with one more thing. "And to your earlier point, don't make this cost me my reputation."

* * *

The sitting members of the committee were on their last round of questions when Senator Littlefield saw the door open. Tasha Samuels entered, nodded slowly from across the room, and sat in the last row. A moment later, Deleon was at his boss's back with a manila folder.

He whispered, "First three pages, sir. The rest you can look at later."

Littlefield opened the file and read slowly. The first page was a copy of an email. The second, a note with a date and location. The third, a bank statement."

Covering the mic he asked, "Where'd you get this?"

"Desk computer." Deleon nodded forward. "His."

"Excuse me. The Chair has a question, Senator Davidson," Littlefield abruptly cut in. The senators flanking him all turned.

Davidson stopped mid-sentence. Littlefield cleared his throat. He looked to his left, to his right, then addressed Senator Moakley Davidson, President Ryan Battaglio's nominee for Vice President of the United States.

"Senator Davidson," Littlefield paused. He bore down on his Senate colleague. "Tell the committee about your relationship with Sherwood Baker, a reporter for *The Hill*, murdered last week in Virginia."

Moakley Davidson stared at Littlefield shocked, thrown off his game. "Excuse me? My relationship?"

"That was my question."

"It wasn't the question so much as your tone, Senator."

"Senator Davidson, the Chair would appreciate your answer," Littlefield replied.

Davidson cleared his throat. "Yes, I knew Mr. Baker." Cupping his hand over the microphone he whispered to his counsel, "What the hell is this about?"

"Don't know. No one brought it up in our preliminaries. Do you have any idea?"

"No!" Davidson said above the whisper.

"Senator Davidson, your answer for the committee," Littlefield pressed.

"*Yes*, I knew Mr. Baker. Everyone of us has relationships with reporters. *No*, I know nothing about his murder."

"I hadn't gotten to that question yet, Senator." The chairman's voice had an icy quality intended to slice through any obfuscation. "But since you raise it, do you have any information relevant to his murder?"

"What I read in the papers. What I hear in the news."

"Let's step back to your last conversation." Littlefield adopted his old prosecutor's posture from his years as a Philadelphia district attorney. "Exactly when and where did you last talk to Mr. Baker? I'll get to the substance in a bit."

* * *

Elizabeth Matthews stepped out of the Situation Room, recovered her cell phone from a drawer and dialed. "Okay, Daniel. I'm out for a bit. What's up?"

"I need to see you."

"You'll have to come here. I'm still tied up at the White House and will be for, I don't know how long."

"Someplace else."

"Can't. Not a good time to run out."

"And there's not a good place to meet considering—"

Of all the intriguing things Reilly could have said, this gave her real pause. She flashed on her conversation with the FBI Director and his message that the Congressional aide believed there was linkage between the reporter's murder and Reilly. She hadn't heard from McCafferty since their walk.

"Okay. The National Mall. The Vietnam Memorial. How soon can you make it?"

"Twenty minutes," Reilly said. "Oh, and only bring your most trusted team."

* * *

Reilly tucked the envelope back into his hiding place. He put his sportscoat back on and took the stairs down from his hotel room. He opened the door to the lobby and stood for a moment. The hotel was busier than earlier. Fifty, maybe sixty people were in various stages of coming, going, and milling about. It was time for afternoon check-in and early drinks for Washington lobbyists and power brokers. At the near and far corners, plainclothes hotel security, one more than he had seen coming in. There was also one uniformed D.C. cop patrolling. Appropriate considering the attack, though if it were up to him he would have had more on the property.

Dan Reilly took his first steps across the lobby. No one appeared to take notice. People were into their own space, their companions, their drinks, or their newspapers and books. Ordinarily he would stop and smile, engage guests in conversations, or evaluate operations. Today he had a single purpose: leave the hotel quietly, meet the Secretary of State, and unload the damned papers.

Midway across the lobby, to the side of the revolving doors, he noticed a stocky man with close-cropped hair locking eyes with him. *Another security guard,* he thought. The right look, the right build, but he wasn't dressed in the usual hotel blue jacket and grey pants. It was when the man shifted his eyes to his left and gave an ever-so slight nod to someone that Reilly felt a sudden chill. Reilly looked over his right shoulder, taking in people at the bar—the security guard, the cop, and people sitting in the lobby. Nothing had changed but he was convinced

a signal had been exchanged. A man at the bar could have seen it in
the mirror, or an older man in a tweed jacket sitting alone reading the
Washington Post.

He looked for others. A brunette wearing a fashionable white hat
leafing through a magazine; a group of four Asian women, standing
and chatting busily; businessmen with briefcases; a teenager with a
skateboard under his arm waving goodbye to his father; a family with a
stroller; an elderly woman with a cane; and the bartender who appeared
to be looking beyond his customers.

Nobody and everybody. Reilly was convinced he'd been made.

He labeled the man in front "A." For now, the bartender was "B."
He didn't doubt that there was a "C," and they had triangulated on him.

Options. He raced through them. If he was right, the entrance was
out. The stairs up would be slow going and "C" was now near the door
he'd just come through. Reilly stood dead center with three hotel security
officers and the D.C. officer equidistant from him. He considered how
public his alphabet trio might get and who was the most dangerous.

He couldn't risk creating a scene, but he had to get out.

New options. Walk purposely to the front desk and walk through the
office to a side passageway. He turned to make the move. That's when
"C" revealed himself and stood no more than fifteen feet in front of him.
And from behind he heard "A."

"Mr. Reilly, don't be foolish. The hotel has already had one incident.
You don't want to be responsible for another."

Options. Fight or flee? He ruled out fleeing as quickly as he did just
walking out with his escorts. But to fight, he would need help. Help,
he hoped, that would act as trained.

Reilly led with his right foot, back to the stairs. "C" moved in kind,
but Reilly cut left in front of a family of four. He picked up an empty
water glass on a low table and launched it toward the nearest guard who
was looking in the opposite direction. It hit the wall and shattered. The
sound drew the hotel security's attention.

"Who the hell did that?"

"I did!" Reilly yelled.

The other two members of the hotel detail rushed over. "A" and "C" backed away. "A" stopped at the entrance, glanced back and shot another look across the room to the still unidentified "B."

"All right cowboy, come on. Hope you had a good reason for doing that," the near officer said.

"I did. And I don't have time to explain." He reached for his wallet, flashed his Kensington ID for barely a second, and ran across the lobby. He stopped just between the sectioned-off bar and the lounge chairs and computed the interest he had created. Everyone froze; curious. He took in the wide shot, then tight. He read each face again. The bartender, the Asians, the man with the newspaper, the skateboard kid, the old lady, the family with their baby, and a dozen other faces.

Something was different. His eyes darted left and right. He turned in a complete circle. The hotel security officer spoke to him, but Reilly had tuned them out. He was looking—looking for the difference. Then he saw it in three parts. First, the magazine lying face up on the chair without its reader. Second, the publication itself—*Puzzles and Games*. Third, he saw a woman just feet away from the lobby door to the stairs he'd taken down. She disappeared through it.

"There!" Reilly shouted.

The D.C. cop was nearest the stairs. He took up the chase. Reilly was steps behind; the door just closing as he slipped through. He heard footsteps racing ahead and a muted pop.

"Careful," Reilly warned. It was too late. As he rounded a landing taking the next flight two stairs at a time Reilly saw the police officer falling backwards. Reilly leapt over the railing to avoid getting pinned. He looked down and saw a hole drilled dead center through the temple. The pop, fired from the woman's suppressed gun.

Three steps up, Reilly saw the guard's 9mm Beretta on the stairway. He picked it up and continued the chase, keeping himself flat against the wall on every turn. Two flights up, he stepped over a woman's hat. Ten more steps, a long black wig. The next floor, a wrap-around dress.

Reilly knew who he was after. Not a woman. That was merely the last disguise. The assassin! And *he* was becoming someone entirely new while running, while killing the Washington cop.

Reilly felt his heart beating hard. He stopped to catch his breath and gauge where he was—between floors eight and nine. He heard running ahead of him and people behind—either hotel security or A and C. The killer had not yet fled onto a floor. Reilly remembered that there was no access beyond the fourteenth floor where the explosion had occurred. He considered the possibilities: The killer might be trapped, but that was unlikely. More probable was that he always had an escape plan and, on the way out, a new face and identity.

71

OFF THE COAST OF NEW ENGLAND

Petty Officer Marcel James focused on his sonar console. He listened past whale songs and other marine life. He listened beyond nature and noise pollution for the nearly inaudible sounds. He listened for a mistake.

He tapped his cans; the earphones pressed hard against him. There was a sound. He looked at his wave scope. The frequency might be in the computer's catalog of recorded sounds. But quicker than cross referencing, it was definitely in his head.

"Commander," James whispered. "I have something."

"What is it, sonar?"

He pressed both earphones tightly. "One, no two. Now three torpedo tubes flooding." He looked around to Commander Policano. "There's another, four."

"Are you certain, Mr. James?"

"One-hundred percent, sir. She's battle ready. But ..."

"But what, son?"

"I've heard recordings of *Admiral Kashira*'s tubes. These aren't ..."

"Say it."

"A minute, sir," he said not knowing if he had a minute. Everything on his sonar was recorded. He scrolled back thirty seconds, froze the video, made a screen grab of the frequency wave, and imported it over to his audio library on his paired computer. Next he typed in "index," then scanned the drop-down menu for Russian Yasen Class-M submarines, including *Admiral Kashira*, Russia's newest, most expensive and deadliest sub. Four-hundred-fifty-six feet long, with ten torpedo tubes located near the central post instead of the bow.

His sound library had a sample. He laid the screen grab over the sample. They didn't match. But it was inclusive. He returned to the drop-down menu and scanned his list of submarines, country by country, based on the latest Navy intelligence.

"Mr. James, You said a minute. What's going on?"

While working, Marcel James heard another missile tube flood. And another.

"Captain, two more tubes flooded. Six altogether," he said while clicking on another sub index. "But *Admiral Kashira* has ten. And …"

James' fingers had been flying over the keys as he listened and talked. He scrolled to another Russian sub class, one that only had six tubes. He quickly found the sound signature, super imposed this screen grab. A match.

"It's not *Admiral Kashira*. It's a North Korean–built Gorae-class ballistic missile sub. I still have to confirm, but its signature aligns with the *Karim Khan*, last in the South China Sea."

"*Karim Khan*. Isn't that—?" He searched his memory.

"Iranian, sir."

Policano mashed his teeth. "What happened to the Yasen? And why another sub in its place with half the fire power?"

James shook his head. He was about to share it when he grabbed both ears and shouted, "Torpedoes away!"

* * *

The problems for Reilly multiplied as he ran up the stairs. His legs ached. His heart pounded. He was exposed. And there was no way out. The doors to the fire exits were locked from the inside. This meant it would be inevitable they'd meet at the top.

* * *

"Sonar, compute target and time," Policano asked.

"No ships in range, sir. But they're running steady in pairs, separated slightly."

"Headings?'

"Calculating, sir."

Policano was most worried about 2nd Fleet ships, particularly the one most vulnerable to torpedoes, the flagship, USS *Harry S Truman*.

"Course two-seven-eight, commander."

"Course two-seven-eight," Policano repeated. He leaned over his chart and noted the last location for the carrier. It was out of the bubble. *Good.* Other promising news, the fish would tail out soon. This had all the earmarks of a test.

* * *

WASHINGTON, D.C.

Reilly slowed as he reached the twelfth floor. One more flight of stairs would take him to the fourteenth. U.S. hotels still avoided the number in between based on triskaidekaphobia—the superstitious fear of the number 13. He cautiously rounded a landing, stepped out. A shot hit the stairway inches away and splintered the concrete. He held back. The killer was trapped but held the high ground, at least until police reached the floor from the elevators. But then again, Reilly thought he was trapped and didn't have the luxury of time. He yelled the obvious, "There's no way out. You can end it here."

He swore he heard a snicker, then footsteps again. Softly. Reilly pressed his body against the wall, bracing for a battle. But it didn't come. Instead of coming closer, the sound was going farther away. Then he heard the fire door open—which he had presumed to be locked.

"Dammit!" he exclaimed. With his legs now stronger from the temporary rest, he could run up faster. He got to the door just as it was about to close. Reilly thrust his arm between the door and the door frame to keep it open and saw a brick on the ground that had kept it open. *Workers or the assassin's escape route. More likely the killer planning ahead.*

Reilly led with the Beretta. As he emerged into the hall, he listened for footsteps. If there, they were impossible to distinguish over the radio and the chatter from the construction crew working to repair the damage.

The hall had the lingering moldy scent of gunpowder, burning embers, and dust mixed with water from the sprinklers. He heard fans throughout the hall, drying the mold. Reilly rounded the corner stairway opposite from where the blast had blown out the wall. He peered left and right, straight ahead and behind. The hotel floor was a wreck. It would take months of exterior structural reconstruction and interior debris removal, scrubbing, rebuilding walls, rewiring, painting, and replacing room and bathroom furnishings, broken tiles, rugs. Expensive and time consuming.

Ahead was a long hall, workers, and somewhere, the assassin. Further along, three other fire exits led back down to the lobby. All the room doors were open. He glanced in each as he passed. His quarry could be hiding anywhere. Reilly dismissed the chance of escaping via a parachute as the killer—he was certain it was the same man—had done in Beijing. *Not enough height to safely unfurl. The stairs or the elevator? The stairs,* he determined.

Reilly approached the first man he saw, a Hispanic worker.

"Someone came up ahead of me! Where'd he go?"

Before the worker answered, Reilly heard a crash and tore down the hall. He stopped at the elevator bank, a four-way intersection in the floor plan. *Left, right or straight?* Stairways at the end of each. A worker doubled over, writhing on the floor, answered his second question. Left.

Reilly quickly assessed his injury. The man's head was bleeding, his arm was broken. He was conscious but couldn't talk.

"Over here!" Reilly yelled to anyone in earshot. "Guy needs medical help!"

Twenty feet ahead, Reilly saw a hotel security guard in his grey blazer and black pants walk toward him. Reilly lowered his gun.

"Someone just ran past me. You looking for him?"

"Yes."

"That way, down the fire exit." He tapped his ear and said, "I've called it in."

"Thanks! Take care of that man."

"Okay."

Reilly ran past him toward the emergency exit. He opened the door, but he had a sudden thought. He looked behind him. The worker was still on the ground. The security officer hadn't stopped.

Multiple images overwhelmed him, as they had minutes ago in the lobby. Flashes of a wig on the stairs. Snippets of what the then-woman had worn: a black jacket. Turn it inside out, maybe it was grey. Under the wraparound dress: pants. Now the man's face. He'd touched his ear, but Reilly hadn't actually seen a radio earpiece or wires.

Reilly raised his gun. "You! Stop!"

The man darted down the hallway, past the elevators, toward the third set of stairs. Reilly sprinted. Just before the corner, he stopped, crouched, and peered low around the corner to the hallway that continued to his left. The assassin fired but he aimed where he expected Reilly's head to be. Reilly was ready to take him down, but a grey-haired Asian housekeeper stepped out of a room with a cleaning cart. She was old and hunched over. Confused.

"Get back in!" Reilly shouted.

She froze.

"Back in!"

She stared at Reilly, who rose. The moment was gone. She had cost him his shot. Now the killer was at the stairwell with another lead on Reilly. He slipped through the heavy metal fire door.

Reilly lowered his gun and continued his pursuit. But in that moment Reilly wondered why the assassin was running. Cornering him, killing him was what the mission was to get the package. Something wasn't right. In the next moment he was aware that the old housekeeper didn't clear the hallway. That's when she pushed the cart in his way. He veered. She did the same.

The woman was no longer hunched over. No longer old. She was at least as tall as Reilly. Maybe taller. Definitely ready for him. She smiled.

"Mr. Reilly, you have something we want," she said with an accent he placed as Korean.

She withdrew a gun from the cart but as she brought it up, Reilly rammed the cart back into her, knocking the pistol out of her hand. Reilly still had his until she rolled the cart away giving her enough room to sweep a roundhouse kick to his right hand. The Beretta fell to the floor.

She pulled two knives virtually out of nowhere; nowhere being sheaths midway down her legs.

Reilly stepped behind the cleaning cart and grabbed a spray bottle. The woman laughed. She swung the blades between her arms and body.

He brought the bottle up with his right and adjusted the nozzle with two fingers. Then sprayed her eyes. Whether it was glass cleaner or something even more irritating, it worked. She swore loudly, "*Yeosmeog-eo!*"

It had the ring of "Fuck you!"

She automatically went to wipe her eyes, impossible with the knives in both hands. She had the sense to throw one behind her and reach for a towel on the cart. This gave Reilly the chance to slam the cart against her again, pinning her to the wall. But she was stronger than Reilly. The woman blinked repeatedly, working tear ducts to wash out the cleanser, while driving the cart back into Reilly's stomach. He dug in his heels trying to stop the woman and at the same time recover his gun. But she had the advantage: forward momentum and the anger of a wounded panther. Meanwhile, Reilly couldn't get his footing on the wet carpet. He slipped, fell to his knees, and backed into the open hotel room, scrambling to get back on his feet.

The woman charged and hit Reilly chest level with her full weight. He fell backwards and she slammed her foot down to his neck. He caught it just before it would have crushed his windpipe. This left her off balance. Reilly twisted her leg. Her body followed. She went down. Reilly vaulted up in a way he hadn't for years. He saw his gun on the floor in the hall. Too far. He grabbed a thin glass lamp on a dresser, smashed it against the wall, and held the broken base in his hand. He had a weapon again.

He waved threateningly. She sidestepped to the right. What he really wanted was his gun and a clear path to it. But he also saw that the file that had been tucked into his belt had dislodged and was near the doorway. She caught the reaction.

"And here we thought we'd have to make you tell us where it was."

She took two steps closer. He thrust the lamp forward and with the same roundhouse kick that first got him, she smashed the lamp. The next kick caught him in the stomach. She spun around and grabbed him from the back with a choke hold. He squirmed. She tightened and leaned into his ear. "Time to die."

Not for him. He brought his elbow up to the side of her head and smashed hard. She staggered back. The momentum returned him to the center of the room, but still not close to his Beretta.

She staggered back, impatient for the kill. She charged. Reilly tripped. She lunged. He planted his feet on her abdomen and flung her over his head and through the window to the street, some 200 feet below; the second body to hit the pavement in a little over a week.

As he lay on the floor, trying to catch his breath, he heard running. *Another round? No, they're getting further away.*

He sat up, regained his wits, and scanned the room. "Christ!" he exclaimed. The file was gone.

72

OFF THE COAST OF NEW ENGLAND

"Still running, sir," Petty Officer James reported.

"What?" Policano asked.

"Long range. Longer than I've seen. *Karim Khan's* torpedoes should have bottomed out four minutes ago. I still hear them. Faint, but true to their course and not running out of steam."

Policano looked up to the low ceiling as if it were heavens. He thought, *If the torpedoes have more than historic range, then what's ahead?* The answer wasn't in the ceiling, but it was in his head. *The mainland.*

He leaned over his undersea chart and based on the heading of two-seven-eight he drew a straight line out from *Karim Khan's* position. "Holy shit!" he declared.

"Holy shit!" James repeated. He was doing the same thing on his computer screen. "Sir!"

"I know. Boston."

James had more specific information. "Plotting the separation of the three pairs, multiple targets. I've got them exactly on course to the Northeast Gateway deepwater terminal east of Boston, the Port of Boston, and the Chelsea Terminal."

"Oil," Policano whispered. "They're targeting oil."

Policano realized that possibly, if not probably, topside wasn't even aware of the threat. Also, according to the last reported headings of the ships, Carrier Strike Group 8 was heading south of the immediate buffer zone, and other ships of the 2nd Fleet could be anywhere between Norfolk and Portland, completely oblivious of the impending situation.

Policano needed to know the fleet's precise location and warn command. However, he couldn't until he dealt with the first problem—the enemy sub.

Every minute counted to Policano. *No, seconds, once Hartford made its intentions clear.*

"Give us some real operating room," he said.

"Sir?" his XO replied, uncertain what his CO wanted.

"Room to fire, Mr. Moore."

"Sir?" The XO looked startled.

"Correct." He explained why. "We can't report in unless we surface. We can't surface unless we reveal our location. We can't reveal our location until we know whether the sub is a true threat."

"This all could just be a test, Commander. Nothing more than an exercise."

"Yes, it could be. But they flooded their tubes and fired in the direction of the United States coast with weaponry that's off the books."

"The way to determine whether it was merely an exercise is to trick them into proving it."

"How?" the XO asked.

"By flooding our tubes. If they react in kind and fire at us, we'll know."

"But they'll get their fish off before—"

"Yes they will. So I'm counting on our skill and training to counterattack and make damned sure we successfully get top side. Can we do it, Mr. Moore?"

Commander Policano's Executive Officer smiled. "Yes, we can. We sure can."

Lieutenant Moore checked the charts, plotted a course, and relayed it to the helmsman. The route would take them around the submerged mountain range. Then came the speed. "Four knots, slow as she goes."

Real operating room would be seven miles from the target.

Eighteen long minutes later, Policano calmly ordered, "All stop." He stood over his communications tech and dictated a message. "You send that once the antenna is raised."

"Yes sir, sending when antenna is deployed."

"One more question for sonar. Mr. James, any change?"

"Negative, sir."

Policano's primary concern was the same as sonar's—the enemy releasing its twelve remaining torpedoes or launching its missiles. The possibilities included short-range surface-to-air missiles, or the longer-range anti-ship cruise missiles.

At twenty minutes, Commander Andrew Policano decided it was time. He braced the control room and word passed crew member to crew member throughout the sub.

"For real?" was the response heard most down the line. "For real. CO says it's not a drill."

Duty, determination, and adrenaline kicked in. The crew of the *Hartford* had trained hundreds of times for such a scenario. But this time it would test everyone's resolve and reveal what *Karim Khan* had conspired with the Russians.

That brought Policano to the other unknown. Where the hell was *Admiral Kashira*?

"Mr. James, I need to know if the Yasen-class is still in range."

"I have nothing," the young lieutenant said, his hands pushing in his earphones close.

"Mr. Moore, your opinion?"

"Only speculation based on sonar's report. *Admiral Kashira* drew us here for a reason. Now she's gone, and we just may be fulfilling that purpose."

To kill the Iranian, Policano thought but didn't say. He turned back to James. "You keep those ears tuned, son."

"Yes sir."

Policano surveyed the control room. He had good men and women serving with him: sons and daughters of veterans, former street gang members, new parents, young people with hopes and dreams. It was his job to keep them alive and defend the country.

"Ready tubes one and two," Policano called over the intercom to the guidance officer.

He flashed on a lecture from his teachers at the U.S. Navy War College in Newport, Rhode Island. "Submarines are really the last place of true autonomy in the United States military."

"Ready tubes one and two," came confirmation.

Policano graduated top of his class. He looked forward to a long career in the service and hoped he'd never have to make a kill decision. On every voyage and with every new command, he shared what he had learned with his crew. "When you submerge, you understand the orders you have through the chain of command, but you may have to decide on how best to execute them. You alone."

"Ready tubes three and four."

"Roger, ready tubes three and four."

Policano never felt more certain of his responsibility.

"Plot target."

"Target plotted, sir."

"Tubes one and two ready to fire," reported the torpedo room. A moment later, "Tubes three and four ready to fire."

Policano nodded. By now, the enemy had heard him and knew his precise location and his objective.

"Sir," Marcel James shouted. "*Karim Khan* flooding tubes."

"Hold everyone," Policano said calmly. "Wait, wait."

"Two torpedoes away," Petty Officer James said. He watched his screen and turned to command. "On course to *Hartford.*"

"Confirm that, Mr. James."

"Aye sir, confirming two torpedoes away. Targeting us!"

Without hesitating, Policano gave three quick orders in succession. To fire control, "Fire tubes one and two," To his defense manager, "Counter measures." And to communications, "Raise the antenna."

"Aye aye, sir," came the responses one after another.

"Time to impact?"

"One minute, twelve seconds, sir," James read off his screen.

"Thank you, Mr. James."

When the antenna broke the surface, the communications officer sent the burst. It was certain to reach as high as the White House.

"Message to 2nd Fleet Command. USS *Hartford* engaging Sinpo-class submarine, nationality Iran. Enemy fired six torpedoes." The communique included their location, the plot of the torpedoes, at present speed time to targets, which Policano was certain would be questioned, and the targets. It ended with, "Andrew Policano, Commander USS *Hartford*."

Seconds after *Hartford*'s first torpedoes were released, Policano launched tubes three and four. Then he took a deep breath and hoped that the sub's countermeasures would pull the enemy's torpedoes away and the speed of his torpedoes would win the race.

He had one more order to give. A warning. "Prepare for impact."

* * *

Captain Ali Shirvani had been assured he was in open, unpatrolled waters. He'd been told that he was only part of an exercise. That his Russian partner would be watching the test of the experimental long-range torpedoes. He had been promised a bonus when he returned to dry land. He believed everything. Now he was thirty seconds away from dying.

Who fired on him? Why?

The *Karim Khan* deployed countermeasures. The crew cheered when one of the oncoming torpedoes was drawn off its course. They cheered more loudly when the second exploded early. When the third and fourth evaded their defenses, Captain Shirvani took the microphone. In the final moments of his life and his crew's, he praised everyone's heroism and proclaimed it was his greatest honor to serve with them.

73

WASHINGTON, D.C.

"What do we have out there?" Battaglio asked haltingly. He sounded like he actually wanted to know and understand.

"CSG-8, Mr. President. Carrier Strike Group 8." Admiral Grimm spoke rapidly without inflection. "A flotilla from the 2nd Fleet under the command of Admiral Rod Koehler. The Nimitz-class aircraft carrier USS *Harry S Truman* is the flagship, recently awarded the Battenberg Cup Award as the best ship in the Atlantic. In support, the guided-missile cruiser USS *Hué City*, ships of Destroyer Squadron 28, and Carrier Air Wing One."

"Please break it down for me."

"Our guided missile cruiser USS *Normandy*, and two guided-missile destroyers, USS *Forrest Sherman* and USS *Farragut*." He went into more detail on the carrier air wing and the destroyer squadron.

"So, we can handle this. Stop it, prevent it."

"I wish it were that easy, sir. The fish are away."

"The fish?"

"The torpedoes. USS *Hartford* destroyed the enemy sub, but the torpedoes have onboard guidance. They're self-contained weapon systems. At the low end of the spectrum, they're simply straight-running undersea bombs. Sharks with explosives on their backs. At the high end, they're smart and can act autonomously with active and passive sonar seekers. To put it bluntly, they have a mind of their own, and they know where they're going." He paused. "And at present, we believe we're looking at a new generation of very smart torpedoes, and we don't exactly know where they are."

Battaglio went right for the word, "*Exactly*?"

"We don't know where they are."

No one spoke as the president took it all in. He stood, walked completely around the table, and stood.

"How much time do we have?"

"The typical range of the Sinpo-class torpedoes is 100 km at 50 km per hour. Two hours."

"But they were launched from further away."

"Yes. We need to assume they wouldn't have released the torpedoes from where the sub lay if they didn't intend for them to reach their outermost targets."

"Then we have …" Battaglio calculated but stopped. "How much time?"

"Less than two now."

"Does anyone have any goddammed good news to give me?" Battaglio shouted.

* * *

Admiral Rand Kenton had deployed in every ocean on the face of the earth for twenty-two years and never launched a missile or fired a shot in active battle conditions until today. Today was different. He received the communication from command. The USS *Hartford* had just sent a Sinpo-class sub to the bottom of the Atlantic with all its souls onboard, but not before the sub released six torpedoes stateside. Sonar picked them up well beyond the point where they should have ended their run. Now it fell to the commander of the Nimitz-class USS *Harry S Truman* and all its resources to get into the fight.

The *Harry S Truman*, a virtual floating city with 6,250 crewmembers, was positioned midway between *Hartford's* nautical position and the last targeting information received from CMDR Policano via USNORTHCOM. Kenton immediately deployed a pair of towed Torpedo Warning Systems (TWS) behind his ship with highly maneuverable Countermeasure Anti-Torpedo (CAT) weaponry designed to seek and destroy the enemy's guided torpedoes generally immune to U.S. countermeasures—specifically Russian type 53-65 torpedoes carried by Sinpo-class subs. And these, according to reports, were well beyond the typical 53-65's.

When Torpedo Warning System (TWS) detects an incoming threat, the information is reported to command. Command can decide whether or not to launch the CAT. That decision was already approved.

The critical questions: Would TWS be able to seek out the torpedoes? And would CAT, developed to protect large warships and tankers, be able to do the job? It's where the challenge met the odds. TWS was designed for short-range, close-in defense. Torpedoes are, in fact, harder to track from a distance. That meant *Harry S Truman* needed to identify the torpedoes within its immediate listening area. If too far out, CAT might not hear them or be able to catch up. Then...

* * *

"We have multiple options, Mr. President." Admiral Grimm began his tutorial, noting the Torpedo Warning System aboard the *Truman*. "Consider that the first line of defense, but by no means the only one. The commander of the carrier is one of our most experienced fleet admirals. He's got more arrows in his quiver. Already aloft, ten helicopters with dipping sonars. They're patrolling a wider perimeter. His F/A-18 Super Hornets are taking off as we speak. They can create a pretty nasty shock wave in the Atlantic with what they have onboard. The *Harry S Truman* and the other ships in the CSG-8 are equipped with arrays of 360 transducers, each one meter square."

Battaglio looked confused. Grimm read the expressions. He wasn't the only one. He stopped at the empty seat.

"Where the hell is Elizabeth?"

Chief of Staff Lou Simon adjusted his glasses. "She had to step out. Someone she had to meet."

"Well, she picked a helluva time," the president exclaimed. "Get her sorry ass back in here!"

The comment shocked the members of the National Security Council.

"I'll make the call," Simon replied. He left the room and picked up his cell phone, held in a drawer outside the Situation Room, guarded by a marine and two Secret Service Agents.

"We were talking about—" Battaglio left it open.

"About the acoustic arrays," Grimm continued. "They're effectively big flat-panel loudspeakers running along sides of the hull below the waterline. When their ship's sonar detects signatures from an incoming torpedo, the transducers fire acoustic shock waves of such immense intensity they can either get the torpedo to detonate or disable itself. The tech comes out of DARPA, our Defense Advanced Research Projects Agency."

"God help us. A dose of heavy metal right out of *Star Trek Beyond*," Secretary Sclar observed.

"But real. We're also dropping acoustic decoys to attract the torpedoes."

"Are any of these guaranteed to work, Admiral?" Battaglio asked.

"Statistically, 50 percent might get through the outer barrier."

"That means three out of six could hit."

"Mr. President, we have other active defense/offense tools. The Mark 60 Captor is one."

Secretary of Defense Vincent Collingsworth interrupted. "Sir, you may have heard that we took them out of service in 2001."

He hadn't.

"They were considered a danger to shipping, including to our own vessels. But we didn't mothball them all. In fact, we put a new generation online and—"

"Stop!" the President declared. "In English!"

"Captor mines," Collingsworth offered. "Submerged mines, in a standing tube, that can release a light torpedo when a target is detected. Instead of a mine merely exploding in place, the Captor can release its own lightweight torpedo, and the chase is on. Its range was, well is, unless the admiral can share any new intelligence, about a mile-and-a-half."

"Newer, better. An added shield for the homeland," Grimm added. "It's an encapsulated torpedo; the Navy's only deepwater anti-submarine mine."

"We're not trying to sink a sub, Admiral," Battaglio noted.

"No, but on detonation they can take out a torpedo or create an extremely high temperature gas bubble, about 3,000 degrees Celsius, and pressure to about 50,000 atmospheres that spreads at 25,000 feet per second. The shock wave pushes outward in all directions and can kill the torpedo or confuse the hell out of it. It all depends on how close we can get to the oncoming threat. If we do, we may be very grateful that we've kept a few around."

"A few?" Collingsworth asked.

"More than a few," Admiral Grimm admitted.

"Is that it?"

"One more option to mention. We call it Quickstrike—air-dropped mines. Navy has them. The Air Force, too. Like the Mark 60, they're intelligent and can sort out acoustic, seismic, or pressure signatures from a vessel. Extrapolating, they could be equally effective against torpedoes. Trouble is getting them to the theater in time. We're working on it."

"Jesus Christ," the president said sharply, rising, ready to storm out. "You're going to fucking start World War III!"

"No sir," Grimm declared. "We're trying to prevent it."

74

"ELIZABETH," Simon began on his call. "You have to get back here."

"A few more minutes," she said. "I'm waiting for someone."

"Now. He's shitting a brick, and the situation is escalating."

Elizabeth Matthews knew she wouldn't get any more information. She'd been ordered back. Reilly would have to meet her later.

* * *

Reilly's phone rang. He was in the stairwell almost to the ground floor. He reached for his cell, saw it was Elizabeth's private number.

"Can't really talk now," he said.

"And I have to get back to the cement mixer." She used the Secret Service code word for the White House Situation Room. "Anything you can tell me while I'm walking?"

"Sorry. Gotta run." He never got to *Really!*

He barged into the lobby and immediately spotted commotion past the bar, leading to the restaurant. A woman was down. Reilly picked up the chase. "Out of the way!" he yelled. People didn't need to be asked twice. He had a gun.

Reilly heard pots and dishes crashing ahead in the kitchen. Screams and swearing. Then a gun shot. A cook on the line was down, wounded but alive. "Tried to stop the motherfucker." He lifted his hand off the floor and pointed toward the back door.

"Call for help!" Reilly demanded.

"I'm on it" a waitress said, taking her phone out.

Reilly continued, not knowing how far ahead the killer was. He stopped at the service entrance and carefully peered around. A white Ryder Sprinter van was just rolling from the garage loading dock down the short driveway. As it turned left onto the street, the driver looked back. He saw Reilly; Reilly saw him. The assassin smiled. He taunted with a wave. Reilly ran onto the street. A grey Mercedes GLB SUV was heading toward him. Reilly raised his gun. The driver came to a screeching halt. Reilly jerked his head to the side to get out. The driver didn't need further encouragement. He opened the door and stepped away. Reilly jumped in the car. The man thought he heard a *thank you*.

Reilly gunned the SUV. Maybe because he was now in a car chase, maybe it was the double meaning, but Reilly gave the assassin a name: *Bullitt*, for the classic Steve McQueen movie. He followed the rental van, making a series of sharp turns, before a right onto 10th NW against the flow of traffic.

Bullitt was five car lengths ahead of him. Reilly had speed, the truck had mass and used it, clipping a Prius on the right and a Lexus to the left. Reilly slowed as he passed between the two cars. Rhode Island was coming up fast—a decision point. Straight, right heading east, or left to the west. It was just like his choice in the hotel.

Honking constantly, he moved past the cars until fifty feet, about five car lengths, separated them. Reilly sped up, betting Bullitt would keep going straight. He was wrong and saw how wrong he was when the van hung a fast left onto Rhode Island Avenue NW, and he was forced through the intersection by a southbound car that blocked his turn.

"Shit!" he exclaimed. Reilly had no room to make a U-turn. He floored the accelerator, waited for three slow-moving cars to pass, and made a left, figuring he'd head south and converge with Bullitt at Logan Circle. At least that was his hope.

As he covered the circuitous route, Reilly pictured the D.C. map and tried to get into Bullitt's head. He was the best at everything. Disguises and killings. Appearing and disappearing. Walking and flying. Probably now driving. He had an escape plan; he always did. And he had the file.

The Ryder van was likely one of many ways to leave the hotel. The team with him, not as experienced as he was. The woman on the fourteenth floor accomplished more than the others. Thanks to her, Bullitt had what he'd come for, but she paid the price.

And now they were in a road race. Car to van. Reilly assumed Bullitt had to know the Capital streets as well as he did and where he was heading. *Which way?* he asked himself. *Not near the closely patrolled White House, that was already clear by the route. Not north, either. West or southwest.*

At that moment he made a sharp turn onto Vermont. One long block ahead was Logan Circle. The white Ryder van was just rounding it. The most direct route out would be to continue on P to Dupont Circle. Thinking like Bullitt, he counted on it. Now he would hang back and keep the van in sight.

Bullitt definitely knew the streets. He drove with real awareness, moving from the left lane to the right, ready to make another turn at the next roundabout.

* * *

He eased back on the pedal, believing he had lost Reilly. From the glove compartment, he removed a wig and a mustache, putting both on as he steered with one hand. Next, he wiggled out of his sports jacket and pulled the front of his dress shirt, which separated a Velcro strip in the back, revealing a blue t-shirt. He was partially transformed. There would be more to complete his new identity. He slipped a German passport into a pocket: Gustaf Frederickson of Bonn. He liked to play video games, so he was now a game designer traveling back home from a DC conference.

He practiced saying his name with the correct accent. "Frederick-sin. Fred-rickson. Fred-erick-son." He had it. The assassin checked his mirrors and shook his head. He entered Dupont Circle at half the speed, ignoring the first four exits and on the fifth split off at New Hampshire.

* * *

Reilly saw the turn. He smiled. He was thinking like his objective now. He expected him to make his next move at Washington Circle. He'd either pick up 29 West or continue down New Hampshire and skirt the Potomac on his way to the Theodore Roosevelt Bridge. Reilly believed west would be more likely, open and faster.

He sped up once he was on New Hampshire. Bullitt was a block-and-a-half away. Then he saw Bullitt make a sudden turn into a garage on the right between M and L Streets. Reilly slowed and passed it. It looked like new construction. Now a new question. *Proceed or wait?* At first, he concluded Bullitt had made him. Then again, he might hide in the building. *Proceed or wait?* He pulled over beside a fire hydrant and turned the car off. He'd give it two minutes, keeping his eye on the passenger side and rearview mirrors.

* * *

The man who now called himself Gustaf Frederickson pulled into an open space in the underground lot. This was not his plan. Garages were enclosed. Egress was limited. He was in relatively unknown territory. He hated unknown territory. Unknown territory presented multiple unknowns: people coming out of elevators, mothers with strollers, kids on skateboards, a random police officer. But this was where he was sup-posed to be for the moment—an order from a plan he did not design.

He didn't know Reilly's experience, but so far, his opponent had sensed the threat in the hotel lobby, fought the woman and tossed her out the window, requisitioned a car, and picked him back up after losing him. He had training or instincts or both. This made him a danger—first in China, now in Washington. He wanted to eliminate the danger, but his only objective was to recover the package Reilly carried from China—which he had done successfully—and then escape.

* * *

Ryan Battaglio had taken the stairs up from the Situation Room two at a time. He stormed through the hall ignoring everyone who addressed him, impolitely held his hand up to his secretary Lillian Westerman, who was absorbed in the senate hearing on TV, barreled into the Oval Office, and slammed the door.

"Fuck!" he shouted. Too much was happening at once, and he didn't have enough people loyal to him in key positions. He'd acted too slowly. He vowed to fix that immediately. The void was costing him, especially now with the crisis in the Atlantic. At first the Pentagon had ID'ed Russia. Now they believed it was an Iranian plot. *Jesus, make up your minds,* he said to himself. *People. Yes, I need my people.* Better ones, he thought, than even Roger Whitfield, who was proving himself a useless National Security Advisor. *Davidson!* He wanted Moakley Davidson by his side to manage and control the fucking military.

Battaglio hit the intercom button. "Get Senator Davidson in here now," he demanded.

"Mr. President he's still …" she paused to find the right description. Answering questions wasn't accurate enough. "Testifying, sir. It's on TV now."

For the past hour she'd watched Moakley Davidson respond with a succession of "I have no recollection … I don't know … I will have to check my notes." Most of the senators on the Vice Presidential confirmation committee, no matter their party affiliation, waived their time to Littlefield. Two close Davidson allies constantly tried to interrupt with their objections. They were gaveled down by the chair. When their time came to question, they returned to the original agenda: laudatory statements and softball questions. Battaglio tuned in to the last few minutes of the round.

It all appeared pro forma to the president. High praise and talk of his patriotism and service to the country. He concluded Davidson would be approved by the committee by the end of the day. Then came Senator Mikayla Colonnello's opportunity at the microphone.

"Senator Davidson ..." She smiled.

"Yes."

"Just one question, after which I'll yield the rest of my time to Chairman Littlefield."

Davidson smiled defiantly.

"Are you responsible for the death of *The Hill* reporter, Sherwood Baker?"

The Kennedy Caucus Room erupted. One hundred-fifty-two voices speaking as one. And under the cacophony, Davidson told his aide, "Get me out of here!"

75

OFF THE COAST OF NEW ENGLAND

The true firepower of the United States, unknown to the general public, was at the fingertips of Admiral Branson Stuckmeyer, commander of the 2nd Fleet. It wasn't the largest complement of ships in the Navy, but because it had America's homeland to protect, it had some very special tools.

"Bran, this is a big job."

"Yes, sir."

The orders from Admiral Grimm, Chairman of the Joint Chiefs, to Admiral Stuckmeyer were clear and unequivocal. "Kill those damned torpedoes!"

"Yes, sir."

Stuckmeyer had a wide array of acoustic weaponry and the ability to trigger mines tethered to the ocean bottom. He'd use those and another tool. Budgeted in 2020, tested under the cloak of secrecy, and now in his fleet's arsenal—the Navy's anti-torpedo torpedo, an Anti-Torpedo Torpedo Compact Rapid Attack Weapon (ATT CRAW). The weapon is an interceptor with sonar-seeking capability and a guidance package that allows it to make precise movements. It lives to kill before a torpedo can take out a super carrier or destroyer. It can ram an oncoming torpedo or detonate an explosive warhead in its path. The ATT CRAW replaced a previously failed system and was, so far, "in development." Admiral Stuckmeyer had them at his disposal, ready to be launched from tubes on his fleet's ships or from airborne drones.

The tactical challenge was distance, operating within a kill chain short enough for the interceptor to be effective. The defensive system must first locate and classify the threat, then deploy within a very tight time period. And to be successful, it has to be close to the target.

The report from USS *Hartford* provided the trajectory. Sonar buoys along the way confirmed that they were on course. What surprised Stuckmeyer and the entire Navy command was the range of the torpedoes. Considering the distance they'd covered so far, he had to assume they could make it all the way ... and all the way was a great deal closer now.

He gave the command. Fifteen drones went aloft from the USS *Harry S Truman*. The destroyers readied their ATT CRAWs. Sonar operators listened. They made contact. The first two torpedoes were taken out by the mines. The resulting churn threw another off course. It connected with an undersea boulder and exploded before it could right its course. Three down, three to go.

Further in, an ATT CRAW from one of the fleet's Ticonderoga-class ships made a head-on hard-kill. Four down, two to go, and only miles to the New England shore, where pleasure boats leisurely sailed and oil tankers queued up for off-loading.

It was going to be up to the drones.

76

WASHINGTON, D.C.

The man who now called himself Frederickson steered head-on into a spot two levels down. He turned the van off, exited, unlocked the rear panel, and climbed in. One minute later, he sat atop a BMW S1000R sport bike, wearing a black leather jacket and black helmet. Inside his jacket, a Heckler & Koch USP9 tactical semiautomatic pistol.

Frederickson, or whoever he was about to become, flipped the visor down, gunned the engine, and flew off four feet forward and two feet down onto the garage floor. Seconds later, he was at the gate, passing between the security arm and the pedestrian walkway and screaming out onto New Hampshire Avenue.

With an eye on his rearview mirror, Reilly had little doubt who was charging down the street on the BMW. He slammed his fist on the steering wheel. *Damn!* he thought. He should have tried to take him inside the parking structure. Now he had to keep up with a motorcycle that could weave in and out of traffic, split lanes, and outrun him.

He threw the car into drive, picked up the chase, simultaneously pressing his cell call button. "Siri, call Bob Heath."

"Calling Bob Heath."

While it dialed and rang, Reilly dodged around a biker and just barely made it through a yellow light. It didn't appear as if Bullitt knew he was being followed, but that would soon become obvious if he merged onto 29 West after a quarter turn around Washington Circle.

"Hey brother, wondering when you'd be back." The CIA officer was light and breezy.

"Need help!"

Heath picked right up on the tone. "What's going on?"

"Pursuing subject presumed to be the killer of the oil execs and nearly one other," Reilly said over the speaker.

"Who?" Heath asked.

"Me."

"Where are you?"

Reilly told him, though he didn't need to. Heath was already typing in the phone number. The agency could track him in real time.

"I'll get you help. Don't do anything stupid on your own."

"Too late for that."

"Then at least don't hang up. I'll find you!"

Reilly swung wide around Washington Circle. Bullitt was on course. From here he'd take the Francis Scott Key Bridge across the Potomac.

"The business at the Kensington?" Heath asked.

"Yup."

"Okay, we're getting an airship up. What are you driving?"

"Mercedes SUV. Grey. Don't know the plates. I borrowed it. Probably reported as stolen by now. Do me a favor."

"Name it."

"Get me off the most wanted list."

It was too late. He heard the siren before he saw the car in his rearview mirror—a Metropolitan Police Department Ford Police Interceptor—all white with red stripes, a single blue strip, and the motto painted on the unit, "We are here to help."

He, or she, was not going to be a help today.

"Got MPD coming up fast on my tail! Get him off me! He's going to blow everything."

"Why?"

"The assassin stole something from me. It's urgent I get it back. Me and no one else."

"Jesus, Reilly. What did you get yourself into?"

"A mess. Now flag that cop off."

"I'll try. Sometimes they don't listen."

Reilly heard typing. Heath said, "Putting you on hold."

The motorcycle sped up. Reilly was just 200 feet behind him. But the police cruiser was gaining on him. All three made the turn to the bridge.

Traffic moved slowly. The motorcycle moved quicker. Reilly decided at least for the time being, he'd use the police siren to his advantage. He honked. D.C. drivers, used to diplomatic caravans and police escorts made way. He whispered thanks to the cop, but still hoped Heath would make him go away.

Two new options off the southbound bridge: North Fort Myer Drive would take them east through Arlington. A right turn onto the off-ramp would lead to the northbound George Washington Memorial Parkway. North, he thought. Open road, especially at this hour. Faster. *Faster to where?*

Reilly was right again. Bullitt wanted out of the District.

"I'm back," Heath said. "Still working it. They don't like the CIA telling them what to do. I've gone a little higher. In the meantime, air support's up."

Reilly leaned in and looked up through the windshield. He didn't bother to ask what support meant. *But it damned well better have some firepower.*

* * *

Moakley Davidson indignantly stormed through the hall, network reporters and video cameras following him. Journalists livestreamed with their cell phone cameras. Reporters yelled questions, all of which he ignored.

"Senator Davidson, what do you know?" "Are you involved in the murder?" "Were you there?" As he got further away, only individual words penetrated. "Murder. Evidence. Reason. Surprise. Statement?"

Capitol Police opened the exit door to the office building. Davidson got into a waiting town car. Reporters continued relentlessly, pressed up to the windows until the driver took off.

* * *

President Battaglio wasn't the first to scream, "Fuck!" in the Oval Office, but he was probably the loudest in years. Four members of his Secret Service rushed in from the outer office and the Rose Garden.

"Sir? Are you all right?" the senior agent asked.

"Out!" he demanded.

"Are you sure, sir? We heard you—"

"Scream. Damn straight. The President isn't allowed to scream?"

The agent nodded to others. "Of course, Mr. President." They backed out.

Battaglio buzzed his secretary. "I don't care how you do it, get Davidson on the phone. Cell, landline, or fucking orange-juice cans."

"Yes, Mr. President," Lillian Westerman replied.

Battaglio continued to watch the coverage on the bank of monitors against the wall. He saw replays of Littlefield's grilling, Davidson's tepid responses, and his rush to escape from the chairman and the reporters. Now the press offered their commentary on the surprise line of questioning by Littlefield and the very direct demand by Senator Colonnello that sent Davidson fleeing. Battaglio could see that Davidson's appointment was dead in the water. He'd find out what this was all about and withdraw the nomination.

Battaglio paced as speculation from the Capitol Hill press corps worsened. He rushed to Lillian Westerman's desk. "Put the phone down."

She was slow to act.

"Put the fucking phone down! Forget what I said. I don't want to talk to him. If he calls, don't put him through. Not today. Not ever!"

"Yes, Mr. President."

"And get me the press secretary."

"Sir?"

"Now! I'm putting out a statement!"

Battaglio returned to the office. He'd leave Davidson to the sharks.

77

FREDERICKSON LOOKED BACK. For some reason the siren had stopped, the police car had peeled off. Best of all, he was pulling away from the Mercedes. It had become more difficult than it should have been. He felt he would have done better if he'd gone it alone—quicker, cleaner, fewer moving parts. But he hadn't plotted this mission. He was simply dropped into it at the last minute. He wanted to get back to Norway after China, relax, and take time off. But the money was too good to pass up, and the client didn't take no for an answer very well. He'd been promised a no-kill, grab-and-go mission. It was supposed to be easy. Others would do the heavy lifting; he just needed to leave with the package.

Amateurs, he thought. *Easy? Right. It would have been if I'd planned it.*

He checked his mirror. The lights were smaller, but his pursuer was still pursuing. He considered slowing, engaging, and ending the nonsense. But now he had a lead that increased every minute. The motorcycle vs. the car. The motorcycle was winning. He'd done his job. Time to get to the exfil point and leave.

* * *

Reilly kept the BMW in sight, intentionally holding back. Heath had gotten to Metro Police, and if their quickly devised plan worked, Bullitt would be cut off. He'd find out in a few more miles.

* * *

The assassin swerved onto George Washington Parkway. He slowed at the crest to get a sense of the slope downward. It was dark. No cars ahead in his lane or oncoming. *Odd,* he thought. He'd been passing vehicles all along. And now no one. Then he saw why. Out of the pitch black came a bright light that panned across the road and found him. Not just bright—blazingly bright. Sunlight bright that cut through the dark. Millions of candlepower focused on him.

Since light travels faster than sound, it took a moment before he heard the rotating blades of the helicopter shining the high-intensity beam. It was rising up the grade toward him. Behind the airship, a line of police cars.

Frederickson came to a sudden stop. His black helmet visor helped defuse the light. Not knowing the terrain to his left or right, and reasoning that reverse would be blocked by now, he opted for going straight. It would be the least obvious route. The stupidest. But they lit the way.

He gunned the throttle and let loose down the incline. His first move was to slip under the helicopter that had to keep adjusting its position and rate of climb. The second maneuver, which he did alternating between speeding and braking, was finding a path through six squad cars. Had they had their doors open wide, it would have been harder. As it was, his decision to barrel ahead was unexpected, and the Virginia State Police were not prepared. Nor were they for the Mercedes that followed.

The helicopter arced upward and around. The pilot aimed his 500-watt xenon lamp across the road. He saw the car, but the motorcycle was gone. He flew on.

The third thing Frederickson did was turn off his lights, pull off the highway, and ditch the bike. The police didn't see it, but Reilly did. He swung right before the police had made their three-point turns, side-swiped the downed motorcycle, flew up and over a mound and landed hard below eye level from the oncoming squad cars. The airbag inflated on impact, pinning Reilly to his seat until he punched through it. Dazed, he opened the door, dropped to the ground, and listened. Reilly cocked his ear toward the woods. He heard rustling.

Reilly patted his jacket pocket for his phone. It wasn't there. *The car!* He reached back in and fumbled more than felt around on the seat, the floor, the space between the driver's seat and the console. *No more time.* Bullitt was getting away. He presumed Heath was in the helicopter or nearby. He'd have to figure it out on his own.

The gun was still in his belt. *Good.* He breathed a sigh of relief that he had the forethought to engage the safety. Otherwise he might be bleeding out with a shot to his leg. He figured that Bullitt had heard his car crash, so surprise was out of the question. Keeping up and finding an opportunity were his only options. Most of all, he needed the package.

Some fifty yards into the woods, the trees opened up to a field. If there was moonlight, Reilly might have seen him. But it was dark. The dark also helped mask him. He ran realizing he was coming up on the Potomac. He heard a boat. *A coincidence or a rendezvous?* Bullitt had accomplices in the Kensington. They could be out here as well. Reilly ran faster.

At the river's edge he saw Bullitt in silhouette against the boat's oncoming light. He waved a laser pin light on the boat. *Rendezvous.* Coordinated via cell phone. And this would likely be one of many transfers Bullitt would make to disappear.

In a movie, he would have yelled a command to stop. That'd be followed by a fast turn and possibly a well-placed volley into Bullitt's center mass. But this was no movie. Bullitt was running, and Reilly decided to take him down without warning.

He pulled the Beretta, clicked off the safety. A gunshot screamed across the expanse, but it wasn't from his pistol. He hadn't squeezed the trigger yet. The boat had a sniper, likely wearing night vision goggles.

The shot hit in the dirt just short of Reilly. He dropped. Bullitt spun around. More shots from the boat. High, wide, and too close. Reilly rolled five times to his right and crawled forward through the tall grass. A moment later, a bright light exposed the boat in the river. Not prepared for a battle with a helicopter that seemed to come out of nowhere, it swung around and sped away. The copter began the chase, then returned to the riverbank, hovered, and illuminated the assassin who blindly fired a shot skyward. Reilly rose to a low crouch and charged. He hit the assassin below the knees. The force knocked the man's gun out of his hand and into the river. The laser fell onto the ground. Reilly still had his Beretta. He backed up on his butt, ready to make the kill, but not far enough to avoid Bullitt's foot. It slammed his hand. Now his gun flew into the grass, the gun he counted on to end the fight.

Reilly had not been in a hand-to-hand fight for years. That was going to be his next training at the FBI's Hogan's Alley training facility. He was limber and fit, yet hardly the equal of Bullitt.

Reilly mistakenly looked to his left for the weapon. Bullitt grabbed his leg, twisted hard and slammed his elbow on his thigh. The blow would have been crippling had Reilly not twisted his whole body. The momentum, coupled with Bullitt's need to get to his feet, gave him a second's reprieve.

The helicopter light shone on the two men who now faced one another. Reilly wanted them to take the shot, but their position was too high, and they jockeyed too much for position.

Bullitt took two steps forward and spun with a high right kick to the head. Reilly threw up his hands in a reflexive defensive move, but Bullitt followed up with a second kick to the stomach. Reilly grabbed his gut; a useless, time-wasting reaction. Bullitt grabbed Reilly's neck, moved behind him and put him in a life-ending choke hold.

Reilly tried to force his right hand under the killer's. No room. Too tight. What his hand couldn't do, his leg could. He stepped forward far enough to make room for a kick backwards. His right foot slammed Bullitt's most vulnerable regions. He released Reilly, doubled-over and swearing. *"Faen deg!"* Reilly had a good ear for languages. It sounded Scandinavian.

Reilly delivered a strong right hook to Bullitt's head. Now he was suffering in two places. Reilly went for a third; a roundhouse kick to the stomach. This one missed and Reilly was thrown off balance.

Bullitt straightened and wound up with his own right hook to

Reilly's chin, followed by a second with his left and a third with his right. Reilly stumbled back. But he dodged a punch that landed in the wall, giving him opportunity to strike fast. A blow to the stomach, an elbow to the ear, a knee to the crotch.

Bullitt slowed, backed away, and stumbled. All Reilly had to do now was keep hitting. Bullitt was on the ground. He reached around to steady himself. That's when his finger touched something metal. He smiled.

Reilly saw the glint of the barrel from the helicopter's light. He dove headfirst. Bullitt turned sideways deflecting most of the blow but catching the shoulder. Both men were back down. Reilly grabbed Bullitt's leg just as the killer was bringing up the gun. Reilly tightened his knuckles and jabbed Bullitt's throat—hurtful, causing him to cough, but not a deadly blow. Just the opposite. It invigorated him. The killer drew on adrenaline. He swung his gun hand around. Reilly swept his leg across his calf. Bullitt fired. The shot missed, but the gun was still in his hand. Reilly only had a few feet to maneuver and no time left to do it. The assassin smiled again.

Reilly was going to die.

* * *

All the ambient sounds seemed to fade away. The whooping of the helicopter. The boat's engine that was going to take Bullitt away. Even the light from above was gone. *No,* Reilly thought, it wasn't gone. *It was coming from the side.*

Still, Bullitt's smile was going to be the last thing he saw. Then came the last thing he would ever hear—the gun shot.

Only feet apart, eye-to-eye, the two men faced one another. Blood rolled down Reilly's face. He instinctively wiped it away. He felt no pain. *Is that how it is? No pain at the end. The thought of a dead man.*

In what seemed like slow motion, Reilly watched the killer's smile turn to dismay and then sheer disbelief as he looked down.

"*Nei,*" he said, seeing his own blood spurting from his chest. His strength was leaving him, but with one last effort, he brought up his gun to kill the American.

A second shot rang out. Bullitt collapsed to his knees and fell onto his face. Bob Heath stood ten yards directly behind him, backlit by the helicopter's powerful xenon lamp. He lowered his rifle.

"You okay, buddy?" the CIA operative called out.

"Been better," Reilly said. "Could use another shirt, though."

"Let's get you out of here."

"Not yet!" Reilly walked to the dead man. He unzipped his leather jacket. "Christ!" he exclaimed running his fingers underneath. He rolled the man he dubbed Bullitt over and fumbled under his shirt, then down his pants. "It's not here!"

"What's not?" Heath replied.

"The file! Papers."

Reilly dropped to his knees and began feeling around the grass. Nothing! "Fuck!" He ran back to where the motorcycle was ditched. Nothing there either.

"Reilly, slow down. What the hell are you looking for?"

"A package. An envelope. I've got to find it. He had it. Damn, Bob, did you have to kill him?"

"As a matter of fact, yes!"

Reilly nodded. "I'm sorry. I owe you my thanks."

"You owe me your life."

"That, too."

Reilly stood over the bike and played the last hour back in his mind. The race down the stairs, through the lobby, the kitchen. He could have passed it off there. *But no*, Bullitt carried it right to the van. He pictured the chase, through the streets of Washington. He could have tossed it to a contact along the way, especially on the blocks that he'd lost him. *No*, he thought. *Where else?*

"Jesus, the garage."

"What garage?" Heath asked.

"The one he drove into on New Hampshire and switched to this." Reilly rested his foot on the downed motorcycle. "It was a dead drop."

"I don't even know who *he* is."

"The man you killed has been very busy recently, and his death is going to make someone very upset."

"Who?"

"Nicolai Gorshkov."

"Jesus. I have to lock down the area."

"Roger that."

Reilly looked at the helicopter in the open field near the Potomac. "Is that gassed up enough to get me back into town?"

"In and back."

"Good. I'm borrowing it."

"Not without telling me more."

"I've been on a wild goose chase and wasting time. The van may still be there and the package with it. I've got to go back."

"That important?"

"Yes, that important."

"What was the address on New Hampshire?"

"Don't know exactly, but between M and L. West side of the street."

Heath began dialing his cell. "I'll get it for you."

"No. Secure it, but no one enters or leaves. I'll explain on the way."

78

A STRUCTURE ACROSS THE STREET from the New Hampshire Avenue building had a helicopter pad. The pilot set down, and Reilly and Heath exited quickly. They ran down the stairs and cut across the street. Metro Police, acting on Heath's request, and confirmed by the department's liaison with the CIA, set up a cordon in front of the building. Nobody in or out. A crowd gathered. Gawkers shot video on cell phones and posted them to Citizen, Facebook, and other portals. No one knew what was happening, including the police officers on duty.

"You can't go in," Metro Lieutenant John McNamara stated, stepping in front of the two approaching men.

Heath produced his identification, low and not to be seen by civilians.

"This is your game? Mind sharing what's going on? Got a lot of upset occupants."

"We'll know in a few minutes. In the meantime, tell people we're investigating a ..." Heath thought for a second, "carjacking. Now let's go in."

"Be my guest." McNamara lifted the police tape. Heath ducked under it. Reilly followed.

Their entrance triggered a commotion across the street.

"I have to get in!" a middle-aged man in a business suit demanded through a thick accent. A cop holding the line nodded a definitive no.

"My medicine! It's in my car. I left it by mistake. If I don't—" He began wheezing.

"All right, all right," the uniformed officer said. "Just wait."

"I can't! I need it now! Please!" he pleaded.

"Wait!"

The Metro policeman went to McNamara, exchanged a few words, then waved an okay. The man came forward.

"Okay, come with me. Stick close."

"Yes, sir."

"What level?"

"Two down."

"In and out fast," the officer said. "Let's go."

*　*　*

Reilly led. They walked the 10,000 square feet of the first parking level. The Ryder rental van wasn't there. Reilly picked up his pace as they circled down the ramp to parking level two. There were some hundred cars, including one white van, but nothing with Ryder logos. One more level to cover.

"You sure you have the right lot?" Bob Heath asked after they completed their sweep of the bottom floor.

"Yes!" Reilly answered. He slammed his fist on the roof of a Prius.

At that moment he heard footsteps. More than one person.

"We've got company. Thought no one was allowed in," Reilly said.

"No one was supposed to be."

Reilly pointed to the up ramp. A moment later he heard two quick pops, distinctive to the trained ear. Heath heard them too and recognized the sound that comes from a suppressed gun, which is never completely silent.

They began running and heard another sound—a car being unlocked remotely. Less than a minute later, back on the second level, they saw a police officer lying lifeless against the back of a van; a white van dripping red. The CIA operative signaled Reilly to go low to the passenger side. Heath, flush with the car, peered around the corner. The driver side door was open.

"Toss your gun out now!" Heath demanded. "Show me your hands!"

No response.

"Now!"

Reilly came up slowly alongside the van with his gun drawn. Feet at first, then inches. Silently. Heath shouted the order again. Reilly made his move, stepping back, taking the firing stance, and sweeping his Beretta up.

"Not here!" Reilly said.

"Shit!"

Under Heath's exclamation Reilly heard running.

"Come on. He's got the envelope."

Heath stepped out into the open. The assailant fired. It caught Heath in his left shoulder. He went down. "Fucker. Get him! Go!"

Reilly scooted around the van. He saw the man running across the lot toward the stairwell. *Not more fucking stairs!*

"Stop!" Reilly yelled.

Reilly assumed a sideway stance showing less of a target. Two shots, one from each gun. The man missed, but his bullet hit a car and set off the alarm. Through the noise he fired again.

The gunman squeezed the trigger a third time. His aim was off. He didn't understand why considering his sharpshooter ranking. He fired again, but he still couldn't draw an accurate bead on his target. Then he looked down and saw blood soaking his shirt and jacket. He hadn't been aware of the shot that Reilly had taken. And then he was.

First, he dropped his Sig Sauer pistol. Next, the envelope he was clutching in his left hand. He stood for another five seconds, feeling what the end of life was like and not having the ability to explain it.

Metro Police rushed in, surveyed the crime scene, and ordered Reilly to the ground. He was immediately cuffed. It was only when Heath hobbled over and talked to Lieutenant McNamara that he was released. Reilly was allowed to approach the dead man. He picked up the blood-stained brown envelope.

"Sir, step away and leave it where you found it," McNamara declared.

"I can't."

"This is an active crime scene."

Heath, needing medical care, stepped in. "Actually, Lieutenant, this is going to end up way above your pay grade and mine. A team will be here in five minutes to clean up. This would be a good time for you and your men to clear out."

"On whose authority? You have no legal right to operate here."

"Lieutenant McNamara, this is a matter of national security."

"As I said, you have no legal right to operate here."

The argument was ended with the arrival of both Reese McCafferty and Gerald Watts—the Directors of the FBI and the CIA.

Heath smiled, then collapsed.

* * *

Heath lay in the ambulance on the way to Walter Reed National Military Medical Center. Through groggy eyes, an IV dripping a sedative, he put the shape of Reilly's face together.

"You got your damned envelope."

"Got it. Thank you, brother."

"Now, care to tell me what's so important?"

'If I tell you, you won't remember."

"There is that," Heath said. "What the hell. At least we're even on the night."

79

APPROACHING BOSTON HARBOR

Twelve miles out of Boston, less than a mile to The Northeast Gateway deepwater terminal, a drone picked up one of the two remaining torpedoes. It dropped its ATT CRAW from 1,500 feet. The fish hit the water. Its active sonar listened, acquired the target, and accomplished its mission.

Five down, one to go.

The last torpedo was on course to the Chelsea Terminal. It had passed all the outward mines and evaded overhead drones. There were no defenses left.

Passengers on an evening Boston Harbor cruise saw what they thought was a shark swimming toward the shore. A very fast-moving shark that was throwing off a wake as it rose closer to the surface. It was deadlier than the deadliest shark. A Navy vet, leaning across the rail with his fiancé on his arm, immediately recognized the threat. Without hesitating he pulled out his cell phone and dialed 911.

"What," Cassie O'Halloran said.

"That!"

The torpedo shot by them with only 50 feet to spare.

"Whoa! Did you see that?" O'Halloran shouted. But Stan Herbert, a recently retired lieutenant from submarine service, wasn't listening.

He was trying to get a call out on his cell. If 911 answered, which so far they hadn't, the operator wouldn't believe him. But his message would be on the record, and at the speed and direction of the torpedo, he knew someone would come to him for a statement after the inevitable.

A half-mile ahead, one of Boston's water taxis was heading from Logan Airport to Rowes Wharf. The shuttle could carry as many as fifty. This evening it had only eight passengers and its small crew. The travelers were absorbed in their texts and emails. The vessel's captain alternatingly kept his eye forward toward his port and glancing at his radar. All was clear except for the torpedo that he was crossing directly in front of. The explosion obliterated the craft, and, as a result, probably saved thousands of lives from a terrible oil explosion.

Six out of six destroyed.

* * *

WASHINGTON, D.C.

Admiral Grimm beamed as he hung up the Situation Room direct phone line to the Pentagon.

"Ladies, gentlemen, all torpedoes accounted for."

The National Security Council members cheered, Battaglio the loudest of all.

"But there was collateral damage." The celebration ended. "A Boston Harbor shuttle craft. The Coast Guard is looking for survivors. The press is reporting an onboard explosion." Grimm shook his head. "Hopefully it ends there."

"Then that's the story we stick with," Roger Whitfield, the president's new National Security Advisor declared.

"There will be lawsuits against the company," Homeland Security Secretary Deborah Sclar noted. "We'll have to come up with something to help them."

"A cover-up?" Elizabeth Matthews exclaimed.

"You want to start a war?" Whitfield argued. "Hell, even Grimm can't point a finger to who launched the torpedoes. Russian? Chinese? North Korea? Iran? Who was it, Admiral? Was it intentional, or a test of a new weapon gone bad? Or a rogue commander?"

"We don't know."

"That's right. You don't know. That's why we go with the explosion," Battaglio proclaimed.

Matthews looked away. She was afraid the argument was only over for now. One-by-one the members of the Security Council left the Situation Room.

* * *

Matthews walked out of the West Portico. She checked her phone—a score of emails, another twelve text messages, but no phone messages from Dan Reilly. He'd missed their meeting on the Mall. He wouldn't come to the White House. Now she was worried. She dialed. He answered on the third ring.

"Where the hell are you?"

"In a cab. You?"

"Just wrapping up."

"Good. I'll meet you at your condo."

"My office. I've been out most of the day. Have to catch up."

"No. Your condo, Elizabeth. Please. And double your security." The Secretary of State's detail were all members of the Bureau of Diplomatic Security, the DSS. "I'll be there in under ten."

"This better be—"

"It is," Reilly declared.

Reilly arrived first. He waited in the cab four buildings down from her brownstone on Hopkins Street, NW. The Secretary of State's driver and accompanying DSS agents in two SUVs pulled in front. Reilly told his cabbie to drive forward. Once the agents were at the door, he paid and exited. Matthews's men cleared him to enter; another led him to the study.

"Secretary Matthews will be with you shortly."

Reilly said thank you and poured himself an eighteen-year

Macallan scotch which he drank quickly. He was into his second when Elizabeth Matthews entered. She was about to launch into a string of questions, but his appearance stopped her in her steps. He was bloodied. His clothes were grass-stained and torn. His face bruised. Reilly looked exhausted.

"Jesus, Daniel! You look like you've been to hell and back."

"Twice." He took a glass from her liquor cart and poured another scotch. "You're going to need this."

Matthews accepted without question. She sat in a red leather chair and invited Reilly to take a matching one directly opposite. He clutched a large thick envelope. It was sealed.

"You're holding that like your life depended on it," she said.

"Or worth dying to get it to you."

"Oh my God, what did you get yourself into?"

"The deepest I've ever been in."

He patted the envelope. "It's all in here."

Elizabeth stared at the envelope. Reilly held onto it without speaking, not yet ready to turn it over.

"Whenever you're ready, Daniel."

He took another sip of his Macallan. It fortified him.

"Twelve years ago, I was in Afghanistan," he began. "I accompanied two United States congressmen on a tour of Shindand Air Force Base. They insisted on taking an unscheduled excursion into the hills. They saw it as a photo op for back home. Command allowed it, a real mistake. The return trip went bad. We were ambushed. My second time under fire. Good men and women were killed because of them, Elizabeth. The congressmen left right away. They were supposed to head back to Washington. They didn't go directly there."

Reilly rubbed his aching chest, wondering if he had cracked ribs.

"Are you all right?" Matthews asked.

"I'll be fine when this is over. And that will be your job."

He took another sip and continued. "They disappeared after landing in Hong Kong, which was supposed to be a short intermediate stop.

Into the second day, their offices panicked. Word went to the Capitol Police, then to the Pentagon. I was called by USPACOM, since I was the liaison to the congressmen in country."

"You haven't said who they were."

"No I haven't," Reilly replied. "USPACOM had worked with a fixer in the region. They ordered me to get on a flight, meet with him, and retrace their steps. First, I figured if they went to Hong Kong, they probably intended on going to Macau. Maybe to decompress from what they saw. Maybe to gamble. Maybe—"

"Got the picture," Matthews noted. "Go on."

"I sniffed around myself. Nothing. Finally met the fixer. Believe me, fixer only begins to describe him. Anyway, on day three he found one of the AWOL assholes. It took a couple more days to find the second."

Matthews replayed what she'd been told so far. "A couple of congressmen went on a bender. I take it you got them on a flight out."

"Yes."

She looked at the envelope still in his clutches.

"Then what's in there?"

"The second guy didn't just go on a bender, Elizabeth."

He flipped over the package. She saw the blood on it. Reilly removed tape he'd put on in his hotel room and opened it, revealing the contents.

"You asked who they were."

She nodded.

"The two congressmen returned to their jobs. In time they ran for Senate and won. One moved up even higher; the other about to. Their names—"

Secretary of State Elizabeth Matthews said them herself. "Battaglio and Davidson."

Reilly handed her the envelope.

80

MACAU

TWELVE YEARS EARLIER

The combination of alcohol and cocaine made Ryan Battaglio very content. He'd fucked his way from hotel-to-hotel for the past forty-eight-hours. One girl, two girls, and a transvestite just because it seemed exciting. He found it all so easy in Macau. They were on the streets and roaming the hotels. They were at the bars and in lounges. His ATM card worked, and in his conscious moments he knew he had to make sure he came back with office gifts to show for the money spent.

He wanted one more night and somebody even younger: a virgin, untouched. It would his last conquest before returning to respectability and the United States Congress.

Battaglio stumbled off the beaten path, onto Dahengqin Island. He took a room at the Zhuhai Hengqin Bay Nightowl Inn, sniffed another hit of his cocaine, downed a shot glass of a Japanese whiskey, and went on the prowl, carrying a plastic bag he prepared for the occasion. He tried to pick up a pair of preteens but was chased away by a chaperone. He crossed to nearby side streets and was propositioned by a middle-aged hooker and an even older prostitute he assumed was another transvestite. Neither was what he wanted tonight. Then he saw a young girl saying goodbye to friends at a taxi stand. She was fourteen, maybe fifteen, fair-skinned, dark-haired, fresh and lively. He approached her. She spoke no English. That didn't matter. He wasn't interested in talking. He smiled and offered her a drink. She nodded no and began walking away. On his last night he wasn't going to let the perfect girl get away. Battaglio grabbed her from behind, twisted her around, and removed a towel soaked in chloroform from his plastic bag. It wouldn't knock her out completely. That would take away half the fun. But it did put her in a daze. Her legs gave way, and Battaglio put his arm under her for support. He guided the teen back to the Nightowl Inn.

"We're going to a have great time together," he said, slurring his words.

She didn't understand and with what little strength she had, tried to resist.

"Shhh shhh shhh," he said.

She squirmed, completely disoriented but not fully knocked out.

"Be a good girl or I'm going to have to give you another whiff."

Battaglio pulled her closer as he unlocked the door. Inside, he tossed her onto the bed. He pulled off her dress. She drew her body up into a ball and screamed. It probably wasn't out of the ordinary for the hotel, but Battaglio didn't want to draw attention. He brought the towel up to her mouth and held it there.

The teen's arms and legs relaxed. Battaglio smiled. She was his.

He finished taking her clothes off, stripped, and stood over her. She stirred weakly with just enough energy in her to make it interesting.

Battaglio picked well. The rape turned the girl into a woman. He intended the rest of the night to introduce her to all of his pleasures. But the cocaine actually made his continued performance more difficult. This infuriated him. He took it out on the girl. He slapped her. Slaps turned into punches. Punches into bites. Every time he failed, he drank, snorted more lines, and returned to abuse her in revolting ways.

In the morning, the old housekeeper knocked on the door. The American was naked and out cold. The girl was dead. She ran to the front desk. The manager called the police. An officer went through the victim's purse.

"*Mā de!*" he exclaimed. He radioed a supervisor. The supervisor phoned Sammy.

WASHINGTON, D.C

PRESENT DAY

Close-up photographs documented the brutal crime scene. Matthews silently watched the video, which showed the death in even greater detail. But it was the footage of an indignant Ryan Battaglio blaming the victim during questioning that made it clear why this package was so explosive. Then she came to the video confession showing him signing the paper, which was also part of the package.

"Who's after you, Dan?"

"Not the Chinese. They wanted me to deliver it."

"Battaglio?"

"Maybe, if he was tipped off. But that would mean he had a secret army or mercenaries to hire." Reilly paused. He knew his next statement came with tremendous geopolitical implications. "More likely it's someone else who stands to gain if there's no change in the White House."

Matthews mouthed the name as Reilly said it. "Nicolai Gorshkov."

He explained what he'd been through on the way to meet her. The chase and fight in the hotel. The chase and shooting along the Potomac. The shootout in the parking lot.

"Well coordinated. There was a plan of attack and a plan of exfiltration. And," he added, "Russian accents. They had people inside China. My flight back gave them time to pull it together.

"All to prevent this evidence from interfering with their negotiations with Beijing. Except Beijing doesn't want to be dictated to by Moscow. They want some negotiating room with Washington but feel they can't get it as long as Battaglio is in power."

"Politics makes strange bedfellows," she observed.

"Oil, Elizabeth. Oil makes strange bedfellows."

For the next hour they talked about strategy: pros and cons, impact and fallout. Matthews explained what had occurred in the Atlantic and tied it into the greater global picture, which now made all the more sense.

"You know he'll deny everything," Reilly said. "He'll call it all a deep fake. We've seen it before."

"Yes, he will. But we may have an ace in the hole."

"Oh?"

"Someone who may be very willing to cut a deal under the present circumstances."

"Who's that?"

"Senator Moakley Davidson."

She explained.

81

AS SECRETARY OF State, Elizabeth Matthews was fourth in the line of succession. Should the President not be able to serve for reasons enumerated under the language ratified in the 25th Amendment, the job goes to the Vice President. That's how Battaglio succeeded Alexander Crowe. But now there was no number two. Next in line, Speaker of the House Sean Allphin, followed by the President pro tempore of the Senate Butch Pruett, and then the Secretary of State.

Matthews huddled with Allphin, Pruett, and Senator Mikayla Colonnello, who chaired the Judiciary Committee. That afternoon, she advised Attorney General Hector Sanchez, FBI Director Reese McCafferty, and CIA Director Gerald Watts. Dan Reilly was in all the meetings. For most of them, he sat quietly.

In each briefing, Matthews was warned of the danger, the political blowback, and the impact on stock prices. Everything came down to what Battaglio would do. The FBI's discussions with Moakley Davidson, holed up in a safe house, would be the determining factor.

The second day, Davidson heard the deal. It took another day and six consultations with his lawyers, to accept the deal.

The fourth day they met at the FBI; each participant coming in different entrances to avoid the press. It was decided that Reese McCafferty would take the lead when they confronted the President. AG Sanchez would stipulate the authority granted by the 25th Amendment. Elizabeth

Matthews would accept President Battaglio's letter of resignation in accord with a law passed by Congress in 1792. The Chief Justice of the Supreme Court would be called to the Oval Office and, with no current Vice President, Sean Allphin would be administered the oath of office.

At precisely 0900 on the fifth day, the participants walked into the White House without an appointment. Matthews brought along Dan Reilly. He had earned the right to be present.

"Lillian, we're here to see Mr. Battaglio," McCafferty said.

The President's secretary was surprised, but only to a small degree. The White House had been in a flurry of activity over the past few days.

"I'll let him know," she said

"That won't be necessary."

They entered without a chance to be announced.

"What's going on?" Battaglio demanded. "I didn't have you down for a meeting."

"That's correct," Reese McCafferty responded. "But circumstances require that we see you."

"I'll have Lillian put you on the calendar."

"Now."

Battaglio scanned the faces. He knew all but one, yet there was something familiar about him.

"Mr. President, please sit."

"Not until you tell me what this is about. I've got work to do."

"And so do we, sir. The people's work."

* * *

Battaglio begrudgingly sat. As planned, the FBI Director spoke first.

"Mr. President, numerous facts have come to our attention. Facts that so far have not become public. Facts that you would not want to see released."

Battaglio honestly appeared puzzled. It seemed to him that the group might be there to help him through a problem he wasn't aware of. "Go on," he said with interest.

"These facts have been confirmed by multiple sources."

"Get to the point."

McCafferty paused and locked on the President. "These facts concern you."

Battaglio blanched. They were accusing him of something. "What the hell are you getting at?"

The Attorney General rolled through the digits on his attaché case lock. *1776.* He opened it and removed a manila envelope. "These, Mr. President," he said handing them over.

Battaglio slowly opened the envelope, not knowing what to expect. "What?"

"Photographs, sir."

He slid them out upside down and turned them over. The first photograph, an exterior nighttime wide shot of a hotel, meant nothing. The second, an interior room shot, also wide, showed a naked girl on a bed.

"Jesus, Hector. Porn? Really?"

"Keep looking, Mr. President," Sanchez replied.

The third photo was tighter. It pictured a naked dead girl lying spread-eagled. Battaglio swallowed hard. The next photos captured more gruesome details from head to toe. The final photograph unmistakably showed him—then Congressman Ryan Battaglio in handcuffs with Macau police and officials beside him.

"That isn't me!" Battaglio tossed the photographs back at Sanchez.

"We also have video and audio," Reese McCafferty said coldly.

"It's all fake!" Battaglio turned to Matthews. "This is your latest gambit, Elizabeth? The best you've got?"

She said nothing.

"You think I don't know what you've been doing behind my back. Trying to line up Cabinet members? Your coup failed. So now this?"

Matthews sat quietly.

"I get it. You regrouped. You have new allies. You doctored photos. That makes you all goddamned conspirators. Fuck every one of you!"

He stood. "Now get the hell out of my office! I want your resignations within the hour. Consider them accepted."

"Point of order, Mr. President," Speaker of the House Sean Allphin interrupted. "Neither I, nor Senators Pruett and Colonnello, work for you. You can't fire us. There will only be one resignation today—yours. Secretary of State Matthews will take it before we leave."

"Like I said, you've got nothing. And who the hell is he?" Battaglio said focusing on the man standing at the door.

Reilly stepped forward, closer. Battaglio scrutinized him.

"I know you."

"Yes, you do. Years ago, as an Army captain in Afghanistan. And again as you boarded a plane out of Hong Kong. I've come back in time for you, *Representative* Battaglio," Reilly said.

"President! President of the United States!"

"Maybe for a minute longer."

"Get out! You can go to hell along with the rest of the traitors."

No one moved.

"I'll have the Secret Service throw you out!"

"Mr. President, we're not finished," the FBI Director said coldly. "There's one more item on the agenda." McCafferty nodded to Reilly who went to the door. Seconds later he returned. Walking behind him, eyes lowered, was Senator Moakley Davidson followed by two FBI agents.

"Thank you," McCafferty told his men. "We'll be out shortly."

Davidson stared at Reilly and whispered, "You're going to be responsible for bringing down a president."

"No, you are, Senator Moakley. To save your own ass."

Davidson lowered his eyes. He was a defeated man, never to return to the Oval Office under any circumstances. Davidson had agreed to plead guilty to a conspiracy charge coming with reduced jail time in the case of the reporter's death. This, for what he knew to have occurred in Macau, backed up by his own twelve-year-old contemporaneous notes he made after their flight back, kept in his home safe, and now in FBI hands.

Elizabeth Matthews stepped forward. "I'll take your resignation now. You've got stationery. Any pen will do. You might want to keep it simple. Cite health reasons."

Battaglio knew he was defeated. With his arms by his side, he crossed to his desk and removed a sheet of paper embossed with the presidential seal. He lifted a pen and stopped.

"You're a real motherfucker, Elizabeth."

"Under the circumstances, I'll take that as a compliment."

Battaglio looked to the Attorney General for support. He didn't get any.

"Now, Mr. President," Matthews demanded. "We have a new president to swear in, and the White House photographer is outside, eager to find out why we have him waiting."

Battaglio stared at everyone with cold, hateful eyes. He stopped at Reilly.

"This is you, Reilly. This is all you."

"No sir, it's the girl in Macau. Fourteen when you raped and killed her. Her name was Ting. Ting Wing Li."

82

THE OATH OF OFFICE concluded with Sean Allphin proclaiming, "So help me God."

The Speaker of the House was now the President of the United States. Ten minutes later, he stood in front of a camera in the Roosevelt Room making his first address to the nation. His wife Carolyn stood by his side. She had a shell-shocked expression, mirrored by most of the press.

"My fellow Americans, much has happened in the past few hours. President Ryan Battaglio has stepped down citing fatigue and health reasons. Without a current sitting Vice President, the 25th Amendment to the Constitution of the United States, ratified in 1967 by the states, stipulates that the powers and duties of the president pass to the Speaker of the House of Representatives."

Allphin noted that he would submit his choice for vice president in the coming weeks. He said nothing about Moakley Davidson.

"To be perfectly honest, this is not a position I have ever sought. I have served my constituents faithfully for eighteen years. And through them, I have proudly served our country.

"To most Americans watching now, undoubtedly I am not a familiar face. However, I have extensive experience in national and foreign affairs. I've met all of the world's major leaders, friend and foe. I listen to advisors and give critics their due. I am capable of making hard decisions. And I stand ready to do so.

"To the members of the press, I ask you to bring my story to the public so they know who I am and what I stand for. You will learn that I'm a consensus builder, but I can be a troublemaker should trouble be dropped at our doorstep. I will serve with honesty and integrity as President of the United States. In the process, I hope to earn your trust."

President Sean Allphin concluded by saying, "I will be ready for your questions in a few days. Bear with me until then. Most of all, today I pledge to you that I will preserve, protect, and defend the Constitution of the United States. Thank you. May God bless America."

* * *

Dan Reilly watched the coverage with Elizabeth Matthews.

"What kind of president will Allphin make?" Reilly asked.

"He'll have good days and bad. He'll get points for negotiating the oil deal with China. But it'll be a short honeymoon. At no time in American history has the Speaker of the House been elevated through succession to the Presidency, let alone one from the opposing party. He'll promote stability, but eventually he'll replace us one-by-one."

"And where will you go, Elizabeth?"

"First stop, Turks and Caicos. A nice vacation."

"Can't help you there," Reilly joked. "No property on the islands. Anywhere else?"

"Probably best I don't look for any favors, considering what might be my second stop."

"Where's that?"

Elizabeth Matthews smiled broadly. "We'll discuss that later."

* * *

Dan Reilly went to Chicago to report to his boss. Before they got to business, EJ Shaw gave him a good looking over.

"You run headlong into a linebacker?"

"Three," Reilly replied. "They eventually got out of the way."

"Care to share?"

"Street fight back in D.C. I walked away."

"Who were the others?"

"Didn't catch their names. No one was charged."

Shaw laughed. "You want my advice? Leave the fighting to Alan. You're business; he's security."

"Sounds like a plan."

"What's your sense about all this Washington intrigue?"

"Makes my head spin," Reilly offered coyly. "From what I hear, it's going to take a while to shake out. On the positive side, we might have new things to talk about with China."

"Well, that's good news. One more question. It's personal."

"Yes."

"Learn anything about yourself on the trip, Daniel?"

Shaw was probing.

"About myself?"

"Yes."

Reilly snorted, wanting to keep it light. "I need to hit the gym more often."

Shaw nodded. "Nice try. No, about your career choices."

"You gave me a year, boss. I think I've still got forty-nine weeks to go."

Reilly left thinking he had time to breathe, to think through the decisions ahead. But EJ Shaw wasn't convinced time was what he needed. Maybe it was a push.

Considering Shaw's years running Kensington Royal Corporation, the political campaigns he'd given to, and the candidates and causes he supported, when he phoned Washington, his calls got answered.

His secretary dialed and notified him when he was connected.

"Madame Secretary, thank you. Let's talk about our boy, Dan Reilly."

* * *

"No!" Nicolai Gorshkov commanded, "Remain standing. I find people listen better when they stand." His chief advisors obeyed.

Arkady Sechin, Markov Kudorff, Gregor Moloton, Igor Bazalvonov, and General Valery Rotenberg faced their president, who sat behind his desk. They had been summoned out of bed—not necessarily unusual for Gorshkov, but always unsettling, especially considering that the armed security that had roused them remained outside Gorshkov's door.

"I thought we'd begin the new day with a review of the past few."

He was given the expected nods: respectful, hopefully believable.

"Wins and losses, gentlemen. Time to take stock of our recent activity.

"The Northern Sea Route," Gorshkov continued. "Global warming is on the side of the Russian Federation. The ice melts, and our influence over the Arctic increases. We will build more icebreakers, but the passage is ours, and we shall charge a hefty price for transit. A win."

Smiles.

"I want to bolster Venezuela. Find me a way to get boots on the ground. It will be our new Cuba, but richer. Once we lock in Venezuela, it furthers my oil strategy."

Rotenberg was the first to volunteer. "Yes, Mr. President."

"Good. Now to America. I'm not happy."

The advisors considered that the understatement of the session.

"A pity we lost an ally with the departure of Ryan Battaglio. I'm concerned about this new man. He is from the opposition party. I view him as a danger, a man who will be hard to control. Markov and Gregor, find out if there are any business entanglements he might have that can work to our benefit in our first conversation. I'd like to turn a loss into a win."

Markov Kurdorff and Gregor Moloton looked at each other. In unison they replied, "Yes, Mr. President."

"Thank you," Gorshkov said good-naturedly. "Just a few more items."

This is when his men began to worry. Gorshkov always left the worst for the last.

"Dr. Sechin." Gorshkov addressed the man in the middle.

"Yes."

"Our oil strategy. How would you sum it up?"

Sechin swallowed hard. "Overall, we have major gains."

Nicolai Gorshkov fiddled with a cigar lighter on his desk. "Overall, yes. The Suez, brilliant. The Strait of Hormuz, a tactical success. However—"

Sechin braced for the words that followed. The fact that Gorshkov addressed him as Dr. Sechin was troublesome.

"The Panama Canal was an utter disaster. The damage to the Chinese tanker and the Chinese-controlled Atlantic port has put all our planning at risk. General Rotenberg's sources tell us the Chinese are investigating. That cannot lead to us. Tell me there are absolutely no loose ends. All of the operatives have been neutralized?

"The team, of course."

"The team leader, goddammit!"

"He's on a flight back now."

"Make certain that flight does not land!" Gorshkov demanded.

Sechin nodded.

"No, not you!" The Russian president turned to his FSB Chief who read the order perfectly.

"Dr. Sechin, do you have any idea how much this could hurt our negotiations?"

Sechin gulped.

"No, I don't suppose you do. Perhaps you should." Gorshkov turned to his banker Igor Bazalvonov.

"How much hurt, Igor?

"In round numbers, Mr. President?"

"As you please," Gorshkov said dispassionately.

"Fucking billions."

"Billions!" Gorshkov bellowed. "Billions that can't be turned into more icebreakers and pipelines, submarines and fighters, or missiles and tanks. All of that goes into the loss column, Dr. Sechin. Yours."

"Mr. President, I'm truly sorry. But it was the North Korean operatives' blunder," he offered in his own defense.

Gorshkov's face turned red. Sechin braced himself for the inevitable. It came.

"Dr. Sechin, would you mind excusing us. I do have one other thing to discuss with these gentlemen." He pressed a button under his top desk drawer. Officers immediately entered. Sechin left pleading for clemency.

With the door closed again, Gorshkov said, "The last point is for the rest of you to consider. Our entire China strategy may be in jeopardy, fucked up by the ship ramming the Chinese port in Panama. I will talk with President Yáo and offer our cooperation. But please tell me nothing will come back to us."

All eyes fell on General Rotenberg.

"Nothing will be traced back to us. Not our training or their travel," Rotenberg said as positively as possible.

"It would be a shame to see those losses show up in your column as Dr. Sechin's blunder did in his, my friend."

Rotenberg forced himself to project strength and confidence rather than weakness and fear. Gorshkov noted the general's obedience, then widened his criticism to the other two men in the room.

"Now, more than ever, I insist on only success from all of you and everyone under you. Their faults become yours, especially as I look toward the Baltic Sea." Gorshkov smiled. "But of course, I know you understand."

The last of Sechin's screams outside the president's office perfectly underscored his point.

EPILOGUE

IN THE WEEKS since the Inauguration, the press tried to get an inside bead on what President Allphin's administration would offer. Caretaker or policy maker? Ribbon cutter or trailblazer? With his vow to only serve out Alexander Crowe's, then Ryan Battaglio's term, he could make a statement or make history. Unknown to anyone but his closest confidants, Sean Allphin set a course to make history. On the last Wednesday of the month, at precisely 9 p.m. ET, he walked the broad hallway on the first floor of the White House connecting the East Room with the State Dining Room. The eighty-foot, twenty-three-second walk along the red carpet trimmed with a gold border of five pointed stars and laurel leaves gave the nation the sense that something of great consequence was coming and commentators the opportunity to make last-second comments peppered with words like "iron-willed ... determined ... consensus builder ... political creature ... hand shaker ... backstabber." Their assessments predictably depended upon the political perspective of the channel, the anchor, or the pundit. They ended their speculation on his last step.

President Allphin stood at the podium bearing the presidential seal and flanked by two flags, those of the United States and the Office of the President.

"Good evening," President Allphin said warmly.

* * *

Nicolai Gorshkov stood in front of the TV in his Kremlin residence watching the live telecast. He wore an open silk robe.

"I can't see," said the twenty-two-year-old blonde behind him in bed.

"Quiet!" he barked, waving his hand palm down for emphasis.

Gorshkov didn't move. The young woman did.

What do you possibly have to say? Gorshkov thought as Allphin began.

"Two weeks ago America witnessed an unexpected change in the White House. Nowhere was it more surprising than in my own household," Allphin said warmly.

Gorshkov folded his arms. In a few minutes, he would turn the TV off and get back to the naked FSB recruit whose name he had forgotten.

* * *

President Allphin seemed to rise up as he spoke, standing taller and looking younger than his years.

"My constituents have known me as their representative to Congress through nine terms. To my colleagues, I have been the Speaker of the House for the past six years. Today I am your President. Like any political figure, I have been painted by many brushes: patriot and scoundrel, deal maker and obstructionist, compassionate and oppressive."

He appeared to echo and rebuff what the TV talking heads had just said.

"Let me be clear, I am a man who believes in the goodness of the United States, but more important today, it is my responsibility as steward of our great nation to protect our people, our borders, and our natural resources from threats foreign and domestic.

"And so, I have come to talk to you about our tomorrows and how fragile they have become. Recent terrorist attacks in Egypt and Panama and what appears to be an accident in the Strait of Hormuz have proven how vulnerable the United States and the world is to economic terrorism.

"After consulting with experts, it's apparent that the Suez Canal will require a unified international effort and billions of dollars to reopen.

Traversing the Persian Gulf and the Strait of Hormuz, a most dangerous passage, has gotten all the more dangerous. Closer to home, the Panama Canal will be easier to clear, but not without time, money, and more stringent, more proactive defense measures.

"It's estimated that it will take at least three years, perhaps longer, before global shipping will be back to normal. During that time we will see major disruptions at the gas tank, in all manner of manufacturing and construction, the money markets, and every aspect of life as we know it.

"As for the terrorists in the field, we will hunt you down. But we know you were only part of the equation, acting as agents of a government, perhaps governments in collusion with one another."

He fixed a cold stare into the lens. The pool camera operator slowly zoomed in with the director's whisper in his headset.

"I can promise you, as we evaluate and confirm our intelligence, the United States, in league with our allies, *will* take action. To that point, I have already spoken with NATO member nations as well as our allies in Asia and throughout the Western Hemisphere. We are united in our determination."

* * *

In Moscow, Gorshkov shrugged his shoulders. "Eh," he said, dismissing Allphin's comments as mere bluster.

* * *

Allphin continued, "I have ordered the USS *Dwight D. Eisenhower* Carrier Strike Group, a key component of our 5th Fleet, to the entrance of the Strait of Hormuz. The *Eisenhower*, flagship of the group, will be accompanied by the guided-missile cruiser USS *Monterey* and guided-missile destroyers USS *Thomas Hudner* and USS *Mitscher* to safeguard the passage for all ships. They will be in position within eighteen hours, with more American ships set to sail in three days from our naval base in Bahrain. This is a step further than my predecessor was prepared to take. Rest assured, it will not be the last to ensure safe passage."

That news was intended primarily for Iran. Allphin's next declaration focused on maritime waters closer to home and different ears: North Korea's Supreme Leader and the President of the Russian Federation.

He began solemnly. "Since December 31, 1999, the United States no longer maintains military installations or troop forces in Panama. Present circumstances, especially the attack on the port, emphasize the need to revisit that decision. Accordingly, I have instructed Secretary of State Elizabeth Matthews to lead a delegation to Panama and negotiate a new agreement designed to give the United States greater visibility in the region." Though he didn't say it, visibility meant ships and ground troops.

* * *

Gorshkov bristled at the last pronouncement but still viewed this new president as a paper tiger and a part-timer with no real authority or will. Until …

* * *

"I have spoken with our principal allies. Based on present circumstances, the time has come for a series of momentous decisions. America has oil in large supply. Other nations will be struggling to deliver their supplies. The United States will help: with ships and reserves, with financial incentives. Working with other oil-producing countries, we are seeking to freeze prices for six months. I can't promise that will be embraced by all OPEC members, but we are talking. And I am making it a priority meeting with Congressional leaders later today. This will also require the titans of industry to come together, something that presents its own challenge. But we will be talking. Of course, talking doesn't guarantee unanimity of purpose or agreement. For that reason, I have at the ready a number of executive actions that will bring government and corporations together to fuel the world's needs.

"That brings us to an even larger question. Do the attacks on oil transportation, which the United States views as an attack against not one country, but all countries, provide the world with greater reason to explore alternative energy? The answer is yes. Do these attacks, whether perpetrated by a terrorist organization, rogue players, or one leader seeking to advantage his country, force us to consider the importance of developing alternative energy production with even more urgency? The answer is yes."

Allphin let the point sink in. His measured delivery demonstrated why he was called the Lion of Congress and one of the best orators in decades.

"Let me be clear. I do not seek to cut off the flow of oil. Life as we know it would come to a grinding halt. We couldn't survive. It would be a world where traffic would stop, planes would be grounded and industries shut down, and products vital to our lives would disappear. Our military wouldn't be able to move on land, sea, or air. But it's not simply the gas and oil that keeps things going. It's everything in our lives that's based on petroleum. Look around your home, the room you're in, the rooms you'll walk through tonight. Your TV and computers, lamps, floor linoleum, shower curtains, toilet seats, refrigerators, and refrigerants. The items you use without thinking: ink, hair coloring, lipstick, ballpoint pens. Sporting goods: basketballs, golf balls, surf boards, sneakers. Your medicine and your food couldn't be bottled or packaged. Your cell phones wouldn't have cases. Virtually everything today depends upon oil in one way or another. But our reliance is killing our planet. And someone … some ones have unwittingly given us a window to make a change on a scale otherwise unimagined."

* * *

"Come back to bed," Gorshkov's fuck cooed.

"Shut up!"

The speech had taken a surprising turn. Allphin or his speech writers had crafted an emotional argument. *Rhetorical*, he thought. *Perhaps political theater, but effective.* Then he wondered, *He's leading up to something.* Gorshkov stepped closer to the TV set affixed to his bedroom wall.

* * *

"While we join the world in condemning these acts and finding and ultimately punishing the perpetrators," President Allphin continued, "the United States maintains that no one country should be solely reliant on another for their economic well-being. It is for that reason that my administration is currently engaged in a groundbreaking trade initiative with the People's Republic of China, created out of good will in what I term an evolutionary period. This agreement, in the final stages of negotiation, will increase our oil exports to China, further easing its dependence on oil imports from the Russian Federation."

* * *

Infuriated, Nicolai Gorshkov screamed at the top of his lungs and grabbed the television monitor with both hands. He pulled hard. The TV, along with the bracket and wall molding, crashed on the floor. Gorshkov screamed louder, like a petulant child who hadn't gotten his way, while smashing his fists to his forehead. Four bodyguards outside his bedroom suite barged in. They saw Gorshkov seemingly in pain and the naked woman scrambling to get out of bed.

The officers had their Serdyukov autoloading pistols out. The two nearest to Gorshkov rushed forward, knocking him to the ground. One laid across him, the other on his knees aimed his weapon at the woman who ducked beside the bed. Another officer ordered the woman to stand. Afraid, and not knowing what to do, she did nothing. The fourth did as he was trained. He eliminated what he deemed a threat with five quick shots. The officer on his knees added more. They weren't needed. The woman was dead.

Their rounds drowned out Gorshkov's own yelling to stop. By the time the captain of the presidential security service arrived, Gorshkov had aimed his rage at his bodyguards, but was really venting against Allphin. He missed the rest of the president's speech.

* * *

"Something for something," Allphin offered firmly. "In return, President Yáo has committed to a course of action we have sought for years. He will reduce his country's carbon emissions. While the precise terms remain on the table and we continue to view China's own aspirations toward Taiwan and its ongoing island-building and base expansion in the South China Sea as perilous, our new initiatives may lead toward greater understanding and a safer world."

Allphin did not reveal that the deal was tied to the removal of Ryan Battaglio from the presidency, brokered by a go-between hotel executive. He didn't get into his suspicion that Russia had likely conspired with the Supreme Leader of North Korea and possibly the Ayatollah of Iran. He also didn't mention he was seriously considering asking the Senate to confirm Elizabeth Matthews as his choice for Vice President of the United States after her return from Panama City.

He concluded his speech with two quotes. One from a Republican; one from a Democrat—both presidents.

"First, President Ronald Reagan who said, 'The greatest leader is not necessarily the one who does the greatest things. He is the one that gets the people to do the greatest things.' And President Kennedy noted, 'Change is the law of life. And those who look only to the past or the present are certain to miss the future.'

"And so today, I call on the world to help make great things happen. For if not now, we may not have the opportunity again."

* * *

The former President had not watched the speech. Ryan Battaglio was in seclusion, on the advice of Elizabeth Matthews, avoiding all requests for interviews. Meanwhile, Senator Moakley Davidson was conferring with his attorneys, who were desperately trying to find a way to spin his story. Soon even that wouldn't be enough. He'd be met by a knock on the door from FBI Director Reese McCafferty, who would give him every reason to resign, cooperate, and plead out for the murder of *Hill* reporter Sherwood Baker.

* * *

Dan Reilly and Yibing Cheng weren't watching the speech. Yibing was sleeping restfully, lovingly in Reilly's arms. It was their fourth night together at his Washington condo. He stirred to the sounds of the city. He felt good, yet wondered if he ... if *they* were moving too quickly. He'd made the mistake before. But he didn't want to slow down. Life was too short. And life had nearly come to a sudden end.

He held Yi, listening to her relaxed breathing. Outside, the sound of a car honking, a bicyclist's bell ringing, and a helicopter flying by. The car passed, the bicyclist rode away and the helicopter? It seemed to hover close.

Reilly quietly tiptoed out of bed, put on a bathrobe, and walked to his window. The low whooping continued. He wondered what kind of police action was going on in the neighborhood.

He opened the shade and no more than fifteen feet away, a drone with four small propellers hovered directly at eye level. Reilly automatically hit the ground. Yibing stirred in the bed.

"Where'd you go? Come back."

Reilly rose slowly. The normal sounds returned. He looked outside. The drone was gone. But not his worries.

ACKNOWLEDGMENTS

RED CHAOS is a thriller about the global hotel industry in a challenging and dangerous world. Gary and I used many fictional characters and incidents which occurred in the forty years I worked with Marriott and the twenty-two years I was President and Managing Director of the International Lodging Marriott. During that time I founded and led the Marriott International crisis committee. I am grateful to the individuals listed below who made our successes possible, who influenced, mentored, guided me, and played key roles in making this latest novel possible. Several of them might find themselves in this creative work. Linda Bartlett, Yvonne Bean, Katie Bianchi, Harry Bosschaart, Stan Bruns, Nuala Cashman, Paul Cerula, Weili Cheng, Don Cleary, Mark Conklin, JoAnn Corday, Henry Davies, Victoria Dolan, Roger Dow, Brenda Durham, Ron Eastman, Joel Eisemann, June Farrell, Franz Ferschke, Jim Fisher, Fern Fitzgerald, Paul Foskey, Geoff Garside, Robert Gaymer-Jones, Jurgen Giesbert, Will Grimsley, Marc Gulliver, Tracy Halphide, Debbie Harrison, Ron Harrison, Pat Henderson, Jeff Holdaway, Andrew Houghton, Ed Hubennette, Gary Hurst, Beth Irons, Andrea Jones, Pam Jones, Simon Jongert, Nihad Kattan, Kevin Kearney, Chuck Kelley, Karl Kilburg, Kevin Kimball, Tuni Kyi, Buck Laird, Henry Lee, Mike Mackie, Kathleen Matthews, Alastair McPhail, Scott Melby, Raj Menon, Anton Najjar, JP Nel, Scott Neumayer, John Northen, Jim O'Hern, Alan Orlob, Manuel Oview, Jim Pilarski,

Belinda Pote, Barbara Powell, Reiner Sachau, Mark Satterfield, Brenda Shelton, Craig Smith, Brad Snyder, Arne Sorenson, Alex Stadlin, Jim Stamas, Peter Steger, Pat Stocker, Susan Thronson, Myron Walker, Bob Watts, Hank Weigle, Steve Weisz, Carl Wilson, and Glenn Wilson.

I want to thank my Orange County friends for supporting me through the writing and publication of *RED HOTEL, RED DECEPTION*, and now *RED CHAOS*. These friends include Haris Ali, M.D.; David Brouwer M.D.; Jay Burress, Lynn Clark, Paulette Lombardi-Fries, Christina Palmer, Micky Rucireta, Dominique Williams, Sharon Sola, Tingting Tan M.D.; and the staff at City of Hope, Nicky Tang and Christy Teague.

Through memberships with various boards, I have received inspiration and engaging conversations. My thanks goes out to The Orange County Visitors Association Board Members, Caroline Beteta, and the team at Visit California, Carl Winston. Additional thanks to Cal State University Chancellor's Board on Hospitality and Tourism, my Boston University Boards, Cal State San Marcos Foundation Board, and Althea Foundation Board. It is a pleasure being involved with all of you.

Several people encouraged me to take a leap from my business book, *YOU CAN'T LEAD WITH YOUR FEET ON THE DESK*, to writing novels. These people include Bruce Feirstein, June Farrell, Pam Jones, Pam Policano, Andy Policano, and my wife, Michela Fuller. Thank you all very much. Of course, I must admit, it's a great deal of fun working with Gary Grossman.

Finally, there are simply no words to describe my enduring thanks to J.W. Marriott and Bill Shaw.

—ED FULLER

THANK YOU to Ed Fuller for our most wonderful creative and truly collaborative run with our *RED HOTEL* series of globe-hopping thrillers. You are a true friend and an inspiration. Your experiences give life to our character Dan Reilly and your friendship fills me up.

Thank you to our extraordinary business and creative collaboration with Beaufort Books President and Publisher Eric Kampmann, Managing Editor Megan Trank, and Assistant Editor Olivia Fish.

Now for the engine behind the effort. Additional thanks to Meryl Moss and her creative crew at Meryl Moss Media; Ed's fabulous PR team Pat Monick and Holly Cliffe; and Film 14 book trailer Producer Adam Cushman. Also, ongoing thanks to book publisher guru Roger Cooper for his ongoing belief in me and for launching my thriller writing career.

Thanks to Barbara Schwartz and Chuck Barquist for lending their eagle eyes to the manuscript; Sandi Goldfarb for her editorial assistance throughout the creative process; Bruce Coons, lifelong friend and technical advisor for all my thriller writing; ThrillerFest Executive Director and author Kimberley Howe; all my friends and colleagues at the International Thriller Writers Association; and ITW authors Jon Land, W.G. Griffiths, Raymond Benson, Steve Berry, Daniel Palmer, and R.G. Belsky. Also, attorneys Tom Hunter and Ken Browning; my Hudson High School classmates (we're a tight group!); and of course, friends Jeffrey Davis, Stan and Debbie Deutsch, Vin DiBona, Jeff Greenhawt, Robb Weller, Nat Segaloff, Fred Putman, Michael O'Rourke, and incredible cook and author, Ryan Fey of TV's *The Grill Dads*.

Special thanks to Dr. Gregory Payne, Emerson College Professor and Chair of the Department of Communication Studies, for hosting a dynamic weekly global Zoom forum that deep dives into the issues and crises of today and those just around the corner. I can honestly say that the incredible guests and the illuminating discussions help make our international thrillers all the more relevant.

And finally with true loving thanks, my wife, Helene Seifer, and our family Zach and Jake Grossman, Sasha Grossman, and Alex Crowe. You inspire me every day with your creativity and dedication, and, as I've said before, you all make me so very proud.

—GARY GROSSMAN

ABOUT THE AUTHORS

ED FULLER, is a hospitality industry leader, educator, and bestselling author. He is president of Irvine, California-based Laguna Strategic Advisors, a global consortium that provides business consulting services to corporations and governments. Fuller is also director of the FBI National Academy Associates (FBINAA).

Fuller's forty-year career in the industry was capped by his role as president and managing director of Marriott International for twenty-two years. As worldwide chief, he directed and administered corporate expansion by 551 hotels in 73 countries, and $8 billion in sales. During that time, he oversaw the creation of Marriott International's Global Security Strategy. His role put him in world hot spots at crucial times, from Tripoli to Cairo, Jakarta to Mumbai, with close contact with domestic and foreign intelligence operations. The plots for *Red Hotel*, *Red Deception*, and *Red Chaos* draw heavily on his experience and exploits.

Ed Fuller has served on numerous industry, educational, and charity boards. He was commissioner of the California Commission of Travel and Tourism. He served as a Boston University trustee, president of the Alumni Association, and now continues as an Overseer. He is a trustee of the University of California and director at California State University, San Marcos. Other boards include Mind Research, Concord Hotels, Mirage Investments, and Safe Kids. He is also president of the Orange County Visitors Association and chairman of the SAE Foundation.

Ed Fuller served as a captain in the US Army and was decorated with a Bronze Star and Army Commendation medals. His colorful and real-world experiences are recounted in his top-twenty bestselling business book, *You Can't Lead with Your Feet on the Desk*, published globally in English, Chinese, and Japanese. Ed Fuller continues to consult on security issues around the world.

GARY GROSSMAN's first novel, *Executive Actions*, propelled him into the world of geopolitical thrillers. *Executive Treason*, *Executive Command*, and *Executive Force* further tapped Grossman's experience as a journalist, newspaper columnist, documentary television producer, reporter, and media historian. In addition to the bestselling Executive series, Grossman wrote the international award-winning *Old Earth*, a geological thriller that spans all of time. With *Red Hotel*, *Red Deception*, *Red Chaos*, his collaborations with Ed Fuller, Grossman entered a new realm of globe-hopping thriller writing.

Grossman has contributed to the *New York Times* and the *Boston Globe*, and was a columnist for the *Boston Herald American*. He covered presidential campaigns for WBZ-TV in Boston.

A multiple Emmy Award winner, Grossman has produced more than 10,000 television series and specials for networks including NBC, ABC, CBS, Fox, CNN, History Channel, Discovery, and National Geographic Channel. He served as chair of the Government Affairs Committee for the Caucus for Producers, Writers and Directors, and is a member of the International Thriller Writers Association. He is a Trustee at Emerson College and serves on the Boston University Metropolitan College Advisory Board, and has produced tributes for the prestigious Ford's Theater Lincoln Honors. Grossman has taught at Emerson College, Boston University, USC, and currently teaches in the Graduate School of Film and Television at Loyola Marymount University.

FOR MORE INFORMATION AND TO CONTACT THE AUTHORS
WWW.REDHOTEL.COM

CPSIA information can be obtained
at www.ICGtesting.com
Printed in the USA
BVHW080946240323
660567BV00007B/17/J

9 780825 309878